ANALIESE
RISING

Also by Brenda Drake

THIEF OF LIES
GUARDIAN OF SECRETS
ASSASSIN OF TRUTHS

SEEKING FATE
CURSING FATE
TOUCHING FATE

THUNDERSTRUCK

ANALIESE RISING

BRENDA DRAKE

Entangled Publishing, LLC
2614 South Timberline Road
Suite 105, PMB 159
Fort Collins, CO 80525
rights@entangledpublishing.com

Entangled Teen is an imprint of Entangled Publishing, LLC.

Visit our website at www.entangledpublishing.com.

Edited by Liz Pelleiter
Cover design by Deranged Doctor
Cover images by Shutterstock/
Martin Capek, Dmitriy Rybin, The7Dew, Anna Zelenska, Nata789
DepositPhotos/magann, iulia_shev
GettyImages/naropano
Interior design by Heather Howland

ISBN 978-1-64063-508-1
Ebook ISBN 978-1-64063-518-0

Manufactured in the United States of America

First Edition January 2019

10 9 8 7 6 5 4 3 2 1

an imprint of Entangled Publishing LLC

For Annika and Fallon,
who are the Keepers of my heart.

CHAPTER ONE

T he classroom smells like a funeral home.

Hushed voices pulse over the pairs of students hunching over trays spaced across the counters. The odor of bodies fresh out of gym class mingles with the scent of formaldehyde.

Hair dampens at my temples. A crematory would be cooler.

Not many have finished their assignments. Only a few overachievers sit in the rows of empty desks on the other side of the room, their tasks completed, proud smiles on their faces.

Mrs. Cryer shuffles around the tables watching over us — a reaper waiting for lost souls, her bony finger pointing out errors. She shuffles around with purpose. She shuffles around without direction. Then she stops at our table, her eyes peering over reading glasses.

"Mr. Bove and Miss Jordan, you two are falling behind," she says, a disapproving *tsk* in her voice. She only uses last names when she wants to emphasize her warning. "Best hurry before class ends."

She continues shuffling around.

Biology is my least favorite class. Mrs. Cryer's assignments are outdated. It's her last year teaching, her retirement long overdue. Stern and direct, she's not the sort of teacher I usually like, but I do. There's an underlying kindness to Mrs. Cryer. A kindness hiding in her eyes, evident in her actions.

One of the things I like about my school: my brother, Dalton, is in the same grade. We're not twins or anything. Actually, we're cousins. His parents adopted me when mine were killed in a boating accident on Lake Como in Italy. I don't remember them. I was two when that all went down.

The thing I hate about school: Dalton's in my biology class.

"Come on, Ana." Dalton slides the dissection tray closer to me. "I did all the setup. Just make the first cut."

The little green body looks rubbery—almost fake—crucified to the tray with pins as it is. I push strands of dark hair from my face with a latex-gloved hand. I could've opted out of this barbaric ritual of separating body parts from an innocent frog.

Why did I even agree to this?

It's because Dalton coaxed me. He knows how to get me to do stuff. All he has to do is throw down a dare. Been doing that ever since forever.

I glare at him through the plastic goggles. "Just give me a sec."

He flashes me a smug look. One that says he knows I won't do it and he's about to get out of doing the dinner dishes for a month. His eyes are almost the color of the frog's body—sort of yellowy green, but alive. That movement he always does to get the sand-colored bangs out of his eyes annoys me.

A smirk twitching the corner of his lips, he drums his fingers against the table. A move to make me nervous. Make me give up. I contemplate tugging off one of my latex gloves and slapping his face with it. Challenge him to a duel. Like pistols at dawn.

Behind me, Rod's goofing off again. Teasing Sofia and Maggie. He's okay, just has it bad for Sofia. Everyone in school is just okay. Your typical cliques, as in all the schools across America. Dalton and I are like chameleons, morphing into whichever group we feel like hanging out with at the time.

"I'm getting old here." Frustration sounds in his voice. I'm not sure if it's because I'm taking so long or because his crush is flirting with the two most popular girls in school.

The tiny scalpel shakes as I ready to make the cut. My stomach lurches as if it wants to leave my body and walk out the door. I don't want to do this. It's not right. The instrument slips from my hand and clatters onto the table.

"I can't." I pull off the gloves, drop them beside the tray, and push the goggles up to my forehead. "This is just too inhumane. Poor frog never hurt anyone. I don't get why we can't do virtual dissections like they do at Grant."

"Ha!" That smug look is back on his face. "Do you concede, then?"

My eyes go back to the frog. Sadness deflates my soul the way a balloon loses air. Had it been hopping in a pond somewhere green and lush, minding its own business, searching for bugs to eat before the net caught it? Had it been scared, struggling against the cords to get out? Had it been docile once it realized there was no hope? No escape.

A girl's squeal sounds behind me just before Rod stumbles and hits my back, pushing me forward. My bare palm lands on the frog, its body cold, firm, and lifeless. A shudder runs down my spine, and I pull back my hand as if I'll catch a disease.

"*Eww*." I push Rod away. "Be careful."

"Oh sorry," he says, a laugh hanging in his voice.

Mrs. Cryer's eyes shift in our direction. "Mr. Stone, settle down, or you'll spend lunch in the office."

Rod returns to his table, Maggie and Sofia's stifled laughs

greeting him.

Dalton shoots out of his chair. "Did you see that? It moved."

I snap back around. The frog is as still as a statue in the tray. "It did not. Stop doing that."

"Doing what? I swear it—"

The frog's eyes pop open, and it struggles against the pins holding its limbs down. A gasp punches from my chest, and I scoot back. This time it's me bumping into Rod.

"Hey," he protests, shoving me back toward my table.

"What is going on over there?" Mrs. Cryer's commanding voice stills the class.

This can't be real.

Dalton hurries beside me. "What the hell? This frog is *alive*!"

The frog tugs a limb from one of the pins. Its head bangs against the tray as it frees itself from the others. It struggles onto its stomach and pushes off, landing on the table with a *thump*.

Screams and table legs scratching across the tiles break out across the classroom.

"Oh, hell no," Maggie yells, scrambling behind Rod.

Everyone moves away from the frog, but I step closer as if there's an invisible tether between us, drawing me in. Those round eyes stare at me, the slits opening and closing, just watching. My heart gallops in my chest, the thrumming in my ears drowning out all the excited voices around me.

A croak belches out of its mouth. It heaves and heaves and heaves until slimy, clear fluid is expelled from its mouth and splashes onto the table, rushing across the top, spilling over the edge, and dripping to the floor.

It stinks worse than Dalton's trainers do after a long run—a mixture of formaldehyde and sour meat.

The frog springs from the tabletop.

Gasps sound. Bodies bump into tables and chairs.

The frog lands on the next table, then takes off for the next and the next and thuds like a rolled-up, wet sock against the window. Slime runs down the glass.

The little thing sits there on the top of a short bookcase pushed up against the windows, just staring outside as if he's longing to be free. I get the little guy. There're times when I feel trapped, which makes no sense because it's not as though I have restrictions. Jane's too busy to keep tabs on us.

Then the frog lunges again.

More gasps.

And it hits the glass pane, again, again, again. *Thud. Thud. Thud.*

On the last hit, the frog drops onto the bookcase.

Motionless.

A swarm of yellow-and-brown wings shoots up from somewhere under the window outside.

"Where did all those butterflies come from?" a girl asks, her voice shaky.

"Those aren't butterflies." I don't have to turn around to know it's Miles talking. He knows stuff. Random stuff like what he says next: "They're death's-head hawkmoths. Like the ones in *The Silence of the Lambs.* That's strange. This isn't their environment."

The flying creatures take off across the lawn and disappear into the trees.

Everyone inches closer to view the frog. Mrs. Cryer parts the sea of students on her way over. She leans over the frog, studying it for several seconds before straightening and turning to face us.

"Very clever prank." Her voice is sharp, cutting through the excited voices around her, causing the classroom to suddenly fall silent. "Who's the mastermind?"

Twenty-two pairs of eyes glance from Dalton to Rod, but

no one answers her.

"All right." Her sigh says she'll be a bloodhound tracking the culprits until they're found. "Everyone, back to your tables and put them in order. Mr. Taylor and Mr. Bove, go to the janitor's room and grab some cleaner and a box to get rid of this mess." Her eyes point to the bludgeoned frog.

Rod slumps his pointy shoulders. "Why do *we* have to clean it?"

She takes off her glasses, which is a sure sign her patience is wearing thinner than a sheet of paper.

Dalton rests a hand on my forearm. "I didn't do this. I swear."

I yank away from his grasp. "Yeah, right. Then why were you *so* determined for me to dissect it? You were setting me up."

"Whatever. Believe what you want." He walks off, flipping the bangs out of his eyes and muttering, "How could I get all those butterflies, anyway?"

"Moths," I say to his back.

"Whatever," he says again, giving me a quick glance over his shoulder.

I turn to go back to my desk and catch another look at the frog's tiny, broken body, lifeless on top of the bookcase. My stomach fists, and it feels like the world tilts on its axis.

It's nothing. Just a prank.

I study Rod's face. He wears a mask of indifference. Maybe he did do it.

Just outside the window, one of the moths clings to a low-hanging branch. Its yellow-and-brown wings twitch. I move closer to the window. The skull marking on its back should creep me out, but it doesn't. I've seen one at my dad's funeral. It was lying flat against his casket the entire service. Stayed there like one of those butterflies pinned to a collector's board until the best man I'd ever known was lowered into the cold, dark ground. At the rattling of the crane, the moth took off for the trees surrounding the cemetery.

"You okay?" Maggie asks.

I nod, my eyes burning as I stare out the window. "I'm good."

Her concerned look reflects in the glass pane. "Whoever did this is so disturbed." She whirls around, her blond hair fanning in the air, and strolls off in the direction of her desk.

The moth launches off the branch and flutters away, its body diminishing to a black dot in the distance.

CHAPTER TWO

The Delaware River is rowdy, bucking and slapping the pile of rocks on its bank. I sit on my favorite rock, writing in my journal. The dark clouds above promise to dump rain soon, but I don't care. This is our place. Dalton, Dad, and me. And I miss Dad. I want him back.

I need him back.

Three months. Such a short time, yet an eternity.

Three months. The last time I saw his face, his expression frozen, covered in makeup to look alive, his linebacker body completely filling the coffin.

Three months.

This is where he died. In our place. An aneurysm. We were hiking the rocks, and he collapsed. In our place.

Our place.

It was him and me. Dalton had gone ahead. He never could wait for us. Dad collapsed, and I froze. I did nothing. To this day, I don't know how long I just stood there. When we didn't show up to the part that sticks farther out into the lake, Dalton doubled back. He called 911.

The doctors said there wasn't anything I could do. He died instantly, but that doesn't stop me from doubting them and wondering if it was my fault.

The wind makes the tears on my face cold. I swipe them away with the sleeve of my hoodie.

I take out Dad's 1950s vintage Ronson pocket lighter. It doesn't work, but it's a part of him, so I keep it with me. His father gave it to him when he was a boy. Probably should give it to Dalton. He's his real kid, after all. I click the igniter off and on.

Off and on.

I'll give it to him eventually. Right now, I need it. Besides, Jane gave Dalton a bunch of Dad's things, so he's all set.

Though he was my uncle, my mother's brother, he'd become Dad. Strong and protective. I felt safe with him. How could a little vein take Goliath down? Leave him crumpled on the ground as if the world was done with him. But I'm not done. I need him. There're so many words left unspoken and too many moments lost.

Off and on.

He left us alone with her.

My aunt doesn't fit into the mother role. A neurosurgeon, Jane is always busy. Dalton is her biological son, and I'm the forced-on-her daughter.

Footsteps sound behind me. I know who it is without turning around. Before he can see the lighter, I shove it into my pocket.

"I thought you'd be here," Dalton says.

There's nothing to say, so I don't respond.

"Analiese Grace Jordan, are you ignoring me?"

I cross my arms over my chest. "I'm not talking to you."

He stops at my side, picks up a rock, and throws it. The stone skips across the water before plunking under waves. "You know, Mom would be mad if she found out you came to Fishtown on your own."

I jut out my chin.

"Really? You're seriously not talking to me?" He picks up another rock and throws it. This time the rock plunks under the water without skipping, and it takes all my effort not to tease him about it.

"On Dad's soul, I swear I didn't do it."

That's big. He'd never risk lying when Dad's soul is at risk. I finally break my silence. "Then who?"

Another rock. Skip. Skip. Skip. *Plunk.*

"Don't know. Probably Rod."

I close my journal then slip it and my pen into my backpack. The journal is where I write my memories of Dad. I don't want to forget anything. And it's therapeutic. Makes me feel connected to him, helps me deal with the dark hole inside me.

I also use it to keep a record of my panic attacks for my psychotherapist, Dr. Herrera. She wants me to jot down what starts it, how long it lasts, and how I feel during each one. There aren't as many entries for them since I started taking my meds. Usually, I have an episode when I forget to take several of my scheduled doses in a row. But now I have them set in my phone's alarm so I won't forget.

I've always had them. The attacks are just more intense since Dad died.

Dad. His name was Eli. Never played favorites with Dalton and me. He treated us equally. Loved us the same.

Like a festering blister, the wanting to know my real parents is painful. It was Dad who brought them to life for me, telling me stories behind the many pictures in the rows of albums lining one of the shelves in his home office. There're many tales of him and my mom growing up together. She got him into trouble a lot. My mother was assertive and excellent at math. One trait I have, the other I'm working on.

I capture all that in my journal, too.

"You know," Dalton says, pulling me out of my thoughts. "Technically, you have to do dishes for a month."

I hug myself, trying to fend off the chilly spring breeze. "No, I don't."

"Yeah, you do. You threw down the glove before Freak Frog woke up."

"Seriously?" I slide a look at him that says he better rethink his statement.

He flashes me the-hard-to-resist Dalton smile—all toothy and dimply. "Too soon?"

I'm not going to budge. He wants me to, but I'm not. That look of his isn't going to win this time. I press my lips together but can't stop the corners of my mouth from lifting and betraying me.

"I knew you weren't mad at me." He hops off the rock. "You want to get a latte?"

"Sure," I say, giving in. Shaking my head, I let my smile win. It's Dalton, after all. How could I stay mad? He's all I have.

My thoughts turn in my head, and it's as if I'm walking in a haze, ambling along the river beside Dalton. "The incident with the frog was no coincidence," I say. "Not to mention the moths. How could someone even get that many? And why?"

Dalton wraps an arm around my shoulder. "Whoever set up that prank better hope I don't find out who they are."

"Even if it's Rod?"

"Yes, even him."

"You're so tough." I laugh, feeling the tension of the day loosen from my shoulders. It was just a prank. Dad would tell me to pretend it was no big deal—don't give the culprit the satisfaction of a reaction.

I bump Dalton's shoulder with mine and smile up at him. "I saw the mail. Congratulations. First place, huh? Your sculptures are going to make us millions one day."

He pulls on the back of his neck. "Yeah, if I live through high school. That mythology final is going to kill my GPA."

"If you let me out of the dishes tonight, I'll help you study for it." I live and breathe mythology. Our dad was a history professor, and that was our thing. I know the obscure gods and goddesses, not just the ones made popular by comic books and movies.

"Deal." Now he bumps my shoulder, but it has his weight behind it and makes me stumble a little. He chuckles. "Graceful."

The streets are crowded with rush-hour commuters. Across the way, some old man wearing a black newsboy cap and a camel-colored overcoat stands in front of the coffee shop we're heading for. His eyes follow our approach, causing a shiver to prickle up my spine. I keep my eyes on where my feet are landing to avoid catching the man's gaze.

The scent of freshly ground coffee beans fills my nose. We spent many Saturdays in this shop after our hikes with Dad. Back then, we were only allowed to drink hot chocolate while he sipped an Americano.

A crash sounds behind Dalton and me, and we spin around. An SUV and a small red car are mangled together. The tires of a black sedan squeal as it speeds in our direction.

It's as though it all happens in slow motion. The sedan jumps the curb, and someone shoves me out of the way and into Dalton. We land hard on the sidewalk. One tire of the car rides the curb until coming off to join the other on the road. The driver weaves around a few cars before disappearing around a corner.

I scramble to my feet and glance back. The old man in the newsboy cap lies on the sidewalk. Blood trickles down the side of his face.

"Call 911," I tell Dalton and drop to my knees beside the man. The gash in his head is deep. I search the crowd now forming around us. "Someone get a towel or something. I need to compress his wound."

A woman removes her scarf and hands it to me. I take it, and I'm about to press it against the gash in the man's head when his gloved hand catches my arm.

"Don't touch me," he says. "I'm dying."

I push my eyebrows together. "You're not going to die. The ambulance is coming."

"My bag," he says weakly. A worn-out leather satchel lays on the sidewalk a few feet from him.

I snatch it up and lift it for him to see. "This one?"

He nods, his lids half closed over soft blue eyes. His face scrunches up in pain. "That's it." He keeps his voice low. "Take it to my grandson. Don't let anyone see you have it. You're in danger, Analiese. Run. Don't stop."

My heart drops like a stone in my chest, and the case falls from my hands, slapping against the concrete. "How do you know my name?"

A fire truck and an ambulance pull up to the curb.

"Wh—" His eyes close, mouth slackens. I don't know why I believe the man, but I do. I slip the strap to his bag over my shoulder, stand, and back away into the crowd beside Dalton. So many faces stare down at the man. Unknown faces. And one could belong to whoever this man feared.

Paramedics rush a stretcher and medical bags over to the old man. A woman places an oxygen mask on his face while another assesses his injuries.

"What are you doing with his bag?" Dalton asks.

"He wants me to give it to his grandson. Maybe his number or address is in it." The man saying I was in danger made me nervous. I search the faces in the crowd again. No one looks menacing or suspicious. "Come on. Let's get out of here." I sprint-walk down the street and away from the accident.

Dalton keeps step with me. "That's stealing. Taking the

bag."

"No, it isn't. He gave it to me."

"What's in it?" he asks.

I dart glances at the people and cars passing us. We have to get off the street. I spot an ice cream parlor and dash inside with Dalton close behind me.

My gaze goes to the window. Sitting behind the large panes of glass making up the front of the store is like being in a fishbowl—trapped and exposed.

"Get us each a scoop," I say, nodding to a table in a back corner. "I'm going to sit over there."

The chair screeches across the tiled floor as I drag it away from the table. I sit, and it wobbles a little on its legs. The tiny buckles on the straps of the old man's satchel are challenging to undo. The smell of leather oil clings to the bag.

The man's injuries looked fatal. The driver who caused the accident never stopped. Had to be some drunk afraid to face the police.

You're in danger, Analiese. Run. Don't stop, the man told me, his sad eyes haunting.

How did he know my name?

I'm worrying too much. No one from the street can see me in my seat in the back corner of the parlor. And there probably isn't anyone following me. The old man had to be delusional.

The accident was real, though. I'm still shaken up from it, because my hands are trembling as I remove items from the bag. My stomach's doing that dip-and-fall thing it does while riding the monster roller coaster at the amusement park.

There are many objects in the bag, along with a tattered notebook—a ring, envelopes, keys, and other various things. I pick up the ring and spin the wheel with letters of the alphabet etched into the round steel. There're two other wheels. One with numbers and the other with symbols.

A decoder ring? I pause a moment, wondering why the man would have one, before returning it to the bag. The envelopes have what I believe is the old man's name and address on them.

Adam Conte. "He lives in Lancaster," I say out loud, which causes the girl at the next table to look at me. I give her an awkward smile and tuck the envelopes back into the bag. Avoiding eye contact with her, I flip open the cover to the notebook. The first four pages hold a list of names. Many of the names are crossed out. I run my finger down the column.

Dalton returns from the counter, holding two cups with a mound of Oreo ice cream in each.

On the third page, I stop at a name with a line drawn through it—Alea Bove Jordan—my mother. Beside her name, written at an angle in pencil, is Jake Jordan, my father. He's like an afterthought. A line runs across his name, too. Underneath them is my uncle, Eli Bove. His name is also marked off. I turn the page and gasp. Halfway down the list, written in thick black ink strokes, is *Analiese Jordan.*

CHAPTER THREE

Dalton's tiny red-with-rust-spots Civic sputters down the I-76 highway toward Lancaster. An hour and a half there and back and I'll be home before Jane ever knows I ditched school. It's almost Spring Break, anyway. I've turned in most of my work, I reason with myself.

Besides, Jane won't care. She's barely around to notice. The hospital is more her home than our house. I'm not even sure she'll be there on Sunday morning to see Dalton and me off to that bereavement camp for kids she insists we go to over the break.

The gas light flashes on.

"Crap. *Dalton*," I seethe under my breath. He's always running out of gas. I'm approaching the next exit and turn on the blinker.

The Turkey Hill Minit Market isn't as busy as I thought it'd be during morning rush hour. I pull up to the pump right beside a black Audi sedan with a front license plate that reads *My God Carries a Hammer*.

"Nice." I snicker and pop open the gas tank cover.

I fill up the Civic and rush inside to get a horrible gas station coffee. The lanky guy behind the counter straightens. His wide-set eyes follow me the entire way to the coffee bar. A man, way over six feet tall, with red hair that's short on the sides and fades up to a dovetail on top, has one of the refrigerator doors open. With his stare on the contents inside, he rubs his neatly cut beard.

The Styrofoam coffee cup plunks from the holder when I tug it out. I pour a premade cappuccino from the fountain.

The man steps back and looks over, his hand still holding open the door.

The air between the man and me feels off—tense. It's probably just me, and the fact I'm practically alone with a suspicious man in a gas station. I secure a lid over my cup and turn to leave.

"Which one do you suggest?" he asks, stopping me. There's a slight accent to his voice, but I can't place it. Possibly Scottish?

I glance around, and my eyes stop on him. "Are you talking to me?"

"There's no one else about." His smile is off. Like he has to remember how to create one or something.

"I don't drink the stuff, but my brother likes the one with the gold star." I want to look away, but something in his eyes captures me. They're like a kaleidoscope of fall leaves—orange, yellow, and brown. Their focus on me causes the tiny hairs at the nape of my neck to stand straight up.

He picks up a can of the drink I suggested and lets go of the refrigerator door, his eyes never leaving me.

Now he's freaking me out.

I pretend to search the pastries near the coffee bar.

"A young girl such as yourself should not be traveling alone," he says. "You should be in school."

The pastries blur out of focus, the display stands are

closing in on me, and the coffee cup shakes in my hand. Great. The creeper knows I'm alone. I have to lie. Tell him Dalton is in the back seat, sleeping.

I glance over at him. "I'm not alone—"

He's gone. I search over the display cases, but he isn't anywhere in the market. The guy behind the counter watches me intently while taking my cash for the coffee. It's as if he's never seen a dollar bill before. Probably hasn't, with everyone paying with debit or credit cards.

"You okay?" he asks.

"I'm fine." I force a smile to back up my statement. "Thank you."

"Have a nice day." His eyes have left me to watch two younger guys shuffling around the display cases.

The front door slides shut behind me. A brisk wind whips dark strands of hair around my face. I wrap my arms around me and dart for the Civic. The black Audi is gone, and I wonder if the man who strangely disappeared owns it. He did look like someone who would have a Thor license plate.

I'm nervous during the rest of the ride to Lancaster, glancing through the rearview window, checking and rechecking that no one's following me. That the black Audi isn't there.

"*In 1.5 miles, turn left,*" the female voice on my phone's GPS directs.

Lancaster is a pretty cool town, with nearby farmlands and Amish country. When Dad was alive, we'd take weekend trips here and do touristy things like buggy rides and hikes. He loved checking out the architecture.

"*In five hundred feet, your destination is on the left,*" the GPS says.

I've never been in this neighborhood before. The houses are older, and the area is quaint. I pull the Civic up to the curb and stare at the home. It's a two-and-a-half-story stone house and resembles a French countryside chateau with its bay windows, dormers, steepled gables, and cone-shaped roofs.

Dalton and I went to the hospital the night of the accident to see how the old man was doing, but he hadn't made it, dying only minutes after arriving in the ER. His family left before I could give the bag to his grandson.

I would've come sooner, but I figured the family needed space to mourn. His obit said they were having a memorial and reception for family and friends. So here I am. At his house. Two weeks after the accident. Feels like a lifetime.

It's almost nine in the morning. He probably would've been at his kitchen table, drinking coffee and reading the paper, as old people do. His day might've been spent tending to the beautiful and colorful flowers in the beds surrounding the lawn.

For all I know, the house might be deserted. His grandson could live somewhere else.

After grabbing the man's bag, I pop open the Civic's door and slide out. The sidewalk is uneven and broken in spots. Because I'm superstitious, I avoid stepping on the cracks. The scent of freshly cut grass lingers over the lawn. The door has several locks and a peephole at eye level. I count them.

Seriously? Five? The door is metal, too. Above my head is a security camera.

Someone's expecting the apocalypse.

I press the doorbell and wait.

And wait.

I press it again.

When no one answers, I turn to leave but then pause. A faint bass comes from around the corner of the house. The stone pavers on the lawn lead me to the front of the garage.

The doors are open, and a guy about my age works a tattered punching bag hanging by a chain attached to the ceiling. He's shirtless, and his shorts are slung low on his hips.

Tall, with dark, wavy hair, the boy isn't bad to look at.

With each throw of his fist or kick, his muscles flex then go slack. The way he's hitting the bag, he's definitely letting off steam. Maybe I should come back later when he's calmer.

This is a bad idea. I could just leave the bag at the front door. But then I won't find out why my name is on that list. Or why the man crossed my parents off that same list. The guy needs some cooling down. I can go find a coffee shop somewhere and come back when he's less angry and more dressed.

His music is so loud, he hasn't noticed my approach, so I ease around and head back the way I came.

"Hey," he shouts.

Crap. He spotted me. I turn back around.

He's walking my way. His bare chest rises and falls with heavy breaths. A nautical star medallion with a silver chain rests just below his collarbone. "You need something?"

"Um." *Don't look at his abdomen.* My eyes betray me and go there. His half nakedness distracts me, and I forget what I was going to say. "Um…"

His lips twist into a smirk, amusement igniting in his eyes, so dark they're almost black. He places his fist on his hip. It's obvious he's doing that to flex his bicep.

The corners of his mouth lower, and his fist drops away from his waist. "Where'd you get that bag?"

My hand instantly goes to the satchel's strap. "He gave it to me."

His eyes fix on mine. "My grandfather would never let it out of his sight."

"I was there. Um. At the accident." I sound insensitive. "I'm sorry for your loss. My name is Ana. Analiese Jordan."

"Thank you. I'm Marek Conte." He grabs the back of his neck, and I look everywhere else but at him. The boys at my school don't look like him. He must work out a lot.

"Nice to meet you," I say.

"Why would he give it to you?" he asks, nodding at the satchel against my hip. "His bag?"

"I'm not sure, but he told me to return it to you." I remove the strap from my shoulder, step closer to him, and give him the bag. Our hands touch, and a rush of adrenaline surges through my body. It's a strange-encounter kind of day. First the Thor worshipper, and now Marek in all his bare-chested glory.

Marek stares at the bag for several beats before walking off while saying, "Again, thanks."

Is that it? I didn't drive all this way to not get any answers.

"Wait," I say.

He looks over his shoulder at me. "What? Is there something more?"

"Yes, as a matter of fact." I level him with my best "*it doesn't faze me that you don't have a shirt on*" look. "There's a list in that bag. It has my name on it. More importantly, it has my parents' names, too, and theirs are crossed off. Do you know why he put us on it?"

A confused look passes over his face, and his eyes drop to the bag. "I don't know. Come inside, and we'll check it out."

"Inside?" *With you?* No matter how hot the guy is, being alone with him is probably not a good idea. Some serial killers aren't bad looking. That's how they trick their prey.

"Yes," he says. "Don't worry. I won't bite. Plus, my gram just made apple bread. Do you drink coffee?"

"That's like asking if I breathe."

He laughs. It's not genuine, but more like the laugh you do when you've heard a joke too many times before. "Good. We have something in common. Come on."

I trail him to the front and up the porch. The house has a small foyer, decorated in warm browns and shocks of red. Paintings crowd the walls. Aging flowers arranged in cut-glass vases sit on a long entryway table with sympathy cards stacked to the side. Probably from the funeral. My heart sinks at the thought.

He drops the bag on a bench by the door, grabs a T-shirt hanging off the edge, and pulls it over his head. I try not to watch the soft blue material slowly cover his extremely fit torso, but can't help it. His eyes meet mine just as I catch the last glimpse of his tanned skin above the waist of his shorts. The smile on his lips widens, and I quickly look away, pretending to study one of the paintings on the wall.

"My gramps's work." He smiles at the one my eyes are fixed on—a boy and his dog playing fetch with a red ball. "That's Bandit and me. I'm six there."

"He was really talented." And I'm not lying, like you do when someone is proud of their kid's work and it's horrible. The paintings are beautiful. "I bet they'd sell well—"

My words jam in my throat when my gaze lands on a painting of a young girl with dark hair, cradling a doll, a death's-head hawkmoth sitting on her arm.

"That girl is me."

CHAPTER FOUR

Marek pours coffee from a French press into two mugs. He failed to mention that his grandmother had left with one of the loaves of apple bread. Says she's at her bridge group. I'm not sure it's a good idea to be alone with Marek. I don't know the guy. He could be dangerous. Well, his muscles are, anyway.

"That painting has to be a coincidence," he says. "How do you even know it is you?"

"The jean jacket. It has the same patches as mine. A unicorn and stars. I still have it. Of course, I don't wear it. It's too small." I'm rambling, trying to string my jumbled thoughts together. "Since I made it, it's one of a kind."

"So what are you saying? That my grandfather was stalking you? He has better things to do. *Had. He had* better..." He trails off, staring at the steam rising from the press as he pours coffee into his mug.

It looks like he isn't going to stop pouring.

"Watch it," I clip.

He blinks and places the press on the table. "Maybe he

just so happened to be there painting when he saw you. He spent a lot of time in Fishtown. By the river. You were his inspiration or something like that."

"Maybe." I sound doubtful. "So then why was he watching me the day of the accident? And he knew my name."

He passes me a sugar bowl. "He said your name?"

I spoon the white granules into my mug. "Yes. He told me to run and that I was in danger. And my name's on that list with my parents'."

"Right, yeah. That is strange." He lowers his head and studies the intricate lace in the tablecloth, then glances out the window. "But he was a bit eccentric."

"Yeah, I'd say." I have the feeling he isn't telling me something. There are times when a warning blares through my mind like the one that announces class is over at my school. And I know not to ignore it. I did that once while riding my bike and ended up at the bottom of a ditch. Long story.

The warning goes off, and it makes me uneasy, right when Marek turns his eyes away from me and stares out the bay window. There isn't anything out there to see but the lush green garden just past the rock-paved patio. And I'm pretty sure he's seen it many times before and wouldn't give it another glance on most other days. Other days than today. When he wants to hide something from me. Hide the fact that he knows more than he's letting on.

I shift in my seat.

Marek tears his gaze away from the window, a serious look on his face, so serious it makes me recoil.

"You should go," he says, the legs of his chair screeching across the tiles as he stands.

I shoot to my feet. "But…but what about that bag? You know something, don't you? You know why I'm on that list with my parents. Tell me why."

He lowers his head to avoid my pleading glare. "I know

nothing."

I let out an exasperated breath and stomp my way to the door to show him my frustration. Before I reach the entry, he stops me.

"Wait," he says. "I don't know anything about that list or what my grandfather was up to. This isn't my home. I live with my parents in Baltimore. I was just here for the…for my grams."

For the funeral, I'm sure he was going to say. "I'm sorry, that has to be tough."

"It is," he says. "Grams is having a difficult time. I practically had to force her to go to her bridge club. Anyway, my gramps was a secretive man. I wasn't blowing you off. Just thinking. Or, more like trying to decide if I should break into the basement."

I lift my eyebrows. "Break into the basement? Why would you have to do that?"

"My grandfather spent most of his time down there," he says. "It was off-limits. Not even my grams could go in. We haven't found the key to the door. She wanted to sort through his things and clean it up after the funeral. But it's lost."

I brighten. "Keys. There's a ring of them in the bag."

He glances around as if he's forgotten where he put the bag. I don't have to search for it. Ever since we entered the house and he placed the satchel on the bench by the door, it's been a leather beacon calling me.

"It's over here." I gather the bag and hand it to him.

He digs through the contents and retrieves the keys. Sadness crosses his face as he flips through them. The metal ring's tarnished by age. He stops on a skeleton key that strangely looks newer than the other ones that are modern.

"This is it," he says.

The light coming in from the windows beside the door glints across the silver key. On the tip of it are two tiny red bulbs. "That's unusual," I say, pointing them out.

He starts down the hall. "Come on. Let's see if it works."
Everything in the house is old. The solid wood doors are tall and thin.

The front of the house is bright and cheery, painted in yellows and creams. This part is dark and decorated in warm browns. We pass what looks to be the family room. Antique furniture and delicate figurines and vases with lace doilies under them sit on the tables between the chairs. There's a black onyx sculpture of a cat wearing one gold hoop earring and a thick necklace with hieroglyphs on it. Bastet. She's the Egyptian goddess of protection. It looks heavy and entirely out of place with all the other stuff.

There're more decaying floral arrangements placed throughout the house. I want to remove them. The drooping petals are like sad reminders of their recent loss.

Marek stops at the door near the back of the house, inserts the key, and tries to turn it in the lock. "It doesn't work — "

A bright red glow illuminates the keyhole. Metal sliding against metal sounds from the other side. A series of clicks go off, and the light goes out.

"That's interesting." Marek turns the knob and opens the door.

"More like creepy," I say.

He searches the wall for a switch and flips it up. The lights below flicker on, and I follow Marek down the steps.

It isn't your typical basement. This one has a stone staircase and wooden beams on the ceiling. The smell of cigar or pipe smoke attacks my nose. Marek reaches the bottom, and four computers on a long cherry wood desk hum to life.

"They must be connected to a sensor." He crosses the polished concrete floor to the desk.

"Wow, this is nice," I say, scoping the place. There're built-in bookcases on one wall and a seating area in front of it with expensive-looking leather couches. "Talk about a man cave."

Embedded in the wall above the desk are rows of security monitors—six down, six across. Marek clicks on the master power switch, and the screens blink to life. Each one is a live shot of a house or an apartment building.

"Was your grandfather in the CIA or something?" *Or worse, a voyeur.* I keep that to myself because the dude just lost the old man, after all.

"No." His eyes scan the images. "At least, I don't think so. He owns a butcher shop. Owned. Sold it. He's retired. Those two," he says, pointing at a pair of monitors on the top right. "That's the front and back of this house."

I try to keep my mind from going there, but there's no stopping it. A butcher? A great profession for a serial killer.

One of the screens catches my attention. My stomach drops. I recognize the red brick structure with the blue shutters. "That's my house. Why was he watching us?"

"I don't know." He searches around the desk and then kneels to inspect the floor. "There isn't a recorder. He must've just been monitoring people."

"Okay," I say. "I'm completely *freaked out*."

Marek straightens. "Me, too. There've got to be answers in here somewhere. I'm going to check the drawers. You see if there's anything in that cabinet."

The cabinet has four doors. Behind the first two are office supplies. On the middle shelf is a stack of passports. I snatch one from the top and open it. The photograph is of Adam Conte, Marek's grandfather, but the name on the passport is Martin Cleary.

I check another one. Same picture, different name—Ted Johnson.

They all have his photo with an alias.

My finger bounces on the spine of each one as I count them. "There are fourteen."

Marek glances up from the drawer he's searching. "What's

that?"

"Passports." I hold one up. "All with your grandfather's picture but different names. Why would he need these? I'll tell you. He was a spy, that's why."

He hurries over and flips through the passports. The look on his face changes from confusion to anger. He throws the stack across the room. "Who was he? What else was he hiding?"

I back up against the cabinet. This isn't really happening. Some old man was stalking me, and probably many others. The thing is, I didn't even know I was being followed or monitored. It's as if bony fingers scratch up my back and over my skull. I've never felt so vulnerable before. Then a new thought comes to me. One that rips my heart completely out.

Did he kill my parents and my uncle?

"The list." My voice sounds shaky, and my legs wobble a little. "He was watching us. Why was he watching us?"

Marek grabs the back of his neck, and his eyes flick in my direction. "I don't know, but we're going to find out. Let's keep searching. The answers have to be here."

I should run. Go to the police. Tell them some crazy—maybe perverted—old man was stalking me. But he's dead now, and I need answers. Why would my family be so important to this man?

And how had he hidden his secret life from his family?

CHAPTER FIVE

My breath tastes sour in my mouth with the thought of Mr. Conte watching me while I never suspected he was there. Eyes staring, camera on me. How can I ever feel safe again, knowing what I do now?

I shake my head to rid myself of the thoughts, but the fears remain.

"All right. I hope there're answers in here." I open the other two doors of the cabinet. An old-style safe takes up the entire space—bottom to top. "What do you think is in this? A body?"

Crap. I just said that out loud.

Marek's brows are a straight line over his dark brown eyes, and his lips are even straighter. "He was a good man," he says, and I wonder if he's trying to convince himself or me. "A loving grandfather."

It sounds like he's quoting Adam Conte's eulogy. "I'm sorry. It's just... Well, put yourself in my shoes. Your grandfather was stalking me." I search the front of the safe for a way to open it. "There isn't a knobby thing on this."

"A knobby thing?" he repeats, watching me curiously. All the tiny hairs on my arms rise, and my breath quickens.

"You know, a spinner. To unlock it."

He smiles. I like his smile. It's a bit crooked and shows his almost-straight teeth. His right canine sticks out just a little past the rest of them. I bet he had braces when he was younger and didn't wear his retainer at night when he was supposed to, like me. My front teeth are a tad off because of it.

I run my hand across the cold gray metal door. There isn't a latch or anything I can find. My fingers bump over an etching near where a knobby thing should be. It isn't light enough in the basement to see, so I use the flashlight on my phone and study the marking. It's a nautical star. The size of a pendant.

I glance over at Marek. He's studying the hinges on the other side of the safe.

"Your necklace."

He looks over at me. "What?"

"It must be the key." I rub my finger over the etching again. "It matches this."

He leans over my shoulder. You'd think he would smell bad after working out, but he doesn't. There's this manly kind of scent to him, mixed with a musky deodorant.

Marek removes his star pendant and slides it across the etching until it fits inside like a puzzle piece. The safe sighs before an unlatching sound comes from it. He opens it, and I swear both our jaws hit the floor at the same time.

There are piles of money in different currencies on the shelves inside. Heaps of bonds and several jewelry boxes are on the lower two. On the very top is a CD in one of those flimsy plastic cases.

I lift a bundle of euros. "What did he do? Rob banks?"

"I hope not. It would kill my gram." He plucks the CD out of the safe. "I wonder what's on this."

"Maybe instructions on robbing a bank or stalking people."

He frowns at me before plodding over to the computers and sitting in the large leather desk chair. "Guess we should find out."

Though it's cool down here in the basement, the tension is stifling. I suppose it's poor taste to keep insulting his grandfather. But really, I'm the victim here, and I still don't have any answers. For all I know, Adam Conte could've murdered my parents. And Marek frowns at me? Now I'm annoyed. He could be more sympathetic to my concerns.

Ana, if you want them to like you, you have to be nicer. That's what my dad used to say when I'd come home upset that the kids at school hated me. He was right. My snide remarks earned me middle school enemies.

Besides, Marek is probably freaking out as much as I am.

"I'm sorry," I say. "I shouldn't say stuff like that. This can't be fun for you."

"Yeah, it blows." He finds a CD player, inserts the disc into the tray, and presses play. Adam Conte flashes onto one of the screens. He adjusts the camera before sitting down in the same chair his grandson now occupies. He has less gray hair and fewer wrinkles, and his suit is tweed with patches on the elbows.

"When was this recorded?" I pull a chair over and settle beside Marek.

He reads the writing on a piece of masking tape sticking to the CD holder. "Thirteen years ago."

Mr. Conte clears his throat. "To my progeny. If you are viewing this video, then I've passed on to the next life. In the time when people worshipped other gods and goddesses, our family, along with five others, rose up to protect the world from the immortals' wrath. Our ancestors have kept the balance between mortals and immortals since called on by the all-powerful one. This is all I can say on this recording. With strength of body and a mind fed with knowledge, you have been trained since the day you could walk to be a caretaker of something more powerful than you can realize. I have left you with a sort of treasure hunt. We have played many games in practice for this, and all you have to do is remember them, and you will know what to do from here."

Adam Conte clears his throat again.

"Should I die, someone will deliver a possession of mine to you. Solve the cipher and follow the bread crumbs, and all will be revealed to you."

Immortals?

"This makes no sense," I say, rubbing an itch from my nose, trying to keep from sneezing. Though the basement is neat and very organized, it's dusty. "Do you understand him?"

Marek shakes his head, his eyes stuck on the screen. "No."

Mr. Conte leans forward and shuts off the camera.

Marek and I sit there, just staring at a wallpaper of the universe on the computer screen. My mind races. I wonder how Marek is feeling. The man he'd loved, maybe even looked up to, had some sort of weird obsession with gods. He was delusional, for sure. Living in some made-up fantasy or something.

"We used to encrypt messages to each other and use a decoder to transcribe them," Marek says. He smiles at what I'm sure is a memory. "It would annoy Grams. She thought he was keeping things from her. I guess he was."

"I'm sorry," I whisper, not really knowing what to say. But even though I'm on the thin line between creeped out and scared to death, I do feel sorry for him.

He rolls his chair closer to me, and my breath does a somersault over my tongue. "Excuse me. Just need to get into this drawer. I saw some of them in here." He yanks it open and scoops up a bunch of decoder rings into his hands. "This is them. Decoder rings. The letters line up to a number for each one. They're all different. Gramps would change them out for each game. It could be any of these. And what am I supposed to decode?"

The sudden recall of the contents of Mr. Conte's satchel jolts me. "There's a ring in the bag. One of those." I point at the decoders in his cupped hand.

He dumps them back into the drawer, the rings clinking against each other. With one quick and extremely agile move, Marek is on his feet, up the stairs, and out of the basement before I can register his departure.

My mouth purses, and my eyes stay stuck on the open door up the stairs, waiting for Marek to return. I want to pinch myself, wake up from this messed-up dream or nightmare. I need a judge and jury to sift through the evidence and tell me if this is real—the verdict is still out—but I'm very much awake.

Marek thumps down the steps with the satchel in hand. He plops back on the desk chair beside me and unfastens the straps. He claws inside the bag and pulls his hand out, the ring pinched between his fingers.

"This has to be the one." He drops the bag behind him on the seat and searches around the desk.

"What are you looking for?" I ask.

He stops and glances over his shoulder at me. "There has to be a message from him. Look for something with lines of numbers on it."

I grasp the bag, plunge my hand inside, and carefully remove the contents, placing them on the desk. The envelopes are different sizes and colors, from ivory to beige. I shuffle through them and stop on one with Marek's name on it.

It's a letter from Marek, with a crayon drawing of two stick figures—one tall, one tiny—under a large tree with some purple leaves and some green leaves. Written in orange at the bottom of the page is Marek's name with a backward "e." The fact he couldn't stay within the lines suggests he was young when he drew it.

"What's that?" Marek's sudden question startles me.

I hold it up for him to see. "You sent this drawing to your grandfather."

His eyebrows push together. "That's horrible. Good thing I gave up on my artistic ambitions. I sucked."

"I think it's cute."

Our eyes lock, and it's the first time that I truly see his face. I was too busy trying to avoid gawking at his bare chest to notice it. His jawline is prominent, his nose straight, his lips are on the fuller side, and his hair is wavy. He's definitely pleasant to look at.

Stop.

Stop. Stop. Stop. He's the grandson of your stalker.

He grabs a lighter resting on the desk between the keyboard and a damaged tissue box. "Invisible ink. He hid the message. It's on this. Why else would he have an old letter of mine in his bag? Open the envelope at the seams."

I slip my finger into the opening of the envelope, slowly tear it open until it's completely free with no folds, and hand him the dissected paper.

He takes it and holds it over the lighter.

"No." I grab his arm. "Don't burn it."

"I'm not." He tugs his arm out of my grasp. "We used to write private messages with lemon juice and water. I don't think he'd use my drawing, so it has to be the envelope."

"How can he make a secret message with lemon juice?"

"You squeeze a lemon, add a little water to it, and then write your message using a cotton swab on a piece of paper." He flicks on the lighter. "Hold a flame to the paper, and the lemon will turn it a different color to reveal the message."

I can hardly believe it, but it works. The hidden numbers turn brown on the white paper. "Now what?" I ask when he finishes exposing the cipher.

"We decode it." He leans over the decoder ring, turning one of the dials. There are three windows. One with numbers, one with the alphabet, and the other with unusual symbols.

"What are the symbols in that window?"

"I'm not sure. It looks like some foreign alphabet. Read the numbers to me, and I'll write the matching English letter down."

I flatten the envelope on my lap. "I thought it was going to be actual invisible ink. Okay, the first one is twelve." I continue calling out the numbers from the envelope until we reach the last one. "What does it say?"

He straightens. "It says, *the first clue is with number three on the list.*"

"That's kind of anticlimactic." I heave a sigh that shows how frustrated I am. The hands on the very plain clock above the monitors are almost at noon. Dalton and I figured that I should leave here by one to get home before Jane. Actually, I can leave by two, since we left some wiggle room in our estimation. "So who's number three on that list?"

"What list?"

I give him an incredulous look. "The whole reason I'm here. That list. With my name and my parents' names on it."

"Oh." He retrieves it from the bag and stabs it with his finger. "Here. Shona Jackson. She's eighteen and lives in New York. Freshman at NYU."

It's over. The clue leads to someone out of town. I stand. "Well, that's it. I'm never going to know why your grandfather was watching me."

"Come on. Do you always give up so easily? I'll Google her." He grasps the mouse by the keyboard and clicks. "It's locked. I don't know the password. Do you have a smartphone?"

"Yes." I lean back and tug my phone out my front pocket.

"She lives on 57th street. Apartment 15B. The address is listed beside her name." He slides the list on the table closer to me.

I enter the address into the search box. The information loads on the screen of my phone. "Joel Jackson owns the building. Must be her dad."

"Great." He pops up to his feet. "It's less than a three-hour drive from here. We'd get there before four."

It takes a few seconds for my mind to catch up to what he's suggesting. My eyes practically bug out, and I shake my head. "No. No way. I can't go today. I have to get home before Jane — my mom does. She'll freak if I'm not there."

He looks down at me, eyebrows pinched, lips in a straight line. "I thought you wanted to get answers. Here's our chance. This girl has a clue my gramps left me. What about tomorrow? Wait. Where do you live?"

"Philly," I say.

"Perfect. I'll come to you, and we can grab the express."

Tomorrow. A Saturday. The day before Dalton and I take a bus to some boring bereavement camp by Thompson Lake in Maine. I can tell Jane I'm hanging out with friends before we leave. Dalton will cover for me.

"Okay," I say. "We have to go at eight in the morning and be back by six at night, no later than seven." I glance up at the security monitors on the wall above the computers and gasp.

The guy from the gas station, in the Audi with the Thor license plate, strolls up the driveway, flipping his keys in his hand.

CHAPTER SIX

My heart jumps and I bang the back of my legs against the chair and bump into Marek.

He stumbles sideways. "What's wrong?"

I point a shaky finger at the screen. "H-him. He's following me."

His eyes go to the screen, and he leans closer to it. "Oh, him. That's my uncle Bjorn."

"Your uncle?" I can't pull my eyes away from the image of him strutting up the sidewalk with so much confidence he looks arrogant.

"Yeah. Come on." Marek flips off the main switch, and the screens go black. "I don't want him knowing about this… um…"

"Command center?"

He slides me a look that's both disappointed and accepting. "Okay, whatever, command center."

My light footsteps follow his pounding ones up the stairs and into the hallway. He closes and locks the door right before a loud chime sounds throughout the house. We stare at each other for what seems like an eternity.

Is he going to answer it? Why is he just looking at me? Then he inserts the key back into the door, and I notice the flap of my jacket is stuck in the crack. He opens it again, releasing me, then locks it back up and hurries down the hall.

Before Marek can reach the front door, it opens.

A surprised expression hits Bjorn's face. "Hullo, Marek. Wasn't told you'd be about. Just stopping by to call on Grams. See how she's holding up. What took you so long to answer?" His eyes land on me, and I swear my gulp echoes against the walls. "Now who's this? Hold on there. I know you."

I look behind me like there's someone else there he could be talking about.

He continues, "At the gas station. That's it. Good suggestion on the drink. Quite delicious, that one." His eyes shift from me to Marek. "Where's Grams?"

Marek steps aside to let Bjorn in. "She's at her bridge club. She'll be back in an hour or so."

"Mind if I hang about until she returns?"

"Not at all, man," Marek says. "Grams made apple bread. It's in the kitchen. I'm going to walk her out."

Bjorn looks nothing like Marek or Mr. Conte. He's really tall, pale with red hair. Marek and his grandfather have darker complexions and average height. Maybe Bjorn takes after Grams's side of the family.

"And who's 'her?'" Bjorn stares down at me.

"Oh, this is Ana. She's a friend." He scoots by Bjorn. "I'll be right back."

"Nice meeting you, Ana," Bjorn says as I pass.

"You, too." I follow Marek out the door and catch up to him.

"Your uncle. Is he from your grandmother's side of the family?"

Marek glances back at the house, then at me. "No. He's not a blood-relative. My dad met him in college. He stayed here one summer before my parents got married. Been coming around ever since."

He went to school with his dad? "Wow. He looks young."

"Yeah, he's got good genes. I think he dyes his hair." We stop by my car. "So tomorrow?"

"I don't know."

"Give me your phone." He holds an open hand up.

"What do you want with it?"

"Relax. Just adding my number to your contacts."

I pull it out of my pocket and place it on his palm.

He inspects it and holds it out. "Lock."

I press my thumb against the button. He enters his number and hands it back to me. "Call me later. We'll make plans."

"But I—"

"Just call me," he cuts me off, pointing his head in the direction of the house.

Bjorn is watching us from the front window.

"We'll talk later." He winks before walking off and heading back for the house.

I hop into the Civic and take off, putting as much distance as I can from Mr. Conte's secrets.

If there's an epically asinine thing to do, I'd find it. Which I do. Here I sit on the Acela Express beside Marek, on our way to New York.

Sneaking off to New York is something Dalton would do, not me. If Jane ever finds out, she'll ground me for an eternity. "Hey, no worries," Dalton said. "I'll run interference. Mom will never know you went."

Dalton would totally be on this excursion with me if he didn't have a shift at the hospital's gift shop. We both work there, and Jane has a habit of checking in on us while we're on the clock.

My stomach rumbles as if boulders are bouncing around in it. I'm either hungry, or all the rocks of doom have dropped inside me.

Marek gives me a sidelong glance. "You hungry? We can grab a bite somewhere."

"As long as it's quick."

"Right. Home by six. We can grab a hot dog from one of the vendors. Don't worry, we'll be back in time." A crooked smile lifts the right corner of his mouth. His eyes scan my face.

My heart does a flip in my chest. I swear that smile and those eyes could stop a river and make it flow in the opposite direction. His lips wrap around the rim of his water bottle. He takes a long swig, and I watch his throat move up and down as he swallows.

Stop staring, Ana. Seriously. It's like you've never seen a guy drink water before. I pretend to look for the restroom, glancing up the aisle and then in the other direction.

"Need something?" he asks.

"Restroom."

"It's back that way." He motions over his shoulder.

A woman sitting across the aisle from us stretches her incredibly long, dark legs out in the walkway. She has one of those perfect faces you only get from an app and hair that shines like an oil slick.

I stand and slide out into the walkway.

"Ah, young lovers," the woman says, her eyes traveling from me to Marek.

"We're not," I say. "He's just a friend."

Her eyes land on me again. They're black as night, and I can't even make out the irises. Almost hypnotizing. "I'm an expert in spotting romantic links. I do it for a living." She extends a pink card out to me. "If you ever need my services, give me a call."

"Thank you." I reluctantly take the card.

The rocking of the train makes it difficult to walk, and I stagger all the way to the restroom. I shove the card into the pocket of my black bomber jacket. My Vans stick to something on the floor, and I squinch my face. I dart a quick look over my shoulder at the woman before closing the door.

Marek thinks the look is for him and nods at me, that crooked smile lifting one corner of his mouth again. I start and bump my head against the door I'm trying to close.

I don't even want to know if he saw that. This is going to be one *long* day with me trying to act unaffected by Marek.

Check yourself, Ana. I can almost hear Dalton tease me for drooling over the guy.

Marek isn't anything special. Our conversations are about his grandfather and that mysterious list. We probably have nothing in common. The door sighs as I shut it.

When I return to my seat, Long Legs is gone.

"Guess it's my turn. Excuse me." His calves brush me as he squeezes by, his butt practically in my face.

I sink farther into my chair to give him more room.

He makes it to the aisle and smiles down at me. "Sorry."

"No problem," I say, trying to sound as unaffected as a rhino with an oxpecker bird on his back. Which is an actual thing. I saw it in a documentary once. The birds use the rhino for protection from predators. Because no one wants to take on such a mammoth animal.

That's what I need to do. Get a tough skin like a rhino.

With Marek gone, I slip the woman's card out from my pocket. It's pink and there are two interlocking hearts in one corner with three simple lines in the middle.

LOVE IN THE AFTERNOON DATING SERVICE
INANNA AMARI, MATCHMAKER

I'LL FIND YOU...

"What the hell?" The woman is one rook shy of a checkmate.

I sneak a look at the seat she was sitting in. A folded sheet of paper is on the cushion. Rising a little off my seat, I check both directions to make sure no one sees me, then snag the note.

A floral scent rises from the paper as I unfold it. The script is precise and curly. The words are like a knife to my throat.

Analiese, you're being watched.

I can't think with the loud and constant honking of cars on the street just outside Penn Station. I've never been to New York City without my dad or Jane. With my head snapping in different directions—side to side, behind me, in front of me—I probably seem like I'm on something. There are too many people rushing by us on the sidewalk.

Vehicles stop so suddenly, I cringe, thinking I'm going to witness a crash, but somehow they either weave around or stop just in time and avoid hitting the one in front of them. I could never drive in this city.

Analiese, you're being watched. Standing here in the middle of the street with the entire city passing us by has me on my toes. My muscles tense, a headache building behind my eyes. Why did I agree to this?

I spot a black car heading up the street.

"Is that our Uber?"

Marek cranes his neck to see around a woman in a very stylish outfit, carrying an expensive-looking bag. "No. We're looking for a Jetta."

"I wish it would just get here already." I glance around again.

"Hey." He places a hand on my back. "You okay? You're not worried about that note, are you? It was probably a joke. The woman was a little out there."

"It's not just the note," I say, fear sounding in my voice. "It's that she knew my name."

"She probably heard me say it."

"Did you see her writing anything when I was in the rest room?"

"No, but I wasn't really paying attention."

I swallow to clear my dry throat. "Maybe she did hear you say my name. But why write that?"

The grave expression on his face isn't anything like the despair eating away at my stomach. "I don't know, but she's gone now."

A black Jetta pulls up to the curb, and Marek hops off the sidewalk and opens the door. "After you," he says, trying to give me his best reassuring smile and totally failing.

I get in and slide to the other side of the seat. That's when I see them through the window. They're across the street trying to look like tourists, huddled together, a map opened between them. The woman from the train and Marek's Uncle Bjorn.

Why are they together? How do they know each other?

"Wh-what the hell—?" I sputter out, my throat closing on the last word.

CHAPTER SEVEN

The Jetta takes off, and I twist in my seat to peer out the back window. "Isn't that your uncle? He's with that matchmaker woman." Adrenaline rushes through my veins faster than the rising speed of our Uber. My arms and legs shake, and fear tightens my stomach.

"What?" Marek turns and glances back just as the Jetta careens around a corner. "I don't see them."

"They were back on the other street." I flip forward and settle into my seat.

The cushion moves a little when he plops back down. "Could have been a couple that resembled them."

"Right. A couple that just so happened to look like both of them." I cross my arms in front of my chest to steady them.

He gives me one of those smiles Dalton does when he wants to placate me. "Well, we've lost them, so there's no way to know for sure it was them."

He doesn't believe that I saw them. I stare out the window, watching the busy streets, not wanting to talk anymore. Too many strange things are happening lately. Meeting the Thor worshipper at the gas station, then finding out he's Marek's uncle, and now seeing him with the woman from the train.

"Inanna," I say so quietly the only evidence I speak is the whisper of fog against the glass. It's a goddess's name. I think back to Mr. Conte's video. Could she be one? No. Why did she leave me that letter? And who's watching me? Other than the obvious suspects, her and Bjorn, is there someone else?

The Uber driver glances at me through the rearview mirror. I didn't notice him when we got into the car, but the man is young, dark, and gorgeous. There's a falcon tattoo on the inside of his lower arm. "Not to worry," he says with an accent I can't place. "I learn driving in Algiers. This is a piece of cake."

He changes lanes, slipping between two cars with what looks like not enough space to fit the Jetta. I swallow my breath. A seed of anxiety sprouts in the pit of my stomach and branches out, strangling my chest with its roots. I want to go home. But my want for answers is stronger.

Marek stares out the front window, watching where the Uber driver is taking us. I'm not sure I should trust this boy I only met yesterday. I don't know him, and yet, I've abandoned all the warning alarms going off in my head. Why? Because he looks like that? Perfect.

Stop it. He didn't have to invite me to come with him. He could've dropped it when I declined to go.

I look past him and out his side window. Central Park. Tall, thick trees canopy the green grounds. A horse with a shiny brown coat pulls a white carriage holding a woman and two little boys down the shaded pathway running alongside the street.

The Uber driver brings the Jetta to a stop and points across the street to a tall, square building with bronze doors and a long awning that covers the entrance.

"Here you are," the Uber driver says and passes a business card over the back of his seat to me. "If you need a ride again, give me a call. I'll be in the area."

I pop open the door and step onto the curb. Marek slides out after me. The Jetta takes off into the rushing traffic. The business card is expensive, the paper thick, and the driver's name is printed in fancy script.

"Horus…" I mumble. Another god name. There's no way all of this can be a coincidence, is there?

Marek runs his fingers through his hair. "That place is nice. Bet it costs a lot to live here. Even has a doorman."

"What're we going to say?" I shove my hands into my jacket's pockets.

"Not sure," he says. "First, we need to get inside."

"We could tell the doorman we're friends from school."

"What if he checks with her and we're sent away?" His hand rests on the back of his neck, his eyes casing the building. "I think we go with a distraction."

"A distraction?" I repeat, uncertainty sounding in my voice.

"I'll take care of it. When it goes down, you sneak to the elevators and go to the apartment."

"What do I say to her?" I don't like that plan. It can go wrong, and I could get caught. Possibly ending in me getting my first offense on an arrest record for breaking and entering or something. Is it considered breaking and entering if you don't break anything when you enter? I don't know and don't want to find out.

"The truth will work." He sounds confident. "I'll ask the doorman for directions. When you feel he's distracted enough, make your move."

Because, apparently, all common sense leaves me when Marek is involved—or I wouldn't even be in New York—I agree with his plan, and we cross the street with a crowd of pedestrians. I try to look as inconspicuous as possible standing by the front door of the apartment building. When Marek approaches the doorman, he's receiving a delivery.

Every possible outcome of this little, maybe illegal, plan to sneak me into the apartment complex runs through my mind. If I'm caught, I won't have just an arrest record to worry about, they'll call Jane. *Call Jane.*

I'll never be allowed out ever again. Going somewhere in Philadelphia without permission would be bad enough, but leaving the state and going to New York City, she'll blow a fuse. A nervous twitch travels down my back, and I stretch out my fingers to keep my hands from trembling.

I peer through the sliding glass doors. The lobby is empty. Marek's arms are flailing around while saying something to the doorman. The man, tall and lean with a long face, follows Marek up the sidewalk.

"You think she's in labor?" the man's saying as he passes me. "Are you certain?"

"Yes, she needs help," Marek answers.

The man's shoes clack against the cement. "We should call an ambulance."

"We have." Marek gives me a quick look and tips his head toward the door. "Move," he mouths.

I dart through the sliding doors and to the elevators, shooting glances over my shoulder, waiting for the elevator to arrive. Just outside in front of the building, Marek runs off, and the doorman yells something at him before turning to return to the apartment complex.

A ding goes off, and the elevator opens. I dash inside and stab the button for the fifteenth floor. My stomach takes a beat to catch up with me. It lurches and drops when the doors to the outside part and the doorman strides in.

I press myself up against the elevator's back wall, hoping he doesn't notice me. The doors slide shut just as his head turns in my direction. The floor lifts, and I swallow a heavy breath.

"That was close," I say to no one and slump against the

wall.

The fifteenth floor has precisely four doors. Two lead to fire escapes on either end of the hall, and two to apartments 15A and 15B.

I push the doorbell to 15B and wait.

And wait some more.

It's pretty silent on the other side of the door. Maybe Shona's out. We didn't come up with a plan if she's not home. Neither one of us even thought of the possibility that she'd be gone.

Do I wait?

I wrench my phone out of my pants pocket, search for Marek's number, and press the call button.

"Did you make it?" Marek sounds out of breath. He must've run for a while.

"I did," I say. "But she's not home."

"Great. We have to wait for her."

"You mean I do," I grumble. He isn't the one illegally in an apartment building. What would the charges be for trespassing? Or I could be mistaken for a burglar. Or maybe even a stalker.

The thumping of heavy boots on the wooden floor causes me to spin away from the door. A tall guy with sandy brown hair who looks as if he just stepped off the runway comes to a halt outside 15B.

I freeze, not able to move.

He glares down at me and snaps, "Who are you?"

"I—"

"Why are you here?" He lets out a feral growl.

My lungs tighten, and I can't breathe. "D-Don't hurt me."

CHAPTER EIGHT

"Cain, back off," a girl's voice orders.

The guy takes a step back.

The girl has black curly hair, her face is flawless, and her long nails are sculpted. She sways as she strolls over to us on expensive-looking heels. "I can't leave you alone for a second," she says.

Cain turns his head toward her. "She's snooping around. Probably a spy."

"Really?" There's frustration in her voice. "She's just a girl. I need to limit your game time. You're mixing up make-believe with reality. Now go cool off in your room."

He unlocks the door and disappears into the apartment.

Brown eyes under perfectly winged eyeliner and false eyelashes land on me. "You do drink tea, don't you?"

I nod, too freaked out to speak.

"Good. Come in." She pushes open the door Cain left ajar. When I don't follow her, she says, "He won't hurt you, I promise."

There is no way I'm going inside that apartment with an

angry model dude in there. "I'm fine out here," I say. "I was just looking for Shona Jackson."

She comes back, rests her hand on the fancy crystal knob, and leans against the door. "Well, you found her. What do you want?"

Now that I'm here, I'm at a loss for words, knowing that what I have to say will come out sounding as if I took a trip to Neverland and was high on fairy dust. Busy running a practice speech in my head, I forget she's waiting for a response.

Shona's hand goes from resting on the doorknob to her waist. "Well?" She sounds annoyed. "I don't have all day."

"Do you always invite complete strangers in for tea?" I'm stalling.

"No." She raises one precisely bladed eyebrow. "But you look like you could use some? It's calming."

"What I came to say is going to sound far out there," I warn. "I just found out about it myself. But you see, there's this list—"

"I know about it," she cuts me off. "So the old man's dead, huh?"

It's as if someone knocks into me. I stumble back. "You know about the list?"

"Yeah, Cain caught the old man snooping around. Just like you." She looks over my shoulder. "You should come inside. The woman in 15A is very nosy. Her days are filled with watching game shows and spying on me." She opens the door wider and steps aside to let me in.

I hesitate, not knowing if it's a good idea to enter without Marek. She's a stranger, after all, and her scary boyfriend seems unstable. "My friend's outside waiting."

She hesitates and just stares at me. Probably trying to assess if I'm lying about having someone with me. "Okay," she finally says. "I'll notify the doorman and let him know we're expecting company."

"Yeah, about that." There's a quiet *click* behind me, and I glance over my shoulder at 15A's door and then back to Shona.

Shona motions me in, and I step over the threshold. The apartment's huge and decorated with jewel-colored walls and oddly shaped furniture. Rows of windows make up one wall with a great view across the park.

A thought catches up with me. How does she know Mr. Conte is dead?

"What's your friend's name?" Shona asks, and my thought fades into the background. She stands in front of a fancy intercom system, punching in numbers.

My eyes wander over the place, trying to locate Cain. I shift uneasily on my feet. I don't like not knowing his whereabouts. "I don't think the doorman will let him in."

A smile pulls across her full lips. "Interesting. What did he do to get himself restricted from the building?"

"He made a distraction so I could sneak in. The doorman is pretty pissed at him."

Her eyebrow rises again. "I see. My father owns the building. The attendant will do whatever I say." She pushes a button on the intercom and leans closer to it. "Marshall?"

A few seconds later, a man's voice comes through the box. "Yes, Miss."

"The boy, the one who took you away from your post, let him through."

"All right, Miss," he says. "Is there anything else?"

"No. That's all. Thank you." She turns and faces me. "Let your friend know he can come up."

I text Marek, then join Shona in the living room. A door on the left is open. Inside the room, Cain sits straight as a pin on a big cushioned chair, his hands resting on his knees and eyes closed.

"Is he okay?" I ask and drop down on the couch beside her.

She glances at the open door. "Oh, him? He's meditating.

He can get hotheaded at times. Just needs a time out."

I cross my legs. "Is he your guardian?"

"Boyfriend. I'm eighteen. He's only a year older than me."

Hopefully, he doesn't take his anger out on her.

As if she knows what I'm thinking, she adds, "He's never touched me. He listens to me. I can get him to calm down. We've been together since sophomore year of high school." Her lips turn down, and she sighs. "He used to be so sweet. He's changed a lot. Ever since…" She trails off, seemingly checking herself. "Listen to me. Complaining. I should be happy he's completely devoted to me."

Devoted? More like her lapdog.

Her eyes give her away. She's not at all happy about that.

I glance around, feeling a little uncomfortable, and my gaze stops on a painting above the fireplace. It's of a woman with red hair pulled up loosely. By the technique and the woman's dress and hair, it has to be from the Renaissance era. Her face is familiar to me. I must've seen the artwork before.

"Do you like art?" Shona asks. "That one isn't an original. It's a Michelangelo duplicate. From a fresco he painted."

"It's beautiful," I say.

A knock sounds from the entry. Shona springs to her feet and dashes across the plush area rug. The air adjusts slightly in the room when she opens the door. Marek leans casually to one side with his arm braced against the doorframe, supporting his weight. His stance lengthens his toned muscles. His dark hair is messy, and beads of sweat glisten on his forehead.

Shona gives him a once-over and looks over at me. "Nice," she mouths.

I ignore her comment. "What happened to you?" I ask. "Did you run a marathon or something?"

"That Marshall isn't a forgiving man," Marek says, breathless. "He wouldn't let me ride the elevators. Made me take all fourteen flights of stairs."

A laugh blurts from Shona's mouth. "Guess he got even with you."

"What's he doing here?" Cain's voice is deep and filled with anger. His eerily vacant eyes are set on Marek. The muscles in his jaws tighten.

"You're supposed to be in your room, cooling off," Shona directs at Cain. "Now go."

Cain doesn't say a word. He just obeys her order. Just like that. No back talk or argument. She commands him, and he goes. He hangs his head and shuffles to his room.

"Please, have a seat," she says, keeping her eyes on Cain's retreat.

I sit beside Marek on the couch and lean closer. "Isn't that weird? He does whatever she says."

"Yeah, the dude is whipped," Marek whispers back.

Shona spins around on her very high heels to face us. "So, Adam Conte. Who's he to you?"

"He's my grandfather," Marek says.

Her eyes go to me. "And who are you to him?"

"I'm on that list." I adjust in my seat. There's something familiar with Shona. It's as though we've met before, but I know we haven't. It's unnerving and comforting at the same time.

A sympathetic smile presses her cheeks. "I don't have any answers. Cain caught him watching me, and I had to pry him off the poor man. He held him while I searched Adam's bag for answers. I found the list and my name. Adam said an entity, can't remember the name of it, hired him to watch over the people on the list. To alert a team who'd protect us if we were in danger. He never said what kind of danger. I assumed my father arranged it because of the trust fund my mom left me. It must be the same for you."

Her voice cracks a little over "mom." She uses the informal

when referring to her and the formal when mentioning her father, and I can't help but wonder why she does.

"We don't have money." I gesture to the room. "Well, nothing like this, anyway. Wait. You knew he was dead. How?"

"He said if he died, someone might contact me. A replacement, I think."

Marek pushes back against the cushions. "My grandfather said he gave you something. Do you have it?"

Her face is a question mark. "Gave me something? No—" A thought cuts off her words. "Wait. He did send me a postcard. I thought it was strange that he knew I collect them. We only met that one time. Let me get it."

While she's gone to get the postcard, Marek and I sit in silence. Is he as hopeful as I am that there will be clues on it? Placing his elbows on his knees, he rests his chin on folded hands. His dark hair curls slightly at the nape of his neck. Probably caused by sweating during his hike up the stairs.

He glances at me, busting me staring at him.

I flick my head in the other direction, pretending to watch for Shona's return. Marek smiles. He so knows I was checking him out. I need to get myself together. Stop letting a guy distract me.

Shona returns and hands the postcard to Marek. He reads the back and turns it over. "Van Gogh's *The Starry Night*," he says, removing the decoder ring from his right index finger and looking at me, then Shona. "Maybe the clue is your address."

"What clue?" Shona studies us.

I look at Marek and raise an eyebrow, seeking his approval to tell her. He nods, but I decide to give her as little information as possible. Because we don't even really know what his grandfather was up to.

"We think Mr. Conte left them for Marek," I say. "Something to do with the list. We're not sure. Just trying to figure it out."

"Do you have some paper and a pen?" Marek asks.

She nods. "Yes. Right beside you in that drawer."

Marek opens the tiny drawer in the fancy end table and pulls out a pad of paper and an expensive-looking pen. He works with the numbers of Shona's address, writing them down. Every combination he can think of, he tries. "It's just a jumbled mess. Nothing works."

"Can I see?" I reach my hand out, and he passes the postcard to me. "He says 'Happy Birthday' in the closing."

"I know," Shona says, pushing a frown on her lips. "My birthday was months away when I received that."

A bubble of excitement rises in my stomach. "Maybe it's the numbers—"

"Of her birthday," Marek finishes for me. "What is it?"

"The first of May," Shona says.

Marek spins the date and year she tells him into the decoder ring and writes down the corresponding letters. He looks up with disappointment on his face. "That's not it."

"Then why would he write that if it wasn't her birthday?" I say, flipping the card over. "It has to be the clue."

Shona rolls the material of her skirt between slender fingers. It must be a nervous tick or something. "Maybe he just got my day mixed up with someone else's."

I check the time on my phone. "We've got to go soon. I have to get home before Jane does."

Marek nods. "Yeah, maybe my grandfather has the birthdays of everyone on that list in his basement somewhere. What's your birthday?"

"November twenty-seventh."

He spins the numbers with the year into the ring, and it's not mine, either. The letters together were incoherent. "Okay. Let's go before it's too late." His gaze goes to Shona. "Thanks for the help. Can I keep this?" He flaps the card in the air.

"Sure," she says and shows us to the door. "Listen, I'm

sorry for your loss. He seemed like a nice man."

A smile tilts Marek's mouth. "Thanks."

She shuts the door.

"So what are we going to do?" I ask once we're in the elevator.

He leans against the back wall. "You go home, and I'll search my grandfather's things. If he has the birthdays for those on the list, I'll run them through the decoder ring."

"So you'll call me if you find anything?"

"Of course."

Marek sleeps the entire train ride to Philadelphia. I want to talk, but he looks peaceful with his head back and mouth slightly open. I keep busy with my phone, checking social media and reading an ebook.

The train pulls into the station, and I tap Marek on the arm. "We're here."

I text Dalton to pick me up, and Marek waits with me.

"Dalton is always late," I say. "Your train is leaving soon. I'll be fine. You should go."

His eyes go to the departures on the screen hanging from the ceiling. "You sure? If I miss it, the next one isn't for a few hours."

No. I'm not sure. I don't want him to leave, but even so, I answer, "I'm sure."

"Well," he says with a smile that makes my heart speed up. "I'll text if I find anything."

"Okay."

It takes several beats of my racing heart for Marek to say, "All right, then, bye."

"Bye."

It doesn't escape me that I'm giving him one-word answers. I just don't know what to say. He walks away with confidence, his back straight and a little swagger to his gait. I can't pull my eyes from him. I watch him the entire way to the corridor leading to his train. Before he turns the corner, Marek looks back at me, and this time I don't glance away, I hold his stare. His lips pull into that smile of his that could melt an iceberg.

My heart squeezes, and I smile back.

And then he's gone.

CHAPTER NINE

Maybe he just got my day mixed up with someone else's. Shona's words wake me. I stare at the night sky that Dad and I painted on my ceiling when I was eight. We added those glow-in-the-dark stars on my tenth birthday. I tug the covers up to my chin.

Someone else's birthday.

I can totally tell which clouds I painted and which ones Dad did. Mine are less realistic. His are works of art.

"But whose birthday," I mutter to my dark room.

Marek texted me earlier. He found the birthdays of everyone on the list—some were crossed out, too. None of them spelled anything coherent. Some were close, but then one letter wouldn't work.

Why does it matter? I'm done chasing the answers to that list.

So what? My name's on a list. Some old man followed me. But that old man's dead now and can't stalk me anymore.

We should have painted Van Gogh's *The Starry Night* on the ceiling. Seeing it on the postcard brought back a memory.

Jane and Dad had replicated it at a night of wine and painting class once. Dad's was nearly perfect. Jane's was a disaster.

Van Gogh.

I pop up, snatch my phone from the nightstand, and text Marek.

try Van Gogh's birthday

I Google it.

it's March 30, 1853

As if he needs to know the number for March, I text it.

3/30/1853

I wait, staring so hard at my phone my eyes water.
Wait.
"Come on, answer," I order as if he can hear me.
Still no response.
I fling myself back on my pillows and groan. "He's killing me."
My phone chimes. It's a message from Marek.

will do

As though staring at my screen will make him go faster, I can't pull my eyes away.

it worked

A yelp escapes me. I want to call him. *Should I call him?*
Imagine Dragons play on my phone, announcing a call. Marek's name flashes on the screen. I smooth down my hair as if he can see me, then answer it.
"Hello?" I sound somewhat croaky, so I clear my throat. "Hi."
"Rome," he says. "It spells Rome."
"That's it? No specifics."
"It's only a few numbers. I checked the list, and there's an

Angelo Michels, Antonia Rossi, and Dane Connor in Rome. And addresses and phone numbers are by their names. Maybe we should call them."

Angelo Michels sounds familiar to me.

"I guess," I say. "But what if they don't speak English?"

"That would be a problem." He exhales a long breath. "I'm going to try. I'll call you back."

He hangs up before I can answer him. I glance at the clock. It's just past two in the morning. Dalton and I are leaving at nine for camp. I'll have to sleep on the bus. A yawn overtakes me, and I hug my pillow.

Come on. Call back already.

He must be reading my mind. Marek's name flashes on my screen again.

I don't bother saying hello. "What did you find out?"

"Angelo's number doesn't work. The other two didn't answer."

I think of the name again. Angelo Michels. Something hits me. Mr. Conte had used Van Gogh for the first clue.

"He switched the name around to hide it. Michelangelo," I said. "Try decoding the numbers in the address and maybe the phone number for Angelo Michels."

"I'm impressed," he says. "Good catch. Hold on a sec."

I push up against my headboard and cross my legs. An eternity goes by, and then goes around again before Marek returns on the phone.

"It spells Sistine Chapel," he says.

I uncross my legs. "As in the Sistine Chapel in Rome?"

"Looks like it. Some of Michelangelo's works are there."

"I don't get it." I glance at my suitcase packed for camp. The mystery behind the list will have to wait until I return. "Is this a game? What was your grandfather doing?"

"Whatever it is," he says, "it was important enough for him to hide it and leave me clues."

"So what can you do? It's not like you can go to Rome and see if you can find another clue there."

"That's exactly what I'm going to do."

"You're going to Rome?"

"Yeah, there are heaps of money in that safe and a passport with my name on it. I think it's what my grandfather wanted me to do. He wasn't an impulsive man. This has to be big. Important enough for all the expensive spy shit he has."

I'd probably do the same thing if it were my grandfather. "Will you let me know what you find?"

"Sure." He falls silent, and all I can hear is his heavy breathing over the phone. "Thanks for the help. Enjoy the bereavement camp."

I laugh. "How does one enjoy a bereavement camp? I bet everyone will be crying most of the time."

"Well, bring lots of tissues." Now he laughs. "Good night."

"Night." I push the end button and fall back on my pillows. Like the shadows surrounding the corners of my room, a smile creeps across my lips. I can't help myself. There's just something about Marek that makes my skin goosepimply and causes twinges in my stomach.

It's going to be difficult to sleep. What's in the Sistine Chapel? And why did Mr. Conte have to use clues? Marek was right. His grandfather went to a lot of trouble to hide them. A person does that for something of importance. Not just for a game or for something trivial.

I Google Michelangelo's artwork in the Sistine Chapel. Many of the frescoes have naked people in them. I scroll through each one without knowing what I'm looking for.

There are his famous works like *The Creation of Adam*. Everyone in the world has seen the image of a nude man and an older man with a white beard reaching toward each other, almost touching fingers. And there are so many lesser-known paintings in the Sistine Chapel, too.

One catches my attention, and I stop on it. A woman with red hair pulled loosely up. It's the original of the reproduction in Shona's apartment. It has to be the next clue. But what is it? Are the two connected? Had Mr. Conte been in Shona's apartment? And if he had, why didn't Shona say so? I have so many questions, and I doubt I'd get any answers to them.

I text Marek the information and attach the link to the website. He messages me back, telling me he's going to Shona's later in the morning to investigate the painting. I'll probably be on the bus heading for camp before he finds out anything.

My head sinks into my pillow, and I continue staring at the clouds on my ceiling. Not able to sleep. Not able to think of anything else but that list and the clues. And definitely not able to erase all the thoughts troubling my mind.

Imagine Dragons going off on my phone again tells me I did fall asleep at some point in the night. It's my grandparents in Israel. My birth father's parents. We Facetime every Sunday morning. Saba and Safta used to come out and see me when I was younger but had to stop when Saba had a stroke. I fly over there to visit now, but I haven't seen my grandparents in almost a year.

I answer it, and both of their faces appear on the screen, heads together, smiles big and warm. It's three in the afternoon there. Safta is always put together well. Her hair changes colors frequently from dark-blond to light, depending on how my aunt does it. Today it's somewhere in between. In old photographs when she was younger, her natural color is as dark as mine. Saba's hair is almost completely silver now, but he looks healthier. They're on a new health thing. Exercise and no processed foods.

"Hello, *Ana'le*," Safta says in that same voice she uses for my baby cousins. It sounds extra special with her accent.

My birth father's family is big. There are a lot of them

in Israel. It's a little overwhelming when I do visit. It takes a few days to get used to things after I arrive, but I do enjoy participating in all the Jewish ceremonies and traditions. It makes me feel closer to a father I never knew.

Saba clears his throat. "You get bigger each time we call."

Meaning every Sunday, I'm either taller or wider.

Safta frowns at him. "What do you mean? She looks the same. A little bed tousled, but the same." She turns a smile to me. "Are you all packed and ready?"

I glance at my bag as if she can see it off screen. "Yeah."

"You're not happy." Safta can read me even on a small screen. "It'll be nice. You can talk out your feelings."

I'm tired of going over the last few months with strangers. But it's not something I can say to her. She and Saba paid for the camp. For both Dalton and me, which is sweet, since he isn't their blood-relative. I know they're worried about me.

So I lie. "I'm looking forward to it. I'm just tired. I was on the phone late with a friend. His grandfather died recently. He's not really a friend. We just met. Dalton and I witnessed Mr. Conte getting hit by a car."

"Conte?" Saba's eyebrows push together. "Eli's friend?"

He calls my uncle by his name so as not to confuse him with his son. Or maybe to remind me who my birth father was, but I can never forget. I think of him and my mother all the time. It takes a few beats for me to get past him calling my dad that before the context of what he said sinks in.

"Wait. Conte? Adam Conte?"

By the look Saba is giving me, he notices the panic in my voice. "Yes, his name was Adam. He visited us after Eli's... A few months back."

Could it be the same Adam Conte? It has to be.

"Do you know where he lived?"

"Outside of Philadelphia somewhere," Safta says. "What's wrong, *Ana'le*? Do you think it's the same man?"

That's why he painted me. He knew my dad.

I ignore her questions and ask my own. "What did he want?"

Safta's face is all scrunched up with concern. "He was in our area and brought something Eli had of your father's."

"What was it?"

Saba rushes off.

"He's going to get it," Safta informs me in case I can't tell what he's doing and I'm worried he won't return.

When he does return, he holds up a black onyx sculpture of a cat, a thick necklace around its neck, wearing a gold hoop earring. It's the goddess of protection, Bastet. Just like the one in the Conte's house.

My throat clogs, and I can't speak. Adam Conte carried that statue all that way to give to my grandparents. By how Saba needs both hands to hold the thing, it must weigh a lot. There's something there. I'm not sure what, but Mr. Conte wanted to protect my grandparents. How did he even know how to find them? How is he connected to my family? Before I worry Safta and Saba, I need to get off the phone.

"Listen, I have to get ready." Which I do. "Don't want to be late for the bus."

"Oh yes, *Ana'le,* we don't want to make you late." Safta smiles, and it's as comforting as warm chocolate chip cookies. "Will we see you for Hanukkah?"

"With Eli being gone," I say, using Dad's first name out of respect for them, "it'll be Dalton's first Christmas without him. I think I should stick around here and come out for New Year's."

Safta smiles. "Yes, of course."

"Then we'll make plans for you," Saba says with an understanding nod.

"Okay, love you both."

"Love you, *Ana'le,*" they say together.

I end the call, throw my legs over my bed, and just sit there. Not sure what to think about Mr. Conte visiting my grandparents. Why would Eli give a possession of my father's to the old man? Why not to me? Or why not mail it? I'll never know, because everyone who knew the answers to my questions is dead.

It doesn't surprise me that Jane can't take Dalton and me to the bus station. Her work is demanding, and she's the only one providing for us. I get that. But there has to be some sort of balance. If not for me, then for Dalton.

The station is crowded. It seems as if everyone is going somewhere this morning. I push my suitcase along, rushing beside Dalton, the wheels clacking against the tiles.

I told Dalton everything that happened the last two days. When I mentioned the Bastet statues, he showed me the one hidden up in Jane's closet. Since I don't snoop like him, I never saw it before. He doesn't say much, just that it's bizarre. That's it. *Bizarre*. He always downplays things, or maybe he isn't sure what to think. I know I don't.

"I wonder if there'll be any hotties at this camp," Dalton says, struggling with his suitcase, the right wheel of it sticking every few steps.

"If there are any, you can have them all," I say. "Which gate are we?"

A wide grin pushing into his cheeks makes me wonder what he's thinking until he says, "A bereavement camp is the perfect place to get two strong, comforting arms wrapped around me."

"Oh, please," I say, rolling my eyes. "I just hope they don't make us sing around a campfire." Last time I sang in public was in elementary school for a Christmas pageant. It's cute to be out of tune when you're six, not so much when you're seventeen.

"Did you remember your meds?" he asks. "You know what happens when you forget to take them."

"Of course—"

Two men and a woman watching us from where they stand under the bus monitors distracts me. They're unusually beautiful, with perfect bone structures and muscles sculpted over their bodies. One man is dark and tall, one man shorter with red hair, and the woman lean yet curvy.

Dalton glances at where my eyes are set. "Damn. Talk about winning the gene pool. Those three are definitely models."

"Don't turn around." Marek's voice comes from behind us, and I gasp. "Keep walking. Go to the bathroom. I'll meet you there."

Dalton leans closer to me. "Who's the guy? He's delicious, isn't he?"

"He's that old man's grandson," I whisper, scanning the terminal for the bathroom. Once I spot the women's sign, I cross the rushing traffic of people.

"Should I come?" Dalton hurries behind me. "I'm not sure I trust that guy."

"Me neither," I say over my shoulder.

A woman gives Dalton a strange look as she's exiting the restroom and we're entering. Her eyes practically bulge out.

"I'm gay," Dalton says to her. "Nothing in here interests me."

The woman hurries out, passing Marek, who's rushing in.

"Is there anyone else in here?" Marek asks.

"Yes." A woman's voice comes from the stall at the end. "This is the women's restroom, not the men's."

"We know," Dalton says a little too loud. "We're helping

my sister with an issue. You might want to leave. It's not going to be pretty, and it may be somewhat stinky."

I glare at Dalton. "Thanks for that."

A wide grin stretches his lips. "Hey, just ad-libbing."

We wait at the sinks until the woman flushes and washes her hands, then she gives me a pity smile before exiting.

Marek pushes the trash can up against the door, his grandfather's satchel slung over his shoulder.

I face him. "What are you doing here?"

"You have to come with me," he says, riffling through the bag.

"I can't." I toss Dalton a sidelong glance, hoping he'll back me up. "We're on our way to camp."

Marek finds what he's searching for and holds it up. "It's about these."

"Passports?"

"You have to see this," he says, opening one and showing me the inside. "The name on it is Olivia Martin, and the photo is…" He taps it with a finger.

My stomach drops as if it's falling into a bottomless pit— down, down, down.

It's me.

CHAPTER TEN

I can't believe Marek talked me into flying to Rome with him, or that Dalton backed him up. If Dalton had a passport, he'd go along; since he doesn't, I'm on my own. Well, without Dalton. Obviously, Marek's traveling with me.

Going back to my house to get my passport almost caused Marek and me to miss our train. I know it annoyed him, but I wasn't about to go as Olivia Martin. It's illegal. Besides, I've had one since I was born. Most of the stamps in it are from Israel from when I go visit my grandparents.

There's no way this plan's going to work. Dalton will lie to the camp counselors and say I'm sick and will be coming to the camp late. He even forged a note from Jane. He'll call Jane to tell her we made it okay and we're both fine. She won't care if I don't call. It's expected. We've been at odds with each other ever since Dad died.

We're back in Shona's apartment. There's a passport in the illegal stack with her picture on it under a different name. So we figure she should know about it, and we need to find out if there's a clue in the Michelangelo reproduction hanging over her fireplace.

Vanilla scents the room. It's likely coming from the candle burning on the table by the front door. It's chilly. The air conditioner must be on high or something. My gaze keeps going to the painting. There doesn't seem to be anything special about it. Nothing that looks like a clue.

Shona huffs, staring at the passport in her hand. "Sally Smith? He couldn't pick a more exotic name for me? Why do you suppose he made these for us?"

"I'm not sure," Marek says. "It must be something to do with the list. I found other passports. I can't be certain, but I bet the photographs match up to the people on it."

Cain enters the room, a deep scowl on his face. "They're here again. Don't they have better things to do than to bother us? I'm going to the bakery."

Shona's eyes follow him all the way until he disappears into the foyer. The front door opens and then slams shut. "He has such a sweet tooth lately."

"Is he always so grumpy?" I ask.

Her eyes flick in our direction. "It's been that way ever since he died."

Did she say *died*?

Marek has the same thought. "Died? What do you mean? He's alive."

"Your grandfather didn't tell you, did he?"

"Tell me what?" Marek stumbles to his feet and looks down at the carpet as if it tripped him.

"You probably should stay seated for this."

Any time someone wants you to sit before telling you something, it's usually bad. And I'm not sure I want to hear it. I'm kind of done with all the damn revelations happening lately.

Who am I kidding? I want to hear what she has to say. I need to know more about that list now that a passport showed up with my picture on it, adding to the mystery. And I fear, whatever the reason, someone's killing the people on that list. That's why their names are crossed off. Why my parents' and uncle's names are marked out.

Shona perches on the edge of a straight-back chair with swirling vines and flowers carved into its wooden legs and arms.

Marek sits beside me on the couch, his hand resting on the cushion and against my thigh. With some effort, I act as if his nearness doesn't send tingles across my skin and up my spine. But it does, so I scoot over, pretending as though I did that to lean against the armrest and not because I need some distance from him or risk him noticing my reaction.

"You see," she says and pauses, clearing her throat. "A car hit Cain while he was crossing the street. He died. I'm sure of it. There wasn't a pulse. I was out of my mind. Crushed." Her face is a mask; not a single emotion shows on it. "I cradled his face in my hands and was about to kiss him when his eyes snapped open. I thought it was a miracle, but the truth is that it was something else. *Something* from the devil."

I now scoot to the edge of the couch. "From the devil?"

She rolls the material of her skirt between her fingers. "I did it. Cain came back to life because of me."

"Did you give him CPR?" I ask.

"No. Just held his head."

"He came back?" Marek lifts a brow. "Maybe he was just knocked out."

Her eyes drill into his. "No. It wasn't like that. I swear he was dead. He hasn't been the same since. Sure, he looks and acts like Cain, but the Cain before the accident was kind and gentle. A health nut. An animal activist. This one is angry and has no remorse. He killed the pigeons the lady in 15A had up on the roof. All of them. Just because they bothered us while we were up there. He went into the cage and broke each of their necks."

Marek moves forward, aligning with me at the edge of the couch. "Maybe he just snapped. People change."

Shona lets go of her skirt and smooths the material down. "I know it sounds way out there."

Marek releases a frustrated laugh. "It's nonsense. There has to be another explanation. You didn't just raise him from the dead like some god."

His words make me remember what his grandfather said on the recording he left for Marek. Mr. Conte believed in gods and goddesses. He was delusional. Gods and goddesses from mythologies are just that—myths. Which makes me think his wild goose chase for hidden clues is a madman's game. I probably should convince Marek to drop it. I don't need answers. My parents and uncle are dead, and I probably shouldn't dig up their secrets—if there are any.

But I want to unearth them. I want to know everything, not just what other people have told me.

Marek stands and shuffles over to the fireplace. "I'm a little thirsty. You have anything to drink?"

Shona eases to her feet and tugs down her skirt. "Of course we do. What would you like?"

"How about tea?" he asks.

"Sure," she says. "Hot or cold?"

The smile on Marek's face has a hint of mischief in it. "Hot. If it's not too much trouble."

The moment Shona's out of the room, Marek searches the back of the painting. When his hand comes out from behind the frame, he holds a tiny wadded-up piece of paper. I lean over his arm watching him unfold it.

"What does it say?" I ask lower than a whisper.

"A clue." Marek reads it quietly. "*Seek the true one.*"

"This is a fake. The real one is in the Sistine Chapel," I say. "We have to get to Rome."

"Yep. We need plane tickets." He shoves the paper in his pants pocket.

"What if all this is just one of your grandfather's games?"

Marek shifts and gazes down at me. "This is real. My grandfather wouldn't put all this effort into a game. All that money. There's something big at the end of this trail of clues, and I think you're a part of it."

There is some sort of connection between my family and his. Mr. Conte even went to Israel to give my grandparents that statue of Bastet. A protection. From what?

I'm scared to face it, though. Something happened to my parents and uncle. Something bad. And it wasn't an accident. I push back on the inner voice that keeps telling me I don't want to know the truth. Because I do want to know. I stare at him for a long while, processing what the repercussions will be if I go. But the thing is, I have no idea what they'll be if I don't.

"Okay," I finally say. "Do you have a plan?"

"We need to find the soonest flight to Rome."

"Well, you aren't going without me." Shona slowly walks across the room, balancing three mugs on a silver tray. "I'm on that list, too. It's going to be expensive this last-minute."

The front door flies open and bangs against the wall. Cain rushes in, practically blowing steam out his nose. He clutches a donut shop bag in one hand. His knuckles on his other hand are bleeding.

"They're out of Bavarian creams again," he barks. "All they make is donuts there. How can they be out?"

The anger on Cain's face causes me to stand, ready to run if needed. "Did you hit someone?"

"No, just the wall." He paces the room, his muscles tense, eyes vacant. "A brick one."

A stunned look passes between Marek and me. We don't move, not sure what to do.

Shona places the tray on the coffee table and frowns at

Cain. "What did I tell you? It's a popular donut. No need to get violent over it. Take a breath and calm down."

Cain inhales a deep breath and lets it out. His glare shifting around and his nostrils going in and out are full-on scary, and he looks about to charge at someone. He's like a bull stuck in a pen, waiting for Shona to open the gate and let him loose.

"Now go wash your hand before you drip blood on the carpet," she says, picking up one of the mugs and handing it to Marek.

With a frustrated growl, Cain slouches off down a hallway at the end of the living room.

"He's not coming with us, right?" Marek studies the contents in the mug.

A frown deepens the creases in Shona's forehead. "I can't leave him alone. He could hurt someone."

"You let him go to the donut shop," Marek counters.

She passes me one of the mugs. "He's been instructed not to harm anyone in the neighborhood."

"That's comforting," I say with a sarcastic tone and breathe in the aroma of the tea. It's a floral scent with a touch of spice. "Why not just tell him to not hurt anyone until you get back."

"Because I have to remind him every morning or he'll forget." She takes a sip of her tea, eyeing me over the lip of her mug. "You don't believe me, do you?"

"I don't know what to believe." I'm suspicious of the tea. She could have poisoned it. I place my mug back on the coffee table. "How can someone forget not to hurt someone? You just don't do it."

Marek must not trust his either, because he puts his mug down next to mine.

"You're not listening." That heavy frown does nothing for her face. If she keeps it up, she'll have horrible wrinkles when she gets older. "He has no conscience. I'm the only one who can keep him from harming others."

"Sounds like a match made in heaven," I drone.

She regards me a moment before saying in a haughty tone, "We were…before the accident."

"We're wasting time," Marek interjects and yanks his cell phone from his pocket. "We should find a flight." His fingers move across the screen.

"Good idea," I say.

He lifts his phone and squints at the screen. "I don't have service here."

"That happens all the time. We have bad cell connection because the brick walls on the outside are thick." Shona pops up from her seat and motions for us to follow her. "We have a desktop computer in the spare room."

Marek follows her, and I trail him into the room.

"I'll contact my friend, Sid," she says. "Have him pick us up at the airport. He lives just outside of Rome."

I plop down on the bed and sink into the expensive, fluffy comforter while Shona and Marek search for flights on the computer. My attention isn't on them. It's stuck on the elephant outside the room. Cain.

"Wait. You have a friend in Rome?" I'm impressed when someone has a friend outside of Philadelphia.

Shona flicks a look over her shoulder at me. I think she's surprised to find me there. If she thinks I'm going to wait in the living room alone with her hotheaded boyfriend in the apartment, she can guess again.

"Yes. I have them all over the world."

It takes all my power not to roll my eyes at her.

Cain walks by and glares inside the room. I swear my heart stops as he passes, then it picks up beating again and my breath returns after he's gone. When he comes back the other way and scowls, I lock eyes with him. I'm determined not to be the one to break. My cold stare says I'm not afraid of him, but inside I'm terrified.

I almost slip off the bed when he looks away first and rushes down the hall. It wasn't Shona who made him go, because she's staring at the computer screen, discussing flights with Marek. He probably got bored of me.

An uneasy feeling bubbles up in my stomach. Our traveling companions concern me. Cain in particular—with his anger and unpredictability, he could go off at any time. What will he do if Shona's not around to stop him? And was it only birds he killed before? I'm too scared to know the answer to that question. Most serial killers start with murdering animals and then move on to humans.

Lovely. Not only is this trip going to get me in big trouble with Jane, but it could also get me killed at the hands of Demon Boyfriend.

CHAPTER ELEVEN

I know it's cowardly of me, but the entire trip from JFK airport to Rome I've made sure Shona was between Demon Boyfriend and me. I figure she chose Cain, so she can deal with him. Deal with his sudden outbursts.

It's nearing the hour mark since we've been on this curb, waiting for Shona's friend to pick us up. It's a hot day even under the metal canopy shading the sidewalk. I down the last bit of water in my bottle.

"Maybe you should try him again," Marek says, offering me his half-full water bottle, and I can't stop myself from feeling a little swoony at the gesture.

Still, I wave him off. "I'm good. Thanks."

Shona perks up. "There he is. Don't call him a she. His pronoun is he, him…never mind, you get it."

A light pink Fiat pulls up in front of us. A guy about our age pops out from the driver's side door with so much energy it makes me painfully aware of how exhausted I am from the long flight.

No matter how tired I am, I can't keep my droopy eyes

off him. He's beautiful, with perfectly styled hair and flawless makeup. Not just your average, cover-a-zit cosmetics, but it's the kind of perfection that beauty vloggers do with fake eyelashes and bright highlighter on cheekbones.

"Sid!" Shona darts around the back of the Fiat and embraces him.

He wiggles out of her arms wrapped around his shoulders. Tattoos on his well-defined arms peek out from under the sleeves of his shirt. "Girl, watch it. You'll squish my Hermès bag. It's vintage, you know." His gaze lands on Marek. "Who's the new boy toy, honey?"

"He's off-limits," Shona says, opening the trunk and motioning for Cain to bring their bags. She leans over to Sid and whispers, but I can totally hear it—and if I can, so can Marek. "I think he's already spoken for."

Sid raises a perfectly shaped eyebrow at me. "She's a cute kitten. Needs help, though. A lot of tweezing."

"I can hear you," I say and lug my suitcase over to Marek, who's trying to fit the bags in the small compartment.

Shona turns to me. "We're just kidding. Anyway, Sid, this is Analiese."

Right. Kidding. For some reason, she wanted to embarrass me. I shut out the thought and smile. "Call me Ana."

"But Analiese is such a pretty name," he says. "Why shorten it?"

Marek steps in front of me, reaching out his hand. "Hey man, I'm Marek."

Sid grasps and holds it a little longer than necessary. "Sid. It's definitely a pleasure to meet you."

"All right," Shona says, cutting between them on her way to the Fiat's back passenger door. "Let's get going."

I give the pink vehicle a once-over. "How are we even going to fit in this?"

"It seats five," Sid says. "You might not be able to move…

or breathe"—he laughs—"but it's a short jaunt to the hotel."

Jaunt?

"How old are you, anyway?"

A smirk spreads over Sid's lips. "I'd say about your age."

What kind of answer is that? "Seventeen?"

"Yeah, something like that." He walks off and joins Shona.

His vagueness is strange. He probably gets off on giving people a hard time.

Marek's able to fit three of the four pieces of luggage in, but since his carry-on is more of a duffle-slash-suitcase contraption, it has to go across his and my laps in the backseat. It's a tight squeeze with Shona on the other side of me.

Why didn't I ask for the window seat?

Being in the middle sucks. I lean forward over the suitcase to prevent them crushing my shoulders. I'm feeling a little claustrophobic, which can be triggering. Not wanting to have a panic attack in the middle of hectic traffic, I concentrate on other things.

The inside of the Fiat is decked out. It has pink pleather seats with white trim, rhinestones decorating the dashboard and stick shift, and a shag carpet. If you could smell expensive, it would reek of it.

At least Cain's not back here. He's in the passenger seat, staring out the window, not saying a word.

"So how've you been, Cain?" Sid weaves the pink Fiat effortlessly around cars as we speed along the roadway.

Cain doesn't answer.

But Sid tries again. "Did you ever buy that drum set?"

Not a peep out of Cain.

"You know, the one we found in that shop in that village." Sid purses his pink-glossed lips as he thinks. "I got it. Greenwich, right?"

When he still doesn't answer him, Sid glances in the rearview mirror at me and shrugs, his smile exposing perfectly aligned white teeth.

I match his shrug and lift a smile back at him.

He slides the Fiat between two cars and flicks on the blinker. "Hun-*ney*. I just love the chaos of Rome's traffic. Do you feel the energy?"

"To your right," Cain mutters.

Sid glances over his shoulder. "What about it?"

Cain returns to looking out the window. "Blind spot."

Sid slows down, and a gray smart car flies by, barely missing us.

A scowl scrunches those perfect eyebrows of his. "Next time maybe you can give me a better warning. *Like* some urgency in your voice."

I lean against Marek when Sid takes a sharp turn. The warmth of his shoulder against mine causes all my nerve endings to ignite.

Shona scoots forward and wraps her arms around the front seat, resting her hands on Sid's chest. "So what have you been up to?"

"Same as usual." He honks the horn at a slow driver. "Partying. And more partying. However, I did go to the Philippines to see my people. Where I did some more partying."

His people? That's a strange way of putting it. Usually someone says they went home to visit family or friends. Maybe he doesn't have any family. Or friends other than Shona.

"My family died ages ago," he says as if he can read my thoughts. "I'm an orphan."

I shift uneasily on the pleather cushion, and it makes an unpleasant noise. No one says anything. Not even a joke. If Dalton were here, he wouldn't hold back. He'd embarrass me until I was the color of these pink seats.

We come to an abrupt stop that makes all of us jerk forward and knock back.

"We're here," Sid sort of sings out as if he didn't just give everyone whiplash, slamming on the brakes.

Shona opens the door. "You still can't brake right."

"Girl, I got you here, didn't I?" He leaves the Fiat running and meets us at the trunk.

The boutique hotel Shona insisted we stay at is expensive-looking. It's the kind you see in movies. The ones with vine-covered stucco, romantic balconies, and potted flowers. With small cars and brightly colored Vespas weaving in and out of traffic on the road in front of it, and with street cafés and baked bread and coffee beans scenting the air around them.

Cain takes out his small and Shona's large suitcases from the back compartment. Marek grabs mine before I can.

He places it on the asphalt. "Here you go."

My eyes linger on his face until I realize what I'm doing and quickly turn away and grab the handle. But I don't latch onto plastic. Marek's hand is still there. A yelp leaves my lips, and I stumble back slightly.

"You okay?" Marek grasps my elbow to steady me, and I'm not okay. Warmth rises to my cheeks, my pulse is out of control, and I'm not sure if he realizes how touching him affects me.

But Sid does, because he gives me a knowing smile and follows it with a wink.

Grasping the handle of my bag, I tug it up the curb, getting some distance from the whole situation. I just want to be somewhere alone. Heal my embarrassment. Avoid Marek until this little incident is forgotten.

"Stay and eat dinner with us," Shona directs to Sid, pulling the attention away from me. Thankfully.

"Can't." Sid slams the trunk door shut. "It's a full moon tonight, and a beautiful boy is waiting for me."

"Boo," she says, her bottom lip protruding.

He hops into the driver's seat, and before he shuts the door, he says, "See you tomorrow."

The Fiat speeds off into the traffic, and I'm relieved to

step into the lobby of the hotel and get to our room.

I didn't sleep well, not with Shona snoring and hogging the blankets. The good part: Shona and Cain are sleeping in. If we weren't chasing some list or fearing Cain will snap and hurt us, our time in Rome would be perfect.

I'm starting to figure Shona out. She's a trust-fund baby with her own high-rise apartment. Daddy got it for her when she turned eighteen. Only goes to NYU for something to do. Barely makes her scheduled classes. We'd have separate rooms if this hotel weren't full.

But for all the money she has, Shona is lonely. Daddy Dearest is absent a lot. Her mom died of cancer a few years ago. All she has is Cain. That's why she won't break up with him.

Marek and I sneak out and find a café with thick espresso and sweetbreads. He sips from his cup, gently holding the little handle between his fingers. It's as if he thinks the porcelain will break in his hand. With his dark, wavy hair and longish, straight nose, he can easily pass as a local. He could be Italian. We never talked about our ethnicities.

"So, what do you think?" he asks, programming the handheld GPS he bought for almost two hundred euros. "A few names on the list live here. Want to go check them out?"

Shona thinks we're only in Rome to search for Mr. Conte's clue in the Sistine Chapel. But Marek and I decide to check out some names on the list without her and her evil boyfriend. We don't want to scare anyone off from giving us information.

"Sounds like a good plan. How far are the addresses?" I take a huge bite of my stuffed pastry.

"One's nearby. The other is a bit of a ride. We'll take the

bus. You have some custard at the corner of your mouth." He points at the spot on his own lips. "Just there."

I lick the custard away with my tongue.

"You're going to make the servers run into each other if you keep doing that."

"Doing what?" I swipe my tongue across my lip again.

"That," he says, a smile teasing the corners of his mouth.

My cheeks heat, and I snatch up the linen napkin at the side of my plate and wipe my mouth. I pick up my tiny cup, drink down a good portion of espresso, and cough it out when I see them.

"Are you okay?" He shoots a look over his shoulder to see what startled me.

"It's—it's them. Bjorn and that woman from the train… and they're with that Uber driver."

He turns in his chair to get a better look.

"What are they doing here?" I say. "Here. In Rome."

"They're definitely following us. We need to go." He raises his hand and flags our server. The man looks over, and Marek pretends to write in the air.

My eyes trail the perfect-gened trio. I recall the other two's names. Uber driver is Horus, and the matchmaker is Inanna. They dart in and out of shops so quickly it's obvious they're looking for something or someone. Or us.

The pastry and espresso swirl in my stomach, and I hold my hands to keep them from trembling.

It's as if my rational side is arguing with my intuition. Maybe it is a coincidence that they're in Italy. Stanger coincidences happen all the time. But all three of them? Together? When we just met them separately back home? No. Not a chance.

"We need a plan," I say.

"I know. You got one?"

"Other than running? No."

Several minutes go by before the server comes back with the check.

"Do you see that bus heading this way?" Marek asks and drops some euros on the table.

"Yes."

"When it passes, we duck out of here." His eyes stay on the bus.

I nod. "Okay."

The bus approaches and stops. People unload onto the walkway, some crossing the street. With a slight jerk and a metal growl, the bus moves forward.

Almost here.

I grasp the side of the table, readying myself to move fast.

Passersby come in and out of my view of Inanna. Her hair in the sunlight looks like slick tar cascading down her back. Some people rush along with determination, knowing where they're going. Others shuffle by, their gazes going side to side and up. They're definitely tourists taking in the sites.

Almost here.

The clapping of water echoes in the square. In the middle of the piazza across the street from us, there's a fountain. Horus watches the water shoot up from a muscular merman atop four dolphin tails. I bite my bottom lip, worrying he will see us.

I push myself away from the table. The bus cuts off my stare on Horus.

Here.

Marek and I jump to our feet and sprint for the alley just past the café. We stop, and Marek peers around the corner.

"They didn't see us," he says.

I hold my side, panting. The alley is a dead end. "Now where?"

"Try the doors." He darts to the first one on the left, and I go to the right.

"Mine's locked." I dart for another one. It doesn't budge. "Maybe next time we need to make an escape, we don't run into a dead-end alley."

Marek turns from the door he just tried and rubs his eyes. He's probably suffering jetlag just like me. "Why didn't I think of that?" he says, matching my sarcasm, then answering his own question: "Well, it could be because I was enjoying myself in a café for tourists and didn't think I'd have to run from stalkers."

"Sorry, I didn't mean to blame you," I say. "I'm just scared. Why are they following us? And all the way to Rome."

"I know. I'm a little freaked out, too." He forces a smile. "Come on. Let's hide behind the dumpster before they see us."

We drop down behind it, and Marek edges out from the side to get a better view of the street. The stench of decaying trash is overwhelming. My stomach rolls now, and I may hurl the pastries and espresso right there in the alley. I swallow hard and mentally tell my uneasy belly to settle down.

"Why don't we get on the bus?" I ask.

"The door is on the side they're on," he says, stretching out farther to get a better look.

"Do you see them?"

"No," he murmurs. "Now I get why my grandfather was always drilling me to case places before going inside. Know the exits, he'd say. I thought it was for natural disasters or terrorist attacks, but he was preparing me for something like this."

Getting to know Marek is like unraveling a ball of twine. He lets a little out at a time, and I wonder if I'll ever reach the core. "Did he teach you what to do if you're trapped?"

"Stay out of sight and look for an opportunity to run for it." He glances at me. "Then get in a crowd until there's an opening to ditch the person chasing you."

That plan doesn't sit well with me. "Is there an option B or something? Maybe we could just wait here until they're gone."

Marek shakes his head. "No. Somehow, they know we're here. Why would they travel all this way and give up? They'll search until they find us. We have to make a run for it."

My heart slams so hard against my ribs it rattles my spine. Pain sears my palm from my nails digging into the flesh. It hurts, so I loosen my tight fists. From my position between Marek and the wall, I can't see the street.

"Get ready," Marek warns.

"I am."

The adrenaline rushing through my body has me alert and anxious. I take a deep breath and release it slowly through my nose. My mind's all over the place, processing everything that's happened the last few days.

It seems forever ago that Adam Conte handed me his satchel, but it was just a couple of weeks. And here I am in Rome, probably considered an illegal runaway. And I'm hiding behind a dumpster, not knowing why three unnaturally gorgeous people are following me — I slide a look at Marek — following *us*. I'm not sure what they want, but it has something to do with Adam Conte's bag.

"They want the clues," I mutter.

Marek turns his attention to me. "What did you say?"

"I think those three are after the clues."

"I think you're right." He dips his head and stares at the ground for a quick moment before returning his eyes to the entrance to the alley. In one swift movement, he ducks back beside me. "They just passed. Follow me. When the coast is clear, we'll make a break for it. Ready?"

I nod. "Yes. Ready."

We stick to the wall all the way down to the end. Marek peeks around the corner, looking left then right. It's a pedestrian street. Cars aren't allowed on it. The tall buildings house shops and cafés. Flocks of people approach the alley.

Marek grabs my hand, and we step out and into the crowd.

He doesn't let go as we rush down the cobblestone sidewalk. My hand lingering in his feels natural, warm. I keep checking over my shoulder, expecting our three pursuers to show up. Every loud noise—a honk, a yell, a car backfiring—shakes me to the bones. My breath burns going in. We barely make it onto the bus before it takes off.

Marek drops my hand so we can single-file our way to two empty seats together. The memory of his touch lingers on my skin. It's warm briefly before it slowly cools, leaving me wanting to feel his touch again.

We transfer to another bus, and it drops us and a few business people off in a residential area of Rome. The GPS takes us to a narrow street with worn cobblestones and vehicles lining both sides. There's barely room in the middle of the road for a car to use. The building has four stories. Its beige stucco is chipped in places, and the elaborate wood trim surrounding its windows and doors needs a coat of paint.

Marek takes out the list and rereads the information. "This is the right building. It's apartment three-a. Antonia Rossi."

"Antonia Rossi," a woman carrying a sack of produce says. She's about seventy, her hair not completely gray. She says something in Italian, and the only word I catch is "*deceduto*," which doesn't sound good.

Marek and I look at each other at once—he wrinkles his eyebrows, and I shrug my shoulders.

"Sorry. I'm so sorry," a woman in her thirties with short hair wearing a crisp suit rushes up to us, struggling with an armful of bags. Her eyes are bright, and her smile is brighter. By the sound of her voice, she's American. "I thought our appointment was at ten."

"We're not here for an appointment," I say.

She gives me a once-over. "You're not here to see the

apartment?"

"No," Marek says. "We're looking for Antonia Rossi."

That bright smile turns into a straight line. "You're looking for Antonia?"

"Yes," I say. "Do you know her?"

"I did."

"Did?"

She places her grocery bags by the door and tugs her keys out of her pants pocket. "She passed away a few months ago. I'm her wife. Was there something you needed?"

I want to ask how she died, but that would be insensitive.

"She's her cousin from America," Marek blurts out.

I give him a look that says it was a dumb play. Someone's wife would know a person's relatives. I force a smile and search my brain, which is now completely blank, for something—anything—to say.

"She only has one relative," the woman says as I start to back away. "Analiese?"

CHAPTER TWELVE

I'm surprised Antonia's wife, Wren, invited us in. We're strangers, after all. Boxes populate most of the floor of the apartment. The steaming mug of cocoa in my hands is warm and comforting after a morning of playing cat and mouse with our stalkers. I'm sitting next to Marek on a sofa so small there isn't a gap between us.

The place smells like she's just cleaned the apartment. Probably for her appointment. There's ticking somewhere, and I search the room for what's making the noise. A box the size of a coffin lies open on the floor by the open window. I can barely make out the face of a grandfather clock.

I feel for Wren. I've been where she is now. It's hard packing up the memories of a lost life. Not the deceased loved one's lost life, but yours. The life you knew with them in it.

Pushing the thought away, I take another sip of cocoa. I'm trying to play it cool. Acting as if it doesn't freak me out that Wren knew my name. But the cocoa sloshing back and forth inside my mug is a dead giveaway that it does.

A woman outside yells something in Italian, breaking the

silence of the apartment. A second or so later, a young boy answers her.

Wren sits down on a chair across from Marek and me with a mug of her own. "Sorry, I haven't much to offer. The lemon cookies are tasty, if a bit stale. Just dunk it in the cocoa. Softens it up some."

I'd better get this going. We need to be back before sleeping beauty and her troll wake up and find we're not at the hotel. Though I don't know why I care. Shona's not the boss of this operation. "How long were you and Antonia married?"

"A little over a year." She sips her cocoa. Her eyes turn glossy, and she looks away for a second. She returns her gaze to me. "When's the last time you saw her?"

"It's been ages," I say, hating the fact that I'm lying to her. She seems like a sweet woman.

I spot a photograph of Wren with a gorgeous-looking Italian woman. They're all smiles and dimples, both wearing white dresses and holding up champagne flutes. It must've been their wedding day.

A sadness pains my heart, and now my eyes are glossing, too. It's the only photo left out. Wren probably couldn't pack it yet, wanting to keep Antonia with her.

Wren pops up to her feet. "Silly me. I forgot. There's a picture of you with her." She hurries into the other room and calls, "And she left you a box."

I slide Marek a look. His eyes are as wide as mine are. I'm not sure I heard Wren right. Did she say there was a picture that exists of me with a woman I never met? Or don't remember meeting, anyway.

Marek adjusts on the seat to face me and confirms what I thought I heard. "A picture of you? How can she have a picture of you?"

"I don't know, and I don't remember her." I put my mug

on the glass coffee table. "It has to be someone who looks like me."

"But she knew your name," Marek says. "It has to be you."

Wren comes back carrying a medium-sized box. She sets it down and picks up a picture frame that's resting on top. "There you are," she says, turning it around so I can see and stabbing the little girl's face in the photo with her pointer finger. The girl's sitting on her dad's lap, who is beside Antonia on a porch swing.

I stare a long while at the photograph, letting my brain catch up to what I see.

"She said the man in the photo is Eli," Wren says.

My dad.

And me.

I'm about three or four in the photograph. I want to hurl, but I push it down. Marek grasps my hand to hide the fact that it's shaking.

Marek stands and brings me up with him. "Sorry, but we have to go. We promised some friends we'd meet them."

"Oh yes, I'm so sorry—" Wren is in the middle of saying when the intercom by the door buzzes. "And there's my appointment."

It's as if she doesn't know what to do. Answer the door or not.

I don't know what to do, either. My brain's clamped shut, and I don't know how to operate without it.

Marek saves us both. "You should get that. Thanks for seeing us and for the hot chocolate."

"Yes. It was my pleasure. Well then, this box is yours." She picks it up and hands it to me. "I was going to mail it, but I thought I'd bring it to the States. Cheaper to mail."

My name and address are neatly printed in the middle of the box. Antonia knew where I lived. It's unreasonable to feel the way I do right now about someone I never even knew.

But there's a sadness settling inside me, gnawing at my gut.

The buzzer goes off again.

Wren hustles to the door, presses a button, and speaks something in Italian into it. She picks up a marker from the counter separating the living room from the tiny kitchen and comes over to me. Scribbling numbers on the top of the box, she says, "If you need anything, call me. A ride. Money. I'll be here another week. Okay?"

"Okay." Now tears are running down my face. It feels like I've known Wren forever.

She hugs me, the box between us. "I know. I loved her, too."

We release each other.

Marek smiles at her. "It was nice meeting you."

"You, as well," Wren returns.

"Thank you," I say and follow Marek out the door. "Goodbye."

We pass a young Italian couple ascending the stairs as we're going down. They're all smiles, and she's wearing a big diamond wedding band. They look like newlyweds, and I imagine Wren and Antonia with the same excitement on their faces as they shopped for their first apartment together.

But of course, I'm assuming. They could have already been living together before their wedding.

At the bottom of the staircase, an older man with curly white hair and a worn-out sweater is locking the door to his apartment.

"Excuse me," I say, startling him.

He drops his keys, and Marek quickly picks them up.

Marek places them in the man's wrinkled hand. "Here you go. Sorry we startled you."

"English?" I ask.

He nods but doesn't speak.

"Do you know how the woman in 3A died?"

He sighs deeply, which he follows with a *tsk*ing sound.

"Such tragedy. So young. She was on her…how you say…
bicycle, yes?"

I nod this time. "Yes."

He continues, "Went around a corner. A truck he hits her.
Never wakes up again."

We thank him and leave the building. It's as if a dark cloud
follows me, sucking out my energy, drenching me with sorrow.

"How come I can't remember Antonia?" I say more to
myself than to Marek. "I never saw any photographs around
the house of her. If she was a relative, wouldn't they have
mentioned her or have pictures?"

"Maybe there was a falling out?"

"Maybe." If that was the case, it doesn't make sense. Dad
was always forgiving. Even to people who probably didn't
deserve it.

"I wonder what's in the box," Marek asks, rushing down
the street beside me.

I'm silent. My mind's still processing everything. I hug
the box tight to my chest. My Vans pound the cobblestones.
Antonia was on the list. She knew my dad. Took a photograph
with me. There wasn't a line through her name like my parents'.

I stop.

That list.

They're all on it. My dad, birth parents, and Antonia.

All of them died suddenly.

Oh God.

They were murdered. I'm sure of it.

But they didn't look like murders. An aneurism took my
dad, my parents died in a boating accident, and a car hit
Antonia on her bike. Could someone have planned all that? I
don't know. I don't do spy games or anything that could help
me analyze it. All I have is a gut feeling.

And my gut tells me there's no way their deaths are a
coincidence.

It takes Marek several steps before he realizes I'm not beside him anymore.

"Hey, what's wrong?" He removes the box that's threatening to tip over from my arms. "Are you going to be sick?"

"I don't think my dad's death was an accident. He's crossed off that list."

"You said it was an aneurysm."

"I know. But what if the autopsy got it wrong." The street is too vacant. A man in a long gray dress coat with a bolt of silver streaking his black, tousled hair and a beard that comes to a point at his chin passes us. An uneasy feeling settles into my gut, and I keep my eyes on him until he turns a corner.

Marek shakes the box slightly, and the contents thump a little. "Maybe the answers are in here."

Cain and Shona aren't in the hotel room when we return. A note is on the desk saying they went shopping with Sid.

I sit on the edge of the bed, staring at the box.

Just staring.

Marek crosses his ankles and watches from his reclined position on the bed. "Not going to know what's inside until it's opened."

I've been trying to work up the nerve to open the box for nearly fifteen minutes. Whatever is inside could change my life. Ruin my life. End it.

"I'm not sure about this," I say, my gaze lifting to Marek's stare. "I'm scared."

He sits up, slides over, and hangs his legs over the bed, with the box between us.

"Let's do this together," he says, stabbing the packing

tape with a butter knife from the service tray left behind with Shona and Cain's breakfast remains on it. That's why the room smells like old eggs and some sort of spice I can't place.

The dull blade runs across the tape, causing a scratching sound to fill the room. My eyes follow the shiny, rose-engraved metal releasing what I hope are answers to my family's secrets.

Marek lifts one flap, two, three, and four. He stops before continuing. "Are you ready?"

I take a deep breath and push it out through my nose. "Ready."

He looks inside, screws up his face, and reaches in, pulling out folded up poster boards. Four of them. Held together by tons of masking tape. Setting it aside on the bed, he glances at me.

"This was attached to a wall or something. Seems odd she'd remove it and pack it up." Marek takes out a photo album and some papers from the box. "It's as if she was preparing to die. Like she knew it was going to happen."

The top page of the stack of loose papers catches my attention, and I pick it up. "It's the list. The same one as your grandfather's."

Marek places the box on the floor and scoots closer to me, the bed shaking with his movement. We read the list, me holding one side, him the other. A line is drawn through most of the names, just like the one that belonged to Adam Conte. In the margin beside each one is a notation.

Left a message.

Barista at Café on Santa Maria.

Can't locate

No answer.

And so on.

By Shona's name there's a notation dated three years ago, and it says, *always in trouble, now homeschooled.*

My name is untouched.

"There's no notation on mine," I mumble, rubbing an itch from my nose.

I stop on my parents' names. Did Antonia know them, too?

Marek removes his jacket and tosses it on the bed behind him. "Probably because she knew where you were."

"Probably." It's getting warm, so I take off my coat and lay it on the footboard of the bed.

"Let's see what's on the posters." Marek pushes up from the bed and gathers them up. "The tape's still good." He unfolds the connected pieces and sticks them to the wall across from us. Attached to the fronts are pieces of paper, sticky notes, and a world map. Holes dot all the countries where pushpins used to be.

We both lean forward at the same time, elbows on knees, chins resting on hands, studying the macramé of information. Each hole on the map has a number, one through twenty-six, along with a date printed in a blue marker and either the letter "D" or "M" beside it.

"Those numbers must match the names on the list," I say, plucking it up. "The names on this are listed in numerical order. Mine is, anyway. See the one marking Philadelphia? That's my home. Number sixteen. Same as on the list. But there's no date beside it."

Marek leans over my arm to view the list. "Shona's matches the one on the map also. And there's no date on hers. Let's call all the numbers. See what we can find out."

"Okay."

Marek grabs the phone. I sit in the middle of the bed and pull my legs into a pretzel. He plops down in front of me and reaches the phone out to me. "You should make the call. It would be less threatening."

"What do I say? No one's going to just give information to a stranger."

"Fake it. Say you're a claims agent for an insurance company. That way we can find out if they're dead or alive."

I take the phone from him and punch in the first number. It rings several times before a woman answers. She sounds Irish.

"Hello. Um… Um, this is…Sharon…Sharon Knox. I'm a claims agent with…Transcontinental Insurance. Is this the family of Jack O'Neill?"

"Yes," the woman says.

"With whom am I speaking?"

"His mother."

"Okay, well, he had a small policy with us, and I need to verify if…um." I widen my eyes at Marek.

"If he qualifies," he whispers.

"If he qualifies," I repeat. "First, what's the date he died?"

A sob comes over the phone. Well, he's definitely in the hereafter. Another sob reverberates against my ear. My heart sinks to a new low. I should've warmed the woman up first. Asked how she was doing. Said I was sorry for her loss.

I do better on the next call. And the next. And so on.

Marek takes notes on the back of the list, registering the answers and using the photo album as a desk. It takes nearly two hours to make all the calls.

With each one, the news gets harder to take.

Deceased. Eleven, including my three parents.

Two didn't speak English.

A hang-up.

Missing. Six.

Three no answers.

And then there's Shona and me.

I feel the world drop away from me. It's as if I'm riding waves on the bed. Blood pulses in my ears, loud and disturbing.

If it's a hit list, we're next.

CHAPTER THIRTEEN

With some effort, I stop the panic attack before it can consume me. I have no idea why someone would want to kill me. I'm nothing special. Just a girl in high school. I press my eyes with my fingertips. *Don't cry.*

Marek wraps a gentle hand around my forearm. "Hey, are you okay?"

I nod, and it's a little too hard for someone who's okay. Because I'm not. How could I be? Nothing makes sense, and everything is terrifying. And that doesn't make sense, either. I think of Dad and what he'd say in a situation like this.

Stay strong. You can't let your emotions take over.

I see his face. The day he died I teased him about his attempt at growing a beard. The hair was sparse, and there were patches of gray. I smell that awful cologne he got from Jane for his birthday that he insisted on using all the time because some woman at the Coffee House in her nineties said she liked it. I feel his hug. Warm and secure.

And I'm better. Thinking of him always brings me out of the dark. Always stops the demons from consuming me.

My hands fall away from my face, and I smile at Marek. "I'm okay. Just processing all this…whatever it is."

He smiles, but it's as if he's not too sure he should.

I glance over our call list. "That's twenty-five. We missed someone."

His shoulder leans into mine as we study it together.

"Here." I point out the notation next to Shona. The writing in the margin is long and goes onto the next line almost covering a name. "Joel Jackson. He wasn't on your grandfather's list?"

"No." He gets up, retrieves the list from his bag, and reads it. "Yeah, he's not on this."

"I wonder why?"

He shrugs. "Maybe Antonia knew something my gramps didn't. Let's figure out the rest."

"Okay," I say, returning my gaze to the posters.

"So what do we know?"

"Well," I start. "The numbers next to the pinholes on the map match the ones next to the names on the list. So D means dead, and M is for missing. Antonia registered the dates of everyone's deaths or disappearances on the map. That means from the six we couldn't understand or reach, judging by which letter she wrote next to their names, five are dead, one is missing."

I let it rest in my head for a moment. I was right. But I'm not going to panic this time.

Stay strong.

Marek drops the list and photo album on the mattress beside him. "Whelp, at least we don't have to travel the world to find these people."

"Don't you get it?" There's no emotion behind my words. Am I numb? "It's a hit list. And Shona and I are on it."

"You should go back."

"Where?"

"Home. It's too dangerous for you here."

"I'm staying. Nowhere is safe. If they want me, they'll find me. My Dad. Antonia. They were home, and they died."

He stares at his hands for several beats. "You're right. You have to stay with me. We have to stick together." His head turns in my direction. "It's safer that way."

Safer? I'm not sure I agree, but the way he's looking at me makes me skip a breath. His eyes say it all. He cares about me. We haven't known each other very long, but I feel the same way. I'm not sure what it means. I just know that this situation has put us both in danger and we only have each other right now.

And it's overwhelming, so I decide to change the mood. Get us back on the topic of what we're going to do about our predicament.

"Shona's in danger, too," I say.

"I'll call her." He removes his phone from his pocket and starts punching numbers on the screen. After a pause, he says, "Went straight to voicemail." He ends the call and drops his phone on the bed.

Even though the girl is a bit annoying and maybe a bit out of touch, I want to find Shona. Make sure she's safe. Tell her what we discovered. She has the right to know there might be a target on her back. Cain will protect her if it comes down to it, but I still want her with me. Safety in numbers. A sort of we're-in-this-together kind of thing.

Marek leafs through the stack of papers. "These are in Italian, or maybe Latin?"

My hand grazes the album. It's heavy when I lift it. I place it on my lap and flip the first cardboard page over. It's old, the linen cover cracked and worn from use and time. The photographs are faded pink with age. Each page contains three rows, and each row has two pictures of the same person.

On the top row, the images are of a middle-aged man. In

the first photo, his eyes are closed with the word *deceduto* under it, along with the date and time, *20 June 1937, 3:22 p.m.* The image beside it shows the man's eyes opened and has *risorto, 20 June 1937, 3:24 p.m.* with *deceduto, 20 June 1937, 3:30 p.m.* beneath that.

The woman in front of Wren's apartment building used *deceduto* when we asked about Antonia. So it might mean dead or something like that. "Can you get a translation on your phone for these?" I tap my finger on each word.

He checks the translations of them and confirms their meanings—deceased and resurrected.

Marek scoots closer to me, the mattress sinking a little under him. He looks over my shoulder, his breath tickling my collarbone. "What's this? Some sort of death log?"

"I don't know." I toss page after page. Faces flash by, men and women, the photographs less aged the further into the album I get. "Why is there a photograph of each person alive then dead?"

"Correction," he says. "They're dead then alive. Look at the times."

He's right. I stop flipping pages and choke on my breath. On the chest of one of the men sits a death's-head hawkmoth. Its yellow-and-brown wings perfectly spread apart, the skull on its back almost mocking. A shiver runs through my body, the album shaking a little in my hands.

It's a coincidence. That's all. It can't be related to the moths that appeared during the freaky frog incident at school. I shake the thought away.

I remember just then what Shona told us about Cain.

"You okay?" he asks.

"Cain." I can't seem to form a complete sentence. Air is rushing too quickly into my lungs.

Marek rests his hand on mine. "Breathe. It's okay. What about Cain?"

"Shona." I take a breath. "She said he died and she brought him back. Could it be true?"

"I don't know. None of this seems possible, but that doesn't mean it isn't true."

"So what do we do?"

"Keep searching for answers."

"What sick person puts together something like this?" I look at the album.

"I don't think Antonia did," Marek says. "The first photographs were in 1937. Writing and pages are faded. And she wasn't alive back then. We should get those note pages translated. Maybe there're answers in them."

The phone to the room rings. Marek leans back and picks up the receiver. "Hello? No. We're not here, and I didn't just answer the phone. Okay." He sighs as he waits for something. "I'm not giving him a hard time. Right. See you later." He hangs up and turns to me. "That was Shona and her lapdog. They're on their way back."

I push off the bed and pick up the album. "We have to hide this stuff before they return."

"*Okay*," he says, sounding as if he thinks I'm unreasonable. "Why? I thought they were in this with us. Shona is on that list. She's searching for answers, too. Besides, she speaks Italian, and we need a translator."

With a deep sigh, I collapse back on the bed beside him. "You're right. I just don't trust Cain. He freaks me out."

"The dude definitely has anger issues." He places his hand on my knee, and I feel a tug inside me at his touch. If we were in a different situation, I might act on my growing attraction to Marek. He keeps pulling me closer with every touch, smile, and kind thing that he does.

And by different situation, I mean if I weren't in mortal danger.

Sid drops Shona and Cain off almost thirty minutes later. Thankfully, it's another full-moon night, so he doesn't come up. He's off to see the same guy he saw last night.

Shona keeps glancing at us as she reads the notes from Antonia's box. "These aren't hers. It's experiment records from a coroner's daughter named Isabella Favero. She studied under her father. Bodies would come in for autopsies, and she'd experiment on them. It's just stuff like subject died by drowning, pneumonia and other diseases, and accidents. Raised at such and such date. They'd come back to life. Doesn't say how."

"Maybe she injected them with something," I say.

Her eyes go wide, and she covers her mouth. "Oh my gosh, then she'd suffocate them. *Kill* them."

I clench the side of the bed. Did they feel anything when she experimented on them?

"There's nothing about how she brought them back?" I ask.

Cain's pacing the floor in front of a fancy wardrobe. "I feel cooped up in here. Let's go out. It's still early."

"Dude, calm down," Marek says. "Your girl is upset. Maybe you should, I don't know, be less of an ass."

A growl originates somewhere deep in Cain's throat, and his chest puffs out, his hands tightening into a fist. "What'd you call me?"

Marek stands and readies himself for an attack. "An ass. Which you are."

Before Cain can make a move for Marek, Shona steps between them, facing Cain. "Stop."

Cain does.

"Take a shower and cool down already." She crosses her arms and stares him down until his hands go slack and his chest deflates.

"He's gonna get his one day," Cain says, grabs his backpack, and slams the bathroom door behind him.

"Why are you with that guy, again?" Marek asks, returning to his seat on the bed.

"I try to remember the good times," she answers, not convincing herself or us.

"There must've been a lot of them." Marek smirks but then sobers when both Shona and I give him a that-is-so-not-funny-right-now glare. "Bad timing?"

"Yes." I elbow him when Shona returns to reading the notes and mouth, "Be nice."

He mouths back, "I am."

"I'm right here," Shona says, her eyes still planted on the page. "I can see you in my periphery. And I agree. Marek, behave. Stop trying to provoke Cain."

Marek chortles. "But he's so easy to provoke."

"Still not funny." Even though I say that, I have to press my lips together to stop the smile tugging at my lips. Marek is too cute when he laughs.

"I'm sorry." He swallows back one last laugh. "I can't help it. Being in this room with him sucks."

Shona looks up from her reading. "Have we forgotten the scary shit going on? Specifically, this." She shakes the paper in her hand. "Stop messing around."

Who could forget? It felt good to laugh a little. Relieve some tension.

After she gets through all the pages, she straightens the stack beside her. "It's basically all the same. The girl was experimenting on dead people. That shit's not right."

"So we should go to the Sistine Chapel tomorrow," I say. "See if we can find the next clue."

"Sounds like a plan," Marek agrees.

Cain comes out from the bathroom—hair wet, no shirt,

low-slung pajama bottoms—and I avert my eyes. Sharing a room with two guys does have its benefits.

My eyes meet Marek's brown ones. My cheeks heat.

And it has its downfalls.

"Cain, put a shirt on," Shona says, slipping the papers into the box with the poster boards and album. "You're making Analiese uncomfortable."

"I'm not—" I catch Marek watching me. That heating sensation returns in my cheeks. "I'm going to take a shower."

Once inside the bathroom, I stand in front of the mirror, just staring. I'm a lot older now than I was in that photograph with Antonia. The porch swing we were on still hangs from our back porch, paint chipped, chains rusty. Safta made the dress with the daisies I'm wearing in it.

The image of Antonia and me together keeps flashing in my mind. Wren said I was Antonia's only living relative. How were we related? I don't know if my mother has any family left. I'm a lot closer to my birth father's family.

My mom had only the one brother, Eli. My dad. Grandfather Bove was killed young in a hunting accident. My mom was three and my uncle barely one. When my grandfather was a boy, his entire family died in a house fire. He was lucky to make it out alive. Grandma Bove was an orphan and died seven years ago from a massive stroke.

They're all dead.

"You'll never know," I tell my tired reflection and run my brush through my dark, tangled hair.

You never need to be afraid; you hold more power *than you know.* Something Dad used to say to me. He said it often. Always emphasizing power.

I glare straight into my hazel eyes. "Dad, why didn't you tell me? What secrets were you hiding?"

Tears dribble down my cheeks. I can hear him in my head again.

Someday, you won't like me as much. He said that at our place by the riverbank on the rocks. I was upset with Jane. She'd taken my phone away for having an attitude at the dinner table. I'd asked Dad why she couldn't be as kind as he was. Looking back, she was right to do it. I was such a brat.

That's impossible, I said to him at our place. *I love you too much.*

The forced smile he gave me right before responding concerned me. *Well, for now, everything's perfect.* But I brushed it off, thinking that maybe he was having a mid-life crisis or something.

I place a shaky hand on the image of my face in the mirror. That was before the happy girl in our place was broken. Back when all she worried about was if Sean McCabe in third period math liked her or not. Before Dad died and left our place.

If I survive tomorrow, if I survive the week, I'll try to do better. Be a little bit easier on Jane.

Be a little bit easier on me.

CHAPTER FOURTEEN

Marek sits at a table on the hotel restaurant's balcony. He barely touches the breakfast in front of him. I join him, sitting across the table. The view of the city from our position is beautiful. The sky is almost a perfect blue. I lift my face toward the sun to soak in its warmth.

"What are we doing?" I ask, bringing my eyes to him.

He stares at the road below. "Making sure they didn't track us."

"Should we change hotels?"

"Maybe," he says, his eyes not leaving the road. "But it'll have to wait until later. We can't waste time, or we'll miss entry into the Vatican Museums."

"I thought we were going to the Sistine Chapel."

"We are. By way of the museum. It closes at six, so we need to go right away. Shona and Cain keep sleeping late, and it's cutting into our time."

"Did someone mention my name?" Shona wears a blue patterned jumpsuit with flouncy long sleeves, a powerful necklace, and shiny rose-gold loafers. Hugging a tan trench coat and clutching a closed black umbrella, she gives me a look, then removes the sunglasses from her head and puts them on. "You are changing, aren't you? It's the Vatican. You should wear something more respectful."

"Is it going to rain today?" I ask, nodding at the rain gear in her arms.

"It did yesterday." She places the umbrella and jacket on one of the chairs. "It's better to be prepared than sorry."

A chaos of storm clouds rolls fast over the buildings, lightning flashes, and not soon after, the cracking of thunder follows.

"See," she says.

"Wow, talk about moody weather," I say. "The sky was a perfect blue just a minute ago."

Sid prances in, wearing tight black pants with a blue silk jacket over a crisp white shirt. His makeup is subdued, but he gets in some flash on his fingers. There are so many rings stacked on each I don't know how he moves them.

I glance down at my jeggings, bomber jacket, and cropped top. It isn't one of those short kinds. It barely shows my tummy with my high-waist pants.

"All right," I say, standing. "I'll be right back."

"I'm helping," Sid says. "I've been dying to get at those brows. Can I use your supply, Shona?"

"My foundation won't match her," she says.

Sid gives her a look like she should know better than to make that statement. "Obviously, honey. Other than that zit forming on her forehead, she doesn't need it."

I search my forehead with my fingertips, and sure enough, there's a small bump forming just above my right eyebrow. "I don't need help."

"Girl, there's no getting out of this. Once I find a cause, I'm relentless." He laces his arm through mine and leads me toward the door.

"And backpacks aren't allowed," Shona calls after us. "Purses are, though."

Great. It's not that I don't know how to do my makeup or dress nice. I used to be into all that stuff before my dad died. It would take me two hours to get ready for school in the morning. I just prefer understated now. Plus, I get an extra hour or so of sleep every day.

The lobby is busier than when Marek and I went out earlier. We weave through people bunched together around suitcases, waiting to either check in or out.

When we arrive at my room, I remember I'd forgotten to take a pill earlier, so I down one and slip the bottle into my purse.

Sid pats the bed. "Sit here. It's time for the master to work his magic."

I shuffle over and drop onto the mattress with a sigh. "I thought we were in a hurry."

"*Puh*-lease, I'm a pro. This will take ten minutes. You can time me."

He plucks my eyebrows and shapes them with one of Shona's pencils that almost matches my hair. He uses a light-colored contour to shadow my eyes and cheeks. After applying mascara to my lashes, he takes a step back and studies his work.

"Not bad," he says. "Would've been better with foundation. But I'm not mad at it. And. Girl. Those eyes are popping."

I can't help but smile. Sid is full of energy and extremely confident. "Thank you, it looks great."

His eyes go to Shona's bed, and he wrinkles his nose. The blankets are all bundled up, and her clothes practically cover the entire surface. "How do you room with her?"

I shrug. "I try to ignore it."

"Do you have other clothes?"

I show him my suitcase, and he searches the items inside.

When he's done, he frowns at me. "It's as if a ten-year-old packed this."

I cross my arms and give him my best annoyed glare. "I packed for camp. Coming to Rome was a surprise."

He chooses a simple blue tunic top with small white flowers that covers my bottom.

"I'm not wearing this alone," I say, taking it from his outstretched hand.

With a sigh, he tosses me my burgundy jeggings. "Give me more credit than that. We're going to the Vatican, not a nightclub. Here." He picks up my nude-colored ballet shoes.

"Nope. Not happening. They pinch my toes."

"So why did you pack them for *camp*?"

Vans will have to do, since I'm not wearing those ballet shoes. Courtesy of Jane. She bought them for me and insisted I bring them to camp for the final night's dance. I take them and toss them aside.

He sits on the bed. "*Hun-ney*, you're killing me."

I dress quickly in the bathroom, and when I come back out, Sid is studying the box of Antonia's stuff.

"What are you doing?" I ask.

He looks up as if it doesn't faze him that I just caught him snooping. "This is interesting. Is it some sort of experiment?"

I practically tear Isabella's record book from his hands. "It's private."

"It's morbid if you ask me," he says, ignoring my outburst, shuffling over to the door and yanking it open. "The others are waiting."

Before following him out of the hotel room, I grab Dad's lighter from my discarded jeans and slip it into the tiny front pocket of the jeggings. The hall smells like pot.

"At least someone's having a good time," I mutter to myself while draping the strap of my purse over my shoulder.

When I join Sid in front of the elevators, he's holding

his chin and scrutinizing a painting on the wall between the two doors.

"That's not an accurate depiction."

Stepping around to his side, I examine the artwork. It's an odd piece to have in a hotel where you want to make your clientele feel relaxed. Not sure why he didn't notice it coming up to the room. The thing is almost too big for the wall. The artist used a lot of red paint to create some sort of Roman battle.

The elevator dings and the doors slide open.

He whirls away from the painting. "Pompey's horse was black, not white."

We step inside. "What, are you some kind of history buff?"

"I am history."

I flick him a confused look right when the elevator goes up and I grasp the railing. "What does that mean?"

We arrive at the top, and the doors open.

He walks out with me trying to catch up to his brisk steps. Back straight, chin up, you'd think he was strolling a fashion runway or something.

Marek is still watching the road below when we arrive on the balcony.

"That's much better," Shona says, swiftly rising to her feet. "Another masterpiece, Sid. Shall we be on our way?"

Shall we? So formal. I mentally roll my eyes, slipping on my bomber jacket. She's trying to impress Sid.

"Where's Cain?" I ask, noticing Marek adjust to look at me in my peripheral vision. At my quick glance at him, he shifts back around to continue observing the street.

Did he just check me out?

Shona raises a brow at Marek and then turns a smile on me. "Cain's sleeping. He took a couple of PMs, so he'll be out for a while."

Oh, so that's what was under the pile of blankets and

Shona's clothes.

"What if he wakes up before we get back?" I ask.

"I've instructed him to remain in the room." She flips her hair over her shoulder and heads for the door. "Why are we wasting time? The clock's ticking. Tick-tock."

That annoys me. She isn't leading us. We're on equal ground here. I lean closer to Marek to tell him just that when he shakes his head and lifts his eyes to the ceiling.

"Someone thinks she's the boss," he says only loud enough for me to hear. We trail her and Sid, staying several feet behind.

I drop a laugh. "My thoughts exactly."

CHAPTER FIFTEEN

When we arrive at the Vatican Museums, the lines to the entrance are down the road and around the corner.

"We're never going to make it in," I say, stepping out of the Fiat and joining Marek and Shona on the sidewalk. The Vatican's vast brick wall soars into the sky in front of us.

Sid leans over the passenger seat and calls out the window, his eyes on me. "Don't have too much fun. I'm off for a lunch romp. Ring me when you're done."

A grin creeps onto Shona's lips. "Don't do anything I wouldn't do."

"Girl, you know I can't promise that." He winks, straightens in front of the steering wheel, and zooms off.

"We're not waiting in that," Shona says, waving at the line. "While you were out messing around this morning, I bought us tour tickets. We're to meet our guide near the entrance. There she is with the white sign over there. It's the woman with light brown hair in the black turtleneck sweater."

Marek and I join the group forming a half circle in front

of the guide. She's already into her spiel about the tour. Her Italian accent is thick. "The Vatican City is its own separate sovereign state located within Rome and governed by the Pope. It's said to be the smallest country in the world."

The guide leads us inside the museum. It's like entering airport security, walking through the metal detectors and having my purse checked by an X-ray machine. Once in, we go up a set of stairs and down another, through hallways, viewing magnificent paintings and artwork from famous artists—Raphael, Caravaggio, Da Vinci.

The air smells as ancient as the artwork. Tall pillars support the high, arched ceiling. The soles of many shoes hitting the marble floors echoes through the corridor. Sculptures of religious people, cherubs, and other objects line each side of the passages, kept safe behind ropes.

Shona glides up to my side and practically shoves her umbrella at me. "Here, hold this."

I grasp it and turn on my best sarcastic tone. "By all means. Maybe you should check your coat, too."

Marek stifles a laugh, his brown eyes sparkling with amusement.

"I didn't see a coat check," she says and slowly turns on her heel, her eyes scanning the artwork. "We need to find an escape from this very boring tour."

Boring? All the history and artwork fascinates me, and I almost forget we're here to find the clue Mr. Conte left for Marek.

Our tour guide takes us into a courtyard with four squares of green yards and sidewalks cutting through them. A colossal bronze pine cone, green with age, sits on a pedestal with a peacock flanking each of its sides. In the middle is an enormous bronze orb.

"This is *Sfera con Sfera*," the tour guide announces. "It means Sphere within Sphere, and it is by Italian sculptor

Arnaldo Pomodoro."

She doesn't linger here very long, ushering us on. After twenty minutes of studying the Renaissance architecture used on the buildings surrounding the courtyard, she heads for the doors leading inside.

I get a feeling like we're being watched and scan the shadows surrounding the courtyard. Something flutters just to our left. I swallow hard and squint, trying to see it better, but it's too far for me to make out what it is.

It's nothing.

Besides, we're at the Vatican. Nothing bad could happen here.

Going through the door, I bump against Marek. Our hands brush against each other, and a wave of excitement hits me. They touch again, and this time I look up at him. The smile on his face says it was on purpose, and my heart is like a skipping rock in my chest, bouncing once, twice, then plunking under, sending ripples through my stomach.

Shona glances back at us. "What are you doing? Keep up."

We walk through hallway after hallway. I can barely concentrate on the tour guide's comments about each piece of art. I tell myself it's because of what we need to do, and not because I'm obsessing about Marek's touch. Problem is, I know when I'm lying.

The Sistine Chapel is practically empty. We need more people here so that our search will go unnoticed. After leaving the chapel, the guide takes us down a long hall and points out the architectural details.

The tour is winding down, and the doors open to the public. Tons of people pour into the hallways. When the crowd distracts the woman, we back away from the others and follow the signs back to the Sistine Chapel.

It's wall-to-wall bodies, stifling hot, and unusually quiet for this many people. Guards call out instructions occasionally.

"No photos," one warns.

"Silence," another says.

"Move along."

"*Shh.*"

We shuffle around the Sistine Chapel with the mass of tourists. The murmur of voices rises every so often and buzzes across the room like white noise before quieted with an order. A guard barks at two young men to stop taking pictures with their phones. I want to grab a few shots, the frescoes are so beautiful, but I don't want to get in trouble or risk the guard kicking me out.

I lift my face toward the vaulted ceiling, admiring one colorful fresco square to the next. The images are vibrant and detailed. I try to find the woman in Shona's reproduction among all the marvelous paintings that crowd the chapel.

I pause on *The Creation of Adam*. Seeing it in real life is breathtaking. The details are amazing. Angels surround God on the right, and Adam is on his left side, each reaching a finger out to the other.

A large man with a striped shirt stops in front of me, and I try to move around him, but there're people on both sides of me. Just over his shoulder, I spot the fresco of the woman with red hair and point at her. "There she is," I whisper as low as I can so as not to alert the guards but loud enough for Marek to hear me.

He looks where I'm pointing. "That's definitely her."

"Where's Shona?" I slowly turn, searching in all directions, tourists bumping my sides as they pass me. "I don't see her."

"I'm right behind you." She joins us.

"How did you get back there?" I ask.

"I got jostled around and ended up here."

Marek points out the fresco. "Ana found it."

She angles her head back to view it. "Now what?"

We study it for quite some time before Marek lowers his

gaze. "I don't see any clues."

"Maybe it's something around it."

There's absolutely nothing around it.

Shona stumbles forward and rights herself. "Crap," she hisses. "The floor's loose."

Sitting on my heels, I press my hand against the white rectangular tile she indicates. It shifts slightly. There's a small etching of a star in the corner of it. In the mural of the woman with the red hair, the same star is over her left shoulder, and her eyes point down as if she's staring at the tile. I dig my fingernails into the seam of the floor and try to lift it and can't.

I stand. "It won't budge. Do you have a file or something?"

Shona searches her purse, and Marek pats down his pockets. "I've got nothing," he says.

"Just an emery board," she says, "but it's too flimsy for that. How about a credit card?" She removes one from her wallet and hands it to me.

A quick scan of the crowded chapel and I pinpoint the guards. They aren't nearby, so I squat back down and try the card. "Doesn't work. It's too bendy." I straighten. "Got anything else?"

She shakes her head.

It's not as if I can ask people for a tool to deface the chapel. I bite my lip, trying to come up with a solution. Light coming in from the stained-glass window hits the silver pendant on a woman's rosary clenched in her old, fragile hands.

The pendant is thin and medal.

I turn to Marek. "Your necklace." I don't have to say more than that. He gets it right away and slips the chain holding his nautical medallion over his head.

"Let's give it a try."

"Pretend to tie your shoe," I say. "Shona and I will cover you."

Marek goes down on one knee and messes around with

his already tied shoestring.

Shona glances down.

"Don't watch him," I say. "You'll alert the guard."

She lifts her chin, and the corners of her lips dip. "Then hurry up. The guard's heading this way."

I step in front of Marek to block him from the guard's view, aiming my camera phone at one of the frescoes.

The guard says something in Italian, and I lower my phone. "English?"

"No photos allowed," he says with a heavy accent.

"Oh, sorry." I slip my phone into my pocket.

The guard nods before spotting something to my left and rushing off in that direction. I rise on my tiptoes to watch his retreat through the crowd. The people separate to let him pass, and I can see him heading for Shona, who has her phone aimed at the ceiling, snapping pictures with her flash on.

How did she get over there so fast?

Marek straightens to his feet and shoves something box-shaped into his pants pocket. "Got it. Let's get out of here."

I weave around tourists after him. "What was it?"

He gives me a quick look over his shoulder. "I'll show you once we're someplace safe—"

Bjorn towers over us. The grin stretching on his face is somewhat disturbing. "Fancy meeting you here," he says. "You aren't a careful lot. What did you find?"

Marek's hand covers the box hiding inside his pocket. "Nothing. What are you doing here?"

"You can trust me." Bjorn's eyes never leave Marek's face. "I've known your grandfather most of his life."

Most of his life? Adam Conte was probably in his sixties, while Bjorn is somewhere in his thirties. Something in my gut tells me we have to get away from him.

"You didn't answer my question," Marek says, and the tone of his voice suggests he might think so, too. "Why are you following us? Wait. How did you know how to find us?"

Bjorn steps closer so there's barely any space between him and Marek. "We be having our ways. Now you're going to have to give me what you found."

Marek backs away. "Why?"

"You be just as stubborn as Adam." He bends slightly and stares Marek in the eyes. "Hand it over and go home, Marek. Take care of Grams. You needn't be in the middle of this."

A group of tourists, faces lifted to the ceiling, shuffles in our direction.

"Did you kill him?" Marek fists his hands.

The group reaches us.

Bjorn's brows shoot up, and his eyes widen. "I'd never—"

I grasp Marek's arm and tug him back into the crowd. People block Bjorn from getting to us. We scuttle around the many people filling the chapel, putting as much distance between him and us as possible with a sea of bodies slowing us down. Body odor and overused cologne hang in the air like an invisible mushroom cloud. It's hot and stifling, and I just want out of here.

"Where's Shona?" I hop up, trying to see over the all the heads blocking my view.

Marek stretches up, looking left then right. "I don't see her. She knows where the hotel is. She'll have to get there on her own. We need to ditch my unc—" He stops and corrects himself. "Bjorn."

I shoot a shocked look at him, making it clear I'm not at all happy that he even suggests going without Shona. "We can't leave her."

"I don't think we have a choice," he says. "I'm not sure what's going on here. Bjorn really wants something in my grandfather's bag bad enough to follow us here. Which makes me think he'll do anything to get it. Like—"

"Kills us? You think he's going to kill us?"

A man in front of me turns his head at my outburst. I go right to get away from his scrutinizing eyes and find a new trail through the crowd. There's hardly any room between all the people. I shimmy around the bodies, the chorus of different languages filling my ears. Marek shuffles down another aisle between a tour group and a couple with interlocking arms.

"I wasn't going to say *kill*." He dodges an older man that stops in his path. He falls in line after me.

"Then what were you going to say? You think he wants to invite us to a tea party?"

"I don't know, and I don't want to find out."

Marek snatches my hand and tows me along with him, edging toward the exit. His fingers tightly gripping mine cause my already speeding heart to rev up.

We make it out of the chapel, and Marek drops my hand. Jog-walking through the corridors, I stare straight ahead, my eyes on the exit.

The vibrant paintings on the walls are flashes of colors in my peripheral vision. I don't dare stop. Our stalker freaks me out. Whatever Marek's grandfather was into had to be bad. And I mean the kind of bad where people die.

At the end of the corridor that leads to Vatican City's exit stands our Uber driver, Horus. I dart for a door and end up in the courtyard we were in earlier with the tour guide. The bronze pine cone is on the opposite side, which means we need to go forward.

"This way," I say, tearing down one of the sidewalks and passing the huge bronze sphere. I glance back. The doors we just burst out of are still closed. "Do you think he saw us?"

Marek gives a quick look over his shoulder. "I don't know, but we're attracting attention. Slow down." He eases into a determined stroll.

He's right. All eyes are on us, along with many disapproving looks and a few shaking heads. I slow down and match his steps. It's no coincidence that Bjorn and Horus are at the Vatican with us. They're definitely after whatever we just found. Though I don't like her much, I worry about Shona.

I extract my phone from the bottom of my bag and punch the call button next her number in her contact page. She answers on the fourth ring.

"Where are you?" She sounds pissed, her words coming over in quick sound bites. "There are too many people. I… can't see you. Are you…still in the chapel?" Her breath is exerted and her sentences choppy, as though she's hopping up and down to search for us.

"Hold on," I stop her. "We're being followed."

"How do you know that?"

"There're two men here. The same ones we ran into back home."

She draws out a long sigh. "This is inconvenient. What do they look like?"

"One man is really buff—looks like a Norse god or something. The other guy is a hot African man. We haven't seen the other one. She's a woman. A tall model-type with dark hair. Looks like that actress Nazanin Boniadi on Homeland…"

"I have no idea who that is."

"Um…beautiful, almost black hair."

"Is it long and straight?" she asks. "All legs?"

"I don't know. That's pretty vague."

"Wait." She's quiet before continuing, "Okay, I sent you a pic."

Her message chimes in on my screen, and I pull it up to view it.

"That's her," I say, stepping around a man with a fancy camera blocking the sidewalk as he snaps pictures of the surrounding Renaissance-style buildings. "Don't let her see you. Get out of the Vatican. Make sure no one is following you. We'll find you outside."

"Okay, if I don't get squeezed to death by this mob." There's no urgency in her voice. I'm about to tell her we may be in danger and to be careful, but she hangs up.

I blow out a frustrated breath, frown at my phone, then drop it into my bag.

Marek gives me a side-glance. "What's wrong?"

"That girl is in a dream world," I say. "I'm not sure she realizes the seriousness of this situation."

How can I blame her? I'm not sure what's going on. It's all too confusing. Yet, I know that for our three model-looking pursuers to track us all the way to Italy, it has to be dangerous.

A crowd trying to funnel into the door leading back inside slows us down. I make the mistake of glancing back. Horus heads in our direction, his gait precise and determined. My legs are tired and wobbly. It's like I'm walking on a wire, teetering and about to plunge to an unknown depth.

I shove Marek's back, trying to hurry him up, but he's blocked. We shuffle forward until we're inside.

Marek shrugs my hands off his back. "Why are you pushing?"

"He's coming." I swallow down the panic rising in my chest. "Horus."

"This way," he says, capturing my hand and leading me through the hallways. We come to a large circular room with a skylight dominating the ceiling and a massive winding staircase with souvenir display cases and shelves surrounding it. Plaster cupids decorate the half walls running the length of the stairs.

The steps are broad, and it takes several long strides to cross one. Marek storms down them, and I keep to his side, dodging slow-moving tourists on our way. At the bottom, we scramble over the mosaic marble floor and find the exit through a large arched door.

Guards dressed in camouflage uniforms flank the gates.

They hold semi-automatic rifles across their chests, surveying the crowds. Tiny cars zoom by on the road that runs along the side of the massive barrier wall protecting the Vatican.

I grip the handle of the umbrella and hold the strap of my bag as we hurry past souvenir and gelato stands and over a blue-and-white striped crosswalk to the other side of the street.

Fat drops of rain fall from the sky, pinging my head and filling potholes. My hand shakes, and I don't dare open the umbrella, fearing it will slow me down.

Several concrete steps lead down to a small road between the five-story buildings lining it. Instead of going down them, we hide behind a white van parked beside the curb and watch the Vatican exit for Shona.

The rain comes down faster, and I open the umbrella. Marek gets under it with me. Time goes excruciatingly slow as we wait for Shona. When I spot Horus coming out of the exit, I gasp and shrink back behind the van.

"He doesn't give up, does he?" I say, my breath rushing in and out, not out of exhaustion but because of the fear clutching my lungs.

"Who?"

"That Uber driver," I say. "Horus."

Marek peeks around the back of the van. "He's going down the street. Call Shona."

I can see Horus through the windows of the van now. His back is to us. I dial Shona's number on my phone.

Shona answers on the first ring. "Hey. I'm almost through. This crowd is ridiculous."

"One of those guys following us just went down the street. Hurry, before he gets back."

"I'm outside now," she says. "Where are you?"

"We're across the street. Take the blue-and-white crosswalk." My insides are in knots like a tangled necklace.

"And go with a crowd. Not by yourself."

Marek stays close to the van as he peers through the windows.

"What's happening?" I hate not seeing what's going on.

"She's approaching the crosswalk." He squints, studying the other side of the street. "*Shit*. Horus is heading back up the street."

He's going to see her.

CHAPTER SIXTEEN

There's no thought to what I do next. I just act, hurrying around the front of the van and charging over the crosswalk. I meet Shona before her foot lands off the curb and hold the umbrella over us, making sure to tilt it in Horus's direction, blocking our faces from him.

I hold her arm, and we hurry back to Marek. Without hesitation, we jog down the steps to the road below and keep going until we reach an intersection.

"Which way to the hotel?" I hope one of them knows where we're going.

"This way." Shona goes left onto a narrow street. She dials some numbers in her phone, listens, then lowers it. "Straight to voicemail. Sid's preoccupied. We need to get an Uber or something."

Marek pushes the wet hair away from his face. "No. We can't trust it. Horus was an Uber driver. We should take public transportation."

Shona doesn't look very happy about that. Her lip protrudes in a pout, and she whines. "I hate public transportation."

"I'm sure you won't die just this one time." My voice gives away the fact that she's starting to annoy me.

If looks could really kill, her side-glance would cut me down. "I'm sure I won't."

The entire ride on the public tram, my heart pounds in my ears sounding like a thousand racehorses running around a muddy track. Though it's chilly out, my palms are clammy, and my face is hot from running through street after street before finding a tram stop.

I glance around. The tram's packed, and the many faces of the riders hold no emotion. Any of them could be dangerous. *Stranger danger*, I could almost hear Jane say. She says it a lot, especially to me. Probably because I have a habit of not paying attention to my surroundings.

I've had many narrow escapes as a result of my lack of awareness. There was that time I stepped onto a crosswalk without looking and a passing car almost hit me. Another time when I was distracted while rushing down a sidewalk and ran into a pole. And the time when I was climbing over the rocks by the river, made a misstep, and plunged into the icy water.

No wonder she's always nervous about me. I'm a walking accident about to happen.

I lean forward in my seat and grab my knees with shaky hands, take a deep breath, and release it slowly. This has to be a dream. No. It's more like a nightmare.

Nothing makes sense. We're chasing clues that don't make any sense. Going on this hunt doesn't make sense. It's definitely one of those poor judgment calls of mine, and I'm not sure I'll escape harm this time.

Marek places his hand on top of mine. "You okay?"

I nod. "I'm good."

"Well, you don't look good," Shona says from her seat across the aisle.

She's really starting to bug me. No. If I'm honest, she's been annoying me since we first met.

"What did you find in the chapel?" she asks. "Let me see it."

Marek looks from me to her. "Not here. When we get to our room. There are too many eyes around."

She focuses on the window next to me. "We're getting close. Our hotel's just a few blocks away."

I shift to see outside, but nothing looks familiar. Dalton would be all over my case for not taking in my surroundings. Dad always told us to keep track of where we were and know the landmarks so we'd never get lost in unfamiliar places. I've been careless since arriving in Rome, but no more. I need to stay alert. Know where I am.

The tram slows, and Shona stands. "We're getting off here."

I give one last glance at the window and pause. There are two men in black trench coats marching down the sidewalk, heading for our hotel. They're just businessmen, I reason with myself. Not everyone dressed in trench coats is dangerous.

A woman in high boots with a fierce look on her face passes by the window. Her expression makes me slide back in my seat.

Stop it. She's only a woman running late for something.

The tram coasts to a stop, and the doors open. I step down to the curb behind Shona. Marek comes out right after me. The hotel is the third building up from where we get off. At almost four, the lobby's practically empty. Guests are probably out sightseeing or in their rooms preparing to go out later.

The doorman stares out the window, waiting for someone to need his services. Lanky and tall, his shoulders are sharp under his red-and-gold jacket, and his chin comes to a severe point. The woman behind the reception desk gives a quick glance up at us before returning her attention to the screen on the computer in front of her.

Marek places a hand on my back, and I jolt forward.

"Sorry," he says. "I didn't mean to startle you."

"It's just one of those freak-out kind of days," I say, covering up the fact that his touch would send jolts through my body even if we hadn't just run from the gene-pool-winning trio.

The elevator dings, and the doors glide open. Cain charges out, his head down and his chest rising and falling with quick breaths. He lifts his eyes, spots us entering the lobby, and charges over.

"Where have you been?" With teeth clenched, jaw muscles tense, he narrows his eyes at Marek. "You trying to make a move on my girl?"

"She's not my type." Marek returns an equally menacing glare at Cain.

Shona rests a fist on her hip. "That's an insulting thing to say. What do you mean I'm not your type?"

Her question only succeeds in triggering Cain more. With two long, fast steps, Cain grabs the collar of Marek's shirt. "Stay away from her, you hear?"

"Get your hands off me." Marek yanks away from Cain's grip and pushes him. "I'll break your arm if you touch me again."

Cain throws a fist at Marek, and Marek ducks.

"*Smettila*," the woman at the reception desk shouts, then fumbles with the knob to the door behind her until she gets it open and stumbles through it. Most likely, she's getting someone to help her, which means whoever it is will probably kick us out of the hotel. I just hope they'll let us grab our bags from our room before doing so.

"*Ehi tu, smettila!*" The doorman storms across the tile floor in our direction and continues yelling something in Italian. Whatever he's saying sounds angry. I shrink back, wanting to stay out of the man's path.

Cain shoves Marek back and turns his glare on the doorman, hate sparking in his icy blue eyes. When the man reaches us, Cain tackles him, and the man's head thumps hard against the tile floor.

Shona pulls on Cain's arm. "Get up. What are you doing? You're going to hurt him."

Cain straightens—his face an emotionless mask.

"Stay put," Shona orders. "And don't you dare move."

He doesn't move, not even a muscle.

Blood pools around the man's head.

"He's bleeding." Marek kneels beside the man and places two fingers on the man's neck.

"Is he dead?" It sounds like someone else asks that question. My voice filled with so much fear and emotion it's almost unrecognizable.

"He can't be," Shona says. The panic in her voice matches the one pressing hard against my chest, practically cutting off my air supply.

"There's a pulse," Marek says.

I drop to my knees beside Marek. "We have to compress his wound."

Marek raises his head, his eyes search around him. "I need a towel or something."

Shona removes her sweater and hands it to Marek. He lifts the man's head and presses the cashmere against the wound. The man's breathing is labored, yet his face looks peaceful.

A gasp comes from the reception desk. The woman who'd run into the other room is back behind the counter, hands to her mouth, eyes wide.

Marek's head snaps in her direction. "We need an ambulance."

She doesn't move, her hands are still covering her mouth, head shaking.

"How do you say ambulance in Italian?" Marek ask.

Shona tosses the girl an annoyed look. "She works in a

hotel. You speak English, don't you?"

The woman nods.

"Call an ambulance. This man slipped on the floor and he's hurt." Shona glances at us and whispers, "There are no witnesses. They'll believe it's an accident."

The woman picks up the phone.

This can't be happening. Cain's a heartless beast. He's dangerous, and I don't want to be around him anymore.

Marek must think the same thing, because he lowers his voice so that only I can hear him. "We need to ditch these two. Cain is a loose cannon."

Several outward pants come from the man and then one long exhale. His chest stops rising and falling.

"Is he—" A sob cuts through my chest. I know the answer before Marek confirms it.

Marek places his fingers back against the side of the man's neck and waits, listens. The expression on his face makes me think he's hoping as hard as I am. Hoping to feel a pulse. Hoping the man's still alive.

That expression fades, a grim look replacing it. Marek slightly shakes his head. A shake that says what I fear. "He's gone," he mutters.

"No." The world seems to be rocking, and I lower my head. I want to go home. Be safe in our house with Dalton. If he were here, he'd know what to do.

"See what you did!" The anger in Shona's voice is frightening—deep and scratchy—like sandpaper dragging across concrete.

Cain hasn't moved from his spot. There still isn't any emotion on his face. He doesn't even flinch when Shona shouts at him.

Marek pushes up to his feet, his face twisting with anger as he glares at Cain. "You did this."

Shona sidesteps between them. "It was the man's fault.

He came after us. Cain was just responding."

"The man's fault? Have you lost your senses?" Marek lets out a frustrated breath. "Your boyfriend has no soul. He's evil."

My eyes land back on the man who was alive only minutes ago. The memory of Dad lying dead on the rocks beside the river hits me hard. I gulp back tears. Is the man someone's father? Will they be as lost without him as I am without Dad? The pain is too heavy to carry. My heart breaks for them. He's younger than Dad. So if he has kids, they'd be younger than me.

I place my hand on his.

"I'm so sorry," I say, quiet and sad. I don't know how to pray. No one ever taught me. So I adjust on my knees, lower my head, and repeat, "I'm so sorry, I'm so sorry, I'm sorry."

"We need to get our stories straight." Shona paces, her high heels clicking against the tiles. "He slipped. As simple as that. We were returning from sightseeing and walked in right when he fell."

"That won't work," Marek argues. "The receptionist witnessed everything. She saw Cain attack me. Remember?"

"Oh, yes, that." She places a long slender finger to her lips as she thinks. "Okay, so you two were fighting over me, and the man hurried to stop it. That's when he slipped."

"Fighting over you?" Marek shakes his head. "Unbelievable. You'd lie for him. I won't. We have to tell the truth. Cain has to be accountable for what he's done."

"You don't understand," she says. "Without me, Cain is dangerous."

"Without you he's dangerous," Marek repeats with a sarcastic laugh. "You were here and this still happened."

There's a pull on my hands before my palm heats and the man's skin warms under my touch. A twitch of his finger. A raspy breath. The man isn't dead. I let go of his hand.

I fall back, my butt landing on my heels. "He's still alive."

The front doors whisk open at the exact second the doorman sits up, a confused look on his face, blood dripping from the back of his head. At the sound of several footsteps entering the lobby, I turn.

Bjorn, Inanna, and Horus march in our direction. A swarm of death's-head hawkmoths follows and passes them. The moths rush around me, forming a whirlwind of yellow-and-brown wings.

I cover my head with my arms and scream.

CHAPTER SEVENTEEN

Marek plunges into the wing storm, the moths pelting him, and he wraps his arms around me, shielding me with his back. His flinching body and grunting tell me they're hurting him.

"Stop!" rips from my throat.

Just as quickly as they rushed in, they fly off.

Marek's cheek rests against mine. "Are you okay?" he says breathlessly. "You're so cold."

I nod because I can't find the words to speak. He unwraps his arms and releases me.

A few of the moths lie dead on the floor, the skull pattern on their backs staring up at me. My breaths ease, and I straighten. My hands feel frostbitten, the muscles and joints stiff.

Shona takes a few steps closer to us. "What are they doing here?"

I pick up Shona's sweater and press it against the back of the doorman's head. "You're going to be okay," I say to him, but he just stares at me, and his eyes are cold and biting as dry ice.

"We're here for him." Inanna heads for Cain. Before reaching him, she removes a syringe with a light-blue liquid inside.

Bjorn grabs Shona from behind. "Tell him to stay still, or you won't like what I do next."

Marek makes a move for him.

"Don't try it," Bjorn warns. "I don't like hurting girls."

Shona's tearful eyes slide over to Cain. "You will stay still," she says, and he obeys her.

Cain doesn't flinch when Inanna inserts the needle into his neck and pushes the plunger down, the contents emptying into him.

"Stop!" Shona struggles in Bjorn's grasp. "What did you give him?"

Horus strides over and grasps the doorman's shoulder.

I look up at him. "Leave him alone."

Horus ignores me.

Inanna turns a sympathetic look to Shona. "I'm sorry. You needn't fear us. We won't hurt you. As long as you behave."

Cain's knees buckle, and he falls forward, crashing face-down onto the floor.

"No!" Shona starts for him, but Bjorn tightens his grip on her arms. She wriggles in his grasp. "Let me go! What did you do to him?"

"I've righted a wrong," Inanna says. "He was a Risen."

"A Risen?" The confusion on Marek's face matches mine.

"He was meant to die in that accident," Inanna says, walking toward me. "But Shona touched him, and he awoke from death's sleep."

"You're not making sense," I say. "Death's sleep? Shona touched him… Are you saying she brought him back to life?"

She stops in front of the doorman and me. "Just as you did to this man." She gives Horus a nod. "Don't let her touch him."

Horus releases the man, grabs me, and drags me away. I thrash in his arms and kick his shin, but it doesn't even faze him. He holds me tight. "Let me go," I snap.

Inanna pulls another syringe full of that blue liquid out of her pocket. She squats in front of the doorman and inserts the needle into his neck, dispensing whatever it is into him. The man falls back, thumping against the floor again.

Marek hits Horus with one of those stands used to hold velvet ropes for a barrier, which had been blocking the entrance to the closed restaurant. Horus crashes to the floor and slides across the tiles. My mouth drops open. It had to take a lot of strength to hit Horus that hard. Marek snatches up my hand and drags me to the doors.

"Damn." He shoots a look back at me. "How are your hands that cold?"

I ignore his questions and pull back on his lead. "What about Shona? We can't leave her."

"We either leave her, or they'll take all three of us."

I give Shona another look and can barely see her face with the tears building in my eyes. Bjorn's arms are tight around her. She looks from Cain's body on the floor to me. Even with the fear written all over her face, she nods and mouths "go" before Marek tugs on my arm again.

I leave her, and my guilt is like a boulder crushing down on me. If only I were as brave as her. We take off up the street. My tears escape, and I let them race down my cheeks.

Marek keeps shooting glances over his shoulder.

We're a ways up the road when the Italian police, lights flashing, pass and screech to a stop in front of our hotel.

Cars are backed up on the street in both directions.

"It's Horus," Marek says, pulling me down with him behind one of the waiting cars. "He's looking for us. I don't see the others."

Sid's pink Fiat squeals to a stop just up the street from

us. He's blocked by the building traffic. "Come on!" he yells, waving us over from the driver's side door.

Marek and I dash around people and vehicles.

I look back. Horus is faster than us and is catching up.

"We're not going to make it," I call after him.

He glances back at me. "Don't slow down."

My Vans slap the cobblestone road. Marek makes it first and hops in the back seat.

"Come on," he grunts.

I climb into the front passenger seat, and Sid takes off before I get the door closed. I slam it shut. Wiping the tears from my face, I watch Horus through the window until I can't see him any longer.

"We left her with them," I say. "They killed Cain and that man, and we left her there."

Marek sits at the edge of his seat and massages my shoulder. "We had no choice. Besides, the police are there. She'll be okay. If we stayed, they'd detain us for questioning. We don't have time for that."

"How can Inanna be so cruel? She just killed them like that. No emotion."

I'm pretty sure Sid flinches when I mention Inanna. He takes a sharp turn, the Fiat shimmying a little before righting.

My hands shake, and I fist them. "Now what? All our things are in that hotel. We don't have the money. Or your grandfather's bag."

"I have the money and everything from his satchel. Also, got your passport. See?"

I glance back, and Marek lifts his shirt, revealing one of those concealing travel bags. "It was my gramps's"

"You took my passport?"

He nods. "You left it in your suitcase. If someone broke into our room and stole it, you'd be screwed."

A thought crosses my mind, and I twist to face Sid. "You're

awfully quiet. How did you know to come for us?"

"Had a missed call from Shona." Instead of paying attention to the road, he studies me with his heavily made-up eyes. "By the look on your face, you don't buy that."

"No, I don't. You know who they are, don't you? Inanna, Bjorn, and Horus—" A gasp cuts off my words. Strolling in the middle of the road. Hands stretched out at his sides, palms up, is the man who passed us on Antonia's street yesterday. The man with the silver-streaked hair.

A strong wind blows trash barrels down the sidewalk, pushes over chairs and tables at an outdoor café, and causes water to spray up from a *nasone* fountain. Over his head, there's a gray cloud following him. It's not until the cloud dives, raining down on people who swat at it, that I realize what it is.

"Are those bugs?"

"Locusts, to be exact." Sid whips the Fiat around and tears off back in the direction we'd just come.

Tiny insect bodies ping the car.

Sid slams his foot against the gas pedal, and the Fiat skids as it turns a corner, and another corner, and another, ditching the locusts and the man.

"Who was that?" I ask.

Marek asks at the same time, "Was he making that wind?"

"He was." Sid takes a hard right. "It's Pazuzu. Wouldn't invite him to a party, that one. He's no fun." He laughs. "Or a funeral, come to think of it. Of all the gods to get power back, he had to."

"The Babylonian demon god? Shut up." I grab the side of my head. "Just shut up. This isn't real."

"Watch out," Marek snaps.

Sid swerves, barely avoiding three guys messing around as they cross the street.

"Okay, girl. I'll shut up." He acts unaffected by his narrowly missing them. "But then you won't get any information about what's happening."

Marek slaps the back of Sid's seat. "Just spill it. What the hell is going on? First, they kill Cain and that doorman and now... I don't even know what that was."

Sid pulls the Fiat over and parks it next to a row of tall apartment buildings.

I drop my hands. "Why are we stopping? We have to get away from that man."

"We're far enough away from him." Sid turns to look at me. "I'm surprised you hadn't caught on, Analiese. What do the names Inanna and Horus have in common?"

My blank stare says I'm not in the mood for guessing games. "I don't know. What?"

"Oh, come on." He gives me an exaggerated pout. "You aren't even trying. You and your father have a common interest. Something your brother and Jane aren't interested in."

I sit up straighter. "How do you know my family?"

"I'll tell you after you answer my question." He leans back in his seat.

"Stop playing games," Marek warns.

A common interest? Dad and me.

I vaguely hear Marek and Sid arguing over messing with me or something.

Mythology.

"Inanna," I mumble. "She's the ancient Sumerian goddess of love and fertility and sometimes war."

"What is she saying?" Marek sounds frustrated.

"Leave her alone," Sid says. "She's processing."

Marek responds, but I'm not listening so I don't hear him.

Sid laughs. "I'm not torturing her. Girl. Sometimes it's best to let the mind figure things out on its own. It's less of a shock that way."

"Horus." It rolls over my tongue so quietly, I'm surprised

Marek hears me. "The Egyptian god of the sky."

Marek gives me an incredulous look. "How do you know this stuff?"

"My dad," I say. "He was obsessed. I thought it was cool to have a common interest with him. Guess he was into mythology because he knew gods existed for real."

"So you know what they are?" Sid claps his hands once.

"Inanna is a goddess, and Horus, a god," I say.

"Bravo." Sid hits soprano on that last syllable. He glances in the rearview mirror "Your girl is smart. And Bjorn?"

I don't even have to think about Bjorn. He's easy. Even Dalton could get this one. Ancient literature has referred to the god by many names. It makes sense he'd use the most common one for our times. Even made a joke about who he is on a license plate.

"Thor." I stare at my trembling hands. The door attendant's blood has dried on them. I need to wash them.

Wash them now.

"Is there a gas station with a restroom?" I can't sit still. "Do they have those in Rome?"

My gaze flashes over the nearby buildings.

Sid swings a concerned look in my direction. "What's wrong, honey? Too much to process at once?"

"Leave her alone," Marek orders.

"I wasn't—"

"I *said* stop."

With a heavy sigh, Sid inspects his nails. "Whatever."

I flip my hands over and back. My breath is raspy. "It's all over the place."

Marek practically flies out the back door and yanks open the front passenger one. He drops into a squat beside me and grasps my hands.

His are bloody, too.

Dried blood.

"Hey," he says, and when I don't look at him he goes louder, "Hey, look at me."

"M-my hands," I stammer. "I-I need to wash them."

He squeezes my hands lightly. "I'll be right back."

The car bounces as Sid adjusts in his seat to face me. He rests an arm on the steering wheel. "Honey, you need a thicker skin. Because, girl, this shit is real."

A thicker skin. As if that's going to help me.

He makes as though he's going to say something, and I hold my hand up, stopping him.

"No. I need a minute."

He goes back to inspecting his nails. "Mortals. So dramatic."

We sit in silence for what seems like an eternity, but the clock says it's seven minutes.

Marek comes back to my side with a bottle of water and a fist full of paper napkins. "Here, give me your hands," he says.

I lean out the door and hold them out over the gutter. As the cold water runs over my skin, Marek gently rubs the blood away.

"How are you not freaking out?" I ask.

"I am," he says. "It just doesn't show."

After he dries my hands, he removes the blood from his and gets into the backseat. He scoots forward and rests his arms on the front seats. "Now tell us what's going on. No games. Just straight up, man."

"God and goddesses exist." I sound oddly catatonic.

"This may shock you," Sid says. "Who am I kidding? You're already there. I'm a god."

"You're from the Philippines," I say. "You had someone to meet because it was a full moon. The boy moon. Your lover. Are you Sidapa?"

"I am." He lowers his head, and it's the first time he looks vulnerable. "I only see my love then. And don't believe the stories. He's not a small boy. When he walks the earth, he's our age. I tricked the Sisters of Fates into aging me down, so we'd be the same."

I try to wrap my mind around everything he's saying, but it all seems so unreal.

"How can this be real?" Marek has the same questions as me, but he can voice his. He pulls his fingers through his hair. "Are there more of you?"

"All the gods from mythologies around the world. So, yes, there are more of us. A few millennia ago, we lost our powers. Well, not completely. Some of us still have a few tricks in our bags. We're immortals, living amongst the mortals here in your world."

I twist in my seat to see both Sid and Marek. "What do they want from us?"

He inspects his side mirror. "How should I know what Inanna and the others want with you? I'm an undeclared god. They don't associate with me. Some immortals can be real bitches. All I know is that more of them are arriving in Rome every day."

"What's an undeclared god?" Marek checks behind him to see what Sid is looking at.

Sid's eyes slide to me before he glances back at Marek. "We're in the midst of a war between immortals. Two groups fighting for power. Both sides have compelling reasons that I should join them. I just can't decide. My situation remains the same no matter who wins. Bulan will always only come to me on the full moon. His powers never changed. Not even when we lost ours."

His eyes flick to the mirror again. "We can't stay here much longer."

A bus rocks over the brick road, heading in our direction.

"That's your ride," Sid says. "You've been seen with me, and this sweet ride stands out like a pink dress at a funeral. I'll ditch it. See what happened to Shona. Find you later."

"Okay. Thanks, man." Marek steps out.

Before I open the Fiat's door, I ask, "How do you find us?"

He drops down the visor and checks his makeup in the mirror. "It's faint, but there's this energy coming off one of you. Immortals are hungry for it. Like a feline to catnip. It means power to them. Don't stay in one place too long. *Capisce*?"

"Come on, Ana," Marek pleads. "The bus."

"Energy? I don't understand."

"Girl. You don't have time to understand." He rubs the corner of his lips. "See that woman down the street? Tall. Expensive clothes. That's Nyx. She senses it and is searching for the source." He slams the visor shut. "Bye now."

I give the woman a quick look. Definitely fits the goddess mold. Her gaze lands on me, and from this distance, almost a half a block apart, I can tell she suspects the energy is coming from us.

"It's going to leave." Marek doesn't wait for me. He takes off for the bus.

The Fiat speeds off.

I sprint after Marek.

CHAPTER EIGHTEEN

Marek makes it first and hops up on the step to the bus, blocking the door from shutting with his body. He shoves it back open.

"Come on," he grunts.

I climb up and enter. He wrenches himself from the door and follows me down the aisle. After paying, I slip into an empty seat and he sits beside me, breathing heavily.

The bus takes off, and I search the street for Nyx. She's gone.

"Damn. This thing is pressing into my bone." He removes the metal box he retrieved from the Sistine Chapel from his pocket.

"What do you think it is?" I ask, leaning over his arm to get a better look at it.

On the front side, the box has a combination lock. Fastened to the top is a gold cross made out of tiny skulls. A series of etched letters line the back panel.

"I think it's some sort of cipher." He turns it in his hand. "We need a keyword or phrase to crack it."

A husky man a few seats up from us belts out a gravelly cough, breaking our concentration.

Marek tucks the box back into his pocket. "We need to find a safe place to examine this closer. Someplace where we can rest."

People sitting in the rows around us make me uneasy. Any one of them could be dangerous. I would've never pegged Inanna as a ruthless, poison-syringe-holding killer.

I can quit. Leave Marek to figure out all this scary shit himself. I no longer want to know why I was on Adam Conte's list. I just want to go home. Back to my regular and somewhat less crappy life.

Dalton would tell me to grow a pair. Which is insulting and sexist at the same time.

Fear has a habit of holding me down, keeping me from doing daring things. I can't count how many times I didn't do something because it seemed too dangerous. Dad used to say that living in fear wasn't living. By not taking risks, I could be missing out on spectacular moments.

But this moment, here in Rome, with the Model Squad chasing us, is anything but spectacular. They killed both Cain and that doorman, and there's no telling what they'll do if they catch us.

"That man was dead," Marek interrupts my thoughts. "There wasn't a pulse. She said he was risen. How can that happen?"

"We resuscitated him. That's all." The nagging feeling that it all could be real sours my gut like I just drank spoiled milk.

He has this deadpan look on his face, and my breath skips. "I've been trying to piece it all together. The list, this scavenger hunt for clues, and now…and now our stalkers and all this bullshit about an immortal war. My grandfather held many secrets. I don't know what to believe anymore."

"What if it's true—?"

More of the man's coughs distracts me.

"That man with the locusts looked real to me." Marek's head turns to where I'm looking. "The only way to know the truth is to keep following my grandfather's breadcrumbs. But if it's too much for you, we'll get you on a plane home. I completely understand if you want to go."

The man coughs again, sounding like he's going to hack up a fur ball. I wrinkle my nose at the disgusting noise.

I should go home. Try to forget all that's happened over the last couple of weeks since that car hit Adam Conte and he gave me his bag full of clues.

Or more like a bag full of confusion.

But I couldn't go home. Not without knowing my role in whatever Adam Conte tried to hide or protect. Whatever the meaning of that list, I'm on it, and so are my parents. Adam Conte might've had something to do with their deaths, or he may have known something about it.

"I'm staying with you," I say.

He glances at the window, then at me, and smiles. "Okay, then. The first thing we need to do is get off this bus. Find a place to hide out for some time."

The bus makes many stops before we exit onto a busy street with shops. We rush across uneven sidewalks, looking for a hotel, rain beating down on us. My Vans slap the pavement, water spraying up from the force.

The rain seeps through my jeggings, wet and cold. Thankfully, my bomber jacket keeps my top half dry. Marek's hair sticks to his head, water dripping from the slight curl at the ends. We come to a familiar landmark. The *Piazza di Spagna*. Standing on the cobblestones, I have a déjà vu moment. I've seen this place in many movies and did a model of it for my geography class.

A long, broad flight of stairs rises to a chapel at the top. If it weren't raining, people would crowd the steps, sitting and lounging in the beautiful splendor of the square. In spite of the rain, there're still a lot of tourists around, holding up colorful umbrellas to shield them from the downpour.

At the bottom of the Spanish steps is a large fountain with a sculpture of a sinking boat in the middle. Rain pings the water in the basin. I stop, emotions stilling me. There's a photograph of my parents in this same spot during an anniversary trip. It's a frozen memory of theirs, and I wonder what they were feeling at the time.

Marek turns back, and there's a worried expression on his face. "Why are you stopping? There's a hotel at the top."

I give the fountain one last look and climb the elegant off-center staircase beside Marek. The magnificent twin-towered church gets nearer with each step up. I know this place well. I've been obsessed with it ever since I found that photo of my parents. It was their last day alive, right before they caught a flight to Lake Como, and they looked so happy.

We pass the pink building where John Keats, a Romantic poet, died of tuberculosis in the early eighteen hundreds. It's a museum now, and I can see through the windows that there are a good many people inside. Probably trying to keep dry.

The Hassler Hotel is to our right as we make it to the top.

"Shouldn't we stay somewhere less crowded?" I say between heavy breaths after the long climb.

Marek's breathing is practically normal. He's definitely an athlete. I probably should work on my aversion to cardio exercise.

"My bet is," he says, "they'll think we'd avoid tourist spots. Sometimes you'll go unnoticed if you hide in plain sight."

"Something your grandfather told you?"

His eyes dart in my direction. "Yes. As a matter of fact, it is."

"Okay, so we hide out here. I'm tired and hungry, anyway." I head in the direction of the hotel. It's another hike up more steps and finally across a cobblestone drive.

Breathing heavily, I push through the circular door and around into the lobby. The reception area is hopping with guests of the hotel checking in and checking out. Water drips from my hair and clothes, and a puddle forms around me. I must look like an unwrung mop slapped onto the glossy, white marble floor.

"This is nice," I say when Marek stops beside me.

There's a metal sculpture of a wolf and two boys suckling its engorged tits to the right of the reception desk. I raise an eyebrow as I study it. "What is that?"

"That's Romulus and Remus, the mythical founders of the city of Rome," offers an older woman with blond hair in a style you only get from teasing and using tons of hairspray. She's carrying shopping bags and must've come in behind us.

"Oh," is all I can think to say. "It's…interesting."

"That it is," the woman says and walks off.

Marek scans the lobby, most likely checking for any threats. "I'll get us two rooms," he says.

"Just get one. This place has to be expensive, and we need to save money." Plus, I don't want to be alone, but I'm not about to tell him that.

"One room, please," Marek says to the woman behind the counter and turns on his megawatt smile that could cause a power surge. It's the same one he flashed me the first time we met. The one when he knew I was flustered at the presence of his bare chest. "Preferably, two doubles if you have them."

The woman eyes him, not in a nasty way, but more of a curious kind of way. Even wet, Marek is charming. "We have a deluxe with twin beds available." Though an accent hangs on her words, her English is flawless.

Marek smiles again. "That'll do."

He passes her some euro banknotes, and she looks confused, as though she's never seen money before.

"Our credit cards were stolen," he answers her questioning look. "Bags, too."

She nods. "How many nights?"

"Just tonight."

Her eyebrows arch higher, but she doesn't question him. She writes a room number on an envelope, places a key card inside, and slides it across the counter to him.

"Very well, Mr. Striker," she says.

Striker? He must've given her a name on one of those forged passports from his grandfather's bag of tricks. My fingertips run up and down the zipper of my purse. A sure sign that I'm nervous. I grab the strap instead so I won't look so suspicious.

My heart jostles inside my chest with a restless anxiousness as we skirt around people in the lobby on our way to the elevator. Marek pushes the button, and we wait.

And wait.

Someone must be holding it up on one of the upper levels.

My tongue sweeps my dry lips, and I catch a view of myself in the mirrors surrounding the door. Wet strands of tea-colored hair stick to my forehead and cheeks, mascara runs from my eyes, and my nose is red from the cold.

Marek, on the other hand, looks effortlessly put together even wet.

I brush my hair away from my face and rub off the mascara with my fingertips.

The elevator doors slide open, and we wait for a couple to exit before we step inside. As the doors close, I spot a man staring at us. His features are sharp, his hair dark brown and beard cut short. His sea green eyes, hooded with thick brows, reflect a fierceness in their depths.

He smiles when he realizes I'm watching him, too. I swallow and step back as if I can get farther away from his stare.

The doors close and the floor rises, leaving my stomach behind.

"Are you okay?" Marek asks.

"There's a man in the lobby. He was watching us."

His head snaps in my direction. "Was it Bjorn or Horus?"

"No. I've never seen this guy before."

"What do you want to do?" he asks. "We could move to another hotel."

A chill slithers across my wet skin, and all I want to do is take a hot shower. "No, we'll stay here. I'm just jumpy. He was probably staring because we look like we were dumped in a lake or something."

"Okay." Marek pushes the button to the third floor.

I stab all the other ones on the panel.

He gives me a puzzled look. "Why'd you do that?"

"If he's following us, he won't know where we got off."

"That's smart."

Yeah, but it doesn't settle the worry sloshing around in my stomach. My left eye twitches. All this stress is getting to me. My tummy rumbles.

"We'll get room service." He rocks back and forth on his heels, his hands clasped behind his back. He's just as nervous as I am.

The room is classy, white, and there's a view of Rome outside the window. There's a complimentary fruit plate, and I pick up an apple slice. The temperature is set to freezing, so I search the wall for a thermostat. After I push several buttons, not knowing what I'm doing, the heat turns on.

Marek orders room service as I take a hot shower, the water warming my bones. I use one of the white courtesy robes and wiggle my toes into the slippers. There's a towel-warming rack, and I hang my wet clothes on it, making sure to hide my panties and leave room for Marek's clothes.

While he's in the bathroom, I stretch out on one of the

beds and watch the ceiling. I try to forget everything that's happened and just concentrate on my breathing. Though the images of Cain and the doorman and that man with the silver streak in his hair and the locusts stay with me, my exercises calm me. Breathe in.

Soothe me.

I'm safe here.

They don't know where we are.

Breathe out.

Calm. Soothing.

My thoughts go to Shona. The police arrived when we made our escape. I'm sure she's with them, but I can't get the image of her mouthing for us to go out of my mind. If it were me, I'd probably beg us to stay. Not her. She's brave. Strong. I need to be more like her.

Stop being a victim.

My psychotherapist's words echo in my head. I replay them often in the hope they'll take root one day and become permanent. *Take control. Use power words. Don't say I can't, say I can.*

A victim stalls. A survivor keeps going. That's what Dad would say if he were here.

I'll keep going.

Just as Marek finishes and comes out of the bathroom, a knock sounds from the door. He looks for a weapon on the desk.

I spring off the bed and grab both water bottles from the small table by the two-person couch. Made out of glass, they look more like wine bottles. I pass him one, and with the other in my hand, I stand on the opposite side of the door from him and ready mine to hit the person if they attack us.

"Yes," Marek calls.

"Room service," the accented man's voice answers.

Marek eases the door open and peers through the crack.

He lowers the bottle in his hand, which is a clue for me to do the same, and he lets the man in. The cart bumps over the threshold, and plates rattle. The man's eyes go to my robe, then to Marek's, and he smiles.

"Ah, honeymooners?" he says.

"No," I practically snap and then quickly adjust my tone before saying, "He's my brother."

He nods as he sets up the cart next to the sofa. "Oh, very well. Twins?"

Twins? I glance at Marek. Could we pass as twins? We are the same age—both have brown hair—but we look nothing like each other. Our facial features are different. His are sharp and angled, mine are oval with rounded edges. My nose turns up slightly at the end, his is more of a Roman type.

"Yes," I say even though it's a ridiculous assumption.

The man leaves, and I'm thankful he's not an assassin or something.

Marek and I sit on the sofa, eating pasta and studying the box he retrieved from the Sistine Chapel. I pick it up and examine the letters etched into the metal.

"I bet you're right about it being a cipher," I say.

Marek takes a sip of water from his glass. "My grandfather was always trying to get me to do them with him. He'd get mad because I didn't have any interest in cracking the codes. I'm not very good at it."

"We had a session on cryptology in my middle-school math class. I need something to write on." I get up and retrieve a pen and pad of hotel paper from the top drawer of the desk. Marek moves our plates out of the way.

I jot down the letters with the spaces and punctuation exactly how it is on the box.

Jung lbh ner abj, jr bapr jrer; jung jr ner abj, lbh funyy or.

Staring at the code, I search my mind. "We did many ciphers in those two weeks of cryptology. A Caesar one would be too easy."

"My grandfather was always talking about a rot-something or other."

"A ROT cipher." I nibble my bottom lip. "It's a shift-based encryption one. That class was so long ago. I can't remember how many letters to count to the right to replace the ones in the code. Let's Google it."

Marek grabs his phone and stabs his finger against the screen. "My internet's not working."

I check mine, and it's not working either. "They must have Wi-Fi here."

"Right." He stands, finds the paper with the password, and enters it into his phone.

While he's waiting for a signal, I turn off my roaming. I'd be grounded for life and for the next life if Jane sees charges from Italy and finds out I left the country.

"Now it's working."

It seems like an eternity before he finishes searching. "This site says that any number rotation can be used. A ROT13 cipher code comes up a lot in the search hits—"

"That's it." I interrupt him. "Your grandfather would've picked the most standard rotation. He'd make it easy for you to know which number to use. We have to replace each letter in the code with the thirteenth one after it in the alphabet."

"That's what it says here," he confirms.

I write the alphabet in a line on the paper just under the code. "So 'J' would be"—I count thirteen over—"'W.' And 'U' is 'H.'"

It's getting dark in the room, so Marek turns on a light, and I continue deciphering the code.

When I finish, I look over at him. "It says, 'What you are now, we once were; what we are now, you shall be.'"

"What does that mean?" Marek grabs the back of his neck, reading what I wrote on the paper. "It doesn't make sense.

The combination is numbers, not letters."

My shoulders slump, and I lean back against the cushions of the sofa. "I don't know. Is there anything else written on the box?"

He picks it up and turns it around in his hands, surveying every inch of it. "Nothing."

Are we at the end of the line with Adam Conte's freaky treasure hunt? A part of me wants it to be over, but a more significant part of me is disappointed. Now that I'm on this quest, I need resolution. For me. For Marek. And for my parents.

Numbers? I straighten. "Let me see that."

He hands me the box.

"There are four wheels to the lock." I check the decoded cipher. "And there are the same number of sections in that saying or whatever it is."

"Okay," Marek says with a confused look on his face.

A full grin stretches my lips. "I think we have to do a little math. Each letter of the alphabet has a numbered position. One through twenty-six."

The lights go on in Marek's eyes. "Oh, right. We get the numbers and add each section together."

"Bingo," I say, sounding a little smug.

"You must do good in school."

Well. I do *well* in school. I want to correct him, but Dalton's always getting on my case when I do that to him. Says it's insulting and rude.

"I do okay," I say instead.

Marek writes down the numbers, and I add them together with my phone's calculator.

I punch in the last number. "It's 189."

"That's too high," he says as he checks the lock. "Each wheel only goes up to twenty-six."

I'm getting tired. My vision is fogging, and I can't think

anymore.

Marek adds one plus eight plus nine together on the paper, and it equals eighteen.

"That's it." I rub my eyes, and we get back to work solving the other numbers.

After a while, we have the combination. Marek spins each wheel and enters the numbers into the lock.

18, 8, 12, 3

The lid to the box pops loose, and he opens it. Inside is a bone.

A *human* finger bone.

CHAPTER NINETEEN

The bed is so comfortable it's like lying on a cloud, but I can't sleep. Staring up at the ceiling, wondering why Adam Conte would put a human finger bone in an antique-looking box haunts me. Actually, it's several bones that make up a finger fastened together with wires. A slip of paper with an address written on it was underneath the finger. Hopefully, it doesn't lead to a dead body.

There's a blue hue hanging over the room. It's coming from a light somewhere outside that's seeping through the sheer curtains. Before getting into bed, neither one of us thought to close the thicker ones in front of it. Hints of furniture polish and our leftover meal linger in the air.

Marek's on the twin bed that's not even two inches apart from mine, breathing heavily, and it sounds like slow waves rolling in and out of a beach. I should be obsessing about how near he is and how we're sleeping so close to each other, but I'm not.

Well, except for just now. Mostly, I keep going over everything that's happened the last few weeks. My stomach should be in bigger knots than it is. Nothing makes sense. What will we find at the end of all this? At the end of this hunt for clues. I need a distraction.

I roll on my side, tug down the robe that has risen up my thighs, and stare at Marek as he sleeps. The sheet doesn't entirely cover his bare chest, and I watch what little chest muscle I can see rise and fall with his breathing. How is he sleeping?

"Why this hunt? He could've just left a letter," I wonder out loud.

"Because." Marek's voice startles me. I flip onto my back, so he doesn't catch me staring at him. "He doesn't want whatever it is falling into the wrong hands."

"But ciphers. They're so easy. Anyone can figure them out eventually."

"It's easy so that *I* can figure it out." His voice has that tired, scratchy sound to it. "Except he didn't realize a teen boy's mind wanders too much and that I'd forget what he taught me about them. The part that was hard, the part meant to keep others from finding the clues, was the envelope with my drawing in it. Only I would've known there'd be a message on it. No one else could've guessed. It's what starts the hunt. Without it, the other clues can't be found."

"Are you scared?" I ask.

Marek bounces onto his side. He props his head up with one hand and gives me a smoldering stare that threatens to melt me into a puddle. "A little. Bjorn and the others could have killed us, but they didn't."

"They killed Cain and that doorman."

His lids lower as he thinks. "I believe they were already dead. At least that doorman was. I swear he didn't have a pulse."

I push myself up against the pillows. "That thing Inanna said…" I drop my gaze to my hands and pick at my cuticles. "She thinks I brought that doorman back to life."

"And what do you think?"

"I think she's right."

Now he sits up. "Why do you say that?"

"I touched a dead frog, and it came to life. Those moths showed up. Just like they did with the doorman."

He reaches across the tiny gap between the beds and grasps my hand. My heart jumps at his touch, and I gasp. His hand yanks away from mine.

"I'm sorry," he says. "I didn't mean—"

"No, I mean, it's okay. You just startled me."

He adjusts to lie on his back and crosses his hands above his head. I mimic him and face the ceiling.

"Where do you think your grandfather got that finger bone?"

"He wasn't a serial killer, if that's what you're thinking."

That's precisely what I'm thinking, but I'm not admitting it, so I choose to ignore what he said. Besides, by the look on his face, this has to be hard for him. After all, he lost his grandfather, and chasing his clues has to be painful.

"Is it another clue? It makes no sense."

He lets out a long sigh. "I've been racking my brain over it all night. I got nothing. Maybe we'll have clarity in the morning."

"Yeah, maybe." I tug the covers up to my chin and continue staring at the ceiling in silence.

The sun's out, and the step I'm sitting on is just high enough to get a good view of the *piazza* and the fountain below. I cross my legs, bask in the warmth, and people-watch. Marek maneuvers the steps on his way down, looking for a place to get us coffee and pastries.

Sleeping didn't give us any clarity on what the severed bone in Mr. Conte's box means. It's a creepy thought, using someone's finger as a clue. Couldn't he have just written down the clue and been done with it? To say I'm a little frustrated is more than an understatement, it's an under-understatement. It's the lowest of understatements.

Just then, a WhatsApp notice goes off in my pocket. I forgot Dalton installed it on my phone so he could contact me internationally. I wrestle the phone out of my pants pocket and read his message.

how's it going? did you find anything out?

I type back.

Some wild stuff. It's too confusing. Explain later.

I pause and wonder if I should ask about Jane. If I know she's found out I'm not at camp, it will add to my stress. I sigh and send it anyway.

Have you talked to Mom?

barely. shes on call this week. your good. check in later

Well, at least Jane has no idea I'm in Rome being chased by delusional people who think they're immortal. Another message from him pops up.

stay out of trouble K?

Okay. Bye.

ttyl

Leaning back, I slip my phone back into my pocket, take in a deep breath, and slowly release it.

"It's a beautiful scene, don't you think?" The man from the hotel lobby last night sits down beside me, leaving little space between us. I snatch up my jacket and purse and rise to my feet, but he stops me with his command: "Sit down, Analiese."

He knows my name. How does everyone know my name? I don't move. "Who are you?"

"I think you should sit for this." He's dressed in expensive-looking clothes. Stylish. Sunglasses. Leather jacket.

I lower back to the step, making sure to leave enough distance between us. "Okay, I'm sitting."

An amused smile tips his mouth, and his eyes watch me intently. He repeatedly clicks open and close a silver lighter in his hand. Rubies form an "A" on one side of it. It reminds me of my dad's in my front pocket. His silence annoys me. Or scares the shit out of me.

Both. Definitely Both.

"What do you want?" I press.

"Shall we make our introductions first?" He smiles as if we planned this meeting. "My name is Ares. I'm a god of war. You, my dear, have walked into the middle of a battle between gods."

"So I've been told." I'm not sure where my sass comes from, but I'm going with it. "I don't see a war or any gods and goddesses. Where's all the earth-moving, ocean-splitting, thunder-cracking power?"

He throws his head back and laughs. It takes him a second to compose himself. "You have spunk, I'll give you that."

I keep my eyes forward because I have a feeling if he sees them, he'll know I'm terrified. If I took off down or up these steps, I'm pretty sure this man could catch me.

"Soon you will have to pick a side," he says.

I raise an eyebrow at him, but keep quiet and let him continue.

"You see, there are those who want to kill you. Others, to use you. I want to make you an offer. Give you all that you desire."

Now I'm pushing my eyebrows together. "An offer?

I don't have anything for you." A quick glance down the stairs and I spot Marek balancing two to-go coffee cups and a bulging white pastry bag.

I want to call out and warn him not to come up here, but then I'd just expose him to this man.

"Oh, but you do." His eyes go to where mine went. "Be careful of your travel mate. His grandfather wasn't your ally. On the contrary, he held your fate in his hands." He pushes up to his feet. "I will tell you more the next time we meet. When you know who you are. For now, I'll let you and the boy play Adam's game. There's something precious at the end of the hunt. Something you'll willingly give me."

"Leave the girl alone, Ares," a heavily accented male voice says from my other side. A leather satchel drops on the step, and the owner sits on top of it. He's a young guy, light brown hair, blue eyes, wearing all white, except for a tan leather belt and shoes. "You do not have to listen to his rubbish."

Ares smiles, but his eyes narrow. "What are you doing here, Jarilo? Don't you have enough to worry about in Russia without concerning yourself with these matters? And where are your other six heads?"

Jarilo? A Slavic god of war and protector.

The guy's gaze travels to a group of four men and two women wearing all white a few steps down from us.

"Of course," Ares says, and there's amusement in his voice. "You wouldn't confront me alone."

"There's no ignoring the energy." Jarilo has an innocent-looking face, but he can match Ares glare for glare. "Immortals flock to Rome. They thirst for power, and soon they realize, a side they must pick."

"Be careful of wolves in sheep's clothing, Analiese." Ares stands and reaches a business card out to Jarilo. "When you're ready to choose a side, call me." His black boots thump up the concrete steps as he climbs, putting distance between us.

I turn to ask Jarilo about the energy he mentioned, but he's gone, and so are his friends.

It's as if spiders skitter across my skin. Ares said some people wanted to kill me. I stand and spin around. My gaze goes from face to face. How can I tell if any are murderers? They all look harmless to me. The warmth leaves my body, my hands shake, and even though I'm outside, I can hardly breathe.

"Who was that man?" Marek asks when he reaches me.

I shake my head.

"Are you okay?" He places the cups and bag on the concrete, then puts an arm around me and guides me back down on the step. "You're shaking."

"He—he said his name's Ares, and he's a war god. And the other one is Jarilo."

Marek scans the stairs above us. "Who? Where did they go?"

"They're gone," I say. "Ares went up the steps, but Jarilo just disappeared."

He sits beside me, and his eyes go to my face. "What did they want with you?"

"I don't know what Jarilo wanted. Ares told me the same thing Sid had. Something about me being in the middle of a war between gods and that I should pick his side. Why would he want me?"

"Not sure," Marek says. "Maybe it has to do with what Inanna said you did. We need answers. All we have are bits and pieces of things. And we're carrying a bone around that could be from a murder."

"But we're at a dead end." I rub my clammy hands across my jeggings, hands still shaking.

He passes me one of the coffees, then opens the white bag. "Let's eat."

"What about Ares and Jarilo?"

He looks over his shoulder again. "I don't think they want to hurt you. Not Ares, anyway. Not if he was recruiting you for *his side*."

"I like how we're talking about this like he's recruiting me to work at Hotdog World or something. I keep thinking we're going to wake up any minute from this nightmare."

"Hey." He bumps my shoulder. "After you finish that, we'll search for that address in the box."

My gaze drops to my coffee. "Yeah, okay."

The cup is warm in my trembling hand, and I take a careful sip. My mind wanders as I eat my second cream-stuffed *sfogliatella*. The pastry with its many flaky layers melts in my mouth. I'm not hungry, but I'm a stress-eater, and this stuff is a stress-eater's dream. The pressure between my eyes loosens, and I'm feeling less scared.

"We need to hide better." I lick the cream from my lips. "Sid says they're sensing some sort of energy coming off one of us."

There's a deep swallow before he answers me. "I thought we did. Maybe we have a stalker." His eyes scan the steps and square below. "Someone who's with Ares. Or that other person. Jar-what's his name."

"Ares was in our hotel lobby last night. He was alone. So maybe he just felt us there." I finish the last bit of my coffee. "If only we knew what this energy we're supposedly emitting is."

"Maybe it's like a dog whistle. Only gods can sense it." He crumples up his napkin and stuffs it into the bag.

"If we ever see Sid again, we need to get more details from him." I ball-up my leftovers.

Our eyes meet, and I can see the worry in his. He smiles to cover it up, but I can still see it. I can feel it, too. Deep in the pit of my stomach. The same fear. It grows inside me like an unwanted weed, strangling.

"We need to find whatever your grandfather left at that address," I say, omitting my suspicion that it'll be a dead body.

He turns away, gathering up our cups and trash. "Okay, I've got the address programmed in the GPS. But first, we have to make sure no one's following us. My grandfather taught me how to ditch a tail. He started teaching me survival techniques when I was six."

"*Mine* taught me how to tie my shoes," I say, a little salty, but not toward Marek—toward his grandfather, who obviously kept Marek in the dark. "He was definitely preparing you for this. I wonder why he didn't tell you about whatever all this is."

"He had to have his reasons." His eyes dart around to the people passing us. "You ready?"

"Just a sec." I pick up my purse and remove the meager contents from the main compartment—passport, wallet, pillbox, and lip balm—and slip them into the pockets of my jacket and zip them up. Traveling light seems like a good idea.

I retrieve my cell phone from the side pocket and I'm about to put it in my jacket when Marek stops me.

"I did a lot of thinking last night," he says. "Replayed things in my head. I recalled my grandfather's instructions. We don't stop long enough for them to catch up to us. Keep moving. Only use cash. Get rid of our phones. We have the GPS I bought for directions."

"I haven't been using my phone."

"Doesn't matter," he says. "They might be able to trace them still. I say we dump them."

"You want me to throw away my phone?"

"Sorry," he says, an apologetic look on his face. "But it has to be done. I think that's how that Ares guy found us. Not some bullshit energy Sid wants us to believe."

He's right, but I worry what Dalton will do if he can't get a hold of me. He'd break down and tell Jane, fearing something terrible happened.

"Okay, but I have to send a message to my brother first."

"All right."

He waits as I type up an explanation and send it to Dalton.

After dropping my purse and our cell phones in a nearby trash barrel, I throw on my jacket and bound down the steps, catching up to Marek.

"So how do we ditch a tail?"

CHAPTER TWENTY

Tourists pack the shops on the cobblestone streets, searching the expensive, cheaply made souvenirs for the perfect gifts to bring back home. So many delicious smells fill the air surrounding the restaurants and bakeries we pass.

I can almost forget why we're here in Rome.

Almost.

Marek pulls me to a stop. We're in front of a shop's window displaying plaster Colosseums lined up on staggered shelves.

He points at them. "Pretend we're interested in the souvenirs. Someone's trailing us. I don't want him to suspect we know he is."

"Okay." It takes all my willpower to act normal.

"Do you see him?" Marek aims his index finger at one of the figurines.

I squint and try not to look suspicious. "No. Where is he?"

"Left of those statue heads of Caesar."

My focus shifts to where he indicated. "Is it the short man with the long nose?"

"No. He just got there. The Spanish man to his right."

Whoa. He's too perfect to be real. His hair thick and falling just under his chin, tall, and big muscles. But there's an edge to him. He's probably as dangerous as he is hot.

Marek slides a look at me. "Now, do you?"

"Um. Yeah, I see him."

"We need to stay in a crowded area. We'll shop. Eat. Then shop some more, keeping an eye on him through store windows. When he lets down his guard, we make our move and ditch him. Follow my lead, respond to my movements." He points at another figurine, and I nod, feigning a response that I like it.

"Good," he says. "We should act like a couple. It'll be less threatening. He'll see we're relaxed and have no idea he's following us. That way there's no fear we'll run from him."

"Okay."

"Are you ready?"

"Guess so," I say. "Let's do this."

Marek and I put on the facade of a couple, shopping for gifts to bring home to all our imaginary relatives. And he's good at faking it. I'm starting to think we are more than co-conspirators.

I know his touches don't mean anything. That we're pretending to be into each other as we browse the souvenirs. But each brush of his hand against my arm or back and every smile directed at me makes my heart tug toward him.

He checks the GPS. "*Via delle Muratte* is a few blocks away."

Every so often, we spy our stalker through a window made into a mirror by the afternoon sun. Marek was right. The man is getting careless. His eyes roam, checking out two women who definitely look American by their colorful clothes. We move along the sidewalk, and it takes him a few beats to notice and follow us, always keeping what he believes is a safe distance.

Leaning closer to Marek, I whisper, "I wonder if he's a god?"

"He definitely fits the part." He glances over his shoulder at the man. "Or he's one of those book cover models on my grams's romance novels."

A chuckle bursts from my lips. I should be scared. There's possibly a dangerous man following us, but I'm not afraid. Something in the depths of my soul tells me that the man doing a horrible job at being inconspicuous behind us isn't one of the bad ones. I catch a glimpse of him as we cross the street.

The man stops to pick up something a baby in a woman's arms dropped. I can barely make out the tiny stuffed elephant.

Marek points at a small shop as we approach it. "This is it."

I glance back to get the location of the man following us. He's still preoccupied with the baby. When I face forward, I almost collide with a postcard stand.

"Watch out." Marek snatches me into his arms before I make contact.

Our eyes connect, and we hold each other's stare for several electric beats of my heart. His gaze switches to my lips, and I suck in a breath, holding it until I can't any longer, then releasing it. He backs up. The expression on his face is serious. He tilts his head slightly to the side and brushes my hair behind my ear.

A smile raises one side of his lips. "You should be more careful," he says and lets me go. He picks up a postcard and holds it up for me to see. "How about this one, babe?"

I shake my head, fake-rejecting it as a contender, and commence my own search for the perfect postcard. My heart is still bucking in my chest. What just happened? Did he feel it, too? I peer at him through the stack of cards. He catches me and smiles. I quickly grab one of the cards and show him, covering up the fact I was just checking him out.

He shakes his head and mouths "no," and I find myself concentrating on how his bottom lip is fuller than the top while he's forming that word.

Marek searches a case filled with figurines.

"What are we looking for?" I ask.

"Not sure," he says, picking up a statue of the Pope. "Something to do with bones?"

"Right." I return to browsing the stand.

He lifts a decorative plate with tombstones and the title *Cimitero Acattolico* painted on it. "Possibly a graveyard?"

"Maybe." I search for postcards of them, but only find tourist spots. So many of them are beautiful, I want to buy them—the Trevi Fountain, Ponte Sant'Angelo, and the Mouth of Truth. My hand hovers over the next one on the stand.

Marek comes up behind me and looks over my shoulder. "You okay? What is it?"

I snatch up the postcard and stare at it. Four pictures make up the front. One is an image of a chapel, the other three are of walls decorated with hundreds of human remains. The bottom left photo is a cross made out of skulls, just like on the metal box in Marek's pocket. I flip the card over and read the caption. *Santa Maria della Concezione dei Cappuccini*; Crypt of the Skulls; Crypt of the Leg Bones; Crypt of the Pelvises. And at the top is the saying, "What you are now, we once were; what we are now, you shall be."

"This is it," I say.

He leans farther over my shoulder, his chest pressing against my back and his hand going to my waist for balance. I am breathless, and it could be a combination of the excitement of solving the clue and the connection of our bodies. My thoughts and feelings are scrambled with fear, curiosity, wonder, and confusion.

Marek takes the postcard from me, as well as the other three in my hand. "I'm going to buy these. It's time we make our move and get rid of our Spanish god back there."

While he pays for the cards, I inspect colorful scarves knotted to a circular rack in front of the door to the shop. I sneak a glimpse of the man who's been tracking us. His attention is on a woman with long red curly hair and tanned skin. By the way the woman smiles at our stalker, she's into him, and by the way he can't take his eyes off her, we have our opportunity to ditch him.

As soon as Marek steps out of the shop, I point out the situation. We dart up the street and turn the first corner we reach. We cut across the road and go up another one.

"We need directions," I say, panting. The GPS is good for when you have an address to enter, not so good when you need a map to search. "Why didn't we think to buy or rent one of those international cell phones?"

Marek crosses the street and approaches a man. I join him. The man points down the road and waves at the buildings as if Marek is Superman and can see through bricks. Marek shakes the man's hand and says, "*Grazie*," and I echo him.

From what the man said in his broken English, the Capuchin Crypt closes at seven and isn't too far away. We stay on this street and do a few more checks in windows to make sure that man isn't following us. We come to a building with a wall blocking steps leading up to an apartment on the second floor. Marek snatches my hand and storms up the stairs, towing me along with him.

"What are we doing?" I ask when we stop at the top.

Marek steals a glance over the wall. "It's the next phase in ditching a stalker. Once you think you've outsmarted him, verify it by getting someplace where he can't see you, but you can see him."

I so want to sneak a look, but I stay put and wait. "Is he there?"

"Yeah, just came around the corner. Guess that woman

wasn't a good enough distraction. *Shit.*" He drops down. "Shit, shit, shit."

"*What?*" I hiss.

He shakes his head and places his pointer finger to his mouth to quiet me. "That demon god's with him," he whispers.

"Pazuzu?" I cover my mouth to stop the terrified sob from escaping.

Inching up the wall, Marek peeks over it. He's up there longer than is comfortable for me. They could spot him.

In every scary movie I've seen that featured Pazuzu, he was terrifying. He's the worst in *The Exorcist*, when he possesses that little girl and makes her do all sorts of evil stuff, and I don't want to find out how he is in real life.

As I sit on my heels, the fear catches up. A *demon god* is after us. In this moment, where quiet rests around me and the only noise I can hear is people on the street and the occasional vehicle driving by, my mind is all over the place. I forgot to take my pill last night. And this morning. I was going to take one with breakfast, but Ares distracted me.

Panic builds like blowing up a piece of gum. It expands and expands and expands until it bursts.

They're going to sense us. Sid said one of us was emitting some sort of energy. Catnip to the gods. That's what he told me. It's just a matter of time before they find us.

They could kill us.

I tug out Dad's lighter from my pocket and tighten my fist around it. Wrapping my arms around my legs, I rock back and forth.

Back and forth.

We're going to die. We're going to die. *We're going to die!*

My heart is rapid and painful in my chest, and I can't get enough air.

It's not a heart attack.

I'm panicking.

Clammy palms. Out of control.

Dad's lighter grounds me.

Marek squats back down. "They're coming this way," he whispers.

Breathe.

Remember what Dr. Herrera taught you. You can control this. Use the 3-3-3 rule. Focus. What do I see? I look around.

Copper vines decorate the length of the wall that we're hiding behind. There's a busted brick at the corner just near Marek's foot. A rust-colored stain on the step in front of me. Could be blood. *Stop.* It's not blood. Probably someone dropped a to-go container of pasta or something.

Marek dares another look over the wall. "They passed us. Spanish god is talking to someone on the phone."

My arms and legs shake.

Breathe.

"Okay, they're gone," he says and pounds down the steps but stops when I don't follow him. "What's wrong?"

I just shake my head, unable to answer. His shirt is blue.

What do you hear?

Cars pass. Voices. A man and woman exchanging words in Italian somewhere. Not too close. Music. Someone's playing a violin or viola. They need more lessons.

He kneels on the top step, right over the bloodstain, and places his hands on my knees. "Ana."

I inhale. Tears form in my eyes and blur his face.

"It's okay," he directs. "They're gone. You'll be okay. We have each other. We'll get through this. If you want to stop, we'll stop. Go home."

What do you smell?

The hotel soap clinging to Marek's skin. A sour smell, like there's a trash can nearby. Someone's cooking. It's spicy.

Rolling my neck, I stretch my fingers and toes.

I blink, and the tears fall from my eyelashes. "I just need

a minute," I say between breaths. "Are you sure...they're... he's gone."

"Yes. A black SUV picked them up."

I study his almost-straight teeth while he's talking.

He doesn't get impatient while waiting for me to gather myself. His concern is genuine. I can see it in his eyes and feel it in the gentle squeeze of his hands on my knees.

The tightness in my chest subsides, and a calmness relaxes my tense muscles. That man who said he's Ares mentioned that Adam Conte wasn't my ally, but Marek sure feels like he's mine.

"I'm ready," I say, slipping the lighter back into my pocket.

"You sure?"

I nod, wiping away my tears, then brushing my wet fingers across my jeggings.

His brows push together as he studies my face. "You don't look good."

"I'm fine," I say. "Just tired. I saw a hotel down the street. We should get a room and go to this crypt tomorrow. Besides, we'd only have a few hours to find whatever clue is hidden there. And I think the finger bone is like a puzzle piece and it's going to take time to locate its owner. Okay?"

"Good idea," he says.

We stay on the side of the road that's covered in shade from the trees, keeping alert for either a black SUV or Pazuzu and his friend.

I really misjudged that Spanish god. He seemed kind. Picked up a toy for a baby, even.

Once while we were reading a tale about Loki, the Norse god who was always causing trouble, Dad teased, "Be careful of the trickster gods, Ana."

Well, apparently, I have crappy judgment.

If I can't tell the difference, I'm screwed.

CHAPTER TWENTY-ONE

The sun is out today, and dappled light slips through the leaves of the trees lining the road that is home to Santa Maria della Concezione dei Cappuccini chapel. The Capuchin Crypt is situated beneath it.

Marek looks different today. Taller? Straighter, maybe? I thought he was attractive from the first time I met him, but there's something more to him now.

There's a small line forming outside the wrought-iron gates, waiting for the crypt to open. Three groups—two couples and four older men. I'm not sure if we should trust them. As it is now, I don't believe anyone.

"Ready to see some dead monks?" Marek smirks and crosses the street.

I hurry to his side, working hard to keep up with his long gait. "Can you quit with the dead references already? Two was funny. You were pushing it at three during breakfast. Now it's just tired."

He stops in the middle of the road. "You wound me."

I grab his arm and pull him out of the way of oncoming

traffic. "If you're not careful, they'll have another dead body to add to their collection in that crypt."

"That's not funny." He frowns.

"See?"

He shakes his head and steps up on the curb.

We get in line and wait.

On the other side of the gate, fixed to the brick wall, is a plaque with a three-dimensional woman in flowing robes. There're two infants at her feet and a crest underneath her. The writing on the stone is in Italian or Latin, so I don't know what it says, but my bet is the woman is Santa Maria, since the chapel is named after her.

Marek faces the street, looking out for anyone recognizable while I read the stuff about the crypt I printed in the hotel's business center earlier this morning.

The pocket in his jacket is bulging out, the metal box hiding there. It's in the shop's bag Marek got when he bought the postcards. If there's security, hopefully the box will pass off as a souvenir.

His head tilts in my direction, and a smile pushes up his cheeks, causing a hint of dimples to appear in each one. There's a worry behind his eyes. He thinks I may break down again. What he doesn't know is that I have it under control. I missed taking my meds a few days in a row and consumed a lot of caffeine yesterday. Add the incredibly stressful situation we're in and an attack was bound to happen.

"I'm okay," I reassure him.

"I didn't say anything." He looks directly into my eyes, then sneaks a glance at my lips, and it stills me.

What was that? He keeps looking there. Do I have weird lips? I make a slow 360 turn, pretending to search the street, running my fingers across my mouth to see if any breakfast remains are hanging out there. I don't feel anything.

The line moves, and we shuffle along with the crowd.

When we enter, everyone's voices lower to a whisper out of respect for the dead. We skip the museum, walking through it and going straight to the crypt.

"I wonder how many people a day say 'I see dead people' while entering this museum?" He laughs, pleased at his joke.

My lips press together to suppress a laugh. "I'm not sure that joke is appropriate in a monk's crypt."

The corridor is lit only by small windows and dim electric candles.

"I see you holding back." Amusement strikes his eyes. "You think it's funny."

I chuckle and abruptly stop in front of one of the rooms.

There are so many bones and skulls, my mind can't process what I'm seeing. Human bones. Thousands. Elaborately stacked against the walls and arranged into a baroque pattern. Thigh bones and skulls fashioned into arches and benches. Some are even crafted into chandeliers that hang from the ceiling.

"Holy shit," Marek says a little too loud. His eyes go wide, and he looks around to see if anyone heard him before lowering his voice. "It's like bone wallpaper."

There's a smell I can't quite place. Damp earth and must with a hint of rot.

"That had to take a lot of time," I say. "Separating every bone from thousands of skeletons, cleaning them, and arranging them into art like this. Who'd do that?"

We continue down the arched corridor decorated with more bones. Each room we pass is closed off by wrought-iron gates. There's the Crypt of Skulls, Crypt of the Leg Bones and Thigh Bones, and the Crypt of Pelvises. In each room, there are full skeletons wearing monk robes, the hoods covering their skulls. None of them are missing a finger.

After several hours staring at the macabre structures, I want to give up. A long sigh deflates my lungs. "I was sure the clue was here," I say.

"The finger bone is the same yellowy color as these," he says and ruffles his hair as if he's trying to shake bugs off.

He's probably feeling like insects are crawling all over him. I know I am.

I scratch my arm. "What do you want to do?"

Marek's eyes run over the bone sculptures again. "I guess we should go."

"I am disappointed." A man's voice comes from behind us. An Italian accent hangs on his words. "The great Adam Conte's grandson gives up so easily."

Marek and I spin around at the same time and come face-to-face with a man in his mid-twenties who's a little taller than Marek and is wearing jeans and a tweed jacket. The man's hair is brown, short, and wavy. Nose long. He crosses his arms as he scrutinizes us. His amber eyes shift between Marek and me.

Not a word passes between us for several breaths. I can tell the man is waiting for one of us to say something.

I bite. "Who are you?"

He smiles, and his teeth are bright white against his olive skin. "I'm Janus."

"Oh for Pete's sake," I snap, using Dad's old phrase because what I really want to say wouldn't be proper for where we are. "Janus, huh? The god, Janus? Like, as in the god of beginnings, doorways or gates, and endings."

"You forgot time and passages," the man says.

"Wait." Marek's attention turns to Janus. "How do you know who we are?"

"Because you're the mirror image of Adam at your age."

"You're too young to know him when he was my age," Marek retorts.

"He probably saw pictures of him back then," I reason.

Janus smirks. "Could be. But I've been friends with Adam since his years at Oxford. Before he took over things for his father."

"He's a god, Marek," I say. "And he's immortal."

"What do you want?" Marek fists his hands, readying to defend us.

"You will only believe me after following where the next clue leads." Janus isn't smiling anymore.

A line of tourists coming from the museum shuffles down the corridor. At the sight of the first bone room, some gasp while others take a step back. Frightened expressions. Surprised looks. The crypt's peculiar decorations captivate them all.

Janus steps closer so he can whisper, "But first, you must show me the treasure he left you."

Marek makes a play for his pocket, and I drop my hand on his arm to stop him. "No. He's a stranger. We don't know if we can trust him."

"Your grandfather came to me many years ago," Janus says. "He asked that I be the keeper of your legacy. Hold out your hand."

Janus removes something from his pocket and keeps it fisted inside his hand.

Marek glances at me, and I shrug. He lifts his arm, and Janus drops a ring onto Marek's open palm.

There is silence as Marek twists and turns the ring in his hand, studying it. The ring, dull with age, is gold with a crest in the middle.

"What is this?" he asks.

"Your grandfather's Oxford ring," Janus says.

"This could be anyone's." Marek holds the ring out to Janus.

Janus doesn't take it. "Read the name and the inscription inside."

Marek examines it. The left corner of his mouth tugs up, then his eyes gloss. He swallows and clears his throat. "It's his."

"What does it say?" I ask.

He hands me the ring and turns his head from us to gather his emotions. I read the inscription. *Adam R. Conte – "What we think, we become." Buddha*

"How do you know it's his?" I ask.

Marek faces us, and I pass the ring back to him. "It's his favorite saying. Said it to me all the time."

"Yes," Janus says. "He was obsessed with it."

"Why did he give this to you?" Marek asks.

"To pass it on to you," Janus says, "and so that you would believe me when this day came." His head snaps in the direction of the tourists getting nearer. "It's about to get crowded here." He holds up his hand in the direction of the tourists, and a blue light blocks the corridor.

I stumble back and quickly balance myself. "How did you... What is that?" I'm not sure which question to ask.

"It's an old parlor trick I learned." He winks as if he didn't just create a blue shield thing in front of me. "You learn a lot of things when you're immortal."

He just made a bunch of people freeze in place, and I'm wondering if we are hanging out in a crypt full of bones and skeletons with a man that just might possibly have the power to send us to the next life.

Janus's mouth is a straight line. "Now, the box?"

Marek yanks the box out from his pocket.

"Open it," Janus directs.

He spins the combination code into the box, lifts the lid, and tilts it for Janus to see.

Janus's eyes go to the box, then to us, and he grins. "Very good." He looks directly at Marek. "I will say, you have put Analiese in danger by bringing her into this. With knowledge comes great risks." Now his eyes go to me. "Do you want to turn back?"

Do I want to turn back? I don't think I have the option.

He said with knowledge comes great risks. Sid's words replay in my head. *You, my dear, have walked into the middle of a battle between gods.* I am in the center of whatever is going on. My parents were, too.

Marek steps a little in front of me. "How is she in danger? We have no idea what's going on. It's all confusing."

I back up, hitting the wrought-iron gate, reminding me that we're in a crypt with the remains of thousands of monks. A chill licks my skin, and I'm sure I hear haunted voices.

I decide to jump in.

"There was a list in Mr. Conte's things," I say. "My name and my parents' names are on it. Do you know what it is?" I leave out the part where everyone on the list is either dead or missing.

Janus stares at my face for what seems like the longest second ever. "If Marek chooses to take you along to where the bone leads, you, too, will find your answers."

"What was my grandfather up to?" Marek searches for answers to his own questions.

"You were his progeny. His successor. Just as his predecessor did, and all the predecessors before him, he was preparing you for this role. That's all I can tell you. You're about to walk through a door where you'll find the answers to your questions."

"What if I don't want this? Whatever it is."

Janus's mouth twists down. My heart beats as fast as a rabbit's facing the fangs of a snake. Janus may be a friend of Adam Conte, he may be sworn to help and protect Marek, but he has no responsibilities to me. My intuition yells at me to not trust him.

"You go home," Janus says. "It's either accept your role or lose out on your inheritance. No gray area. No door number three. It's a sizeable sum of money, so you should consider that. You and your grandmother will be penniless otherwise."

Bingo. I knew there was a catch.

"They're not my rules," Janus says, his voice calm and calculating. "Blame your predecessors."

Marek turns and takes a few steps away from us. He stares at the thousand or so skulls piled neatly, faces out, and formed into arches against the wall across from him. A chandelier made out of human bones hangs from the ceiling. It's a reminder of what we all end up being when we die. Just a pile of bones. Except for Janus. He can live forever.

Janus and I avoid eye contact as we wait for Marek to turn around. When he does, Marek has a determined look on his face. He comes to me and takes my hands in his.

"I'm going forward," he says. "You can go back. I won't blame you. This is some messed-up shit."

A slight smile tugs at my lips. He's delusional to think Janus would let me leave here and go home. He said it himself. I know too much. There was a point when I could've walked away from all this, but that time is gone. I'm in as deep as Marek is now. There's no return for me. I can only go forward. Find out why everyone knows who the hell I am and why Ares thinks I'll give him whatever we find at the end of this journey.

"I'll go with you," I say. Dalton is always telling me I have a blind spot for trouble—I never see it coming. I walk straight into it. But this time I see the trouble, and I'm heading straight at it anyway.

There's concern in Marek's eyes, his hands gripping mine, firm and gentle at the same time. "Are you sure?"

Of course I'm not, but I lie, "I am."

Janus waves at the blue electric barrier, and it disappears. "All right, you two. Follow me."

The tourists are moving again, the spell broken.

Marek and I give each other confused looks as we follow Janus up the steps, through a gift shop, back to the street, and into an alley.

Scary alley. Check. One immortal god who's a little unstable. Check. Sitting ducks, AKA Marek and me. Check.

"This is it." Janus turns to face us. "What's wrong?"

He must notice the fearful thoughts scrunching up my face. "I thought the clue would be in the crypt," I say.

He laughs and shakes his head. "Silly mortal. We would never desecrate a holy place. Now, the bone is the key. It fits into that hole." He points down to what looks to be a manhole.

"We're not going underground, are we? I thought you said it was a door."

Janus doesn't answer, so I lift my head. He's gone, disappearing seemingly into thin air.

"Where'd he go?" Marek's head turns left, then right, searching the alley. "He vanished."

"Well, he is the god of passages and doors and apparently manholes." I frown at the rusty, circular metal. "So are we going down?"

Marek lifts a brow at me. "No going back now."

"Okay," I say. "Let's do this. I just hope it's not a sewer."

He unlocks the metal box, removes the bone, inserts it into the hole, and pulls it back out. There's a scraping sound as the cover slides away. All I can see is the top of a ladder. It looks old and not at all clean. I scratch my arms.

"Do you want to go first or should I?" He puts the bone back in the box and stuffs it into his pocket.

I give him a look that says hell-yeah-I-want-you-to-go-first-into-the-dark-creepy-hole. "You first."

He smirks, and it's not his usual confident one, it's more of a nervous one. "Okay. Wait until I call you."

"See. If we didn't throw our phones away, we'd have a flashlight app to use while going into the black hole that leads to God-knows-what."

He glances up at me. "You're going to use that every time we're in a situation where we could've used them?"

"Yep."

He laughs and continues down.

The ladder shakes a little as he moves. It creaks with each step down the rungs. His foot slips.

"Shit." He steadies the ladder and looks up at me. "The wood's getting slippery. You'll have to be careful coming down."

"You pay attention." I nod my head, motioning him to continue.

There's a thump and Marek's breath punching out. "Okay, I'm down."

I get on my knees and squint, trying to see him at the bottom. I can barely make out the outline of his body.

"Hey," he calls. "There are kerosene lanterns and matches down here."

"Well, that's convenient. We get to see whatever scary things live down there."

A strike of a match. Another drag across the matchbox. It ignites, and he touches the flame to the lantern. A soft orange glow illuminates the hole.

"Sure, I'll go with you. No, I don't want to go home where it's safe," I mock to no one, yanking up the zipper to my bomber jacket before going down. "Great idea, Ana."

The ladder wobbles, and I cling to it. A memory slaps me like an old enemy. My stomach twists. I tremble, not able to move, my knuckles turning white from the tight grasp I have on the top rung. All I remember is falling and hitting the ground hard. The next memory is waking up in the hospital with a severe headache and a cast on my arm. I was about six, and I was wearing the dress with the daisies.

I can't move.

The ladder shakes, again, and before I can get in two breaths, Marek is behind me, one rung below, his arms around me. "You're okay. We're going to go down together. All right?"

Without a word, I nod.

"Now," he says.

We move down one rung.

"Okay, next one." His hand is firm on my waist, the other on the ladder.

Another step down. His mouth is resting against my neck.

We move again and continue until we reach the bottom. I don't notice where we end up. I'm busy trying to recover. Marek looks good in the glow coming from the kerosene lantern. It dances over his face and lights up his brown eyes, which are watching me with so much concern in them.

"So," Marek finally says. "You're afraid of heights?"

"Not heights. Just falling."

"Don't they go together?"

"No. Maybe. I can stand on a high platform. Even climb to get there, but coming down, I freeze with fear. And it's only with ladders."

"I'll keep that in mind." He smiles and picks up the lantern. "Shall we see what's down the rabbit hole?"

"You know that's overused, right?" I smirk and follow him into a tunnel I'm pretty sure won't lead us to Wonderland.

CHAPTER TWENTY-TWO

The light reveals the cavern we're in. Arched ceilings, brick walls packed tight, rough floors, and no spiders, from what I can see. Against all common sense, we trudge through the tunnel. It curves, bringing us to a small chamber.

Shelves dug into the walls—several rows and stacked four high—encompass the room. Skeletal remains rest on each, bits of cloth that had once wrapped the bodies still clinging to the bones. A few of the bodies are more intact. Like they hadn't died too long ago. Ancient artwork decorates the walls.

"We're in a catacomb," I say.

Marek slowly turns, holding up the lantern, casting the light over the many tombs. "I wonder who they are."

"This is it?" I spin around with him. "I thought it was supposed to reveal all your answers. Actually, I'm not sure what the questions are."

"I'm not sure on that one, either."

I shuffle around, moving the dirt on the floor with the toe of my Vans. "Maybe it's buried. There's a pile of cigarette butts here. Why would anyone smoke down here? It's already hard to breathe as it is."

He comes to my side. "They look old. Probably didn't know the health ramifications."

I squat down, pick one up, and inspect it. "Whoever it was, she was staring at the artwork on the wall for a long time to smoke this many cigarettes."

"How do you know it was a woman? And it could've been more than one person."

Raising my arm up, a cigarette butt pinched between my fingers, I say, "Red lipstick. All the same brand. And there's a broken fingernail with the same color polish."

He ruffles his hair, then combs it in place, probably trying to shake off imaginary bugs again. Because I know I'm dying to scratch my head. I swear there are tiny, creepy-crawly legs skittering across my scalp.

"What was she trying to see in the artwork?" I sit a foot away from the discarded cigarettes. My legs are sore when I pull them into a pretzel position. All the running around and climbing gave them a workout they've never done before.

I imagine the woman with the red lipstick smoking and trying to figure out the scenes painted on the walls surrounding the tombs, a hazy cloud hovering over her head.

Marek places the lantern on the ground and grabs a seat on my other side.

"There has to be a message in the pictures," I say. "I wonder what the writing is underneath them. Hmm…they must tell a story. Did your grandfather teach you any strange languages or how to uncover fables within the artwork of earlier times?"

He drops his head, a little laugh moving his shoulders. "That man had patience. He'd try to teach me stuff, but my mind was always distracted. Hopefully, I retained some of it."

I rub an itch away from my nose. "My dad and I spent hours studying ancient paintings from books and museums.

He used to say I was a natural. It's pretty easy. Understanding a lot of the symbols just takes some common sense."

"It sounds like he was preparing you, too."

"He didn't have to work hard at it," I say. "All he had to do was say he liked something and I would bust my butt to be perfect at it. I wanted him to love me. So I thought if I was into the same things, he would. Maybe even more than Dalton. That's pretty messed up, right?"

"Yeah," he says, smiling. "It's called sibling rivalry. Trust me. My brothers, sisters, and I are always in competition for our parents' attention. So don't beat yourself up. You're normal."

I laugh. "Good to know."

"Okay." Marek stretches his legs out in front of him and crosses his ankles. "Let's see if we can figure out the story."

"All right." My eyes burn against the dim light and the dust hanging in the air as I study the images on the wall. "The first set depicts gods with worshippers surrounding them, placing offerings at their feet—animals, grain, young women. There're several of the same scenes representing different gods from around the world. The next set shows the people less interested in the gods. In the following group, the gods unleash their wrath on the people."

Marek rubs his chin, nodding. "I get that. Good. There's one almighty god that oversees them all. See him there on top?"

"I do," I say. "He's angry, his hand comes down, and he takes power away from the other, lesser gods. At least that's what I think is happening. The painting shows light leaving the gods and going into what looks like a talisman in the mightier one's hand. I think he's like *The* God. Our God."

"I see it," he says.

"Next, a god is rising up from the grave. His palms are open, and there are skeletons on them. He's a god of death. I've seen that image before. There's a creepy painting of him in my dad's office."

"Who are the small people at his feet?"

"That's the gods' children. Gods had children with mortals all the time. Most are demigods."

Marek pulls up his knees and rests his folded arms on them. "He really got around, didn't he?"

I lean back on my arms, arching my back to stretch my muscles. "I wonder which god of death it is."

"It's Soranus," Marek says. "He's walking on fire, and there are wolves around him. The other death gods are in the underworld below him."

I flash him a smile. "You listened to your grandfather more than you think."

"I guess so."

"Because no one worshipped him, Soranus didn't lose his power."

"There's plenty of people into dark shit nowadays who would," Marek says.

"I bet so." Deciphering the artwork, I almost forget we're in a creepy catacomb. "Because Soranus didn't spite mortals, he was spared the others' fate."

The artwork wraps around the entire catacomb. I stand and pick up the lantern to get a better look at the other images. "The gods who lost their power raid Soranus's grave to get the talisman. They need it to regain their magic. Before the gods reach Soranus, he breaks it into six pieces and gives it to his most beloved daughter."

I point to the image of a woman. "See how her face is shaped like a heart and Soranus's other children's are boxes. That means she's his favorite."

"You're good at this," he says, getting up and following me around the catacomb.

"The daughter summons six elders from the mortals and anoints them and hands them each a piece of the talisman."

"Whoa." Marek grabs the back of his neck. "There's some sort of battle over there."

I pass a group of shelves holding bodies on my way to where the story continues. "The paint is more vibrant here. It's newer, or better materials were used. I don't get it. Gods are fighting against other gods. Soranus's children are there. See the square heads?" I point them out. "Who are these men? They don't look like the humans in the other images. And they're fighting gods."

"Gods without power," Marek adds.

"Could be." I almost stumble at seeing the next painting. "Look here. Soranus's favorite child has her hand on a man's chest. He has *X*s for eyes, meaning he's dead. The next image shows him alive. And the next has him fighting a god with just as much strength as the god. He doesn't look human. See his pointy teeth and long fingernails."

"So is that it?" Marek glances back at the artwork we've just walked by.

"No." I hold the lantern to a bleeding dove with a flock of burning birds flying up and over the adjacent tombs. "See this?"

"Yes." His eyebrows pinch together as he studies it. "The symbol for war."

"It is." I point to the others after it. "Ares's flaming spear, the Flower of Aphrodite, Inanna's whip, Thor's hammer, and so many more. It indicates a great war between all the gods."

"Hey, look. There's one of those moths that attacked you in the hotel lobby. See, it has a skull on its back."

I lean closer to the wall. "It's a death's-head hawkmoth."

"What does it mean?"

"I don't know." My voice sounds far away, muffled in my ears. "But both times something came back to life—the doorman and the frog—they appeared."

I don't want to say out loud what I think it means. I don't

want to believe it. Because I don't understand how it's even possible.

"I remember part of a story my grandfather used to read to me." His eyes go to the favorite child. "The death god, maybe Soranus, borrowed the freshly dead from the underworld to build an army. Something about the gods' powers being taken away and them attacking the underworld to get it back. Soranus defeated them, and the gods scattered around the world, hiding among the mortals. There's more to the story, but it's foggy."

I give him a *how could you forget that* look. "And this is something you just remembered now?"

"In all fairness," Marek says, "I was really young. It's just coming back to me after seeing all this."

"How can this be real?"

I can't ignore it anymore. Not now. I feel it in the pit of my soul. A darkness.

He puts an arm around my shoulders. "Are you okay?"

"Just letting it all settle in." I can barely feel the weight of his arm. "How is it even possible. Raising the dead. *Me.* I'm just…well, me. Janus did say I would find my answers down here. So is this what he meant?"

"That doorman was dead. He didn't have a pulse. You touched him, and he came back. Then those moths…"

"I think my dad's been here before." I rub the dust from my eyes. "These symbols are familiar to me. Maybe I've seen them in his things. In his sketch books."

"Do you remember anything else?" he asks.

I inspect my hands. "No."

They're just normal hands. Nothing extraordinary about them. A blister forming from climbing down the ladder. I flip them over. The cuticle on my middle finger is torn from where I kept picking at it. How could they be powerful enough to bring someone or something back to life?

But I can't ignore this nagging feeling. It started at the hotel after the doorman woke up from apparent death. There was a tugging feeling in my palms, and all the warmth in my hands left, leaving them icy cold.

Marek drops his arm from my shoulder and heads back the way we came, scanning the artwork. "I don't see my answers down here. What's my role in all this?"

"I'm sorry." I join him where he's staring at the death god. "Let's search around some more."

We comb the entire catacomb. It feels like I've breathed the same air twice or maybe ten times. It's thick and dank.

"There's nothing," he says. "Let's get out of here. Maybe Janus can help me."

Beside one of the newer mummified bodies is another polished red nail. "I think this is our chain-smoker. She never got out." My breath catches, and my heart speeds up. "What if we can't?"

"We can't get lost. There's only one way in and out."

"Then why didn't she make it out?"

His eyes go to the pile of lipstick-stained cigeratte butts. "She probably smoked herself to death."

"Who buried her, then?"

"Come on, before you start freaking me out," he says. "I don't see anything for me down here, anyway."

I stay close to Marek through the corridor. We go around the curve, coming to a fork where two tunnels branch off in different directions—one left, the other right.

"That wasn't here before," he says.

"Is this a trick?"

"I don't know." Marek's eyes go from one opening to the other. "The right looks like it goes nowhere. There's a brick wall at the end."

We go left. The tunnel is longer than the one we came in through. It twists and dips. We go up and down steps and around corners that weren't here before, ending back in the catacomb with the ancient artwork.

"What the hell." Marek stops in the middle of the room.

I bump into his arm. "Maybe we should've taken that right."

"Okay, let's try it." He darts out of the catacomb with me on his heels.

We make it to the fork in the tunnel and go right. It's a dead end. Marek pounds his fist on the bricks. I grab his arm and stop his next blow.

"You're going to hurt your hand." He already has. Blood trickles from his knuckles down his wrist.

"How do we get out? We're going to run out of kerosene soon." He kicks the dirt, trying to get rid of the rest of his frustrations.

"Are you sure your grandfather loved you?"

He shoots me a startled look. "Why do you ask that?"

"Well," I say. "Because for one, if you didn't accept this jacked-up legacy, he'd leave you and your grandmother penniless. And two, he sent you on this hunt and into this underground catacomb and no telling if there's a way out. It doesn't matter. We'll probably die in here."

My heart is beating at a breakneck speed, and I think it'll rip out of my chest and find its own way out of this dismal crypt.

Morbid thoughts rush through my mind. Would we die of starvation first? Or lack of water? Will the air run out down here? When the lantern goes out, will a bunch of catacomb critters come out of hiding and eat us?

Any of those options sound like they'd be drawn-out deaths and possibly painful.

CHAPTER TWENTY-THREE

Marek grasps my face in his hands. "I'm sorry if I scared you. I shouldn't lose my cool. It'll be okay. We'll find a way out."

I nod against his hands. "Promise me if I die first, you won't eat me."

He chortles. "I can't. There's no telling what people will do to survive. If I kick the bucket first, you can eat me. I promise not to haunt you the rest of your life." As his hands slide away from my face, I feel cold metal on his right one against my skin.

"The decoder ring."

His fingertips touch my cheek, and concern crosses his face. "Did it scratch you?"

"No. It's the symbols on it. They're the same as the writing under the artwork on the catacomb's walls. It's the Phoenician alphabet."

"Back to the catacomb?"

I nod and race back with him to the chamber of tombs.

He removes the decoder ring from his finger. "Do you

have anything to write down the letters as I translate them?"

Back in the purse I ditched. "No," I say. "I can write in the dirt." I squat and ready my finger. "Go ahead."

"The first letter is I, the next is N, and—"

"Just give me the letters. I get what order they're in."

Marek rattles off the first line's letters.

In the beginning, the people loved the gods.

I straighten, wiping off the dust covering my hands on my pants. "Stop. It's just telling the story in the artwork."

He steps back. "Then what?"

"There has to be something different," I say, following the line of the fable. "A clue or something."

Neither one of us speaks as we shuffle along the walls, searching. It's so quiet, definitely as silent as a tomb. The Phoenician letters under the paintings go from black to red.

"See here." I wave a finger over the six elders receiving the pieces of the talisman. "I think we need to decode it. The words are in a different color from the rest of the story."

"Okay, let's try it." He tugs off the decoder ring.

I drop back down and get ready to write the letters in the dirt. I nod when I'm ready, and he calls them out.

We get the first word. It's a lengthy passage to decode. When finished, we stand over the transcription.

Progeny, spoken thee an oath to forfend mortals from gods with the aim to take away free will. Six families. Each holds a piece of Divinities Keep, containing the power of the gods. With each piece joined, doth power return. Sacrifice life to keep the talisman safe.

Guard Death's children, for they shall be the weapon to triumph in the great battle between the gods.

Marek gives me a sideways glance. "Really? You had to punctuate it."

I shrug a shoulder. "Habits can't be broken."

"What does forfend mean?" he asks.

"Protect," I say. "Do you remember giving an oath?"

"Yes." He scratches the back of his neck. "'My life I give to the Divinities Keep. I will protect it at all costs.' That's it. I thought it was a game at the time."

"I wonder why your grandfather didn't just tell you about all this."

His head lowers, as if the weight of whatever memory he's having is too heavy. "If only one person knows a thing, the chance of it leaking is slim. My grandfather once said that when I was older, he had something to tell me." He looks up, and his dark gaze meets mine. "Guess he thought I couldn't handle *all this* yet. Probably the same with your dad. Not wanting to end your innocence until it was absolutely necessary."

"Now what? I thought it would show us how to get out of here."

The light coming from the lantern is growing dim. I don't want to think about what will happen when it goes completely out.

He sits down as if he's giving up. "Me, too."

"There has to be a way out. Something in this artwork must tell us how." I walk a circle along the circumference of the catacomb and then retrace it.

My measured steps kick up dust as I walk the length of the wall between two shelves. The shrouded skeletons are silent reminders of what will happen to Marek and me if we don't solve this clue. I come up to the one with the broken red polished nail. There's a scuff mark on the shelf and on the one above it.

"This isn't her body," I say, thinking out loud.

"Did you say something?"

"Chain-smoker. She didn't die." I grab the bottom of the next shelf up, pushing back the thought that there were remains on it, and boost myself up.

Marek hurries over to me. "What are you doing? Be careful."

"There's something at the top. The burning birds point to it. Why didn't I see it before?" I climb to the next and the next. The ledge at the top of the tomb blocks a latch if viewed from below. I yank on it, dirt and tiny pebbles hitting my face, causing me to lose my hold. I fall backward, and Marek tries to catch me. Before we crash to the ground together, he turns so he lands first, cushioning the fall for me.

My head drops onto his shoulder. I turn to look at him. Our faces are so close now. There's pain twisting his, and I'm pretty sure there's only admiration showing on mine. He broke the fall for me. No thought. No hesitation. Instinctively, he wanted to protect me.

"Are you okay?" I finally find my voice.

He groans. "That f—k—hurt. I thought you were afraid of climbing."

I roll my head back and laugh. It's so cute that he didn't want to say the big bad f-word in front of me. "I can climb. It's the getting down part. That's the problem."

"So you were just going to ignore the fact that what goes up must come down?"

I sober. He's right. I was too excited to get out of this grave to think. "Yeah, I didn't think that through."

"Your elbow's in my stomach," he grunts.

"Oh sorry." I roll off his body, stand, and offer my hands to him.

He grasps them, and I help him up.

We feel the draft at the same time and turn our heads in its direction. There's an opening in the wall, leading into another tunnel.

Excited screams come from both of us, and we hug tight, then quickly let go.

"Um…" I'm not sure what to say.

"Come on. Let's get out of this death trap." He grasps my hand, tows me out of the room, and suddenly stops.

I come around him. On a marble stand resembling an upside-down bird's leg with a talon sits a silver canister the size of Saba's cigar tube that he keeps hidden from Safta. The soft green light coming from it fills the area. It reminds me of the glow-in-the-dark stars stuck to the ceiling in my room.

Marek just stares at it.

"Take it," I say. "I think it's for you."

He looks back the way we just came and then to the left where the newfound tunnel leads. "What if it's a trap? You go before I remove it."

"I won't leave you."

He shakes his head. "No. I'm not touching this until you're safely out of here."

The resolve on his face tells me he means it.

My eyes burn, and I know the tears are about to well in my eyes. "If anything happens, I'll find you."

"I know," he says with a wink. "Take the lantern and go."

Picking it up, I rush down the tunnel, orange light bouncing against the brick walls with my movements. It's longer than I expected. I reach a set of stairs and pound up them, careful so as not to trip over the many broken railings scattered over the steps. Overhead is a manhole cover. It doesn't budge when I try to move it. There's a hole in it the size of the finger bone we used to get into this catacomb nightmare.

"Great." Marek has the finger. I come down a few steps and sit, elbow on my knee, resting my chin in my hand, and wait. Wait either for the walls to crumble around me or for Marek to catch up. With my luck lately, I'd put my money on the former.

A soft moaning sound comes from the dark tunnel that led me here.

"Marek?"

Only the moaning answers. I stand.

"That's not funny at all."

A faint white light flickers and fades.

"Come on, Marek. Quit messing around."

A smell of sulfur wafts through the air.

The light nears and grows, forming into a body. Into a ghostly-looking man. Anger is set on his almost transparent face. The sockets where eyes should be are dark and empty. I know his face. A face seemingly hanging loosely off sharp bones. A face I've seen in duplicate.

Deceducto, risorto, deceducto.

Isabella Favero's experiment.

I scramble on my back up the stairs, make it halfway before I lose my footing, and slip back down. Pain sears my back.

"What do you want?" I try to yell, but it comes out more like a croak.

The ghostly figure moans and keeps moving toward me. Several similar lights begin to form behind him, and I want to close my eyes, but I'm not sure that will make them go away.

They move closer.

The others form faces, and there are so many of them. I recognize some of them from their headshots taped in Isabella's record book.

The moaning grows louder, piercing. A chorus of pain. A chorus of sadness.

A chorus of hatred.

I slowly move back up the stairs, afraid to go fast.

There are so many faces. Old and young. Men and women. Bile rises in the back of my throat when I spot a little girl in the mix.

"What do you want?" I'm sobbing, my words are wet, and there's no air behind them.

The moaning turns to screeching.

"I'm not her," I shout. "Isabella did this to you."

They stop at the foot of the stairs. Faces turn up to me, watching me with hollow eyes. Expressionless faces. All their emotions are saved for the hideous moaning. It's full of pain and anguish. Torture.

I can't breathe.

Their second deaths flip through my mind, and I can't stop it. Each the same. They wake up suddenly and look around dazed. I can see the mortuary. Other bodies on tables. Confusion. Isabella says something, but I can't understand her. It's in Italian. She makes notes. Picks up a plastic bag, covers a man's head with it, and suffocates him.

The lantern dims.

"No. Don't go out," I order it. "Please don't go out."

It flickers in response.

The images and moaning stop, and the whispers hiss around me.

Riser. Riser. Riser. Riser. Riser. Riser. Ri— I cover my ears.

Scratching noises come from behind the wall on either side of me. No matter how tight I cover my ears, I can still hear the hissing chants of the spirits and the frantic scraping of whatever is on the other side of the walls.

"No! Leave me alone!"

It's like demons have control of my head. This isn't real. Something is making me see these things. Push it away. Stop it.

And the lantern goes a little dimmer.

"Marek!" Where the hell is he?

Something breaks through the wall on my left.

The flame puffs out.

CHAPTER TWENTY-FOUR

Something claws into my arm, tearing skin.

A scream rips from me.

I writhe on the stairs, trying to get free.

Another something tugs my leg. The wall breaks to my left.

Riser. Riser. Riser. Riser…

My back and hips hit hard against the corner of the steps. Cold twig-like things grab my shoulders and grasp my throat.

"Marek!"

I kick my free leg out and connect with something. There's a rattling sound. A crash.

The pressure on my neck tightens, and I'm getting light-headed.

The ghostly lights move closer, and I can now see what's holding me.

Hands.

Skeleton hands.

I frantically pull at them, tug and tug, until they snap in my hands and fall away from my neck. Air rushes into my lungs, burning, painful. Bony fingers grasp my hair and yank me back, dragging me up the steps. I stretch for a piece of the railing off to the side and fall short.

My head and spine bang against the corners of concrete.

The fear of death clutches my lungs and squeezes, and I can't scream out.

The hissing increases to a storm in my ears. The spirits float above and around me. Moaning and hissing.

Riser.

Another desperate reach for a pole. My fingers graze the cold metal.

I kick off another skeleton, half in and half out of the wall, and pieces of it scatter around me. My hand lands on a pole. I snatch it up and swing it, again and again, crushing the skeletons' hands, arms, and what I couldn't see in the dark, bodies and skulls. Some of them escape into the walls.

A green glow illuminates the ceiling.

"Ana!" Marek's voice cuts through the hissing. Marek runs through the spirits, and they scatter.

The hissing stops.

It's quiet. The spirits are gone. I catch my breath and swallow.

I can't move. But I'm not panicking. It's numbness.

Marek stops at the bottom step.

"What the hell is that?"

The skeleton parts slide away, retreating for the crumbled parts of the walls.

I don't know if Marek's face is green from the marble stand he carries or from getting sick at the sight of my attackers and the color leaving his face.

"They-they attacked me." I push myself up and stumble to my feet. Everything hurts. Scratches on my arm and ankle throb. My back and hip scream with pain. I feel like throwing up, and I'm shaking as if I've just come out of an industrial freezer.

Marek puts down the glowing stand.

"Are you okay?" he asks, his voice trembling.

"I'm fine. L-let's just go before…before they come back." I move aside to make room for him and glance up at the manhole. "It's locked. We need the finger bone to get out."

He takes the bone out of the metal box, inserts it into the manhole, and it opens. The air rushing in, brushing across my face is crisp and fresh, and I breathe deep, filling my lungs with it.

"You go first," he says, lifting his pant leg and stuffing the silver canister into his sock.

I'm not arguing with him on that. I can't get out fast enough. At least it's stairs this time and not a ladder.

It's still daytime, and it takes my eyes a few minutes to adjust after going from dark to light. We're not in the same alley where we entered the catacomb. At both exits, each about a half block away, there's pedestrians and traffic rushing by.

Marek comes out and wraps his arms around me. "What the hell just happened in there? Are you okay?"

My body slackens, and I can barely hold myself up. Burying my face into his chest, I sob. He lets me get it out until I can speak between shaky breaths. "There were people." Breathe. "Dead." Breathe. "From record book." Breathe. "Isabella's. They attacked me. Called me Riser."

"Hun-*ney*," a familiar voice interrupts us. "Why would you go down there?"

Marek and I look over at Sid at once.

Sid strolls over as if he has all the time in the world. "Down there is no place for her. That's for the likes of him." He pushes my hair away from my shoulder, examines the markings on my neck, and *tsk*s. "Girl. The damned sure do hate you."

"Why?" I swallow hard. Marek's arms around me are warm

and strong, and I'm less shaky.

Voices from the end of the alley carry over to us and fade when two women pass.

"I saw Isabella's torture book in your hotel." He flicks his gaze right, then left. "That girl was one sick puppy, I tell you that. When I first met her, I was intrigued. Then it just got boring. She didn't raise those people once. She did it many times. I hear that shit hurts. It's torture."

"How did they get down there?" I ask.

"One of his people"—he nods at Marek—"found the bodies. Buried them in this catacomb to hide what Isabella did. This is where all terminated Risen end up. Down there. Their bodies no longer look normal. They're feral-like, honey, and it's not pretty. So burying them where they might be discovered wasn't an option, and burning them is against some religious belief."

Marek and I startle at the sound of a car horn going off somewhere on the street at the end of the alley. It doesn't even faze Sid.

"But I'm not her," I say. "Why did they attack me? I didn't do that to them."

He brushes some dirt off my shoulder. "Why do haters hate? They're mad at the world. It's misplaced anger, honey. Those poltergeists despise Risers for what Isabella did. And that's what you are, Ana. A Riser."

I don't even flinch when he calls me that. The ghosts hissed it so many times in my head, I believe it. Not sure what it means to be one. What powers go with it. But if it tortures people and makes them evil, I would never raise anyone from the dead.

"I know what you're thinking," Sid continues. "That you'll never bring someone back from the dead. Isabella thought that, too. Think about it, would you bring your father back if you could? Someone you love." His eyes shift to Marek then back to me. "Isabella was a newlywed when her husband fell off a horse and broke his neck. She couldn't live without him. Brought him back. Watched him slowly turn evil. Her experiments were a search to cure him."

"I won't ever bring anyone back." I twist out of Marek's arms. "Not ever."

Sid just smiles. "Sometimes it happens without thinking. Like with Shona and Cain."

"Shona?" His mentioning her reminded me that he went to investigate her whereabouts. "Did you find her?"

"She's alive and well," he says. "Hiding out in a safe place. We'll join her soon."

I should be relieved to hear that, but the pain in my body consumes my thoughts.

"Why would Janus send us down there?" Marek asks. "If he knew those things would attack her."

"As long as she was with you, they wouldn't," Sid says. "He didn't think you'd separate."

I step toward him. "How do you know that? And how did you know where to find us?"

"Janus rang me," he says. "You see, we all went to Oxford together. Living forever, gods and goddesses can get bored. I used to attend colleges here and there. Janus, too." He removes an old photograph from his pocket and hands it to me. "That's me and Janus with Eli's father, Richard. Your grandfather, Ana. On the right, at the end, is Adam."

I pass it to Marek.

"Who's the woman?" he asks.

"Oyá," Sid says, a wide smile spreading across his lips. "Smart, beautiful, and tough. They all had a crush on her. I would have, too, if I weren't infatuated with Richard. Ah, unrequited love. It's the best kind. The pain is a reminder you're alive."

"How did you all just so happen to come together?" I'm

skeptical. "I'm assuming my grandfather was a Riser and Marek's grandfather was a…what do they call them?"

"Keepers," Sid answers. "Since they are custodians of the Divinities Keep."

"Okay, so you have them and a bunch of gods that just so happen to go to this prestigious school together? Not a coincidence."

Sid waits for an English-speaking family to pass before saying, "Lugh, he's another member of our group. Brought us together because of a dream. He saw your families come together for the big war between gods. We wanted to protect them. So Oxford offered them scholarships for different things when they never applied. That was my handiwork. But we all know how that story ended. We had the wrong family members."

This little revelation that there are gods that want to protect us has me feeling a bit better.

"You think it's us," Marek says.

It's a statement, not a question, but Sid nods anyway, glancing at the exits to the alley.

"Now that our little history lesson is over and you seem less freaked out," he says. "We need to get you sewer rats cleaned up. We're near Trevi Fountain. There're shops. Fresh clothes are a must."

Sid leads us down the alley and onto the street. A few passersby glance at how filthy Marek and I are. Ducking into the first clothing store, I instantly want to run out. It's fancy, and all eyes are on us.

"Not to worry," Sid says. "This is one of the kinder shops."

The woman that helps us is surprisingly nice for how dirty our clothes are. She even lets us clean up in her bathroom in the back. I don't wear lying well. Honestly, I'm surprised the woman believes me with all my stuttering while explaining how we got so dirty. "That's never happened before," was her response when I told her that one of the walls in the catacombs open to tourists collapsed.

So it wasn't a total lie. We were in a catacomb.

I buy the black skinny jeans and sweater Sid insists I get and pass on the torture boots. His nose wrinkles slightly when I slip my Vans back on. The woman raises her perfectly shaped brows at me when I ask to toss my shirt and jeggings in her trash.

It feels good to be in new clothes. What I really want is a shower, but that will have to wait. I'm starving, and by the way Marek's stomach growls as we exit the shop, he is, too.

Sid takes us to a pizzeria near the Trevi Fountain, and we sit at a table outside. We eat salads and share a margherita pizza. The street has less traffic than the ones closer to the famous landmark.

When he finishes, Sid stands. "I have an errand to do. Stay in this area. Visit the fountain. And by all means, don't get into trouble."

"Sure, we'll be good little tourists." I press a wide grin.

After Sid disappears around the corner of a building, Marek removes the silver canister from his pocket. "Guess we should see what's in this. I'll watch my way, and you watch yours. Let me know if you see anyone suspicious."

"You think we should do it right here? In the open?" It's a narrow street. The buildings are tall and close together.

"You know what they say…hidden in plain sight."

Holding the canister against his chest, he pops off the lid, pinches the rolled up paper inside, and removes it. He stares at it for a few seconds before passing it to me. The parchment is thick, a cream color, but I'm not sure if it's naturally that way or if it's aged. I read it.

Elena Kristoffer Prevot

I look up from the slip of paper. "Do you know her?"

He shakes his head. "Never heard of her."

The server comes over and picks up the bottle with still water on our table. He bends closer as he fills our glasses. "Finish your meal," he says with an Italian accent. "Then go east. There are eyes west." He thumps the bottle down and rushes off for the kitchen.

I want to turn around, but I keep my eyes on Marek. "Do you see anyone?"

"No," he says, picking up his glass and taking a sip of water. "We'll do as he says. Finish up and act as if we don't know someone's watching us."

I lean over the table and whisper, "How do we know we can trust the server?"

The look on Marek's face tells me he hadn't thought of that. I slide my eyes in the direction of the kitchen.

After paying, we stroll in the opposite direction from the one the server warned us against going. A woman down the way catches my attention. A little too beautiful to be normal and a bit too interested in a teen couple walking down a narrow street.

Approaching an alley, I catch Marek's hand and guide him in its direction, whispering, "I think we have another friend waiting for us down there."

"Who?"

"A woman. Beautiful. Dark hair. Dark skin. At the end of the street."

Once inside the alley, we sprint to the end. Gushing water sounds somewhere close by and grows more intense when we turn a corner onto another narrow road. Many of the streets in Rome are tight, squeezed on all sides by tall buildings in different shades of yellow, beige, and orange.

Falling water reaches a crescendo when we enter a square with a large crowd surrounding a fountain. I'm a little bummed at the moment. I've always wanted to come here, but not under these circumstances.

Marek checks the GPS. "We're at the Trevi Fountain. I'll try to find a hotel nearby."

An enormous structure with a palace as its backdrop, the fountain is made out of some sort of white stone. It's not marble, though the statues are. I forget what my teacher had said the material was in class, some kind of limestone, I think.

A massive sculpture of a man in a chariot, pulled out of the sea by horses, dominates the center. Some think it's Neptune, but it isn't. He's Oceanus. On either side of him are two women figures shielded under arches—Abundance and Health.

"Which way do we go?" I ask.

He lifts his gaze from the GPS and searches the *piazza*. "It's that way." He motions across the square with his head.

The crowd is dense, filled with strangers and unknown dangers. We move into the throng of tourists.

A man aiming his phone at the fountain backs into me, and I stumble against Marek. His hands go to my waist, steadying me so I won't fall, his eyes holding mine, and I forget where we are. I forget about the woman who may be following us. And I forget to breathe.

His hands drop away from my waist, and the spell is broken. I take a deep breath and twist around to find a break in the crowd. Maneuvering around bodies, dodging tourists too busy gawking at the fountain to pay attention to where they're going, I've barely gone six feet.

I pivot, making sure Marek is still behind me. He gives me a half smile that seems to indicate he wonders if there's anything wrong. Before I resume cutting a path through the jungle of people, the crowd on the far side of the fountain shifts. A chorus of screams drowns out the thunderous clap of the water falling into the basin.

Like a wave, the crowd moves, picking up speed, people

running for the many streets that connect to the square. Marek's and my hands instinctively come together. We turn around, hand in hand, and sprint for the road we just left.

Mixed in with the screams are growls, crashing sounds, and car alarms all bouncing off the tall buildings encompassing the square—echoing—magnifying.

Marek abruptly stops, causing me to bump into him. He stretches an arm out in front of me as if he's going to protect me from something. I push by him to see what it is. The woman from the alley towers over us, her leather jacket flapping in the wind, her dark eyes determined.

"Not this way." Her voice is accented, commanding, the look on her face fierce. "Or you'll run into men who wish to harm you."

Backing up, Marek pulls me to his side. "Who are you?"

"My name is Oyá." She steals a quick look at each of us. "It will not be long before you are found. Come with me, if you wish to survive."

Now that I look at her, she is the woman in the photo with Marek and our grandfathers. Her hair was longer then, and she was smiling, but it's the same woman.

Marek tugs on my arm, urging me to go the opposite way as the woman.

"She was in the photograh Sid showed us," I say, pulling back.

Oyá waves her hands in a circular motion, and two swords appear. "I could kill you now, should I desire it."

A woman with a little girl clinging to her side screams at the sight of Oyá's blades swooshing through the air.

Marek leans back and whispers, "Yeah, I say we trust her."

I'm hypnotized by the light glinting against the steel. I nod. "Yes. Okay."

"Good." The swords in Oyá's hands disappear. "I shall make a distraction. You must run into the fountain. I will follow."

"What?" I glance back. I'm frozen, unable to move, not able to speak, holding my breath deep in my lungs. Men leap over the viewing tiers surrounding the fountain. People run from them with fear-stricken faces, ear-piercing screams. "Who are those men?"

"There isn't time," Oyá snaps. "I will tell you all when we are in a safe place. You must go now."

People run past us, bumping our shoulders and pushing us against each other.

I look from Oyá to Marek. His eyes are just as questioning as mine.

"Those men are that way," I yell. "We have to follow the others."

Oyá grips my arm, and I turn my stare at her. "Go the way I told you."

"Ana, we need to trust her." Marek's eyes search my face. "We don't separate."

"All right," I say, and Oyá releases my arm.

We dart off toward the farthest side of the fountain from where the scary men are. I grab a look over my shoulder. Oyá's hands are raised. The wind swirls and grows on her palms. With my attention on her, I almost trip at the first set of steps. I pound down them with Marek, and we reach the bottom.

One of the scary, rioting men blocks our path to the fountain. His face is twisted like a feral animal; a beast with inhuman eyes—primal. He snarls. Claw-like fingers swipe at Marek. He hops back, the nails barely missing him. Another swing misses and lands on the side of the fountain, breaking it and sending pieces flying.

A powerful whirlwind brushes past me and lifts the beast-man up, carrying him away. I turn to see Oyá riding a hurricane. Her arms extended, one inside the tunnel, the other outside, her feet spread apart, knees bent into a squat, it's like she's riding a wave.

Marek climbs over the basin of the fountain and plops into the water. "Ana, come on!" He reaches a hand out to me. I can hardly hear him over the chaos going on around us, and the howling of the wind.

There are injured people on the ground, bleeding from gashes, some unmoving. I can't pull my eyes away.

No! Stop! I scream in my head. *Please.*

The humanlike beasts—men and women—a range of ages—pause, heads tilting from side to side, blood dripping from their hands and mouths. All their heads slowly turn in my direction.

They don't make a sound. The only noise comes from people somewhere in the distance—crying, screaming, feet pounding—and the clapping of water against water in the fountain.

Almost silence.

CHAPTER TWENTY-FIVE

"Analiese!" Marek breaks through my trance. I clutch his hand, scrambling over the edge and into the freezing water.

Chaos rings out over the plaza, again. Screams echo against the buildings.

"Now what?" I search for Oyá.

Her hurricane knocks many of the beasts over, and it spins toward us. When it hits the fountain, water sprays up. A door opens under Oceanus and his chariot. I wade through the fountain beside Marek to the door, and we spill into a small chamber. Lifting up on my hands and knees, I'm a fish out of water, gulping for air. Marek rolls on his back, panting.

Oyá rushes in, and the door slams shut. Dim blue light comes on. It's cold, and I'm dripping wet, shivering, my teeth clattering together.

Marek pushes himself up from the floor.

I'm breathing better now, so I stand.

"We must get somewhere warm," Oyá says, and a panel in the floor opens as she approaches it.

I wrap my arms around myself to try to get warm. My legs are numb as I follow her down a long, narrow corridor. Marek's wet shoes squish behind me.

"Those things…their faces were scary. Like animals." My breath stutters over the words.

"They were Risen," she says.

"We've seen a Risen before," Marek answers. "He didn't look anything like that guy out there."

Oyá hesitates before she responds, "He must have been a newly Risen. The longer a Risen lives in their second life, the more evil and stronger they become." She looks at me as she says her next bit. "They are controlled by the one who raised them from death. At first they have free will, but it is lost the more they develop into a beast, only doing what their Death Riser tells them to do. That is why the people weren't killed by them. Just the ones who got in their way were injured. They were after you. I tried to determine who the Death Riser was, but there were dummy ones to throw me off. Killing the Death Riser terminates all of their Risen as well."

Cain would've changed. I can't imagine a meaner Cain, and even though he was a complete ass, I feel horrible for him. Shona did say he was once a kind person.

"Can a Risen be changed?" I ask. "You know, go back to the way they were when they were alive?"

"They are alive," she looks back at me. "You mean back to how they were in their first life? Maybe. There is a tale about the favorite child of a god of death being able to restore life to how it once was. To make it right. But only if the person died before it was their time. Though it is only a rumor."

How do rumors get started? Because there is a grain of truth in them. It doesn't matter. I'm almost sure Cain is dead for good now.

We walk for what feels like two city blocks before going up a set of stairs.

Oyá brings us out of a half door in the back of a shoestring hallway. The walls are a soft yellow with white molding. Smells of lemon and fried food waft in the air. She leads us up a polished marble staircase that winds around and around until we reach the fourth floor. It's an apartment building.

She unlocks the door and holds it open for us to enter. The apartment is pretty standard for a warrior woman.

"My home is yours. Please, you are to make yourselves comfortable." She secures the four locks on the door and heads for a back room. "Just a moment."

Marek and I stand there by the door, our wet clothes dripping on the floor.

I shiver. "How are we supposed to get comfortable? I'm freezing. And we're too wet to sit on the furniture."

"We can ask for some towels when she returns." Marek steps behind me and repeatedly rubs his hands up and down my arms. "Better?"

His light caress is comforting. I'm not sure which goose bumps are from being cold and which are from his touch. I don't even notice when my head leans back and rests on his shoulder. My eyes stay open. I'm afraid of the images I'll see if I close them.

Oyá returns, carrying thick towels and what look like robes. "Here, dry off and put these on. We shall talk after you've finished. Bring me your wet clothes to dry."

In her tiny bathroom, I peel off my wet clothes and slip on the terry cloth robe. I inspect my injuries. The bruises on the sides of my neck are purple now. The scratches on my arms, stomach, and back have stopped bleeding. I retrieve my pillbox from the pocket in my jacket, remove a pill, and pop it into my mouth. Cupping my hands, I catch water from the faucet and drink down the tablet.

I remove the rest of the things from my pockets and place them on the counter and gather up my wet clothes. When I come out, Oyá takes the soaking bundle, her eyes briefly going to my neck. She nods and heads to the back rooms.

The smell of something floral and spicy fills the apartment. I ease down the hallway the opposite direction as her, steadying myself with my hand on the wall.

Marek is on the sofa, already back from the bedroom and wearing a blue robe, a blanket draped over his lap. He sips something steaming from a big pink mug. I sit down beside him, and he covers my legs with the plush material.

He turns to face me and places a gentle hand on my shoulder as he inspects my neck. "I'm sorry that happened—" A rush of emotions choke off his words and his eyes gloss, his hand slipping away from me.

"I'm fine." I stare at a colorful abstract painting of a tiger on the wall, trying not to cry.

Oyá strolls out from the kitchen and places another pink mug in front of me. "Tea. Drink. It will warm you."

"Thank you." I pick up the mug and take a sip. There are so many questions in my head, I'm not sure which one to ask first, so I just throw out the first one that comes to mind. "Are you a goddess?"

"In your words that is what I am," she says. "My people call us orishas."

Marek places his mug on the coffee table. "How do you have magic? I thought it was taken away from all gods and goddesses."

She lowers the mug from her mouth. "It was. Ages ago. Our power was put into a talisman."

Marek stares off at something across the room.

I can't tell what he's looking at, maybe nothing, maybe everything. I stop trying to guess.

"Right," I interject. "And that talisman was broken into six pieces. Hidden away."

"Your ears have heard the story?"

"Yeah," I say. "But you—you made those swords appear and rode a hurricane. Last I checked, that's magic. And we've seen another god with power."

She puts down her mug and leans back against the cushions. "The rumor is that someone has recovered two pieces of the Divinities Keep. They're called Parzalis. As each piece is put together, the gods and goddesses whose powers are held within those parts receive some of their powers back. When it is whole again, our magic will be returned to all of us."

"So your power was in those two pieces? Those *Parzalises.*"

"That is correct," Oyá says.

Marek snaps out of his trance on whatever it was across the room. "How did whoever it was recover them? Why didn't the keepers of those pieces prevent it?"

"All the gods have been searching for Keepers since the birth of the talisman. A god we haven't been able to identify has gotten lucky as of late." She gives Marek a quick glance before continuing, "When they find one, the god kills the Keeper, then follows the progeny on their quest to moving their piece of the talisman and steals it. And, usually, another murder follows."

"Why even move the Parzalis if it's safely hidden?" My frustration is evident in the tone of my voice.

The pain throughout my body is subsiding.

Oyá just smiles and shakes her head as if I didn't give my comment much thought. "When one passes from this world to the next, we take our memories with us. Adam carried the location of where he hid your family's Parzalis with him. There are creatures in the between place who steal these memories and bring them back to the god or goddess they are loyal to. You mortals believe that from death to what you call Heaven happens in a blink of an eye. But in reality, it takes many night skies for the spirit to arrive in the next life."

Oyá pauses, picks up her mug, and takes a long sip. She

places the cup back on the table, her eyes landing on Marek. "That is why you must move what your family has promised to protect. For its location is compromised. It is my assumption that you have not but a fortnight before a creature makes it to this realm with its whereabouts."

"Fortnight?" Marek asks.

"It is about two of your weeks," she says.

Marek and I don't say anything, and the silence stretches on for longer than what's comfortable. I'm not exactly sure what to think. It's like glimpsing in the rearview mirror, watching my perceived reality growing smaller. It doesn't seem possible that we've only been in Rome for a few days. It feels like a lifetime.

I remember what both Sid and Ares mentioned, and I decide I need clarity. "I was told that there's a war between gods going on. What are they fighting over?"

She puckers her lips before answering. "Wars are usually fueled by different beliefs. One side wants to return to the days when gods and goddesses were worshipped. The other is fighting to leave things as they are. Then there are those who haven't decided one way or the other."

Brows pushing together, Marek leans forward. "What god or goddess wouldn't want power?"

"There is always an imbalance where power is concerned," she says. "Less powerful immortals would be dominated by more powerful ones like in the days of old."

"That makes sense," I say, downing the rest of the tea and placing the mug on the table. I feel good. I rub my arm, noticing the deep tears in my skin have healed and are only red marks now.

What did she put in that tea?

"Why did you leave your homeland?" Marek asks.

"Gods and goddesses," she says, "or divinities, if you will, sense the magic pulsing over Rome. It draws us to it."

An extended sigh releases from me. "What's this energy everyone keeps talking about?"

Her eyes hold mine for a quick pause. "No one knows. All I know is it's coming from you two. I sensed it. That's how I found you today. In ancient text, this seducing energy is the sign that the war between gods is here. More immortals will arrive in Rome before the week is out."

"It's an immortal convention." Marek snickers, resting his hand on mine. It's his way to remind me I'm not alone.

I don't find the amusement in his statement. I'm too worried. My brain is too cluttered with information and questions.

I gather up the nerve to ask, "Which side did you choose?"

"Neither choice will affect my people. They have remained faithful to us, and we will not treat them any differently should our powers be fully restored. But when it comes down to it, I will join the side with the morals that match my own."

Oyá tosses her throw blanket aside and stands. "Your clothes should be dry shortly. Then you must go. It is best to keep to yourselves. Do not travel with others, especially those with powers." She stares down at Marek. "Finish your task. Hide your Parzalis."

When I was younger and didn't know how to swim, I would hold on to the edge of the pool, going hand over hand around it, watching Dalton and our friends play Marco Polo. I'd taken lessons, but still, I was scared to venture out into the middle. Dad tricked me. Brought me out to the deep end and said before letting go, "You'll either sink or swim, kiddo. Which is it going to be?"

That's precisely what Oyá is doing. Dropping us in the middle of the vast city of Rome and seeing if we'll sink or swim.

CHAPTER TWENTY-SIX

The sun over Rome is almost entirely gone, a blue hue blankets the buildings, and the lights are golden blossoms in the distance. I stand on a balcony of a quaint hotel, waiting for Marek to return. A cool breeze rolls over my skin. The bruises all over my body have almost vanished, only a hint of them remain. Oyá healed me.

It's our fourth night in Rome. Before crossing over the Tiber into the Trastevere neighborhood, Marek and I stopped in a library so I could use the public computer to send a message to Dalton through his Snapchat, letting him know I was okay. We also Googled Elena Kristoffer Prevot and found nothing. The decoder was useless. It just gave us a bunch of numbers and translated the name into Phoenician.

The door handle jiggles. I step back behind the wall next to the balcony door, a part of me saying it's only Marek, the other part scared it's someone else. Someone dangerous.

"It's me," Marek calls from inside the room. He's unloading items from a shopping bag and placing them on one of the beds when I come in from the balcony. "Take a seat. Thought we'd have a picnic. I got meats and cheeses. Some fresh bread. And..." He pauses, reaching inside the bag. "This." He pulls out a classic glass bottle of Coca-Cola.

I overexaggerate my excitement and sit on the bed and ask, "Do you have a bottle opener?"

"Shit. I didn't think of that." He places his finger on his chin. When he goes for his belt, I raise my eyebrows.

He removes it from his waist and uses the buckle as a bottle opener, then hands me the cola.

"I've been thinking about what you said." I take a swig from the bottle, the sweet fizzy drink reminding me of home, making me miss Dalton. "About your grandfather's games. Which ones did you play?"

He tears a piece from the loaf of bread. "Well, you know about decoding messages and espionage tactics. We did mazes, puzzles, chess, and solving things like riddles and anagrams. He was really into fitness."

The smell of *soppressata*, a sort of salami, teases my nose, and my stomach grumbles. He slaps a few slices on the bread and tops it with a piece of Asiago cheese. He offers me the tower of yumminess, and I gladly take it.

"What kind of puzzles?" I open my mouth wide and take a bite.

He fixes himself an open-faced sandwich. "Crosswords, Picross, logic, and math puzzles."

I swallow and take a swig from my bottle. "Did you ever hear your grandfather mention an Elena? Maybe she was a family friend?"

"Not that I know of." He goes to take another bite and stops. "Oh wait. Anagrams. He always used names. First, middle, and last. And I would tease him that they were all old women's names. Probably all his ex-girlfriends."

I put my sandwich down on a napkin and grab a pad of paper and pen from the nightstand drawer. "Okay, let's try it."

Marek retrieves the slip of paper with the name on it from the silver canister and rereads it.

Elena Kristoffer Prevot

I stare at it. "So how do we do this?"

"We make words from letters in the name. Then put them together until it's a sentence that makes sense."

"Got it." I study the names so hard my eyes start to water. "There's 'off' or 'offer.'"

"No. That's too easy. Those letters line up in the name. My grandfather would scramble them. Those words are to throw off someone other than me trying to solve it."

Just in case, I write them down on the paper anyway and spot more words. "'Top,' and there's 'life,' 'stone,' 'star,' 'plate—'"

He laughs. "You're doing it wrong. Once you use a letter, you can't use it again. 'Life' is good. My grandfather was attached to sayings about life. Here, let's separate the consonants from the vowels."

I scribble the letters down.

AEEEEIOO FFKLNPRRRSTTV

"Oh, yeah, that's *so* much better." I'm not even hiding my sarcasm.

"Well, we have 'life' so let's take that out."

AEEEOO FKNPRRRSTTV

"My grandfather would include 'sport,' too. Used it all the time. He did that so I'd be able to solve this. If he made it too hard, this would take forever. Remove the letters."

I rewrite the remaining letters.

AEEEO FKNRRTV

I'm getting annoyed that I haven't come up with any words. Squinting at the letters for so long is causing my vision to blur.

"How about 'take'?" I ask.

"Okay, remove it and let's see what we have."

EEO FNRRV

Marek stretches his arms over his head. "I need a break." He goes to the bathroom, and I continue shuffling letters around until I have "for" and "never."

I straighten and bounce a little on the bed. "Marek! I got it," I call.

life sport take never for

The door opens, and he hurries over. He leans over my shoulder, some sort of chemical still scenting his skin. Probably something used to keep the Trevi Fountain waters clear.

"Right here." He points out two of the words. "Flip them. It'll make more sense."

"Okay." I rewrite the words.

life sport never take for

And I write:

Never take life for sport

"You got it." There's excitement in his voice. He pats my shoulder, and his hand lingers there.

"What do you think it means?" I ask, trying to ignore the fact that all my attention is zoned in on where his hand is and it's making my pulse flutter.

"I don't know."

I hop off the bed and spin to face him. "Of course. We're

in Rome. *Life for sport.* It's the Colosseum."

His face lights up. "You're right."

"We can go tomorrow."

"Sounds like a great plan to me," he says.

After we pack the food back into the bags and clean up, I take a shower. The courtesy robe is like a plush hug. I crawl in the bed closest to the balcony and listen to the shower run in the bathroom. Marek's growing on me.

When this is over, and we're back in our ordinary lives, will Marek and I stay in touch? More importantly, can we go back to being normal teens and possibly even go on a date? Who knows.

The door opens, steam rushes into the room, and he comes out wearing the other robe, hair wet. He pads to the bed across from me with a confident walk that I've noticed before but not really appreciated until now.

Yeah, I would date him.

Alone in the room with him, enjoying an Italian picnic, drinking Coca-Cola, and solving an anagram, I almost forgot all the stuff going on outside this hotel room. I flip onto my back and stare at the ceiling.

The room grows dark when an outside light somewhere turns off. I can't sleep. Not with everything that's happened the last few days. Not with Marek sleeping in the bed next to mine. And definitely not with the skeletons from the catacomb and the beasts at the fountain haunting my dreams.

I sit up and turn on the lamp on the nightstand. Marek sleeps with the pillow over his head, so I know the light won't bug him. I grab one of the magazines from inside the drawer and flip through it. The articles are in Italian, filled with the hotel amenities and things to do around Rome.

It sucks that Marek had us dump our phones. I'm bored out of mind without it. Want to torture a teen? Throw away their phone. I could be checking my social media right now.

Or catching up on the YouTube channels I follow. I angrily turn a page.

"Perfect." I land on a page with a photo of the Trevi Fountain.

Pinching the glossy paper, I toss it over. The Colosseum dominates both pages. If I were here in Rome as a tourist, it would be on the top of my list to visit. I drop the magazine on the nightstand, turn off the light, and resume staring at the ceiling.

I roll over to my side, and my eyes blink — close, open, close, open, close.

B irdsongs float into the room, sun teases my eyelids, and the smell of coffee fills my nose. I smile but still can't open my eyes. Marek must've woken early and gotten us coffee. He's always so considerate.

I sit up and stretch my arms over my head.

"Your boy shouldn't be leaving the balcony unlocked while you be in here alone."

A man's voice with an Irish accent startles me. I scramble back, hitting the headboard hard. The man is tall with dark auburn hair and a beard. He's so tall he barely fits in the small chair across from the bed.

The man laughs. "You be as scared as a mouse with a kitten on its tail, that you are."

"Who are you?"

"Settle down." He takes a sip from a to-go coffee cup, his green eyes sparkling with amusement. "I brought you a coffee."

I don't move. My eyes search wildly around, trying to find an escape or a weapon.

CHAPTER TWENTY-SEVEN

"P erhaps," the man says, "I should have changed into something less threatening before visiting." He begins to morph. His hair slowly grays and thins until it's bald on top. The taut skin covering his muscles moves until it's sagging and wrinkled. Ears and nose grow longer. He shrinks, his clothes now a bit too big for him. The green eyes that were just sparkling a few moments before are now dull with age under bushy gray brows.

"H-how did you do that?"

"I be one of the lucky gods. Me powers are restoring." He places his coffee cup down on the tiny circular table. "I come because of a promise made to a woman I admired."

"Answer me. Who are you?" I try to make my voice sound commanding, but the shaky words give my fear away.

"My name is Lugh," he says, picks up the other coffee cup, and carries it over to me. "Here. You slept poorly last night."

I'm in a daze and not sure why I take the cup from him, but I do, and it's almost too hot to hold. "You were watching me?"

He vigorously rubs his nose, his droopy lids almost hiding his eyes. "You make me sound perverted. I've merely been trailing you since your arrival in Rome. I was across the way. Could see you through the window."

"Trailing me? What for?"

As he lifts the cup to take another sip, his hand shakes, not because he's nervous, but because he's now as old as sin and seems to be aging to the grave by the minute.

He swallows. "You've been watched all your life."

Now I'm angry, which makes me anxious. I throw a bunch of thoughts I can't hold back at him. "Are you going to kill me? Because if you are, you should just do it already. Stop toying with me. And will you please stop aging. It's creepy and freaking me out."

A laugh bubbles up from his chest, and he coughs around it. "Me heart can't take such excitement. You don't seem to understand. If any of the gods wanted you dead, and I be one, you'd be pushing up daisies already."

I'm not sure what to feel. Scared? I'm not. Sad? I'm not. Anxious? Not anymore.

He adjusts in the chair, wincing in pain. Fingers bent with arthritis, he grips the armrests. His bones under paper-thin skin look fragile and could easily break at any moment.

Curious? That's what it is. I want to know what he knows.

"I'm okay," I say. "You can change back before you die."

Watching him grow young is just as fascinating as it was when he aged. His fingers slowly straighten, hair changes to auburn and more of it sprouts on his head, filling in the baldness, wrinkles smooth out. His back straightens. He grows taller and fills out his clothes.

"Much better," he says and slurps coffee from his cup. "Me name is Lugh, as I said. I knew your mother well. She was a great woman. Beautiful. Just like her daughter." He removes a photograph from his pocket and passes it to me. "That's at her wedding to your father. She made me best man. I knew your uncle, too. Most of your family were dear friends to me. Great people, none better. Your grandmother was a firebrand."

"And my grandfather."

"Richard? Ah yes. Great man, that one."

The picture is of my birth parents in a garden. They must've had a non-religious ceremony because my parents were raised in different faiths. My mother's dress is pale yellow and conservative, something you might wear to a tea party. He wears a blue suit, and his matching tie is messy. To their right is a woman with tight curls, then Lugh.

The digital screen of the alarm clock on the nightstand shows it's almost nine in the morning. I have no idea what time Marek left the room or when he will return. Since my biological parents died when I was a baby, I only know what Dad told me about them. He left out the part that they were friends with gods and goddesses.

"How did you meet my parents?" I ask.

He leans forward in the chair, his knees almost pushing up to his chest. "At university. Just as I did your grandfather. Since I never age, I enjoy attending colleges and making friends. I've been sticking to your family ever since I met Angelique in the Italian countryside." He scratches the back of his neck. "Let me see. That had to be somewheres near 1820."

I stare blankly at him. I've never heard of the woman before.

Noticing my reaction or lack of it, he clarifies, "She be a relative of yours. One of your grandmothers with all the greats in front of it."

"I see." Never heard of her, but it looks like he has more to say, so I don't ask any questions about my quadruple, or something, great grandmother.

"It's a lonely life being a god without power. Immortal. Never to age. It raises eyebrows if you stay in a place too long."

"I guess that would suck." I actually feel bad for him.

"Especially when you fall in love with a mortal." He glances at nothing, from what I can tell. "It can't last long. She ages while you stay young. There be about ten good years, before the questions. It starts with comments about how well you age. That's when I know it's time to go. To save me loves from searching for answers, I fake me death. It helps them move on, so it does."

There's sadness in his voice that weighs on his words. I know that misery well. I've never met my birth parents, but I long for all the what-could-have-been moments—school plays, holidays, and family vacations. Instead, I had those times with my uncle's family. I'm not complaining, though. I was lucky to get a fantastic dad and a brother who only annoys me part of the time. Jane and I tolerate each other at best. Without her, I wouldn't have a roof over my head, and all that stuff parents provide.

And that is why, while I'm looking at my mother's smiling face, that feeling of what-if comes rushing back.

"What was she like?" I mutter, forgetting about my other questions, forgetting that this man is a stranger and I have no idea what he wants.

Lugh's eyes are glossing like mine. "Have you ever seen sunshine dancing on water?"

"Yes." I give him back the photo.

He stares at it. "She was like that but a thousand times brighter." A sigh lifts his chest, and he shakes off the spell the image has on him.

A few tears escape my eyelashes and drop onto my cheeks. I swipe them away and sniff.

"Ahem." He clears his throat as if he's trying to hide his emotions. The chair is so snug around him that it almost comes up with him when he stands. He extends a flash drive to me. "A message from your mother."

It's then that I realize I'm still pushed against the headboard. I scoot forward and hold out my hand. He drops the flash drive, and it lands on my palm.

"As long as I breathe, you won't be alone." He opens the door and hangs inside the frame. "It's a promise I made to your mother and one I'm making to you. My phone number is on the drive."

I'm not sure what to say, but I don't have to come up with anything because he leaves, the door closing behind him with a soft click.

I fixate on the flash drive in my hand, playing with the sliding button, watching the metal USB plug extend and retract. A message from my mother? I've only seen photographs of her. My dad said all videos of her were lost. Was this a recording of her?

My stomach is all in electrical knots. Excitement sparks from within me and zaps across my skin, over my skull, and down to my toes. I'm about to see my mom in real movement, maybe even hear her voice for the first time.

I decide to distract myself and get dressed. That way I'll be ready when Marek gets back, and we can leave right away. The public library isn't too far from here. We can view it there.

The library isn't busy. The flash drive is in the port, but I can't bring myself to click and open it.

Marek's been on guard since finding out about Lugh getting into our hotel room. Doesn't matter that the god didn't do anything harmful. But Marek's too busy looking for someone that resembles a god to see Lugh. He's in his old man state, and I've already spotted him twice. Once on the street and now sitting at one of the tables with a stack of books. Come to think of it, I may have seen him over the years before he broke into my room this morning.

"We might have to use your grandfather's rules for ditching a tail again." I move the cursor over the navigation pane, drag the mouse down to the drive, and click. There's a frozen image of my mother on the screen.

"Why? Is he here?" Marek casually rotates, scanning the room.

"Old man at the table over there." I nod my head in Lugh's direction. "With the books stacked as high as the Leaning Tower of Pisa."

Marek rests his butt against the edge of the table. "That's him?"

"He can make himself young and old at will. He's a Celtic god. Known as a trickster and other things—smith, craftsman, and warrior." Acting as if I'm getting something out of my jacket draped over the back of the chair, I do a sneak-look over my arm at Lugh.

"You're stalling," Marek says when I straighten. He holds out a set of old headphones.

I snatch them from him. "No, I'm not." I totally am, nervous about what my mother had to say. It's like having a ghost visit from the grave. "All right, I'm ready."

The headphones wobble every time I move. So irritating. I try to keep as still as a pole in concrete. My mother's young, maybe in her mid to late twenties, and she resembles me. Same brown hair and hazel eyes. Same body build, more on the curvy side. Same dusting of freckles over an upturned nose. She wears her hair away from her face. Doesn't care about showing her widow's peak. I hide mine under side-swept bangs. It makes her face look like a heart. It's almost as if I'm staring into a mirror. I click on the play arrow.

"Now," a man's voice says somewhere offscreen. It could be my father. I use the mouse and drag the play bar back to hear him again. "Now." Deep and confident for such a small word.

My mother smiles. She's sitting at a table inside a small kitchen. "Hello, um…I'm sorry. Can we start over?" She has no accent. Her family immigrated to America from Italy in the early 1900s.

"Of course," the man says. He does have an accent, just like Safta and Saba, his parents. "I'll edit it out." He obviously never did.

Taking a deep breath, she continues, "Hello, my dear Ana'le … um …Analiese. I'm your mother, Alea." A nervous laugh escapes her lips. "But you probably know that. So, if you're viewing this recording, then Mommy and Daddy are gone. We wanted so much to be with you, our little butterfly."

"It wasn't a butterfly, it was a moth," the man offscreen says.

A moth? Could it have been a death's-head hawkmoth?

My mother frowns at him. "I don't care. It didn't look like a moth to me. Now you'll have to edit that out, too."

"I know. I know. Continue."

"Okay, where was I?" She lowers her head and then looks up. "It doesn't matter. Analiese, know that we love you deeply." She chokes on a sob and pauses to regain her composure.

Her glassy eyes stare back into the camera. "Sorry. This is hard. Saying goodbye to you is tearing our hearts out. Our baby. You're so tiny. Uncle Eli will take wonderful care of you. What I'm about to tell you shouldn't be too shocking. We've instructed Lugh to only deliver this recording once you've learned of the hidden secrets within our world. I hope that you never have to see this. That you live a happy life without the knowledge of what you are."

She picks up a glass of water, takes a long sip, and puts it down. "You are a descendant of the death god, Soranus. Which means you are a Death Riser. Just like me, just like Daddy and Uncle Eli and our ancestors. You can raise the dead.

"Those brought back to life can also be controlled by

you. The Risen, that's what they're called, will do whatever you command. At first, the Risen seem normal, but they will turn into beasts. Beasts that can tear gods to pieces. Powerful and without a conscience. You must not bring anyone back from death. Gods will want to use your power as a weapon in their war. No matter what a god may offer you, don't give in. Don't be that weapon for them. For all humankind will become their slaves again."

Tears run down her cheeks. "Daddy was adopted, so Safta and Saba don't know any of this. You mustn't tell them. It is why we're sending you to live with Uncle Eli."

She looks over the camera at who I think is my father. "Did I miss anything?"

"I think that's it." A chair scrapes across the floor somewhere in the kitchen. A man comes into view dragging it. He places it beside my mother and sits down. Lanky, sporting dark hair with unruly curls, he holds my mother's hand. "Ana'le, it's Daddy. I want you to always remember that I love you with all my soul. There isn't the proper word to express how deep that love is."

My mother places her free hand on her heart. "I love you, butterfly."

He says something in Hebrew like what Safta and Saba use, but I don't understand him.

She frowns again. "Jake, she might not know Hebrew. She'll be raised in America. Eli isn't Jewish."

"You're right." He grabs the back of his neck. That's when I notice that both my parents look tired. "It means," he says, "love is like the wind, you can't see it, but you can feel it." He grabs my mother's hand. "Feel our love, Ana'le. We are always with you—"

The recording freezes, my mother's lips pressed together and my father's mouth wide open as if he was going to say more. I remove the headphones and place them on the table.

"What did they say?" Marek asks.

He puts the headphones on and listens to the recording. When it ends, he looks at me with concern. As if I'll fall apart. I've never seen my birth parents in motion—living and breathing. At the same time my heart is swelling to capacity, it's also losing air at my mother's puncturing reveal.

Marek's hand covers mine, bringing my attention to him. "I'm here. You're okay."

I'm okay.

My skin is sensitive to Marek's touch—every slight tremor registers high on my internal Richter scale.

I take a measured breath, filling my lungs and releasing it slowly through my nose. There's a poster of a woman reading to a boy. It's in Italian, so I don't know what it says. Most likely something promoting literacy. The hum of a water fountain breaks the shell of silence over the library.

I'm okay.

The anxiety bubbling up my chest recedes. I am okay. Today is a spectacular day. Today I've seen my birth parents alive within a recorded time capsule. But their sadness crushes me. Their final hours of life marred by the idea they'd have to give me away. And I want answers.

I charge over to Lugh. Marek's footsteps behind me are muffled against the carpet. Lugh's old hunched shoulders straighten just a hair. He's fragile in this state, and I'm glad for it. Because if he were in all his god glory, I wouldn't be as brave as I am right now. I sit in the seat across from him. Marek drops on one beside me.

"Why did my parents send me away?"

He gives me a questioning look and scratches inside his ear. "You know, the old sure do grow a lot of ear and nose hair. I wonder why that is."

"No, you don't," I snap. "No distractions. Just answer my question."

"All right," he says. "Don't give me the evil eye like that. I'll tell you. Your mother was discovered. It was only a matter of time before they killed her. She sent me off with you. I brought you to your uncle."

"Why? Who killed her?" The chair is solid, but I'm sinking. I place my hands on the tabletop to steady them.

"You see," he says. "Death Risers went into hiding when the first piece of the Divinities Keep be found centuries ago. Some keepers of the talisman decided that getting rid of all Death Risers would prevent gods from using them as weapons. They formed a group, Lares, the name for ancestral spirits, deities that guard each family. The Lares believe they be protecting mortals by eliminating the Death Risers."

Marek shifts in his seat. He probably has the same question that I have. I stay quiet and let him ask it. "Was my grandfather a Lares?"

Lugh's face is growing younger, his shoulders expanding. "If he were a Lares, Analiese would be dead already. He protected her. Eli knew your grandfather well. They'd even meet in the park while you played in that jean jacket with the unicorn and stars patches."

"How do you know that?" I sound croaky, so I clear my throat. "About the jean jacket."

"I be there a few times." He's back to his younger self.

I glance over both shoulders to make sure no one saw his change. The tables are empty.

Lugh smiles. "I take care changing. Make sure no eyes be around to see. Now then, the two of you were devising a plan to ditch me. Best get on with it. I'm in the mood for games today."

"We weren't—"

Marek cuts me off. "You're worried I'll side with the Lares. That's why you're following us."

"You're not as careless as I thought." Lugh looks from

him to the librarian passing by. She's an attractive woman, short hair, average height, a little weight in all the right places. Something behind the woman catches his eyes. He's rapidly aging. "Your wish is about to come true. You're going to lose me. Go out the emergency door. It's behind me. Don't look back. Just go."

The librarian stumbles, noticing Lugh's change.

"What is it?" I ask, but Marek is up, tugging at my arm, urging me to go.

"Don't ask questions," he says. "We have to go."

I take a few steps, turn around, and whisper, "The Colosseum."

Lugh nods, and I can see the side of his mouth lift.

Marek and I weave around the tables to the emergency exit. The alarm goes off when he pushes the door open. A chorus of screams belt out, and the crashing of furniture follows, and I catch a last glimpse of the library before the emergency exit shuts.

I see them. I see him. And I just stare at the closed door. Two beasts. The Risen that can tear a god apart. They could rip Lugh to pieces. With the Risen was a man commanding them. A man I'd seen before in the photographs around Shona's apartment. Her father.

Our missing number twenty-six.

Joel Jackson.

CHAPTER TWENTY-EIGHT

Shona's father is a Riser, and he's on whichever side is after us. Maybe I made a mistake. It could be someone who resembles her father.

It doesn't matter. Nothing does. I just want to go home.

I want to know if Lugh is okay.

Traffic speeds by on the narrow roads as if there isn't a level of difficulty in braking and swerving around parked cars. My fingers tingle. I'm floating, the numbness making me feel weightless. I'm in another world. My brain is foggy.

As my mind clears while I hurry along the sidewalk with Marek, the images of that frog and that doorman coming back to life keep flashing in my thoughts.

I did that. Brought them both back.

Riser. Riser. Riser. The ghosts of Isabella's tortured victims knew what I am.

Death Riser. Just like my parents.

I stop and glance back. Lugh is my only connection to them. To parents I never knew. He saved me. Took me to Dad when I was a baby. What am I doing? Those beasts can rip immortals to pieces. Could kill him.

"Hey," Marek calls. "Why are you stopping?"

The wind flips my hair into my face when I snap my head in his direction. "We can't leave. They'll kill him."

"What can we do?" Marek is practically stomping over to me. "He's a god, and we're not. We're mortals. He can take care of himself. Besides, he told us to run."

He holds his hand out to me. "Come on."

Another glance in the direction of the library. I can barely see the roof from where we stand. "How did we get so far?"

"We've been walking a while." His hand slips into mine, and he gives it a light squeeze. "Remember, he's a trickster god. He was changing into an old man when we left. He'll be all right."

"I hope so." I let him lead me down the narrow sidewalk, if you could call it that. It's a slight ledge at best.

"Look, there's a bus," he says with saccharine optimism.

We take off, my Vans hitting the cobblestone street hard, hurting the soles of my feet. Marek bounds up the steps. "*Scusate*," he apologizes to the round Italian man behind the wheel. He doesn't move, making sure I get in before the door shuts.

"*Grazie*," I say, my eyes locking with the driver's. It's like someone hit him with a stun gun.

He smiles. "American?"

I don't answer him.

"Is okay," the man says. "Bus comes every twenty-two minutes."

After paying the fare, we find two vacant seats, but they're not together. I sit across the aisle from a Chinese man in a wheelchair with shocking white hair and beard. He's braiding thin red strings into a bracelet, a canvas knapsack on his lap. Marek gets the only other seat on the bus, toward the back. I smile at the man, then look out the window.

"Having a good time in Rome?" the man asks. His voice is smooth, a sound that if you listen to it too long, it could lull you to sleep.

I pull my stare away from the window and put it on him. "Yes, it's such a beautiful city."

"It's a city for young lovers." He smiles, his gaze forward, and I realize he's looking at Marek.

"Oh, we're not…" I'm staring at Marek. He runs his hand through his wavy hair. His face is weighed down with the strain of the morning. Not focusing on one thing, he's searching for any threats. Making sure no person or thing is following us. There are shadows under his eyes. He must be as tired as I am.

I want to rub his shoulders, give him some relief. He keeps looking better and better to me. We've come so far. If we make it out of this alive, I don't think I could let him go. With every kind thing he does, he takes a little bit of my heart.

"It is a great city for young lovers," I say instead of finishing the other sentence I'd started. "What are you making?"

"Reminders," he says, tying a knot at the end of one of the braided strings. "An invisible red thread connects those who are destined to meet. Do you believe in fate?"

"I'm not sure."

His smile reaches to his eyes, deepening the wrinkles around them. "Those destined to meet will, regardless of time, place, or circumstances. Just as you and he. It was meant to be. Do you see the red thread between you?"

I try to keep all emotion off my face, not wanting it to show that I think the old man is a little bit out of touch with reality. But who am I to say. I lost my grasp on reality a few days ago. My gaze travels down the aisle of the bus to Marek.

"I don't see anything."

"Have faith," he says. "Look again."

Having faith isn't my strongest trait. There was a time

when I was happy. A time when Dad was around and our family was whole. All my scars are hidden, but they're still there marring my heart. Losing parents will do that to a person. Faith is something for happy people. Not for someone jaded like me.

The bus slows, preparing to stop.

"Even the most broken of people have faith," the man says as if he heard my thoughts. "If a man without the use of his legs can have it, so can you. Look again, Analiese."

I'm starting to get used to people knowing my name. "Who are you?"

"My name is Yuè Lǎo."

The Chinese god of marriage and love.

"It's nice to meet you," I say.

A smile so warm it heats my face spreads across his lips. "The proof is right there."

I look at where he's pointing. There's a red line, so faint that if you didn't know to search for it, you wouldn't see it. The thread is wrapped around my wrist and stretches out to Marek's.

I shift in my seat to face the man, and he's gone. His wheelchair is almost down the ramp exiting the bus. A man in his twenties rushes over to aid him.

"I am not in need of assistance." Yuè Lǎo smiles. "Just because I'm in this chair doesn't mean I'm helpless." He comes off the ramp without help.

I lower my head and smile. A peace settles inside me that I know is the god's doing. My hand brushes against something on my lap. It's a red thread bracelet.

"I have faith in you, Analiese," his voice whispers in the air to me.

I glance out the window, and he's pushing his chair down the cobblestones. Pinching my fingers together, I slip the red thread bracelet over my hand and around my wrist. It reminds me of something my cousin wore when I visited my family in Israel a few years back. Many cultures have their versions of the tradition.

The red thread going from me to Marek isn't visible anymore, but something is breathing new life into me.

The line into the Colosseum moves at a relatively fast pace around the spiral structure. The grand facade commands the sky, a noble ruin with the whispers of thousands of untold stories. Of people put to death for merely living in the wrong place or having the wrong belief. Of the roars and whimpers of animals silenced for sport. It's a monument to a brutal past.

I rise on the tips of my toes, trying to see over everyone's heads. *Where is he?*

The towering columns remind me of how small we are. How short our time is on this earth. The creators of this place, the spectators who cheered in the stands, this is their legacy. This is what they chose to leave behind for generations to remember them by.

Maybe he didn't make it out of the library. I try not to think about what those beasts could do to Lugh. And trying not to think about it makes me think about it.

"He's not coming," Marek says. "It's been over an hour. He'd be here already."

He's probably right, which crushes me. I haven't known Lugh that long, but he was my parents' friend. They trusted him. He helped them.

"I hope he's okay."

"Stop worrying," Marek says. "You said yourself he's a trickster. He probably just didn't want to lead them to us."

"Yeah, maybe."

The line moves through the gate, and we enter the arena.

I might not like what the Colosseum represents, but the architecture astonishes me. We follow the other tourists along the designated pathway through the ruins. I pause, imagining the arena filled with over fifty-thousand spectators. A losing gladiator waits for his fate, the crowd pointing their thumbs down, his opponent ending the gladiator's life with a blade across the throat. It almost feels real to me.

I shake the thought away. "So, any ideas of what your grandfather would've left here for you?"

"I've been here before," he says. "When I was twelve. My brother was eight. This is the same walkway. My brother and I kept running around, pretend-fighting, and our mom kept scolding us. Gramps would tell her to leave us alone. That we were burning off energy."

"Fitting for this place." I pause and peek through one of the window-like arches at the many other ruins surrounding the Colosseum. It's a fading memory of a time when people worshipped gods and goddesses.

I spot a woman with dark hair the length and style of Inanna's nearby the Arch of Constantine.

CHAPTER TWENTY-NINE

I hurry to the next window to get a better view, but the woman disappears behind one of the arches. It's hard to tell from this height if it was Inanna or not.

Marek shuffles up to my side. "That's a long way down."

The woman walks across the next window, holding the hand of a little girl who resembles her. It's not Inanna.

"Any idea where your grandfather would hide the clue?"

"Nope." He backs away from the arch. "Maybe if we walk around, something will come to me."

A few hours pass and still nothing jogs Marek's memory. Every sign and marking we pass, we look for clues. Something to decipher. But there aren't any.

I'm about to tell him we should give up when he suddenly halts in the middle of the walkway.

"The Forum," he says. "We were bored out of our minds. My grandfather played a game with us once we went to the Roman Forum. A treasure hunt for coins. It had to be secret. If we were caught, we'd get kicked out, and that would've pissed off my mom."

"Okay. So let's go there." Even though it's a chilly day in April, the bright sun beating down on me heats my skin. It's hot. I'm thirsty and hungry.

The Forum is a vast graveyard of crumbled buildings with some columns and arches remaining intact. A pathway for tourists snakes through the ruins. Marek stops every few feet, examines the area, sighs, and moves on. It continues like this until we come to a large complex beside the Forum. We learn it's the House of the Vestal Virgins and where priestesses lived.

"This is it." Marek's pace quickens, his head turning right and left, searching the grounds. In the middle is a grassy yard with a square pond. Marble statues of women, many missing their heads, line one side of the path.

I follow close behind a tour group, curious about the place. The woman speaks in an accent thickened by her excitement, explaining every tiny detail. Six virgins lived at the temple, keeping the sacred fire lit. If the flame went out, whoever was on watch would be beaten. One priestess was buried alive after being accused of losing her purity. When the tour guide notices me, I pretend to study one of the statues.

Marek is staring at one of the statues with a missing head. I double back to him.

"Whatcha doing?"

"This," he says. "Tell me when the coast is clear."

"Why? What's 'this' mean?"

He checks up and down the pathway, then whispers, "I got upset. My brother kept finding his hidden treasures and had more coins than I did. My treasures were more difficult to find. It was right in this spot. I yelled at Gramps. Said I quit."

"He was harder on you 'cause you were older?"

"Yeah, I think so." He glances over at me. "This is the spot. Where I wanted to give up. Gramps told me it's when people are closest to reaching their goals that they give up. It's why so many fail. Then he walked off. Joined the rest of the family.

He just left me there."

I try to picture a twelve-year-old Marek standing in the exact spot we're in now. "What did you do?"

"I kicked some dirt around. Tried to hide the fact I was crying." He chuckles. "I must trust you enough to tell you that."

I laugh. "I'll take it to my grave."

He moves the soil around with the toe of his shoe. "So I was kicking around in the dirt, and I see it." A smile tips his mouth, and he motions to the wall with his head. "One of the bricks, behind that bush, is missing mortar."

From where I'm standing, I spot him, but he hasn't noticed us. "We need to go. *Now*. Horus found us."

Marek doesn't care who's around now. He darts around the statue and searches behind the bush. He's struggling with something. Horus is about to turn the corner and will see us.

"Hurry," I urge, my heart racing as fast as a hummingbird's wings. "What are you doing?"

"It won't come out. I need a tool or something. A knife or screwdriver."

I roll my eyes. He knows we don't have that stuff with us. My stomach is bouncing—rise, fall, rise, fall—and my hands are shaking. We need to get out of here, and fast. I frantically search the ground. A stick. No. Doesn't look strong enough. Rock? No. Too thick. A rusty nail. Yes! I hurry to his side and hand it to him.

People walk by, but they don't say anything to us. Horus is at the end of the row, about to come on this one.

"We have to hide," I urge.

Marek abandons his work on the brick, and we hide behind the statue.

I can't believe I'm going to say this, but I do anyway. "I'm going to lead him away. You get whatever is hidden behind that brick. We'll meet…" I'm not sure where the safest place would be.

"Meet me at the Mercure Hotel," he says. "When you leave, you'll see a cluster of hotels. It's a few buildings down. Only place I know around here. It's where we stayed with my grandfather."

"Okay." He catches my hand before I go out from behind the statue, and I glance at him.

He's worried. "Be careful. If they—"

"I will." Before I can freak myself out of doing it, I nonchalantly move around the statue, pretending to study it, folding my arms and tapping a finger against my lips.

Horus comes around the corner. He doesn't see me at first, but when he does, I act as though I don't notice him. I stroll down the path and catch up with the tour group. Not daring to look back, I can feel him behind me. The tiny hairs on the back of my neck prickle. When the tour group leads me around another corner, I lower my head and peek through the hair draping my face. Horus goes right by Marek. He's following me, and my stomach flips.

How am I going to get rid of him?

As soon as I'm out of Horus's sight, I sprint-walk for the almost two or so city blocks of the Forum. Wherever Horus is, usually Inanna and Bjorn aren't too far behind him. Every movement in my periphery makes me jump a little. I pass the Arch of Constantine and end up on a busy road that runs in front of the Colosseum. I'm not sure if the hotel is right or left.

I spin around to see what is nearby. Maybe some sort of landmark or hotel signs. To my right, the way everyone is going, where the gelato and food trucks and buses are lined up, is Inanna. Her back is turned. I take off in the other direction up the sidewalk. There's a slight incline, and it kills my legs.

Bjorn towers over the tourists he's trying to mix in with, but I spot him from my position down the sidewalk. I cross the street. His head snaps in my direction. He sees me, too. The road I'm on has restaurants and bars on one side, and a fenced-off area with ruins on the other, which doesn't give me any cover.

When I reach the top, I go right, then I take a left. I need to hide, but the cut-through I'm on only runs along the back of buildings. My heart thumps hard, in sync with my pounding feet. Turn after turn, and I'm getting lost. Not that I know where I'm going in the first place. I'm on a road with a parking lot on one side that ends at a broader street.

Traffic zips back and forth. I wait with an older couple for an opportunity to cross. My heart leaps into my throat. With their backs to me, Inanna, Horus, and Bjorn head down the street in the opposite direction. Just one of them has to turn around, and this cat-and-mouse chase is over.

I shadow the couple to the other side of the road, keeping them between the gods and me. The building in front of me is ancient. It's made of brown brick and has a large arched door with a tiled mosaic of a saint and a cross above it.

The couple goes into the next door over. I keep going through an arched tunnel that leads to a thin road between two high walls. The stucco is marred and showing the brick underneath it. Dark water stains drape the tops. I come to a square. Cobblestones cover the ground and cars are parked against the buildings. Potted palms line one side.

The wind stirs dried leaves around my feet.

Analiese, it seems to whisper, and I pause, whirling around on my heel. I'm alone. There's no one there.

I pass under several more arches. Tiny cars line the road, and it ends at an expansive three-level staircase that leads up to a commanding Roman-style church.

The soles of my feet burn. My legs are about to fall off, so I sit down on the steps. I'm definitely lost. I place my elbows on my knees and rest my chin in my hands. No phone, maybe thirty euros to my name.

"I'm so screwed," I mumble to myself.

A cool breeze ruffles my hair and pushes a discarded Styrofoam cup across the ground in front of me.

Analiese. That doesn't sound like the wind. It's a voice. A woman's? I shoot to my feet and walk in a small circle, searching everything that comes into view as I go—the steps, trees, the parked cars, more trees on the other side, and back to where I started.

Analiese. It's in my head. The voice. And it's not my internal thoughts. It's too feminine and soft to be.

I feel a presence behind me. It's just the whispering in my head freaking me out. I stay forward, not sure if I want to see if something's really there. No one's there. Only my shadow stretches out before me.

A pungent smell wafts past me. It's sort of a cross between the mothballs in Safta's attic and sulfur. The crunching of gravel under heavy feet causes me to choke on my breath. A hulking shadow joins mine on the steps of the chapel.

I spin around.

Pazuzu's menancing glare could turn me to ash. My skin's suddenly hot, like that time when my fever was so high Dad had to rush me to the emergency room. I back up on trembling legs.

"Wh-what…" I can't find the words. He looks like an ordinary man in some ways. A little unkempt, but dressed nice. Except for those eyes.

Eyes dark and rimmed red.

I back away and trip on the step. He snatches my arm before I land, his tight grip cutting off the circulation. It hardly takes him any effort to drag me over to him.

"Let me go," I say, finding my words, but they're weak and not threatening at all.

He stares down at me. "Where is it?"

I can't speak. There's movement in his irises. People. Thousands. Millions. Bodies writhing in a sea of molten tar.

Faces contorted in pain. Eyes pleading for help.

"You have it," he says in the deepest voice I've ever heard. "I sense it on you."

Tears run hot down my face. I can't pull my eyes away from his. Away from the people drowning in dispair.

He could easily crush my head in his hands. I'm pretty sure he will.

I don't want to die.

CHAPTER THIRTY

I mages of Dalton, Safta, Saba, and even Jane flash through my mind. But the one I hold on to is Marek, and it gives me a little strength. I'll beg for my life.

"*Please*, don't hurt me." My voice is barely audible.

Distraction.

Keep him distracted.

"Wh-what? What do you want?"

"The Divinity's Soul," he says, his voice hissing like an echoing serpent. He holds his free hand a couple of inches away from my face, guides it down as if it's a metal detector, and stops at my front pocket.

He tries to remove my dad's lighter, but the pocket is small and my jeggings are tight.

"Give it to me," he demands, and it's a sharp, loud *crack* like when thunder goes off directly over the house. And it shakes me. Stuns me.

My eyes go to his again, and I can barely see through the tears burning mine. But I know they're there. The people in pain. I blink, clearing my vision briefly, and I realize all the faces are his. Thousands. Millions. All him.

He releases me suddenly. "Bastet," he growls and runs off.

I drop onto the step, shaking, watching him disappear over a brick wall. Burying my face into my lap, I hug my knees and sob. There're people in the chapel. I should get up and run inside for help, but I can't move. Or think.

I take a deep breath.

And another.

What chased him off?

I'm lost. I don't know where Pazuzu went or if he's hiding somewhere waiting for me to leave.

I need a phone. With trembling fingers, I wipe away my tears. There are people in the chapel. They can help me. Someone has to have a phone. But Marek doesn't.

A black cat comes out of a nearby bush and slinks up to me, arching its silky back and rubbing up against my leg.

I reach down and rub behind her ears. "Are you lost, too?"

There's a collar hanging from her neck. It's gold with light blue stones. I pick up the tag and read it.

"Bastet? As in the Egyptian goddess?" I run my fingers down her back.

Pazuzu said her name before he ran off.

"Did you chase him off?"

She purrs under my touch. *Analiese.*

"You did."

I'm here with you. You're safe. I won't leave you.

"Why are you helping me?"

Richard.

"My grandfather—I mean, Eli's father?"

Not many mortals I can tolerate. I loved him.

I raise an eyebrow.

Was not as you think. He was my pet.

"Wait. I've seen you in photographs with him." I run a more steady hand down her back again. Her fur is plush.

"You have to be old."

I am immortal. You are better. We must go.

"No." I shake my head "He's out there waiting."

You are safe with me.

I raise an eyebrow. I'm not sure if I believe her.

I chased him away, didn't I?

"Well then, I guess I should get directions to that hotel." I stand and wipe some dust off of my black pants.

Before I can go up the steps to find someone to ask, Bastet practically trips me, snaking her body between my legs.

"Hey," I say, edging her away with my foot. "You're going to make me fall." I pound up the steps, and Bastet jumps in front of me. "What is it?"

She dashes down the steps and turns to face me.

"You want me to follow you?"

She darts a few feet away from me and sits as if waiting for me to chase after her.

"Why don't you just say so." I sigh and drop my shoulders, crossing the gravel drive to her.

We almost backtrack the way I came, except we go through smaller roads and alleys. When I left the Colosseum earlier and went up that thin road, I was close to the hotel, but I took one wrong turn and missed it.

Two palm trees flank the Mercure Hotel's awning-covered entry. Its modern architecture looks out of place with the ancient Colosseum as its backdrop.

Bastet doesn't stop; she darts away. *I will be nearby. Pazuzu will not come while I am here. Whenever you want to hide from an immortal, get near copper. It will block the energy coming off you.* She disappears before I can say thank you.

Copper?

That explains why Pazuzu didn't find us when we were hiding behind that wall with those copper vines. Probably why no immortals find us when we're in hotels. The pipes. Except for Ares, but he could've spotted us on a street or some place else and followed us to our hotel.

Marek meets me before I enter the hotel lobby. He pulls me into a hug. "I was worried when you weren't here. And I thought—" He swallows hard and releases me. "You're shaking. What happened?"

"I was chased by Horus and Inanna, and Bjorn joined them. I ditched them, and Pazuzu caught me at a chapel."

"That man with the locusts?" The pitch in his voice sounds a little higher than normal.

"Yes, him. Bastet chased him off." I tug my dad's lighter out from my pants pocket. "He wanted this. Said I have something called the Divinity's Soul."

He covers the lighter with his hand and glances around the lobby. "Let's go up to our room."

The room is small with one double bed pushed up against a wall. I don't even care if we share. I'm so tired I could sleep on a hard floor.

I stretch out on the bed and lean against the headboard, turning the lighter around in my hands. "I don't get it. There's no writing on this. It's nothing special." I flip up the cap and dig my nail into the seam, trying to pop the top off, and it doesn't budge. "It's stuck. I need a knife or something."

Marek searches the drawers. "There's nothing here that'd work."

My thumb spins the spark wheel.

"*Ana, come on. You don't always have to follow the trail.*" I can almost hear Dad's voice when I refused to go off the path during a hike once.

"Of course."

"What?"

I smile and spin the wheel the other way, and the body of the lighter pops open. Inside is a gold medallion with a death's-head hawkmoth on top of an intricately woven wreath.

"When did those moths start appearing? Before or after you got that?"

"After," I say, flipping it in my hand, examining the front then the back.

"It looks just like the one on the catacomb wall."

"Yeah, I wonder what it is."

"Does it come with instructions?"

I inspect the lighter. "No. Nothing."

Marek sits on the edge of the bed and takes out the silver circular canister he retrieved in the catacomb. "Well, guess we should see what's in this." He removes a rolled note from inside.

"What is it?" I slip the medallion back into the lighter and close it.

"A note from my gramps." He unrolls it.

I notice the letterhead on the stationary. It's from Caesars Palace. "Your grandfather was in Las Vegas." I tap the gold lettering at the top of the paper.

"All the time. My grandma loves it there. Let's see what it says." He reads it out loud.

Danny,

Last time we met, you were young. Quiet as you were. Wise as an owl. Keen on doing your own thing. Happy to be alone. Fearful of the future. Lonely on a bench. When I left, you cried. Boy as you were. Rightly so. I shouldn't have gone. Only if I knew. Lost time is never returned. Joking didn't help ease the pain. Kindness always wins. We are the same, you and me. Very much so. Kindness always wins. Happy once before. Very much so. Pondering the past. Lonely as I was. On that bench. Happy no more. Very much alone.

Adam

"What does that mean?" I ask. "Do you know a Danny?"

Marek tries to straighten the note on his thigh. "Danny is code. This letter is a clue. We used to drive Grams nuts with them. She never knew why we'd write things that didn't make sense."

"So how do you decode it?" My stomach growls.

He smirks. "Let's eat and then we'll work on it."

We eat stuffed Italian bread and fruit that Marek grabbed at a market on his way to the hotel. After finishing, we wash up. I wrap my hair in a towel and join Marek back on the bed.

Sitting beside each other, backs resting on pillows pushed up against the headboard, we put our heads together as we study the letter. The hotel pad of paper balances on my knees, and I'm ready to write. The pencil is one of those short ones. Like the type they'd give us to keep score at our bowling tournaments before they came out of the Stone Age and got computerized.

"Ready?" I gaze at him.

He rolls his head against the wall to look at me. Our faces are so close, I can feel his breath on mine. So close, I can feel the heat coming from his body. Close enough that one movement from either of us and our noses will touch.

I suddenly forget how to swallow.

His deep brown eyes search mine. "I never noticed you have a widow's peak. It makes your face look like a heart."

Um, thank you? I'm not sure what to say to that, so I just stare into those eyes of his, so captivating I lose the ability to function normally. A wet strand of hair must've escaped from the towel wrapped around my head, because he brushes it away from my forehead, making me shudder. There's a thin red thread linking us together, and I know only I can see it.

I shudder again.

"You cold?" His voice is raspy. Like you get from overuse or first thing in the morning after waking up.

I love everything about Marek's face. I should look away, but I can't. I'm caught in a spell, and I'm hopeless to break it.

So he does. He returns his attention to the letter on his thigh. "Let's see. My gramps's cryptic notes would change every time. The letter for the clue is always in the same position in each word. I'll call out the first ones, and you write them down."

"Okay. I'm ready." I hope he doesn't hear the shaky tone in my voice.

He rattles off the letters, and I write them down.

LQWKHFLWBRIOLJKWVVKHVPLOHV

"Doesn't spell anything," I say.

We try the next letter position in all the words of the note and it isn't coherent, either. We continue through all of them, and none of them spells out anything. We even look at them backward.

Staring at the paper, he lifts it closer to his face, and I notice indentations at the bottom right corner.

"What's that?" I touch it.

He studies the spot. "They're marks. Like you get when you put two sheets of paper together and write hard on the top sheet. Whatever is written on the top one transfers to the bottom one. Let me see the pencil."

I hand it to him, and he shades the lead over the indented letters, exposing the word *decipher.*

"He had to cipher it," I state the obvious. "Probably another ROT13 code."

I move through each line of letters I wrote on the pad. It takes time, but when I'm done, nothing's coherent. I throw myself back against the pillows and sigh. It's a little dramatic, and I don't even care. It's a release to emphasize my frustration.

"This is *so* annoying." I cross my ankles.

Marek stares at the note as if it's going to suddenly reveal all the answers. "What are we missing?"

"Exactly what will happen if we solve this clue?" I shift onto my side, pointing my frown at Marek. "Is there going to be another one, then another, and another? Will this ever end?"

He moves to his side, too, and he's not frowning. His lips are curled up, and his eyes are dancing all over my face.

I wrinkle my eyebrows at him. "What?"

"You're cute when you're agitated."

"Agitated? Really? Who uses that word?" Wait. He just said I was cute. Is that in a good way or in a way that you'd think about your best friend's kid sister?

"My grams," he says. "She uses it on me all the time. And I've figured it out."

Figured what out? That I'm kind of, maybe, sort of, possibly falling for you? "Well, are you going to tell me or what?"

He holds up the stationery. "It's in plain sight."

I'm not seeing it. Just the note and the elegant writing.

"You don't see it," he repeats what I'm thinking.

I shake my head. "Nope."

He finally gives in and points to the letterhead. "Ceasars Palace."

"It's a Caesar Cipher. So is ROT13." It surprises me that he doesn't know that.

"Yeah, I know," he says. "Look at the address."

I read the address. The first number in *3570 S Las Vegas Blvd.* is circled. "We use a shift of three."

I sit up, and Marek joins me.

We decode the first line containing the first letter of the

first word in each sentence of the note.

So this *lqwkhflwbrioljkwvvkhvplohv* becomes this *inthecityoflightsshesmiles*.

I bounce a little, and the mattress shakes. "We have it."

"That was a tough one." He pulls his fingers through his hair. His eyes are droopy, and he yawns.

I put brackets between the words, then write it out so we can read it better.

In the City of Lights, she smiles.

"Paris," I say. "Though I have to say, I believe he has it wrong. It's the City of Light. But he'd think you would know the one Americans use."

"Or maybe he just needed an S for the code."

"Yeah, that could be it. Anyway, the second half of the sentence must mean the *Mona Lisa*. Why spend all this time in Rome, then send us to France? Why not just give one clue and be done?"

"He's drawing all the gods and goddesses here." He swings his legs over the side of the bed. "The things my gramps taught me. Nobody else could know his thought process. The clues in Rome are to throw off anyone following me. To keep them away from the real location of the Parzalis."

"So, we need to sneak to Paris," I say. "Without being followed."

"Looks like it."

I skim over Mr. Conte's note again and a thought hits me. "I think your grandfather knew he was going to die that day. He was looking for me. Giving me his bag to put you and me together. He wanted us to team up on this search. That's why he and Eli were meeting. They were training us."

He leans over his knees and sighs. "They thought it was them, but it was us. The ones to end the immortal's war."

As if it's the most natural thing to do, he holds my hand, and we just stare at the wall for a long while until he faces me.

"We're going to be okay," he says, and he means it.

I gaze into those hypnotizing eyes, and I almost believe him.

I'm stuck between Marek and the wall, so I scoot down the bed and stand. Removing the towel from my head, I avoid eye contact with him. I don't want to get snared in those brown eyes again. Not with my emotions all over the place as they are.

There isn't time for infatuations or whatever I'm feeling. We have to figure this out. I do need to get home eventually. Dalton probably has read my direct message by now. Hopefully, it was before he panicked after not hearing from me and told Jane I was missing. It would be inconvenient to have the Italian police searching for us, too.

Dalton. I'm not sure why the thought hadn't hit me before, but it does right now, and I drop the towel.

Dalton!

CHAPTER THIRTY-ONE

In one quick movement, Marek is swiftly off the bed, worry pinching his eyebrows. "What's wrong?"

"If Eli was a Death Riser, Dalton could be, too. He could be in danger." I flip around and face him. "I have to warn him."

I don't realize I'm shaking until Marek places his hand on my cheek. "It'll be okay. We'll buy a prepaid calling card and use the phone here."

I nod against his hand. "All right."

After I quickly dress, we leave the room. The elevator is crowded and it bumps a few times when it lands on the first floor. Sitting in the lounge, beaten and tired, is Lugh. I hurry to him.

"What happened? Are you okay? Do you need water? How about—"

He holds up his hand to stop me. "I be fine. Do you have a room?"

"Yes," Marek says, reaching his hand out. "Let me help you."

Lugh takes Marek's offered hand, and they hobble to the elevator.

"How did you find us?" I step inside with them and push the button to our floor.

"Bastet brought me to you."

There are still wrinkles at the corner of his eyes. Silver streaks his sideburns. He hasn't entirely renewed after aging himself.

The elevator lifts, and I grip the railing attached to the mirrored walls. "What happened in the library? Did those beasts get you? Those Risen."

"They weren't aware it was me. Not in me old state. I was too slow in getting out of their way. They hurt many others, as well."

We return to our room, and Marek helps Lugh to the bed.

Lugh looks from Marek to me. "Only one bed?"

"It was the only room left," Marek says quickly.

I hide the heat rising in my cheeks and rush into the bathroom. The cold water spurts before smoothly running out of the faucet. I grab a face cloth and drench it, wring it out, and bring it to Lugh.

"Here, wipe the cut over your eyebrow." I extend the cloth to him.

He takes it and places it against his wound. "Thanks. You two were heading out."

"Yeah," I say, sitting on the desk chair. "We were going to call my brother. I need to check in. Make sure he hasn't told Jane...my mom where I am."

Marek leans against the dresser. "We think her cousin might be in danger."

Lugh lowers the washcloth. "Why do you think that?"

"We're related, and his father was a Death Riser." I twist the chair left and right, back and forth, back and forth, back and forth. I stop when Lugh frowns at me. "Don't you get it? He has to be a Riser like me. They'll go after him."

"Oh." Lugh returns the cloth to his brow. "He'll be safe. You needn't be worrying about that one."

Marek gives him a doubtful look. "You heard her, right? He's her cousin. Raising the dead runs in her family. There are people out there who want to kill them."

A smug look settles on Lugh's face. "I very well understand. I wanted to avoid this, but I see no other way. Eli wasn't Dalton's biological father."

I stand so quickly the chair rolls back and crashes into the desk. "What? Is that true?"

"Unfortunately, it is," Lugh says. "Eli was a great man. I knew he'd be a loving father. He couldn't have his own children, so I helped Jane and him out."

"You…and Jane?" I plop back onto the chair.

He throws his head back and laughs. "No. Not like that. I gave a donation. They didn't know I was a god. Eli and Jane just thought I be a school friend of your parents. I met them at your parents' wedding. I stayed with them a few times while I was in the States. That's why your mother thought I'd be the best one to deliver you to them."

My head feels like it's going to explode. "What does that make Dalton?"

"A god's son," he says. "And when he gets his power, someone who'll be protecting you."

"You did that…just so I'd have a protector?" I'm having a hard time threading a coherent thought together.

"Not entirely. It's just an added bonus." Lugh tosses the washcloth on the bed. "I saw an opportunity to help a friend. That is all. Dalton was loved by his father…and is by his mother. He's more than a protector for you. He's my son. As long as I'm alive, he'll be taken care of."

"You know Dalton is a great guy."

He smiles. "I know. After I brought you to Eli and Jane, I lived in Fishtown for six years. To make sure you be safe and to be with my son. Eli and Jane were quite kind to me. You two be closer than real brothers and sisters I've seen. But if it makes you feel better, I'll send Sid on a flight tonight. He'll watch over them."

"Thanks. I need some fresh air. I'm going to explore the roof." I push myself up from the chair, open the door, and let it close on Lugh's and Marek's protests behind me.

The door opens again, and Lugh's voice carries down the hall. "Get her back here. There are immortals all over the area."

Marek rushes for the elevator but doesn't make it before the doors close. I don't even try to hold them open for him. I push the button for the top floor. The elevator arrives, and I step out, pausing at the view. The sun has just gone down, leaving the sky a dark blue, and the Colosseum is lit up in gold lights. Headlights from vehicles rushing across the streets flash like stars over the dark pavement.

I walk to the edge and take in several fresh breaths. What do I do with this information? Do I tell Dalton? Or wait and let Lugh come clean? Jane might not want that to happen. I'm thinking I don't want that, either. Eli is Dalton's dad. He's mine, too. No amount of blood can change that. Can change every special moment we spent with him.

No. I won't tell Dalton.

I brush the tears now dripping from my eyelashes.

It's so unfair. Some people are dealt crappy cards in life. My parents barely had any time to live. I can't guarantee I'll have a long life, either. Even if I'm a master of death, or whatever I am. Raising the dead? Gods? It's all so absurd. These are things that happen in movies or video games, not here. Not in real life.

The air behind me adjusts, letting me know that Marek has caught up with me. "It's not safe out here."

"Do you see the heat lamps?"

"Yeah," he says.

"They're copper."

"And?"

"It keeps me off the gods' radar."

He steps closer. "And you learned this how?"

"Bastet told me. It's why Pazuzu didn't sense us when we were behind that wall."

"Well, maybe we should make armor out of the stuff."

I wrap my arms around myself. A gust whips my hair around, and I push it away from my face. "Last week I was at school taking finals before Spring Break. Now, we're here. I don't even know who I am. I'm definitely not who I thought I was."

"Come on, you're not going to let a little thing like being a Death Riser define you, are you?" He comes up to my side. "Man, this is a great view."

I press my lips together, a chuckle bubbling up my chest. "You're not funny."

"What can I say? I'm trying." He bumps my shoulder with his. "What'ja say we get back to the room. Besides, we need to plan our route to Paris. I think we should go right away."

"Yeah, okay." I give the Colosseum one last look. Nearly four hundred thousand people died over the time it was in use, a million animals slaughtered. Where were the Death Risers then? Did they do something? They could have raised an army of Risen, let them turn into beasts and kill those cruel rulers. If we have the power to bring people back, it's a shame we can't use it.

"Hey." Marek wraps his hand around mine. "Where are you? You're miles away."

I flash him a smile. "I'm right here. Let's get to Paris."

Going to Paris will bring us one step closer to finishing Adam Conte's hunt. One step closer to finding Marek's family's piece of the Divinities Keep. One step closer to going home. And several steps away from Marek.

Driving in a sardine can with an extremely tall god and a nearly six-foot Marek almost wholly eliminates leg room. Add Bastet taking up residency on my lap, and to say I'm uncomfortable is an understatement. I twist my body and rest my legs on the seat beside me. Bastet gives me a look before going back to sleep.

Ten hours.

That's about how long it'll take to get to Paris. Lugh wouldn't let us take public transportation. Not with immortals searching for me, particularly a demon god and some creepy group called the Lares. Not to mention, Bastet wouldn't have been able to come, and having her around is comforting.

When Lugh was asleep, I used the medical tape Marek got for him at a nearby pharmacy to secure my dad's lighter just above my ankle, and I covered it with my sock. Something called Divinity's Soul sounds too important to be in the hands of a teen. I'm pretty sure Dad meant for it to stay in the safe. Now I get why he kept his collection of Norman Rockwell copper plates in it. Jane was always complaining about how silly it was that he had them.

I just had to take the lighter. I sigh.

"This is not a very fun road trip," I complain. "Where's all the junk food? We need to get some when we stop for gas."

Lugh glances at me in the rearview mirror. "That food will kill you."

"I know a lot of other things that will, too." I tug on the seat belt that's threatening to strangle me.

Marek looks over the back seat, the sun setting behind us making him squint. "I'm with you. Junk food is a must." He winks, and I reward him with a bright smile.

"All right," Lugh says. "There's no need to gang up on me.

We must have an understanding."

"An understanding?" I repeat. "Over snacks? We all get what we want. That's the rule of road trips."

He shakes his head, and the stiffness in his jaw tells me it's something serious. "No. It's not that," he says, and he gives Marek a nod. "I'm not going all the way to Paris with you. I be putting you on a train at Milano Centrale."

Raindrops ping the windshield.

Marek is nodding his head as he listens. As if he isn't shocked.

I decide to do the protesting for us. "You have to go with us. What if more scary gods find us?"

Lugh turns on the wipers. "Your grandfather was a smart man, planting the clues in Rome." He gives Marek another sidelong glance. "They be looking for you there. They sense you all over Rome. They won't suspect you've left and are in Paris. Unless…" He leans forward and wipes the fog away from the window with his hand.

"Unless what?" Marek asks, sounding impatient.

Lugh settles back in his seat. "Unless I stay with you. Those Risen in the library weren't looking for you. They followed me. Probably have been for a while because of me relationship with Ana's parents. Someone suspects I'm in contact with you. They'll seek me out. It'd be too risky for you to be with me."

I slide down a little in my seat, disappointment taking the wind out of me. The thought of Lugh going with us to Paris gave me hope that Marek and I could survive this wild hunt. I'm pretty sure Bastet won't be allowed to travel with us. But Lugh isn't done hitting us with distressing news.

"The last time a Keeper died," Lugh continues, "the possibility of stealing their Parzalis during the progeny's hunt caused a frenzy. Much like we see now."

Marek scratches the side of his head. "How do they know when a Keeper dies?"

"The ancient dead whisper it to their god. Give the name."
I finally join the conversation. "Why don't they just go to Heaven or wherever and leave us alone?"

"In life, the ancient dead worshipped gods and goddesses. People in that time had a favorite one. They attached to their god in death and couldn't move on. They remain in the place between here and the afterlife, feeding on the secrets the newly departed carry with them on the way to their final resting place."

"And tell those secrets to their god," I add. "Which causes a race to get the talisman before the progeny can. We've heard some of it. Is there anything else?"

"That's it," Lugh confirms.

Marek grips the back of his seat so tight his knuckles turn white. He's nodding his head, letting it all sink in.

"You'll understand," Lugh says. "Analiese can't be continuing with you. She's in great danger. I must get her into hiding, now that she be discovered."

That makes me sit straight up and earns a protest hiss from Bastet. "I'm going with him. You can't stop me."

Marek shakes his head at me. "No. He's right. I have to go alone. If they get you, think of what your power in the wrong hands can do. Those beasts can kill tons of people."

I'm sure they're right. I should go into hiding with Lugh. I can't leave Marek alone, though. He conceals his fear well, but I feel it seeping out of him. It pulses around me, clings to my own. It's what connects us.

You must not let the boy go alone. Bastet confirms for me. *You are stronger together.*

Okay, do you have any ideas on how to do that? I pull my legs under me and press my forehead to the window, watching the scenery go from city to country.

An opportunity will show itself. Do not hesitate. Act on it.

I close my eyes and think about what she's told me, letting the rattle and hum of the ancient Alfa Romeo lull me to sleep.

CHAPTER THIRTY-TWO

*B*ang.

I jerk awake.

BangBangBangBangBang.

I'm alone, and it's pitch black outside. I can't see a thing. The Alfa Romeo rocks. My pulse quickens. Both front doors are wide open, and the overhead lamp spotlights me while everything around the car is dark.

I pop open the door and roll out onto the ground. Crawling on my hands and knees, I go around the back of the Alfa Romeo to the driver's side door, reach in, and turn on the headlights. Lugh and Marek are fighting a large man with a halo of dark curly hair. He's dressed in khaki pants and a white shirt with red stains.

Blood?

"Quit it, Bacchus!" Lugh shouts. "I thought we were friends."

"We are," the man bellows, effortlessly tossing Marek off his back. "You have your power. I want mine. We need the girl."

Bastet sits at the edge of a copse of trees. *Opportunity.* She darts into the woods, disappearing into the dark.

Lugh slams a fist into Bacchus's side. Bacchus lands in an earth-shaking thump against the ground. "I can't believe you sided with them," Lugh says, standing over Bacchus. "You have all you want. Your vineyard. Family. What do you need the power of a god for? Those times are past. Let them go."

Small dots of light move down the hill between the rows of grapevines. We're near a vineyard.

"That can't be good," I mutter and climb onto the seat. The key is still in the ignition, so I push on the gas and turn. The Alfa Romeo sputters and stops. I try it again. It stalls.

Bacchus struggles to his feet, and Marek hits him with a rake. The man turns and backhands Marek, sending him flying into the tall grasses surrounding the clearing we're parked in.

Once again I turn the key, and the Alfa Romeo coughs to life. Lugh hurries to the passenger side door, carrying Marek. He drops Marek on the seat and looks at me.

"Guess you'll be going with him after all," Lugh says. "Drive east and don't stop. Get on the train to Paris at the Milano station. Only stop for gas, nothing else. You hear me?"

"Yes, but aren't you coming?"

"Those aren't mortals coming down the hill. They're Bacchus's sons and daughters. Demigods. I'm going to stall them so you can get away." Lugh slams the door.

I grip the wheel tight. "No. Come with us. There're too many of them."

He bends over so I can see him through the window. "I'm a god of many skills. A warrior. Growing old is just a parlor trick. I'll be fine." He winks. "Now, off with you."

Tires spin when I push on the gas. The Alfa Romeo bounces over potholes in the bumpy dirt road. Marek groans in the seat beside me but doesn't wake up. Tears pool in my eyes, and I don't try to stop them. Not daring to take my hands off the steering wheel, I let them run down my face and fall off my cheeks.

He'll be okay. He's strong, I reassure myself.

The Alfa Romeo hops onto the pavement. It's a small road, and I'm not sure which way is east.

"Marek." He doesn't respond, so I shout, "Marek!"

His eyes open, and he seems dazed. "Where are we?"

"I don't know." The road has a lot of curves, so I don't take my eyes off it. "Get your GPS. We have to go east. To the station in Milan."

Wincing, he searches the glove capartment where he stuffed the GPS eariler and pulls it out.

"Where's Lugh?" He enters our destination.

"That man you were fighting. His name is Bacchus. He's the Greek god of wine and fertility. He has a lot of kids. Oh, and agriculture. I almost forgot that." I'm anxious, and when that happens, I get rambly. "Anyway, those kids were coming for us. Lugh's holding them off."

Marek frowns at the GPS screen. "You're going the wrong way. Make a U-turn."

I slow down and whip the Alfa Romeo around.

"Shit," he snaps.

I risk a glance at him. "What?" The car swerves a little, and I straighten it.

"My money belt ripped." He lifts his shirt. "It's gone." After looking around him, he searches the back seat. "Where are our jackets?"

"They're missing?"

"Yeah, must've fallen out during the attack. Shit. The money's gone. Our passports. What're we going to do?"

My pillbox.

I so want to yell right now, but it won't do us any good. *Stay Positive.* Dad's motto.

"I have money," I say. We'll have to make it work." I'm

not sure I have enough, but right now he looks a mess, and I don't want to worry him.

Shifting my eyes from the road to him then to the road again, I ask, "What happened back there?"

He flips down the visor. The tiny light attached to it barely illuminates his face as he inspects the damage. "We pulled over so Lugh could drain the dragon. That man came out of nowhere. Attacked Lugh. We fought. I went flying. Woke up here. That's all I know."

"Bacchus must've sensed us. I'll be glad when this is over."

Just as I say that, I think it may never be over for me. Not unless someone destroys all the pieces of that talisman. If the gods have no way of getting their power back, they have no reason to fight. That means they have no reason to use me.

A realization hits me. The talisman can't be destroyed. If it could be, the Keepers would have done it ages ago.

I glance at Marek again. "Do we still have the train tickets?"

Lugh bought them online using the business center at the hotel.

Marek flips the visor shut, opens the glove compartment, and retrieves the printouts. "Got them, Olivia." He usues the fake name Lugh entered for mine. It's from one of Mr. Conte's fake passports.

"How about money. Do you have any on you?"

He gives me a long stare before my question registers, then searches his pockets. Counting the coins in his hand, he says, "Three, four, um…about six euros."

"I have forty-three," I say.

"Not enough for a hotel," he says. "We could stay up all night and go to the museum in the morning."

"I've always wanted to go to Paris. See all the places my parents went to on their honeymoon." I half-laugh. "Sort of like walking in their footsteps. Reenact the photos I have of them. Never thought I'd be going like this."

I grip the wheel tight. The bumpy road has a lot of curves, and it makes me nervous.

"It's going to get cold at night," he warns.

I bite my lip, thinking. "Maybe there's a thrift shop. We can get some thick jackets on the cheap."

I make it to a better paved road that actually has directional signs. I'm heading the right way. That's the only positive thing of the night.

A t a thrift shop in Paris, we buy a distressed leather jacket for me and a black dress coat for Marek for five euros each, along with one-euro scarves. We head into the labyrinth of Paris streets. The buildings are tall, and their facades are an eclectic blend of medieval, Revolutionary period, and Haussmann-style architecture. We hike backstreets, hidden passages, and arcades.

There are plaques on the walls honoring fighters during World War II and other famous people, and we make a game out of spotting them. Street art is everywhere.

We keep moving.

Stay warm. Awake.

Alert.

"It's going to be a tough night," he says. "I'm sorry. I really screwed us. Once we get the clue in the morning, we'll go to the embassy. Get emergency passports."

"We're underage. They'll contact our parents."

I'm trying to stay awake, trying to keep warm, wrapping the yellow scarf around my neck twice. It's not at all the French way, but I'm not going for fashion.

I lag behind. Marek slows his steps.

A mischievous grin curls the corner of his full lips, making my heart take a few skips. "How many strides would it take to cross this road? I bet four."

He's trying to distract me so I won't think about the cold or my tired legs.

"It depends. Who's crossing the street?"

"I'll cross."

"Okay," I say. "Are you taking short, average, or long strides?"

"Does it matter?"

"Yes. I need all the variables to make an educated guess."

He adjusts his bargain jacket. "Okay, then, long ones."

I study him with newfound interest. His playful side is cute, and I hold back a smirk, but the amusement in my voice gives me away. "So your guess is still four?"

"Yep."

"My guess is five, then."

He backs up against the building and makes his first stride. "One," he calls.

Poor guy's going lose.

"Two."

I'm not sure it's fair. While we were talking, a couple trying to avoid people lined outside a red door crossed the street, and I measured their gaits in my head.

He reaches the other building. "Five."

When he ambles over, he exaggerates a pouting face. I meet him with a broad smile on mine. "You're good," he says.

I glance around the street. "I wonder what time it is."

He stops and reads the sign beside the red door.

"Come on," he says. "It's playing *Rio Grande* with John Wayne. Special price for those under twenty-six."

I back out of the way to let an older couple enter the theater. The sign says the movie starts at ten thirty.

Shaking my head, I start to walk away. "No. We can't

waste our money."

He steps in front of me. "We're tired. The movie is a few hours long. We can get some sleep and get warm. And it's not much. A few euros each."

"I could close my eyes for a bit."

"Great." He yanks open the door and waits for me to pass before following.

It's a small theater with red walls and cushy chairs. We grab a spot in the back, and I'm asleep before the opening credits finish.

"*Excusez-moi*," a woman's soft voice wakes me.

"What?" I glance around, dazed, not sure where I am.

"Oh, you're American." The woman's really put together. Her auburn hair is pulled back in a tight bun. She wears a tight white dress shirt, black pants, and spiked heels. "The movie is over."

Over? We've been sleeping for almost two hours.

Marek is still out beside me, so I shake his arm, startling him awake.

He looks around, eyes half open. "Huh?"

"Time to go." I stand and side-shuffle down the row.

The woman watches Marek stumble after me before her eyes go to me. "It's you," she says. "I saw you would come and you are here."

Marek grasps my hand. "Come on. Let's get out of here."

I don't move. "You know me?"

"Mel," a man with a lot of muscles and hardly any hair calls. The woman turns to face him. "*Oui?*"

He says something in French to her.

"They found us?" The look exchanged between Mel and the man makes the tiny hairs on my arms stand up. "And English, please. I've only had four French lessons so far."

The man continues in English, "Attacked the celebration. Thankfully, you were detained, or they would've killed you."

"Go," Mel tells him. "Warn Clio and Erato. I'll get the others. And remember, no phones."

The man nods and darts out of the auditorium.

Mel's eyes snap in our direction.

"It's not safe here," she says. "We must go, or you'll meet a great tragedy. They can't know you are in Paris. Follow me."

Great tragedy. Who talks that way?

When we don't follow, she spins around and narrows her eyes on us. "Did you not understand me?"

I whisper, "I think we should go with her."

A poster on the wall halts me. It's of a muse in a flowing white dress, her brown hair is curled tight around her head, and she's wearing a wreath of vines and grapes. She holds a knife in one hand and a tragic mask in the other.

"I'm not going to harm you," Mel says, pulling at her face and dropping to her knees. "They're here. It's too late."

I pound down the steps and wrap an arm around her back. "Let me help you up."

We stand together. Marek joins us, holding Mel's other side.

"Where do we go?"

"The back room." Her face is distorted, resembling the tragedy mask on the poster.

Marek and I help Mel to the back room.

"Are you Melpomene, muse of tragedy?"

"You know your mythology," she says and nods to shelving that displays books and old film canisters. "Move it."

I get on one side, and Marek takes the other. It's a heavy bookcase, but we're able to push it enough away from the wall to get behind it.

Melpomene snatches up a crystal bottle from the desk, dumps golden liquid from it into a tumbler, and drinks it down. Her face relaxes, and she straightens.

"We go out this door." Melpomene wipes her mouth with

the back of her hand. "It leads to an alley."

"No," I snap. "Not until you tell us who we're running from."

"Who *we're* running from?" she repeats and laughs. "They're after me. You two were just in the wrong place at the wrong time. And about that, how did you happen upon my theater? It's on an obscure road."

"We were just walking by," Marek says.

Just before I say, "We got lost."

"The Fates." She smiles. "As they say, they are on our side. They helped you by providing a place to sleep and me by providing a delay so I wouldn't be at that celebration. Now go."

I step through the crude hole in the wall and into a narrow tunnel and move down it as quickly as I can. Marek and Melpomene shuffle behind me.

"Who's after you?" I ask over my shoulder.

She doesn't answer right away. I'm not sure if it's for a dramatic effect. We are in a theater, after all.

"The Keres," she finally answers. "They're spirits of violent death. Craving blood, they feast on evil mortals' dead bodies after their souls depart. Keres can't touch humans while they're alive, but they can tear gods and goddesses, muses, Keepers, to pieces."

Now I wish I hadn't asked.

"Why do they want to kill you?" Marek asks. He grasps my arm and keeps a hold of it.

"Did you not hear her, Marek? Keepers. They attack *Keepers.*"

"I heard."

"The Keres are the daughters of Nyx," she adds. "My sisters and I refused to be the muses for her son, Moros. Such a spoiled and gloomy deity. He's the god of impending doom. That was thousands of years ago. She holds a grudge."

This has to be one of the longest tunnels ever. My meds

were in my jacket, so I'm going solo on the panic thing. I try to breathe, but the air is thick with mortar dust. I just need to get out.

I need to get out.

I move faster, sliding my feet together, apart, together, apart—

The walls muffle a screeching sound coming from the theater. It's not one, but many of them—high and low pitched.

Fear punches my gut and chokes my throat. I can't move, clinging to the wall as if it's the only thing that can save me.

The screeches are deafening now. Closer. Too Close.

I need to *get out*!

CHAPTER THIRTY-THREE

Ahead of me, there's a golden light. A streetlamp. We're almost out.

Scratching noises come from the other side of the wall. Like nails trying to dig through the brick.

I trip over an uneven cobblestone and land on my hands and knees. The pain doesn't register. I don't care. I'm out.

Marek exits after me.

I push myself up and wipe my hands on my pants. We weren't in a tunnel. It's just a space between two buildings.

Melpomene steps out and stands beside Marek. "You don't have to be afraid. They want me, not you."

Darkness blankets the road between the golden blooms of light coming from the street lamps. Shadows seep from the gap we just exited. Their shapes are almost human, gray as the mortar between the bricks, not entirely lost in the night. They move toward us like rolling fog. I can't count how many there are. Their bodies merge and detach from one another. Six, maybe eight.

"Okay, now would be a good time to run," Marek says.

Melpomene turns her head in his direction. "It's too late for that. They'll catch me before I step off the curb."

One launches with two right after it, flying for Melpomene. Without thinking, I step in front of her, hands out, palms aimed at them.

"No!" I yell.

The Keres instantly recoil from me, slipping away through the gap between the buildings.

"They're gone." Marek places his hands on my shoulders. "Are you okay?"

"I think so," I say.

With wide eyes, Melpomene takes a few steps toward the gap. "You're a descendant of a death god."

Did my hands do that? I inspect my palms. They're ordinary, nothing abnormal about them. Or was it my voice? My command. Those things were afraid of me as much as I was of them. Is it some sort of power? Or just some ability I have, like rolling my tongue or wiggling my ears. What am I suppose to do with this?

Melpomene takes my hands in hers. "I have to warn my sisters that the Keres found us. "

"The nine muses," I say quietly, lowering my gaze to the ground, my mind still processing thoughts.

"Yes." She drops one of my hands and lifts my chin with her finger. "Being a demigod is not a bad thing. Be proud of who you are."

Her hand drops away from me.

"But a death god?" My eyes go to Marek. The shadows hide his eyes, and they seem to be a darker brown than their normal lighter color, and I can't help but wonder what he's thinking. "So I'm evil and scary. Like omens and curses, fire and brimstone, and all that stuff."

"It's not at all like that," she says. "Death gods are respected. They're not as you see in movies. Not all of them are evil or menacing. Some are gentle and caring, guiding us to our final spiritual place. We only fear death because we don't know what lies beyond life."

Marek steps into the light, and I can see his eyes now. He's not afraid of me, he's concerned and something more. I've never had anyone look at me like that. I mean the something-more part—of course Dad and Dalton have been worried about me before. It makes me both nervous and excited. "You're nothing like fire and brimstone," he says with that something more in his voice.

"Now, listen." Melpomene pulls my attention back to her. "You need to get as far away from me as possible. I'm Tragedy, after all. No telling what else will happen if you stick with me." She heads down the street, her spiky heels stabbing the cobblestones, and says over her shoulder, "Keep moving until you get to your hotel or wherever you're staying. The Keres, the little gnats, will spread the news about you like a disease."

She disappears into the shadows, the click-clack of her heels fading into the night.

I take off in the other direction. My Vans pound hard against the cobblestones. Marek is panting behind me.

"Ana, slow down!" he yells.

Only when I go around a corner do I cease running. I grab my side and catch my breath.

Marek eases to a stop beside me, breathing heavily. "I thought you were ditching me."

"I couldn't stay there," I say. "Not with those things around."

Marek checks the time on the GPS screen. "We need to keep moving. It's a little after one. The Louvre doesn't open until nine."

"What are we going to do?"

"We're going to keep walking. See Paris. Maybe get coffee when a café opens. Try to get our minds off what just happened."

"Sounds like a plan." I shiver. "It's so cold."

We walk. Sometimes there's a bench, and we sit. My face and hands are like ice. My head is throbbing, so are my feet. I need coffee. Or better, a bed.

The quaint backstreets of Montmartre are quiet at almost three in the morning. We reach the square, and I stand on one of the corners. Streetlamps line the block, giving little light, but I recognize the buildings.

"Right here," I say. "This square is filled with artists displaying their work during the day. My parents took a photograph in this exact spot."

Marek ambles over and pretends he's holding up a camera. "Say cheese."

It takes a second for what he's doing to register, but when it does, I'm suddenly warm inside, and I flash him a smile.

He clicks the pretend camera.

We make our way up the hill toward Sacré-Cœur Basilica. Its spotlighted facade calls to us. The white stone chapel with its three considerable arches in front, dome roofs, and bell tower overlooks Paris. The city is a black sea at night with beacons of light spreading across its surface. The Eiffel Tower is hidden behind buildings and trees.

I sit on a step. "In one photo, my mother sits here alone. I bet my father took it."

Marek raises his hands and takes another fake picture. His nose is red from the cold. "How are you holding up?" he asks.

The wind brushes my hair away from my face, and a chill slips down my back. "I'm numb. Can't feel my toes."

"We could ride the Metro. Get warm." He pulls the collar of his coat up and tucks his scarf inside.

"No. We need to eat."

"You're tough," he says.

"We have to budget." I skip down a few steps. "Tomorrow, after we're done at the Louvre, we'll go to the embassy, then

I'll call my grandparents. Have them wire money."

"Come on." He grasps my hand and leads me to the side of the chapel.

The wind bites at my skin. I stuff my free hand into my pocket and stare through some trees, and I can barely make out the Eiffel Tower in the dark. Only a few lights and its silhouette can be seen at this time of the morning.

Marek's still holding my hand, and we lace fingers. It's more intimate this way than how he's held it before.

"I bet it's beautiful during the day," I say, turning away, uncurling my fingers from his, but he keeps hold of my hand and tugs me back to him.

His expression is serious. He steps closer. "I'm going to kiss you in five seconds, Analiese. If you don't want me to, then say so and I won't."

I count to five in my head, *One thousand and one, one thousand and two …* Each number raises the anticipation another notch.

Without saying a word, his eyes speak novels. He needs me, just as I do him.

One thousand and five.

If I fall, he will catch me. And I'll do the same for him.

I must count faster than he does.

I could be crouched in a corner, a panic attack disabling me, and he wouldn't leave me. He'd let me know I wasn't alone.

Then it happens. Marek brushes away the hair tossed around my face by the wind, and his parted lips finally meet mine. I close my eyes, savoring the softness of his mouth. He doesn't taste of anything. Maybe night air. His arms wrap around me, and I grasp his scarf, pressing into him, not wanting this to end. I smell the city on him and a hint of mothballs from the old coat he's wearing. The kiss deepens, causing heat to spread from our lips through my body. My fingertips and toes tingle.

I'm not cold anymore.

Lost in his kiss, I'm not scared.

More importantly, he's not, either.

It doesn't matter who I am or what I can do, because he sees the real me, and he's still kissing me.

My heart is like a thousand butterflies, and with each special moment spent with Marek, a few take flight. Before long, he'll steal them all.

His mouth leaves mine, and he leans back to look into my eyes. The shadows just behind Marek shift, and I flinch.

"S-somethings there!" I sputtered.

"What?" He spins around, squinting into the darkness.

I stay perfectly still, waiting, listening. There's no noise, no rustling of leaves, and no moving shadows. "It's nothing," I finally say. "I'm just on edge."

"Well, just in case, let's go." He brushes my hair back again. "You okay?"

"I'm good."

Because of me, our kiss ended too soon. I want more, but he's right, we should go. We're in the dark. Where those shadow things live.

Marek keeps his eyes on the foliage lining the walkway.

The steep, winding roads are silent. Almost deserted. At the bottom of the hill, we pass the famous Moulin Rouge cabaret.

I catch him sneaking a glance at me, and he busts me doing the same. It's like we're running around with a secret.

He laces his hand with mine, and we keep up a good pace, trying to stay warm, down Rue Montmartre, across Grands Boulevards, around Tour Saint-Jacques square, and over the Seine River to Notre Dame Cathedral.

Marek glances at the GPS again. "It's almost four thirty."

I want to collapse. But I shouldn't be disappointed with the time. We've been trying to kill it since arriving in Paris after six the night before. Soon it will be twelve hours that we've been exploring Paris. Only two of it involved sleeping.

I yawn.

Which causes Marek to as well.

I pose for another fake photo in front of the medieval-looking cathedral in the place right at the edge of the street where my parents most likely had a passerby take theirs. Marek mimes clicking a camera.

He lowers his hands and gazes at me with that something-more look, and I have to glance away. I probably imagine it. He most likely just thinks I'm amusing or strange or both.

I think he's both, but he's also hot. Especially when one side of his lips lifts in a smile, and he directs it at me. Like he's doing now.

Not staying long at Notre Dame, we cross the Seine, trekking along the river, heading for the Eiffel Tower. The river lapping against the banks matches the rhythm of our footsteps. The city lights and lamps lining the river reflect in its darkened waters. Each time my Vans hit the ground, pain shocks the soles of my feet, shaking my legs. My eyes droop, and my shoulders ache.

We don't stop. Keep moving. Keep warm.

Another hour and another fake photograph in front of the Eiffel Tower. A thirty-minute walk to the Arc de Triomphe. I give up on taking pictures.

"Come on," Marek urges, holding his pretend camera. "It's the Arc."

"I'm too tired."

He lowers his arms. "I know. It's almost six. Hopefully, a café will open soon."

The Champs-Elysées goes on forever. I'm dragging my Vans across the pavement, and I don't even care if they get ruined. The Arc de Triomphe grows smaller behind us, and the sky gets lighter.

CHAPTER THIRTY-FOUR

Marek and I access the Louvre through the Le Carrousel du Louvre entrance. He has the great idea to buy a notebook and pen at the gift shop. People crowd each other to view the *Mona Lisa* in the Salle des Etats room, snapping photos on their phones. Some older couples use actual cameras. Finally making our way to the front, we lean against the banister that creates a half circle around the painting.

The *Mona Lisa* is behind thick glass. There's nothing that stands out. She's in a gold frame, plain dress, hair down. Her face is lacking eyebrows and eyelashes. Staring off to the side with a half smile on her face that suggests she's amused or distracted by someone other than the painter.

I lean closer to Marek. "Do you notice anything?"

"No." He scratches the back of his head. "My grandfather was obsessed with this painting. He was in Europe with my grandma a month before he died. She said there were several times that he went off on his own for long periods. Must've been hiding the clues."

I don't say it, but if Adam Conte was hiding their Parzalis a month ago, he must've known he was going to die. When Marek lowers his head, seemingly in deep thought, I wonder if he's thinking the same thing.

"Do you remember what he said about the painting?" I ask.

A man, light hair, ruddy skin, bumps into me while trying to get closer to the *Mona Lisa*. His wife pulls on his sleeve and scolds him in what I think is German.

"He did say once that there's always another story behind a painting. Not just what you see on the canvas."

"Maybe the clues are hidden in the paintings surrounding her," I say.

We stroll around the room, stopping at each painting and studying it intently. He couldn't hide the Parzalis in the Louvre. There's no way. The security is too high. Has to be a code somewhere.

Marek's hand goes to my back as we're studying *The Animals Boarding Noah's Ark* by Jacopo Bassano, and my stomach does that fluttering thing that's becoming a habit around him.

"It's gotta be code," Marek repeats my thoughts. "I need a restroom."

"Okay, I'll start making notes."

He gives me the notebook and pen and rushes off, weaving around people on his way out.

There are twenty-five other paintings in the Salle des Etats room with my girl Mona. I jot down the title to all the works and the painter's name for each. The restroom must be far. I only have one left, and Marek still hasn't returned.

Footsteps sound behind me. I try to write the last painting's title and artist—*Portrait of a Man* by Dosso Dossi—faster in the notebook so I can get out of the way.

"Think of my surprise when the Keres' whispers are about you." The voice belongs to Ares. He's behind me, and

I can't move. "Paris. It's my favorite city. Have you and your boyfriend been enjoying yourselves in the City of Light?"

I keep my eyes on the painting. "He's not my boyfriend."

"Who's not?" Marek says.

I whirl around, searching over his shoulders for Ares. I don't see him. He just disappeared. "Ares was here."

He rushes into the crowd.

I chase after him. "Marek, wait."

"The Keeper is getting closer to his prize," Ares whispers in my ear, and I fling around, looking for him, but he's not there. "Remember, you'll give me his Parzalis. Willingly."

"Where are you?"

A woman aiming her phone like she's recording a video gives me a confused look and heads to the next painting over.

I hurry after Marek. The crowd slows him down, and I'm able to catch up.

"I don't see him." Marek turns to me. "What did he want?"

"Something he won't get." I hope Ares is still listening. Because he's not getting what he wants. "He's after your part of the talisman. Says I'll give it to him willingly."

Marek gazes down at me. "I say we find a quiet place for coffee and look over our notes."

The sun is out and almost directly over Paris. Marek and I sit at a table at an outside café near the Louvre. Working the name of the painting or the artist or both, I try to figure out which one Adam Conte might've used for the next clue. Trying to find a code in one of them.

I stare at the *Mona Lisa* and Leonardo Da Vinci's names. "The code isn't in the other paintings. So it has to be here." I stab the M with the tip of the pen.

Marek pushes back in the chair and watches the pedestrian road again. He hasn't let his guard down since we sat at the table.

I'm not worried about Ares. He's waiting for us to find something. I'm a pawn he's playing to get what he wants.

I drop my head into my hands. "I just can't figure it out."

"My gramps wouldn't make it this difficult," Marek's hand goes to my back, the warmth of it pausing me for a beat.

I recover. "What are we going to do? There's nothing here. Are you sure you don't remember your grandfather saying anything about the *Mona Lisa*?"

"Not said so much as…" Marek leans back again, his hand falling away from my back. "Well, he had photos of the painting in the basement. My grandma mentioned them having to push through the crowd to see her when they visited the Louvre. That's all I got."

I drop my napkin next to my plate and stand. "Then we have to go back. Take another look. Maybe we missed something."

We return to the crowded room, and it seems like the *Mona Lisa* is never alone. I wonder how the real woman would feel to know she's this popular. That so many people know her face.

Two hours pass, and we're running out of time. My jaw is tense, and a headache is building behind my eyes. It's time to give up, but neither Marek nor I want to admit it. So I give in.

"We have to get to the embassy before it closes." Both of us need to sleep. I'm not sure what they'll do to us. Are we runaways? Jane will be pissed when they contact her. I realize just now that I don't know what Marek told his family.

"What lie did you give your parents? You know, where are you supposed to be?"

Marek pulls his stare away from the *Mona Lisa* and puts it on me. "My parents think I'm with my grandma, and she thinks I'm at home."

There is no avoiding it, we'll have to face the music sometime, as Dad used to say. But it's Marek's quest. I want him to decide when to give up. I don't want him to resent me for forcing him to abandon our search. Stress tightens my neck and shoulder muscles, causes my stomach to sour. My lids weigh heavy on my eyes.

I just hope he will decide soon.

I catch a glimpse of long dark, curly hair just outside the doors, moving with the crowd, and my pulse quickens. It was a flash, so quick I'm not even sure it was a woman, but every time I see someone with that attribute, I'm going to think of her. Inanna.

It's only a matter of time before she finds us.

Me. Finds me. Because she wants what I can do. I witnessed her kill Cain and that doorman. I'm guessing she's on the wrong side of this immortal war. Maybe Ares is on the right one.

Maybe there's no right side.

Marek checks the time on the GPS. "We should go. Walk-ins at the embassy end at two forty-five."

There's no need to correct him. But I'm pretty sure runaways fall into the emergency category and not regular business hours. Might as well go early, though, just to be safe.

I give the *Mona Lisa* one last look. No one knows for sure who she was. There've been so many investigations into her identity. She's as elusive as that smile. It's her secret.

Guess you'll keep another one.

CHAPTER THIRTY-FIVE

When the embassy contacted Marek's parents, they were concerned for his well-being. Sure, they were upset, but they trust him to get back to the States. They want him home.

When Jane received the call, she lost it. Said she knew I'd be like them. Who she meant I'm not too sure. Probably my parents. Maybe my uncle. Instead of "dealing" with me on her own, she called my grandparents in Isreal. Which makes no sense to me, since I never get in trouble. Not like Dalton. I get straight As. Unlike Dalton.

One time.

One time I do something careless, and I'm the trouble child.

When Jane finally reached my grandparents, it was too late for them to get a flight to Paris. Saba and Safta got me a hotel room right next door to the American Embassy and wired money. They'll arrive in Paris sometime past noon. I'm spending a few days with them to give Jane "time."

Dalton. How can I hide that Lugh's his sperm donor father

from him? Thank goodness I couldn't talk to him, because he can tell when something's wrong with me. He's still at that grieving camp and won't be home for two days.

I'm in a lounge with a lot of gold trim, fancy chandeliers, and a grand piano. There's a cloudy sky painted on the ceiling and marble on the walls. This hotel is expensive. My grandparents have money, and they throw it around all the time. Not to be snobby or showy, but to help others. They're good people. I'm lucky to have them.

Showered and wearing the new outfit I got in one of the expensive shops down the street, I actually feel better. I could pass as a twentysomething Parisian woman with my new black pants, white shirt, and gray jacket. I look sort of innocent, except for the soul of the Devil or something taped to my lower leg. I play with the ends of the yellow scarf Marek picked out at the thrift store for me. How am I already reminiscing? It was just a few hours ago.

Steam rises from the cup of coffee I cradle in my hands. When I see Marek stroll in with the confident stride and the tilted smile he turns on as soon as he sees me, he grabs more of my heart.

He sits in the chair beside me and holds my hands on the table. There are bags under his eyes, and they're glassy, and I'm sure mine are, too.

"So I'm leaving in a few for the airport," he says. "My parents want me home as soon as possible. It might be some time before I can see you."

I stare at our hands, fingers entangled. "I'm not sure when I'll be back home. Jane needs *time*."

He knits his eyebrows together. "Time? Isn't she your mother?"

"She adopted me." I swallow because I really need to hold it together here. I'm already crumbling inside, knowing that any minute now I'll have to say goodbye to Marek. "I think my uncle forced her into it. Sure, maybe she was down with it when I was a baby, but something changed the older I got."

His eyes close for a quick second, and when he opens them, he slips his hand around the back of my neck, guides me toward him, and waits. I lean the rest of the way and press my lips to his. The kiss is soft and not that long. We are in a fancy hotel, after all, and PDA is probably frowned on here.

He releases me, and we straighten. His kiss still hinting on my lips.

I look over his shoulder. A few groups are sitting at the other tiny tables around the room. No one noticed our kiss. "I'm sorry we couldn't solve that clue," I say.

"Yeah, that's a letdown." He absentmindedly fidgets with my fingers. "It makes no sense. He made it too hard. I've played back things he's told me in the past. Nothing fits."

"I guess it's only a matter of time before a spirit gives the location of it to their god or goddess."

"Yeah. More immortals with powers. Great." He lowers his head as if he's ashamed. As if he's let the world down. "I wonder what life will be like under their rule."

I squeeze his hand. "It's not your fault. We tried."

I don't mention his grandmother. I'm sure he's already beating himself up about her losing her money.

The man from the embassy comes into the room and stands by the entrance. He spots Marek and waves for him to leave.

Marek releases my hand. "There's my ride. Walk me out?"

"Okay." I grab my new tan leather bag, now holding my replaced passport, new prescription, and recently purchased makeup, and I sling it over my shoulder.

We clasp hands and shuffle slowly for the exit, not wanting our time together to end. Hoping that by some miracle time will stop.

Fitting my mood, it's raining when we get outside. The

man who waved Marek over in the lounge stands beside a black Mercedes sedan.

I pull the hood to my new jacket over my head, rain clapping on the cotton and polyester blend. "Wow, you're going in style."

He looks behind him. "Yeah, I guess so." Even though he's getting wet, he still stands there with me in the rain. Eyes holding my stare, he grips both my hands, and we stand face to face. "God, I hate leaving you. Stay in the hotel room until your grandparents get here, okay?"

"I'll be fine," I reassure him.

"Call me as soon as you can. I'll have my number switched to my old phone when I get home."

"I will."

He cups my face in his hands and presses his lips firmly against mine. We kiss, not caring who sees. I don't want to let go. I don't want him to leave. I don't want to stay without him.

We were just getting started. Just coming together. I'm not sure when I'll see him again. I want to keep him here with me.

But he lets go.

And so do I.

CHAPTER THIRTY-SIX

Her smile is taunting, teasing. What secret is she hiding? There's amusement in her eyes. It's as if it's a game to her.

I probably shouldn't have come to the Louvre alone, but my ticket is still good for today, and it doesn't close for another hour. I need one last look. Adam Conte had a reason for sending Marek here. There's a clue hidden in this room.

It's less crowded than it was earlier. I stroll slowly around the room, stopping at each painting, studying each one like I'm an art dealer, trying to find something that stands out.

A woman with short brown hair in a pencil skirt and dress shirt leads a small group into the room. "I prefer to end my tours with our special lady, the *Mona Lisa*. I'll tell you a little history about her, and then you'll be free to wander the museum on your own for the rest of the hour. She was painted by Leonardo da Vinci. It is…"

I move away from the group, taking measured steps, eyes roaming over paintings—a naked Venus with cupids, two hounds, a wedding, Noah's Ark—searching for something in them, finding nothing.

Two women, maybe in their fifties, one with short silver hair, the other brunette, hold hands as they stare at the floor-to-ceiling artwork by Paulo Veronese titled *The Wedding Feast at Cana*. It's so large the artist had to use a ladder or something to paint it.

The next one I pause at is *The Raising of Jairus' Daughter*. It's the image that Marek and I thought for sure would hold the clue. It's of a young girl being raised from the dead.

Someone stops to the right of me. I don't look right away. "I was there." His voice is soft, but it still makes me flinch. "It wasn't as dramatic as that. The girl simply awoke."

"Why are you following me, Ares?" I finally take a look at him.

"I'm only curious," he says. "The shadows have eyes, even during the day. They inform me of your whereabouts."

"Why do you want the pieces to the talisman?" I turn my best glare on him. "Don't you already have power? There're wars all over the world."

His head tilts a little as he watches me. "Good question. It's only a fraction of my power. I need all of it for there to be a war between the immortals. A war mortals have never seen before. One that will return glory to deities around the world. I'm not a selfish god. I want all of us to rule as we did in the beginning."

Lugh and Oyá wouldn't let him do that, and I bet other gods and goddesses feel the same way. I decide to tell him just that. "I doubt you can get them all on your side."

"You doubt my ability to influence others. I'll demonstrate." He steps behind the two women standing in front of the marriage painting, leans forward, and whispers.

The brunette says something to the woman with short silver hair, and they argue. It gets heated, arms flail, then they stomp off in different directions.

Ares comes back to my side. "With my full power, I can do that to the immortals. Do you believe me, or would you like me to demonstrate it again?"

"No, I don't want you to demonstrate it again." I glance from one woman to the next. "Are they going to keep arguing?"

"Unfortunately, yes. It will end their relationship. If you asked them later in life why they went their separate ways, they wouldn't be able to tell you."

I didn't think I could get any sadder after saying goodbye to Marek, but another wave of it hits me. Crashing. Stinging. Because of me, because Ares felt a need to show me his powers, a couple is breaking up.

I tighten my hands into fists, trying to keep them from shaking. "What do you want?"

"Analiese, I've already let you know my intentions. I just thought I'd come and keep you company. Now that the Conte boy is gone."

I need an escape. Sliding my eyes left, then right, I search for an exit.

"I see you're up to your old ugly tricks, Ares." A woman's voice comes from behind us. I've heard her before, and she usually carries a syringe full of poison.

Whirling around on my heel, I almost collide with Inanna. "H-how? Where…?"

"At a loss for words?" She grins like a cat about to stick its claw into a birdcage. "Ares doesn't believe in love."

"Now that's just hateful," he says. "What do you call what we had a millennium ago?"

"Lust. There's a big difference. Excuse me, I have to clean up Ares's mess again." Inanna saunters over to the woman with silver hair and says something. Inanna'a smile deepens as she passes us, crossing the room to the other woman. Another whispered word, and she returns to us.

"There," she says.

The women are still ignoring each other.

"What did you do?" I ask. "Nothing's happening."

Stay calm. Find a way out.

Inanna's smile turns into a smug look. "Wait for it."

Ares chuckles. "You're losing your touch, my dear. I had them arguing within a second."

The woman with silver hair looks over her shoulder.

Not too long after, the brunette does also.

With tears in their eyes and longing expressions on their faces, they dart for each other and collide into a hug.

Inanna crosses her arms and gives Ares a disdainful look. "See. Love takes longer to coax than hate."

I take the opportunity their arguing gives me to slip away and stand next to the tour guide and her group. Safety in numbers. I sneak a glance at Inanna and Ares. Their body language suggests they're arguing—her foot tapping impatiently, his arms flying up in frustration.

I have to get out of here.

"Yes, some say that," the tour guide's confirms. "In 2005, Lisa Gherardini, married name Lisa del Giocondo, was identified as the model for the *Mona Lisa*. Leonardo was commissioned by her husband to paint her portrait."

That's it. What was it? Marek said his grandfather told him there's always another story behind a painting, not just what you see on the canvas. The clue isn't the *Mona Lisa*. It's the model used for the image.

I need a computer. Or a library. And I definitely need to ditch the stalkers.

CHAPTER THIRTY-SEVEN

The tour guide is giving her group directions when I return my attention to them. "We should make our way to the exit. The museum will close soon. Follow me."

I move into the crowd, keeping a large man between me and Ares and Inanna. Once we're out of the room, I jog down the corridor, ignoring comments that I don't understand because they're in French. Most likely, it's to slow down.

My new shoes slip across the marble floor. I'm not going to the pyramid entrance. I don't have a ride back to the hotel. And Inanna and Ares will think I went that way.

I head for the inverted pyramid and turn right. Through a small underground shopping strip, up two escalators, and I'm at the Metro station. The platform is like its own museum, adorned with replicas to simulate art from the Louvre. My eyes stay on the entrances until the train arrives and I'm safely on it.

I sit on a seat closest to one of the doors, near an older man, leaving an empty one between us. Gray curly hair, button-down sweater, and leather loafers. Probably someone's grandfather. He seems less threatening than the group of guys in their twenties on the other side. The aroma of liquor and cigarettes surrounds them.

"Your judgment's a little skewed, Analiese," the older man says.

"What?" I move another seat away from him.

Okay, breathe. You're okay. Know your surroundings. What do you see?

A guy carrying a long narrow box. A woman on her phone doesn't look too happy with whoever is on the other side of that call.

"You've become quite the popular girl. Everyone...or should I say, every immortal knows of you." He crosses his legs. He's wearing purple-and-grey argyle socks. "The Keres love spreading rumors—true or not. I had to come and see for myself. Another Riser. What powers do you hold?"

The train pulls up to the next station, and I'm out of my seat before the doors open. As soon as they part, I push my way through and charge up the stairs to the street. A woman with straight dark hair falling around her shoulders and carrying a grocery bag matches my steps.

"You can't get away from me that easily," she says, her voice melodic and accented.

"What?" I pick up my speed, and she keeps up with me. "Leave me alone."

You're okay.

"I can be anyone you want me to be. A fox in sheep's clothing."

"Who are you?"

The woman gives me a confused look and says something I don't understand. She stops, letting me get ahead of her.

Now this guy with short dark hair and a beard with a silver stud piercing in each cheek and one in the middle of his bottom lip is marching next to me. "Maybe this is more your style."

I stop. "Okay, I give. Who are you and what do you want from me?"

"Good," he says. "Because I have about one good change left in me for the day. We should talk somewhere private."

"No. Talk here." There's absolutely no way I'm leaving this crowded street.

His lips spread into a slow grin. "If that's how you want it. Seeing that you won't go somewhere private, our talk will have to wait for another day."

"I'm not thickheaded enough to go somewhere alone with you."

His eyes bug out, and he backs away. "I say nothing to you."

"Sorry, I was talking to the other guy." I rush off. That was beyond freaky. Think. What god can body-hop? *Think. Think. Think.* Okay, a few come to mind.

Wait. He said a "fox in sheep's clothing." It's Kumiho. He has nine tails and can change bodies. Usually, he transforms into beautiful women to lure men. When he has them, he turns back into a fox and eats their hearts and livers.

Perfect. He could be anyone.

When I get back to the hotel, I go straight to the business center and do a search on Lisa del Giocondo. I go through several sites, searching for information on her.

After her husband's death, Lisa lived in the Convent of Saint Ursula and died there. Nearly an hour searching, I now have two possibilities. Adam Conte either hid his family's piece of the Divinities Keep in the Convent of Saint Ursula, where Lisa was buried, or Santissima Annunziata Basilica, which held her family's crypt.

I scribble down the addresses to both on the hotel's paper, rip it from the pad, and shove it into my purse. Next, I search for the fastest, soonest way to get to Florence. It's ten hours on a train and about two hundred dollars for a flight, which only takes an hour and forty minutes.

No matter what I do, I'm in trouble. Safta gave me her credit card information to buy the clothes, but just thinking about using it is causing welts to form on my chest.

I fill in my information for the flight, enter Safta's credit card information in the required fields, and stop before hitting send.

"Safta, what would you do?"

She'd put the fate of the world first before herself. So what if I'm grounded forever, or I'm thrown in a foster home because Jane doesn't want me anymore. At least we'd all be alive. I hit enter and instantly have buyer's remorse. I hope Safta forgives me. I print out the tickets.

I go to the room, call my grandparents, and tell them I'm okay. Safta says to order room service and get whatever I want. Which makes me feel even shittier for using her credit card to buy the plane tickets.

My stomach grumbles, reminding me that I need to eat. I'll just have to feel guilty later when I get back. Since I can't figure out how to order room service, I decide to go down to one of the dining rooms.

Coming off the elevator, I pause in the middle of the door track.

I'm not sure whether what I'm seeing is actually real or my tired brain playing a trick on me.

"Marek?"

The door starts to close, and I step out before it hits me.

"Hey," he says, as if it's no big deal he's standing in the middle of a fancy hotel lobby instead of being on Flight 56.

"What are you doing here?"

He takes two long strides and tows me into a hug. "He said...said you were in trouble. There's no way I could leave you."

I pull back and gaze up at him. "Who told you that?"

"We should go somewhere less open."

For a minute, I forget where I was going. Then my stomach decides to remind me. "I was on my way out to get something to eat. I can't read the menu here, and it's all too fancy."

A smile lifts his lips. That kind of smile you do when you know you should respond to something but your mind is too preoccupied and you give it half an effort.

"Okay, where to?" he asks.

Marek and I stroll down Rue Boissy d'Anglas and find a cute place with sandwiches, salads, and a yummy macaron desert with basil and raspberries. We decide to wait until after we eat to talk about any of the messed-up stuff going on around us.

I place my spoon beside the remains of the macaron desert, which is pretty much the cream I couldn't scrape off the plate. "So who told you I was in trouble?"

He takes a sip from his water glass. "I know this sounds messed up. It was several people, but I think it was someone, or whatever the hell it was, hopping from body to body. Like the damn thing was possessing people. Using them to talk to me."

Him, too? Suddenly everyone in this café becomes a potential danger. The face of evil comes in all shapes and sizes. The least suspect could be the most threatening. The couple in the corner with their heads together and feet tangled, the three couples in their thirties sitting together on our left, two men ignoring each other as they scroll on their phones—any one of them could be a host for whoever or whatever it was trying to talk to me on the street earlier.

It can't be Kumiho if he's warning Marek. I thought the Korean god was evil.

Marek's hand covers mine resting on the table. "Ana,

what is it?"

"We need our bill." I raise my hand, flagging the man serving us. "I know where your grandfather hid the next clue. I have to get you a ticket."

"Where are we going?"

I glance around. "I'll tell you when we get back to the hotel."

I hold back the fact that it may be illegal and involve crypt digging. After all, the shadows have ears.

CHAPTER THIRTY-EIGHT

Florence seems frozen in time. The narrow streets away from the city center are obscure; the old buildings squeezing them hold shadows and secrets of the past. Like living in history.

I'm on the edge of my seat. I haven't relaxed since leaving the hotel earlier. Marek and I made sure we were at the Louvre right when it opened. We went there before the airport to throw off anyone following us. After entering through the pyramid entrance, we immediately exited by way of the Metro and went straight to the airport.

The bus we got on nearby the Florence airport stops a building away from the Santissima Annunziata Basilica. Our driver tells us it's considered the mother church of the Servite Order. We nod politely as if we understand what that means and exit.

Its facade is in the same Renaissance style of the buildings surrounding it. Marek holds the wooden door open, and I enter. He comes in behind me. The chapel is decorated in a heavy and dark baroque style with an abundance of marble and gilding adorning its walls.

We ask a man polishing the benches where we can find the crypt of Francesco del Giocondo, and he graciously takes us to it. The tomb is beneath a floor stone. A design of swirly lines, fleur de lis, stars, flowers, and what look like butterflies are etched into the sandstone.

"It's not here," Marek says assuredly.

A woman in her late thirties or early forties, blonde and wearing a black dress and suit jacket, sits in one of the pews, watching us. I grip the strap of my purse. Not to keep it from falling but because I'm anxious.

I look at the stone but keep darting glances at the woman. "How do you know this isn't it?"

"My grandfather wouldn't disturb a chapel. Also, he'd have a difficult time putting it in that crypt. He'd worry I couldn't get it out."

"Okay, so we go to the convent." I turn to leave, and the woman in the pew is gone.

It's a ten-minute walk through the tight streets. There are so many motorcycles and Vespas lining the roads it looks like a dealership. The Convent of Saint Ursula's windows are bricked off, the walls gray and stained with graffiti. It's a shell of what it must've been back in Lisa Gherardini's lifetime. The building almost takes up the entire block.

"Great," I say, glancing up the three-story building. "How are we getting in there?"

Marek backs up as if it'll help him see over the top of the building. The street is so narrow it wouldn't fit three Vespas lined up tire to tire. "There has to be some way."

"An illegal way."

He lifts a shoulder. "We've faced worse."

"That's encouraging," I say.

Acting like tourists, we roam the streets surrounding the convent. By the looks we're getting, I think they don't get many visitors.

I slip my arm around his and lean close. "I don't like this. Where are we?"

"We'll be fine," he reassures me.

I see it then, above one of the grates at the bottom of the building, written like the other graffiti: *Keram Etnoc*. I point at it. "That's your name backward."

A guy gets on a Vespa and drives down the alley. When it's clear, Marek squats and sticks his fingers through the grate. "Keep a lookout," he says.

He tugs and tugs on it, and the bottom moves slightly. Another pull, metal scraping against concrete until it's up. "Wait here."

"Be careful."

Dropping to his belly, he slides inside. "Come on," he calls.

I shove my purse in and follow it, inhaling dirt, scraping skin because my shirt rises a little as I go through. My eyes water from the dust floating around us. Marek pulls the grate back into place. The convent looks to be under construction.

"Do you think this was going on when your grandfather hid the clue?" I slip the strap of my purse over my head and wear it across my body.

"Yeah," he says, his steps careful as if the ground's going to cave under his feet. "I've seen a picture of this before. It was a selfie of my grandfather in front of dug-up graves. He texted it to me with others from his and my grandma's Europe trip. Come on, let's find the crypt and get out of here."

Scaffolds cling to the walls encircling a courtyard with piles of construction materials. There's a large octagon-shaped hole in the middle the size of the Trevi Fountain. Not sure what it was used for, but I can see the basement down below. Moving along the perimeter of the courtyard, I can almost see what it looked like all those years ago when Mona Lisa was here.

In Italian, monna is a shortened version of madonna, which means lady. Which means Mona Lisa would be Lady Lisa. Another fun fact I learned from the tour guide.

Seeing this crumbling building reminds me how quickly a place, a person, love can fade away with time. Marek and I both lost someone special in our lives. Their deaths brought us together.

It's as if Marek has a sensor connected to my moods. His hand covers mine, fingers slipping between fingers, assuring me he's here. He keeps hold as we pass every arched doorway and window until we come to an excavation site. Squares, or more like graves, the size that could fit a body, are carved into the ground. Archaeologists' box grids.

"I wonder where he'd hide it."

It's not a question, I was just thinking out loud, but he answers, "I don't know. Has to be here. I feel it."

I kneel down by the excavation.

"Not there." He stops me. "It'd be somewhere permanent. Less likely to be disturbed."

I tilt my face toward the ceiling. "What about the beams?"

Marek comes up behind me, wraps his arms around me, and looks over my shoulder. "Too high. He was alone. He'd need help to get up there."

"Okay, there's not much to search, then."

He untangles his arms from me. "It'd be in plain sight. You'd be too busy looking in all the nooks and crannies to see it."

I laugh. "Nooks and crannies?"

"My gramps's words, not mine."

In plain sight is proving to be challenging to find. By the position of the sun and where the buildings are casting their shadows, it's about one in the afternoon.

I go in the opposite direction as Marek.

"Plain sight." I swing my arms, my purse bouncing against

my side.

"Maybe I was wrong," Marek says. "I'm going to search the courtyard. You look here."

"Okay."

It's about twenty minutes into my search, and I want to give up. The walls and floors are so barren there's no way Adam could hide the clue here. As I'm turning to leave, I notice something different in the bricked in window beside me.

The mortar around the bottom row looks newer than the others above it.

Just like at the Roman Forum.

I dart for the courtyard to get Marek. Several shadows slither past, and I stumble to a stop. My eyes follow their path.

Marek. They're after him!

I sprint, hitting the ground hard. The shadows screech. It's that terrible sound like metal scratching against metal. Marek scans the courtyard for the noise.

"Run, Marek!"

He spots me a second too late, and the shadows drag him down.

CHAPTER THIRTY-NINE

The screams coming from Marek tear my heart out of my chest.

"Marek!" I shout.

He's writhing on the ground, his body bending left, then right. Shadows cover him. Squeezing. No. *Feeding.*

They're feeding on him.

I grab Marek's arm, touching one of the shadows. It shrills and races away.

One after the other, I touch the Keres, chasing them off. Marek's howls shake me. Tears drop from my eyes.

"Get off him!"

The Keres scatter away from Marek. I drop to my knees and hug him.

"Are you hurt?" I ask against his shoulder. He doesn't move, so I lay him on the ground. His face is pale. I place my palm on his cheek. "Marek?"

It doesn't look as though he's breathing.

CPR. Okay, open airway. I gently tilt his head back, then lift his chin.

His eyes open. "What are you doing?"

I sit back on my heels. "I didn't think… Are you okay?"

"Yeah. I just—need—" His voice breaks, and he winces. "To catch my breath."

We stay there on the ground until he's ready. When we stand together, I do my best to hold him up. He struggles to keep upright and rocks a little on his feet.

"Sorry," he says. "Just a little light-headed. CPR, really?" His laugh is weak. "Not sure a Death Riser can do that."

He's right. If he were dead, I would have made him into one of those things. I wait while he steadies himself and stops leaning on me.

"Can you walk?" I ask.

He nods. "Yeah."

"Good. Because I think I found it."

"You did? Where?"

"This way." I grasp his hand and lead him back to the excavation site. "But we need something sharp."

I find a broken piece of something metal. It doesn't take very long for us to remove the two bottom bricks. The mortar used to seal them was more water than powder. It crumbles easily, and the blocks slide out, revealing a cavity in the windowsill.

Hoping there aren't any spiders or other creepy crawlies, I reach inside because my hands are smaller. My fingers touch burlap. I wrap them around the material and drag it out, my knuckles scraping against the brick.

I untie the bag. There's a smooth triangular block the size of my hand inside, and I remove it. The edges are gold, and the front and back have elaborate swirls that don't make any particular design. There are other indentations, but I can't tell what they are.

"It's the talisman." I turn it over and over in my hand. "I thought it would have gems or something."

"There's more inside," Marek says and pulls out a small leather notebook from the sack.

I slip the talisman back into the bag while Marek flips through the notebook.

"It's my gramps's book. It's instructions on how to be a Keeper. What my responsibilities are." He lifts his eyes. "After finding the talisman, I have to go on a quest. On my own. To hide it. Our family's divinity will guide me."

"So you don't just pick a spot and put it there?" A quest sounds like a long time to me. I don't like the idea of Marek being away. But right now, I just want to get out of here and back to Paris on our scheduled flight. Return to the hotel before Safta and Saba arrive.

"Wait." Something mentioned in the notes Marek read hits me. "Divinity? Like a deity in Hinduism? Who is it, and where do you find whoever it is?"

"I don't know. It says the divinity will show itself now that I'm in possession of the Parzalis." Marek tucks the leather notebook in his back pocket. "Let's get out of here."

"Yeah, before those Keres tell the world where we are."

I slip the burlap sack in my purse and put the strap over my head to wear it across my body. Marek fits the bricks back into place. We climb out through the grate and onto the road. A man yells at us in Italian, and we run down the street, turning corner after corner until we're confident he isn't chasing us.

Our hands instinctively find each other, and I'm light on my feet, floating. It's over. We made it here. Found the Parzalis. The flight back to Paris takes off in a few hours. Maybe I can even mend things with Jane.

"I think we're lost." Marek stops in the middle of the narrow road. He looks up and then down it.

I copy him, as if I can figure out where we are. I'm direction challenged.

He retrieves the GPS from the pocket of his jacket and

pushes the on button. The screen stays dark. "Battery's dead. I couldn't charge it. Lost the charger with my money belt."

"Let's find someone who speaks English and ask for directions."

The next street looks just like the one before it, and the one before that.

A man is standing in the middle of the road quite a way down from us. I squint, trying to see him, and freeze. Before I can tell Marek, he says it.

"It's Pazuzu." Still gripping my hand, Marek takes off for the road on the left, and I'm yanked forward. "Don't stop. We have to keep moving."

I swallow my fear down, it's sour and bitter in my stomach, and I run. Fast. Right behind Marek. Past all the motorcycles and Vespas lining the streets. Marek stops this time, and I bump into him.

"Don't stop. Why are you stopping?" I come around him. A man and a woman, both on the tall side, block the street. And they don't look friendly. I pull Marek's arm toward the road on our right. "This way."

Three women with demon eyes block our way this time, and we whip around and double back to a street we just went by.

"They're trying to drive us somewhere," Marek says.

We turn another corner, and my heart jumps into my throat. It's Pazuzu again. Just strolling down the road as if he has all the time in the world.

"Back the other way," Marek says, and we go, not stopping, our feet pounding the pavement.

I spot dark flowing hair, and I know who it is before she comes into view. Inanna is sprinting up the long road toward us. I glance back, and that way is blocked by Pazuzu.

"Hold up." Marek stops me, and we shuffle around, losing hold of each other, searching for an escape. "How did they find us?"

"Can't be the Keres. They got here too fast."

We're cornered.

And then I see him, all six-feet-something of him. Lugh is behind Inanna.

"This way!" Lugh shouts.

I meet eyes with Marek. He seems as surprised as I am.

Lugh raises his voice louder. "By all means, take your time!"

Before his sarcasm registers in my brain, we're off and heading in his direction. Stucco and bricks rain down from the tops of the buildings and break against the sidewalk, pieces pelting my legs.

When we reach Lugh and Inanna, they run with us to the end of the road.

My lungs burn, and my legs wobble as if one more step and they'll give in. "Why is she with us?"

Lugh must sense my mortal weakness and stays by my side. "Keep going. Think only of what's ahead."

"Why is she with you?" I nod my head in Inanna's direction in front of me.

"I'm appalled," she says. "It's Ares and Pazuzu you should be concerned about. I've been helping you. I distracted Ares in the Louvre so you could get away. His men were at the Vatican, and we stopped them there as well."

"What about Cain? You poisoned him. And Shona?" Now my ankles threaten to buckle under the exertion. "Where is she?"

Inanna slows her pace and pushes between Marek and me, causing him to fall a little behind us. "I would never poison anyone who didn't deserve it. We tranqued him. He's someplace where he can't hurt anyone. And Shona is at the compound. Safe."

Not waiting for a response from me, she picks up speed

and moves ahead. Lugh drops back. When we make it to the next road, Bjorn and Horus join us.

"There're beasts crawling all over the place," Bjorn says, running beside Lugh. "Watch the roofs."

Horus keeps up with Inanna. "We found a park. The others are there. It'll be a fight to get them out."

"So be it." Inanna takes a quick look over her shoulder at Marek and me. "We can't let him have her or the Parzalis."

I almost trip over my feet at the mention of the Pazalis. "How do you know we have it?"

"Because it alerted me," Bjorn says, holding up his hand so we can see his palm. The veins there are raised and blue and are in a swirl pattern that matches the ones on the Parzalis in the burlap sack.

"What does that mean?" Marek asks through exerted breaths.

"I'm your family's divinity. That's why I've been around your family for centuries."

Lugh shoots us a stern look. "Pay attention. You can be talking about this stuff later."

We're ahead of the beasts, but I can hear them hopping from roof to roof behind us. Fear pumps adrenaline through me — pulsing hard and hot in my veins — and I run. Run faster than I ever have. Run for my life.

A loud scratching, tearing of bricks, comes from both sides of us. Creatures crawl down the sides of the building and onto the street. The Risen rush us so fast I don't have time to think. Bjorn charges in front of me, blocking one from my path.

Marek catches my hand, and I run with him.

A young-looking guy wearing headphones about to take off on his Vespa notices the chaos happening up the street from him. He scrambles off and darts back into the building.

Marek hops on the abandoned Vespa, and I get on behind him. He takes off. I glance back. Lugh is swinging a sword, cutting down the Risen. Inanna and the others have blades, too.

Where did they get those?

A beast jumps down, almost hitting us. Two more join him.

"Can you go faster?" I shout.

Marek looks over his shoulder. "I'm going as fast as it can."

A loud *thump* hits the ground behind us. I glance back again. In the middle of the road, a winged lion blocks the beasts from getting to us. It easily plucks one of the Risen from the ground and tosses it far into the air. The Risen hits the side of the building.

"What was that?"

"It's a Pixiu," I say. "She has two antlers. So she's a Bixie and wards off evil spirits."

A car turns onto the road, and Marek swerves to miss it, crashing the Vespa into a row of parked ones. We fall over on one side.

My hip and shoulder slam against the pavement, and a loud and gutteral grunt tears from my throat. I clench my teeth against the pain.

"Shit," Marek barks. "That hurt. Ana, are you okay?"

"No."

"Is anything broken? Can you move?"

Get up. I can't be weak now. I'm a human in a god's war, and I will surely die if I don't get the hell out of here. Anger flushes my face. I take a deep breath and push up the Vespa and roll out from under it. Marek crawls out after me.

We stand and assess the road. It looks like something out of a video game. From what I can see around the Bixie, there are blood and body parts strewn across the street. Inanna effortlessly swings her sword. Bjorn hits Risen with his hammer.

Dark storm clouds roll in, lightning bolts continually stab the ground, and angry thunder rattles the windowpanes in the buildings surrounding us.

"Let's keep going," Marek says.

I pull my eyes from the carnage. "Where are we going?" He looks up the street. "As far as we can get from that. Come on."

I take off beside Marek, every bit of my battered body screaming in protest. We don't get very far before Pazuzu turns the corner. He strolls up the street as if he's just out for a Sunday walk and not out to damn our souls or something.

There's a door to our left, and I grab Marek's hand and hurry for it. It's an apartment building.

"Now what?" Marek says, looking up the stairwell.

"Let's find a back door."

Around the stairwell we find one. Marek cracks it open and peers out, then quickly eases it shut.

"We can't go that way."

I glance back the way we came. "Front door isn't an option. Basement is too much like a grave. Up?"

He nods. "Up."

Halfway up the stairwell, the front door opens and slams.

My heart practically jumps out of my chest.

The door leading out sticks, so Marek throws his body against it until it bursts open. We run across the roof to the opposite side from the fight below. There's a fire escape.

And it's a long way down.

The blood rushes from my face and pumps hard in my chest. A ladder? I can't.

"Okay, we go down together." Marek straddles the ledge and reaches a hand out to me. "I won't let you fall. Trust me."

A Risen jumps over the gap between roofs and crashes into Marek. The ladder breaks away from the wall, and Marek goes flying back with the man.

"No!" I reach for him, but his hands pull away too fast. I cover my eyes.

And there's a loud *bang*.

CHAPTER FORTY

"Marek!" I'm afraid. Afraid to see his body on the pavement below. Afraid he's dead.

I step closer to the edge and look down.

The ladder got wedged between the buildings. There's a body on the pavement. I stare at it until I realize the body on the pavement isn't Marek, it's the Risen. Marek hangs from a rung.

"Marek!"

"I'm okay," he shouts, kicks his leg over another rung, and lifts himself. "There's a window down here. I'm going to try and go through it. Meet me in the stairwell."

"All right." The ledge crumbles under my foot, and I slip. Strong arms grab me before I can fall over. When I'm steady on the roof, he releases me. I turn. "Pazuzu," I say with all the terror sounding in my voice that I'm feeling right now.

"The Divinity's Soul," he commands.

"No." I'm trapped. I glance over the edge. Marek is working to get the window open. Pazuzu can't know he's down there. Even though I'm terrified, I bring my gaze back to Pazuzu.

"Bastet isn't here to protect you." His head inclines as he studies me. "You, I will not harm, but I will break your companion's neck."

Marek? *No.*

The writhing bodies in the tar pit of his eyes convince me he means what he says.

I reach down and yank the lighter off my leg. The medical tape pulling from my skin stings. "What are you going to do to me?"

He just stares at me with those eyes holding so much torture.

The metal lighter is warm in my hand. I open it and remove the medallion. The death's-head hawkmoth glints in the sun.

His fingers grasp it, and he tries to take it, but it won't budge from my palm. He tries again. A growl escapes his lips twisted in a snarl.

"It is yours. You are afraid of me, yet you and I are the same," he hisses.

"What is it?"

"When all the pieces of the Divinities Keep come together, the Soul connects them. One cannot live without a soul. After all receive their power back, and if the soul isn't attached, by the next full moon, the immortals will die."

"Can't they just pull the pieces apart and stop it?"

"Once joined, the pieces will not separate again. When the time comes, it will be up to you to decide. Their fate is in your hands."

"All gods and goddesses will suffer the same fate?" I inch to his left until my back isn't pointing at the edge.

"Good or bad. They either live or die."

"I can't make that choice."

The lava waves are building in his eyes. I want to look away, but I can't.

"You're evil."

He regards me for a quick second. "My people both loved and feared me. I could bring my wrath when they weren't good, and I could protect them against outsiders' attacks. One is not entirely evil or entirely good. It just depends on what side your scale tips."

"I don't want this."

"You haven't a choice."

He raises his hand, and the medallion heats on my palm. It flies back at me and hits my chest, throwing me on my back against the roof. I writhe in pain over the tiles. Suddenly I'm in the tar lake with all the tortured faces of Pazuzu. My arms flail, frantic to stay above the surface. The black liquid rises and falls in inky waves, trying to pull me under. High-pitched screams cut through the darkness, and I'm not sure if they are mine or theirs. My chest burns and I can't breathe.

I want to give up. Let go. Go under the tar lake and sleep.

Just as suddenly as I was pulled in, I come out. I'm lying on my back on the tiles of the roof, looking up at Pazuzu. I'm no longer in pain, except for a scorching sensation in my chest. I strain to see it. There's a circular burn in my white shirt.

"What did you do to me?" I ask, fingering the hole. There's a bump, so I pull aside the shirt. The medallion is embedded in my chest just under the skin and above my heart, the gold outline of the moth visible.

"You are the Divinity's Soul. It is easier to carry there than taped to your leg."

Seven Risen land on the roof and stop.

I push myself up and stand. "Then is it over? Call off your Risen beasts. Leave us alone."

Pazuzu gives the Risen a bored look. "These are not mine. I do not need to borrow from man to have my army." He holds up both of his palms, and fire shoots out of them. The flames open, and horned creatures with sharp teeth hop out.

The instant they hit the roof they grow to Pazuzu's size and attack the Risen, tearing them to pieces.

At the first attack, I double over and throw up. I cover my eyes, only removing my hands when the noise stops. The demon creatures are gone, and the Risen are just burning heaps of flesh on the tiles.

"Pazuzu!" A fierce voice comes from the roof of the building next to the one we're on.

It's Ares, and he's pissed.

"Those were mine," he continues shouting. "You are forbidden to interfere in my wars."

"Your beasts threatened me first." Pazuzu throws his hand up, and a wall of fire blocks Ares from us. He turns to me. "You aren't safe here. Return to your people."

He bows before strolling off. I keep my eyes on him until he goes through the door, giving Pazuzu a good head start, so I'm not going down with him.

The wall starts to flicker, and I dash for the door.

There isn't time for me to process what just happened. My mind is blank as I barge down the stairs. When I reach the fifth floor, I hear a pounding. Marek is trying to get the window open. I unlock it and let him in.

I wrap my arms around him. "I thought you—"

"I'm fine. Let's get out of here." He holds my hand, and we rush down and push out the door.

"There they are," Lugh yells and runs for us.

Inanna and Bjorn follow.

When he reaches us, he doesn't stop. "Come on. You need an invitation?"

"It's Ares," I tell him, trying to keep up with him. "He's behind all this. The Risen."

Inanna trots beside me, and I'm a little insulted by how easy it is for her to stay at my pace. I was always horrible at running track in gym class.

"I told you it was him, Lugh," she says. "He loves a good war. You can be sure there are older immortals behind it. Powerful ones."

"Them leeches are gaining on us," Horus says.

I make the mistake of glancing back. Those creatures look like paranormal predators, hunched over with sharp teeth and fingers deformed to look like claws.

The Risen chase us a few blocks.

"They're all over the place," Bjorn says, the beating of feet in rhythm with his words.

Horus stops at a gate. He grabs the iron bars and shakes the gate once, then twice, and on the third time, it busts open. He waves us through.

I don't stop. I'm not as fast as Inanna, she's not exerting herself, but I stay on her heels. Marek keeps to my side. We're in a vast garden with tall trees, sculpted bushes, a large pond, and early spring flowers all surrounding a large gazebo.

At a clearing in front of the greenhouse stand men and women, some I've met, others I haven't. Gods and goddesses. They hold various weapons—modern and old. Oyá and Janus break from their line to flank Marek and me. I guess Oyá and Janus picked a side.

Lugh, Inanna, Bjorn, and Horus join the line.

More gods and goddesses approach and face us. Behind them, Shona's father controls the beasts he brought back to life. His commands are garbled from where I stand. The beasts are like rabid dogs on a leash—clawed hands thrashing the air, teeth gnashing.

Our side doesn't move. I want to run. We're in a battle line.

The other side stops not even a half football field away. They're armed, too. It's a standoff. Like *West Side Story* but with immortals.

Shona's father calls out orders to the couple of dozen or so Risen around him. The men and women must have been dead a while, because they are full-on beasts. Their faces distorted like feral cats, teeth and nails sharp, they look ready to pounce. To kill.

Lugh hands Marek a spiked club and me a dagger. "Stay out of the way. Don't hesitate if you're attacked. Strike. Immortals get hurt and take time to heal. Run before that happens. Got it?"

"Yes," Marek says, testing the weight of the club in his hand.

The sky darkens, and a strong wind hits us. It whips my hair around with such force it stings my face. Oyá sends her hurricane, blocking the beasts' path to us. Her swords materialize in her hands.

Oyá glances over at Marek and me. "Stay behind me."

We don't question it, we just do as she says.

A god on their side breaks the line, clouds rolling on his palms. Oyá waves us back.

"Get down."

The god fires the swirling spheres, and the orbs hit Oyá's hurricane, dispersing it until only rain falls on us. He returns to the line, a smug smile on his face.

"Who is that?" I ask, not expecting anyone to answer.

Oyá does. "Jupiter. A weather god. His powers returned at the same time as mine."

"I hope Posedien is on our side," Marek says.

"He is not," Oyá says. "Lucky for us, he has no powers."

It's eerily quiet; neither side makes a sound. The only noises are of birds and engines coming from the street. There are no people in the garden. It must be between two or three in the afternoon, and no one is enjoying the gardens.

It happens so fast, I don't have time to blink. Both sides charge at each other. Swords *schling* and bang together, and bullets fly. Fists hitting immortal flesh sound like thunder. Bodies crashing to the ground and sliding across the grass tear up the foliage.

Marek grasps my hand. "Come on. It's too dangerous here."

"No. She told us to stay behind her." I push the wet hair out of my face.

"He's right," Oyá says over her shoulder. "They've brought guns to an immortal fight. Bullets only injure immortals. Slow us down so one of those beasts can catch us. It will most definitely kill you. Take cover in that greenhouse. I'll come for you when I can."

My shoes slip in the mud, and Marek catches my arm before I fall. We're almost to the greenhouse, and it explodes. Glass shoots up in the air, Marek tackles me, the dagger flying from my hand. We roll under a bench, shards showering around us.

Marek inspects me. "Did any hit you?"

"No. I'm fine. You?"

"I'm good."

He holds me tight against his body and whispers, "We need to get out of here. There has to be another way out. Run with me. To the back of the garden. Don't stop. No matter what you hear. Okay?"

I nod, my body trembling. He slides out from under the bench, and I follow. But I don't run. I can't.

On the stage of the gazebo, Ares holds Dalton's arm, a smile on his face so evil it freezes my blood, my legs, everything around me.

CHAPTER FORTY-ONE

Fear twists Dalton's face. His eyes bounce wildly around, taking in the battle in front of him. I only notice the other three captives on the stage when Ares shouts, "Stop!" It's thunderous. So loud it shakes the buildings surrounding the garden.

Everyone in the battle freezes, heads turn in Ares's direction, then there's a collective gasp.

Jane!

Beside her is Sid. Eyes closed and his hands stretched above his head, he's tied to one of the rafters of the gazebo. His mascara is smeared, and his lipstick is a faded memory.

Jane has a terrified look on her face, her eyes shifting nervously around the crowd. She's in scrubs. They must've grabbed her just as she returned home from surgery.

My mind is blank. I don't care what happens to me. My entire life is on that stage. I can practically feel my heart shattering. I take off for Ares and Dalton. "No! Let him go!"

Someone grabs both of my arms. I think it's Marek, but it's not. Inanna holds me, her fingers digging into my skin.

"Stay still," Inanna orders, then yells to the others. "Cease! He has Gaea."

It doesn't register who Gaea is; my only concern is Dalton. My brother. Best friend. I don't even look at Jane. Nor Sid. I'm too distraught. I focus on Ares's hand on Dalton's neck.

Marek reaches me, the club in his hand stained with blood. By the confusion on his face, he doesn't get what's happening.

"My brother." That's all I have to say. He gets it.

"Shit," he snaps and pushes his sweaty hair from his forehead with his free hand.

And it registers. Gaea is Earth, the mother of everything.

"If he can control Gaea." Inanna turns me around, lets go of my arms, and faces me. "Get all her powers back. He will be master of all. Even the most powerful immortals. She could kill an immortal as easily as snapping her fingers. That fear will control us."

Gaea is young. She looks twelve. She seems helpless to whatever Ares has planned for her. Then there's Jane. She's frail-looking under the hold of the god behind her. I do feel a pain in my heart at seeing her here. I love her even if she doesn't like me.

"Put down your arms, leave or join me, I don't care. If you don't, Gaea will suck the air out of you."

"We have to leave," Inanna says.

I don't have time to tell her I'm not leaving without Dalton. Ares's eyes are on me.

"Bring me the Parzalis, Analiese," he orders. "Or I will kill your brother."

Lugh puffs up his chest. "You won't touch him, or I'll tear you apart."

Ares's grin widens. "Oh yes, I forgot. He's your son. Had an affair with his mother, right? Kept it secret. You pretend you donated for his birth. Well, the cat's out of the bag."

Dalton's gaze shoots to Jane's frightened face.

My eyes snap to Lugh. He keeps his attention on Ares.

He lied to us. An affair? I hope Dad never knew. That would've torn him to pieces. I take two slow steps forward, and no one notices.

"This display by Ares will only ensure my father will join our side," Bjorn says, grabbing Lugh's arm. He leans over and says something in Lugh's ear, and Lugh nods.

My stare meets Dalton's fearful eyes. Tears drench my cheeks. I don't know what to say.

What happens to Marek if I give Ares his Parzalis?

Inanna addresses the immortals on her side. "We go now and fight later. The risk of losing all of you is not one I want to take."

"You heard her," Horus says, weaving around the pairs of fighters. "Grab your things. We'll meet at the compound."

"I'm growing tired," Ares warns, staring right at me. "Shall I just kill the boy, or will you give me what I ask? I'll throw in the mother for good measure."

My tear-filled eyes find Marek's worried ones, and he whispers for only me to hear, "Give it to him."

I'm not sure I hear him correctly until he moves.

"Run." He pushes me forward and blocks Inanna.

I sprint for Ares and Dalton, his gods and goddesses moving behind me like a wall when I pass, blocking Horus and Bjorn from catching me.

When I reach the gazebo, I stop at the steps, reach into my purse, and yank out the burlap bag.

"Send them down, and it's yours." I hold up the bag and shake it.

He lifts an eyebrow at me. "Show me."

I remove it from the burlap and hold it up.

"Good. Now bring it to me, and we'll do a trade."

I don't move.

"I can break his neck now and take it from you," he says.

His tone is dark, makes a chill slither up my back, but I stay strong. "I'll shatter it before you can."

"Okay," he says. "We trade at the same time."

"Release my mom first, and then I'll bring it to you."

Ares smiles. "You're a tough bargainer." He looks at the god holding Jane. "Release her."

The god's hands drop away from Jane, and she clambers down the steps, stopping at my side.

Before I can take my first step up, Jane grabs my sleeve. "No. He'll kill you."

I search her eyes. She's scared for me. "I have to. For Dalton."

She lets go, and I ascend the stairs. I look at Sid, beaten and hanging there from the beam. His chest rises and falls, and I'm relieved he's still alive. I reach the top.

My hand shakes as I reach the Parzalis out to Ares. "Release him."

"Ana, watch out!" Marek shouts.

The god who was holding Jane snatches the Parzalis from my hand.

The smile on Ares's face turns into a sneer. One that dries up my blood and sucks the air out of my lungs. It all happens in slow motion, and I'm caught in the same speed, unable to do anything. Unable to stop him.

Ares twists Dalton's neck and releases him.

Dalton lands on the wooden planks of the gazebo with a *thud*.

"I said I'd release him. Didn't say alive." He cackles, turns, and motions for his immortals to follow him. "Kill the mom. The Keeper. And bring the girl," he orders two gods and a goddess as he passes them.

Jane screams from behind me.

"No! Dalton!" I dash to him, dropping to my knees bedside him.

"Don't touch him." Jane's voice sounds frantic.

The bones in his neck are jagged and pressing against his skin. His face is peaceful. Like so many Saturday mornings when I've gone into his room when he's sleeping to wake him.

I know what you're thinking, Sid said to me once. *That you'll never bring someone back from the dead. Isabella thought that, too. Think about it, would you bring your father back if you could? Someone you love.*

My heart is crumpling inside my chest. It's like Ares reached in and wadded it up and threw it away. There's nothing there now. Just a hollow space.

And the tears run down my face, across my cheeks, over my nose, into my mouth. I'm drowning in the dark sorrow pulling me under.

"No," comes out, barely audible. But he's so young. Images of our past flash through my mind. All our talks and fears. Our laughs and frustrations. Dreams. We experienced them together. What would life be without him?

I'm suddenly cold.

Lonely.

I can't let him go. I can't never see him again.

He's lonely.

He's cold.

I can't let him go.

I pull Dalton into my arms and rock back and forth with him.

A breath hits my collarbone, and I glance down at him.

His eyelids flutter. Jane falls to her knees on his other side and tugs him out of my arms and into hers.

A swarm of death's-head hawkmoths swooshes around us. A murder of crows darkens the sky. I stand and glare at the immortals rushing Marek. The moths attack and pelt them, multiplying until I can't see the immortals within the storm of wings. They bury them, suffocate them.

Ares. I'll kill him.

I flip around and charge across the stage and down the other set of steps. The moths are with me, flying overhead, turning as I turn around a hedge. He's there. About to exit the gate. Grasping Gaea with one hand, the Parzalis in the other.

"Ares!" I want to rush him. Smother him. Kill him.

The rage burns through my veins like the tar lake in Pazuzu's eyes.

The moths feel my emotions. They multiply and race for Ares, striking him. Gaea falls to the ground, and so does the Parzalis.

Gaea screams and covers her head.

Ares can barely move in the yellow-and-brown hurricane, but he pushes forward, Gaea and the Parzalis forgotten. He struggles to get to the door of a waiting Mercedes. He opens it, collapses on the seat, and slams the door. The vehicle speeds off.

I can feel the moths trapped in the car with Ares. Swatted. Slowly dying.

My legs are unstable. I can barely walk on them, but I manage to cross the distance between Gaea and me. She takes my offered hand, and I help her stand. The Parzalis is heavy when I pick it up. Gaea says something, but I can't hear her. I can only hear a loud thrumming in my ears.

What just happened?

Dalton.

Ares broke Dalton's neck. He died. I brought him back.

I *brought* him back.

CHAPTER FORTY-TWO

The compound is a vast structure that's approximately one hundred thousand square feet. It's under a chateau in the French countryside. It's like living in an underground town. It's equipped with a theater, a medical facility, a gym, a pool and spa, game areas, dining rooms, and coffee bars.

The people missing on Adam Conte's list are here in the compound. They were rescued by Inanna and the others before the Lares could find them and terminate them. That's what it's called when the Lares kill your parents and your uncle. Terminated.

They were terminated.

Just like that.

Bastet arches her back and rubs against my leg. She can sense my worry.

I twist the red string Yuè Lǎo gave me. The one that connects me to Marek. He's on his quest to hide the Parzalis with Bjorn. He should be done in a week. We barely had time for a goodbye in Florence. And the one we did have was quick.

I miss him. Need him.

I'm in the medical facility watching my brother through a thick window. Dalton's in a hospital bed with all kinds of tubes connecting him to machines. The transfusion will slow down his metamorphosis into a beast.

One day, I'll have to kill him.

Shona wraps her arm around mine. "He's going to be fine, you'll see. Cain is back to normal." She's doing better since learning about her dad. It has to be tough. Her strength impresses me.

"How long will it keep him normal?" I place my hand on the window as if Dalton can feel my touch. I hope he can sense me. Cain and the doorman had the treatment, and they're doing well. I actually like the real Cain.

"It depends on the individual." Shona glances over her shoulder when someone enters the room. "The earliest change happened in three months. The longest, almost a year. I heard they are going to try a second transfusion on a Risen. See if they can delay the change longer."

"How do you live knowing that's going to happen? That he'll change one day." It's a question more for me than for her.

"I have hope. They're working on a cure. Maybe they'll find it in time." She tugs on my arm. "Come on. It's going to be a while before he's ready."

Jane comes to my side and covers my hand with hers. "I've been afraid of you ever since—" Her voice cracks, and she clears her throat. "Ever since Eli brought my brother back to life. He turned into one of those things… Eli didn't stop him. He couldn't do it. Three men died on a golf course before the police shot my brother."

So that's why she kept her distance. Always on edge when I was around. Making me feel unloved by her. I'm not going to get into it with her here. Not with Dalton in this state.

"And Lugh?" I ask.

"It was a mistake." Her hand withdraws from mine. "Eli and I were separated. We had been fighting a lot. Mostly from the stress of in vitro fertilization. I never lied to Eli. He knew Dalton wasn't his biological son. Eli loved Dalton as if he were."

I didn't doubt that. Dad showed both Dalton and me his love every day.

"I'm tired," I say. "I want to check on Sid before bed." It's my way to escape whatever this is. A confession?

Shona gets my cue and opens the door. "You want a snack first? I have to stop at the food court. If I don't bring Sid candy when I visit, he gets grumpy." She ushers me out, and I don't look back. Jane has what she's always wanted.

Me gone.

CHAPTER FORTY-THREE

So there's this thing. Gods and goddesses don't know how to teach. They have to go to school just like us to get a skill. Living as immortals in a mortal world for millennia, you'd think they would have mastered all kinds of them. But our studies bore them.

To save immortals from having to teach us—*us* meaning Risers—they send us to an American international boarding school just outside Paris. Except for the few gods and goddesses who do enjoy it. Like Oyá and Lugh. They pose as teachers at the school to keep an eye on us. Make sure we're safe.

Along with my new wardrobe and textbooks, I have a new name on my passport.

Ana Ryan.

My Vans squeak against the very polished wood floor in the long hallway. The school looks like a castle on the outside. The inside has more of a university vibe, with high ceilings and lavishly furnished classrooms.

Dalton sidles up beside me, wraps an arm around my

shoulder, and leans closer. "I have a surprise for you."

"No, thank you."

"Ah, come on," he whines. "I haven't even told you what it is yet."

Sid comes up on my other side. "She hates surprises, remember? Don't tease her. Now me, you can tease all you want, honey."

Dalton's smiles are bittersweet to me, but I savor every one of them. I want to hold on to him for as long as I can. Protect him from knowing about his future. Keep that nightmare from haunting him as it does me.

"It's a good one," Dalton taunts.

I shake my head. "Uh-uh. Your last *surprise* involved anchovies and pizza."

"Okay, then." His arm falls away from my shoulder. "I'll just tell him you won't ditch math to see him."

"Him?"

"Yes." He gives me that coy smile of his.

Dalton loves to torture me. I'm an easy target. "Who? Stop teasing me."

"If you don't want him, I'll keep him." He winks.

"Marek? Where is he?"

"Out front." He stuffs his hands in pockets, a wide grin stretching his face.

Oyá's going to be pissed if I miss her class, but I don't care. Marek is here.

I kiss Dalton's cheek, then Sid's, and take off down the hall. "Thank you," I call over my shoulder.

"Don't mention it," he says. "Someone has to get some around here."

"Go get him, girl," Sid calls.

The hall seems longer as I sprint down it. I reach the door, yank it open, and stop on the porch.

Marek waits at the bottom of the stairs. His face brightens

when he sees me. His hair is a little longer, and it looks like he's been in the sun. His eyes, a kaleidoscope of colors in the light, are on me. It makes my pulse race, my heart frantic, and I can't get to him fast enough.

With each step down, wings take flight in my chest, and he has all of my heart. At the bottom, I jump into his arms, and he catches me. Our mouths connect as if they are magnets finally brought back together. His lips are soft and warm and taste like basil and honey. And I don't want to stop kissing them.

I drag my fingers through his wavy hair, clenching fistfuls. It's soft like the plush blanket Jane got for my bed. He smells fresh like the morning dew clinging to the grasses and plants around us. And I'm not dreaming. Like every night since he left.

He's here.

ACKNOWLEDGMENTS

Writing Analiese's story has been challenging and theraputic at the same. We both have a panic disorder. Panic attacks are terrifying and can prevent the suffer from doing things that trigger an attack. There is a way to feel better. Everyone affected with the disorder will have different experiences, different triggers that bring them on, and different ways of combating it. Getting help is the key to managing it. If you have reaccuring panic attacks or have an other mental health issue, please reach out to a parent, a family member, or trusted friend, and visit a medical professional for treatment. For information about mental health and guides for getting the help you need, please go to mentalhealth.gov.

With that said, I want to extend my gratitude to everyone who has worked on this book or supported me while I was writing it.

First and foremost, thank you to my publisher and editor, Liz Pelletier, for being excited about this book enough to want to publish and help mold into the story it is today. Thank you Lydia Sharp and Hannah Lindsey, for helping to get this book into the best shape possible with your insightful edits. Thank you to Greta Gunselman and Kelly Elliot for reviewing and helping to make the pages shine. And to the entire Entangled Publishing team, Stacy Abrams, Curtis Svehlak, Heather Riccio, and everyone else who worked on this book from creation to marketing and everything in between, thank you for getting it into readers' hands. And to Deranged Doctor, thank you for the beautiful book cover.

An infinity of thank-yous to my agent, Peter Knapp, for always being there to guide me, assure me, and for having my back. I can hardly believe it's been over five years since getting that exciting email from you about representation. Here's to many more!

Thank you to my family and friends for all your love and understanding when I have to pass on things because I have a deadline or some other pressing matter.

To my special girls that I dedicated this book to, Annika Anderson and Fallon Anderson, thank you for keeping me young at heart. I love you more than the entire universe and beyond.

And thank you to my husband, Richard Drake, for supporting and encouraging my dreams. I'm lucky to have you accompany me on this life journey, and like Analiese and Marek, I would face the horrors of a haunted catacomb with you any day—you go first!

Finally, to you, dear reader, thank you for joining Analiese and Marek on their hunt for clues to digging up their families' secrets. I hope you enjoy reading their journey as much as I enjoyed writing it.

Keep reading for an excerpt of Brenda Drake's *Thief of Lies*...

Gia Kearns would rather fight with boys than kiss them. That is, until Arik, a leather clad hottie in the Boston Athenaeum, suddenly disappears. When Gia unwittingly speaks the key that sucks her and her friends into a photograph and transports them into a Paris library, Gia must choose between her heart and her head, between Arik's world and her own, before both are destroyed.

CHAPTER ONE

Only God and the vendors at Haymarket wake early on Saturday mornings. The bloated clouds spattered rain against my faded red umbrella. I strangled the wobbly handle and dodged shoppers along the tiny makeshift aisle of Boston's famous outdoor produce market. The site, just off the North End, was totally packed and stinky. The fruits and vegetables for sale were rejects from nearby supermarkets—basically, they were cheap and somewhat edible. The briny decay of flesh wafted in the air around the fishmongers.

Gah! I cupped my hand over my nose, rushing past their stands.

My sandals slapped puddles on the sidewalk. Rain slobbered on my legs, making them slick and cold, sending shivers across my skin. I skittered around a group of slow-moving tourists, cursing Afton for insisting I get up early and wear a skirt today.

Finally breaking through the crowd, I charged up the street to the Haymarket entrance to the T.

Under a black umbrella across the street, a beautiful girl with cocoa skin and dark curls huddled next to a guy with equally dark hair and an olive complexion—my two best friends. Nick held the handle while Afton leaned against him to avoid getting wet. Nick's full-face smile told me he enjoyed sharing an umbrella with her.

"Hey, Gia!" Afton yelled over the swooshing of tires across the wet pavement and the insistent honking of aggravated motorists.

I waited for the traffic to clear, missing several opportunities to cross the street. I swallowed hard and took a step down. *You can do this, Gia. No one is going to run you over. Intentionally.* A car turned onto the street, and I quickly hopped back onto the curb. I'd never gotten over my old fears. When the street cleared enough for an elderly person to cross in a walker, I wiped my clammy palms on my skirt and sprinted to the center of the street.

"You have to get over your phobia," Nick called to me. "You live in Boston! Traffic is everywhere!"

"It's okay!" Afton elbowed Nick. "Take your time!"

I took a deep breath and raced across to them.

"Nice. I'm impressed. You actually wore a skirt instead of jeans," Nick said, inspecting my bare legs.

My face warmed. "Wait. Did you just give me a compliment?"

"Well, except…" He hesitated. "You walk like a boy."

"Never mind him. With legs like that, it doesn't matter how you walk. Come on." Afton hooked her arm around mine. "I can't wait for you to see the Athenæum. It's so amazing. You're going to love it."

I groaned and let her drag me down the steps after Nick. "I'd probably love it just as much later in the day."

As we approached the platform, the train squealed to a stop. We squeezed into its belly with the other passengers and then grasped the nearest bars as the car jolted down the rails. Several minutes later, the train coasted into the Park Street

Station. We followed the flow of people up the stairs and to the Boston Common, stopping in Afton's favorite café for lattes and scones. Lost in gossip and our plans for the summer, nearly two hours went by before we headed for the library.

When we reached Beacon Street, excitement—or maybe the two cups of coffee I had downed before leaving the café—hit me. We weren't going to just any library. We were going to the Boston Athenæum, an exclusive library with a pricey annual fee. Afton's father got her a membership at the start of summer. It's a good thing her membership allows tagalongs, since my pop would never splurge like that, not when the public library is free. Which I didn't get, because it wasn't that expensive and would totally be worth it.

"We're here," Afton said. "Ten and a half Beacon Street. Isn't it beautiful? The facade is Neoclassical."

I glanced up at the building. The library walls, which were more than two hundred years old, held tons of history. Nathaniel Hawthorne swore he saw a ghost here once, which I think he probably made up, since he was such a skilled storyteller. "Yeah, it is. Didn't you sketch this building?"

"I did." She bumped me with her shoulder. "I didn't think you actually paid attention to my drawings."

"Well, I do."

Nick pushed open the crimson door to the private realm of the Athenæum, and I chased Afton and Nick up the white marble steps and into the vestibule. Afton showed her membership card at the reception desk. I removed my notebook and pencil from my messenger bag before we dropped it, Afton's purse, and our umbrellas off at the coat check.

Pliable brown linoleum floors muffled our footsteps into the exhibit room. A tiny elevator from another era carried us to an upper level of the library, where bookcases brimming with leather-bound books stood against every wall.

Overhead, more bookcases nested in balconies behind lattice railings. The place dripped with cornices and embellishments. Sweeping ceilings and large windows gave the library an open feel. Every wall held artwork, and antique treasures rested in each corner. It was a library lover's dream, rich with history. My dream.

A memory grabbed my heart. I was about eight and missing my mother, and Nana Kearns took me to a library. She'd said, "Gia, you can never be lonely in the company of books." I wished Nana were here to experience this with me.

"Did you know they have George Washington's personal library here?" Afton's voice pulled me from my thoughts.

"No. I wonder where they keep it," I said.

Nick gaped at a naked sculpture of Venus. "Locked up somewhere, I guess."

The clapping of my sandals against my heels echoed in the quiet, and I winced at each smack. Nick snorted while trying to stifle a laugh. I glared at him. "Quit it."

"Shhh," Afton hissed.

We shuffled into a reading room with forest green walls. Several busts of famous men balancing on white pedestals surrounded the area. A snobby-looking girl with straight blond hair sat at one of the large walnut tables in the middle of the room, tapping a pencil against the surface as she read a book.

"Prada," Afton said.

I gave her a puzzled look. "What?"

"Her sandals. And the watch on her wrist… Coach."

I took her word on that because I wouldn't know designer stuff if it hit me on the head.

Nick's gaze flicked over the girl. "This is cool. I think I'll stay here."

"Whatever." Afton glared at Nick's back. "We're going exploring. When you're finished gawking, come find us."

"Okay," Nick said, clearly distracted, sneaking looks at the girl.

I slid my feet across the floor to the elevators, trying to avoid the dreaded clap of rubber. "Are you okay?"

"I'm fine." By the tone in Afton's voice, I suspected she didn't like Nick ditching us.

"At least we get some girl time," I said.

I must have sounded a little too peppy, because she rolled her eyes at me. She pushed the down button on the elevator. "Yeah, I can give you the tour before we get to work. The Children's Library has some cool stuff in it."

I didn't see the point of riding an elevator when you could get some exercise in. "We could take the stairs. You know, cardio?"

"How about *no*. My feet are killing me in these heels." The doors slid open, and we stepped inside. "Did you know there's a book here bound in human skin?"

"No. Really?" The elevator dropped and my stomach slumped.

Afton removed her sweater and then draped it over her arm. "Really. I saw it."

"No thanks."

"You can't tell it's actual skin," she said. "They treat it or dye it or something, silly."

"I bet they *die* it." The doors rattled apart. There was a slight bounce as we exited the elevator, and I clutched the doorframe. The corner of Afton's lip rose slightly, and I knew her mood was improving. I released my death grip on the frame then followed her into the hallway. "Besides, isn't it illegal or something?"

"Well, the book is from the nineteenth century." Afton shrugged a shoulder. "Who knows what was legal back then?"

"Why would they even do that?" This entire conversation was making *my* skin crawl.

"It's a confession from a thief. Before he died, he requested his own skin be used for the book's cover." The spaghetti strap on Afton's sundress fell down her arm, exposing part of her lacey bra, and she slipped it back in place.

A thirty-something guy passing us gaped, then averted his eyes and hurried his steps, probably realizing Afton's underage status. I rolled my eyes at him. *Jeesh.* Every single move Afton made was sexy. Nick was right. I walked like a guy. I leaned into her side. "Did you just see that perv check you out?"

"Oh, really?" She looked over her shoulder. "He's not all that bad for an older man."

Ugh. "You seriously need a therapist. He's almost Pop's age."

She laughed, grabbed my arm, and turned on her scary narrator voice. "They say this library is haunted."

*Grab the Entangled Teen releases
readers are talking about!*

MALICE
by Pintip Dunn

What I know: someone at my school will one day wipe out two-thirds of the population with a virus.

What I don't know: who it is.

In a race against the clock, I not only have to figure out their identity, but I'll have to outwit a voice from the future telling me to kill them. Because I'm starting to realize no one is telling the truth. But how can I play chess with someone who already knows the outcome of my every move? Someone so filled with malice she's lost all hope in humanity? Well, I'll just have to find a way—because now she's drawn a target on the only boy I've ever loved...

TO WHATEVER END
by Lindsey Frydman

Quinn Easterly is cursed—with one touch, she can see the end to someone's life. She has finally learned to go about life as usual until she meets Griffin. With one touch, she sees a death she simply cannot ignore. Not when, dying in her arms, Griffin whispers three simple words that change everything. Even if Quinn can't save him, she at least has to try. Even if it means taking the bullet meant for him.

ILLUSIONS
by Madeline J. Reynolds

1898, London. Saverio, a magician's apprentice, is tasked with stealing another magician's secret behind his newest illusion. He befriends the man's apprentice, Thomas, with one goal. Get close. Learn the trick. Get out.

Then Sav discovers that Thomas performs *real* magic and is responsible for his master's "illusions." And worse, Sav has unexpectedly fallen for Thomas.

Their forbidden romance sets off a domino effect of dangerous consequences that could destroy their love—and their lives.

PAPER GIRL
by Cindy R. Wilson

I haven't left my house in over a year. The doctors say it's social anxiety. All I know is that when I'm inside, I feel safe. Then my mom hires a tutor. This boy…he makes me want to be brave again. I can almost taste the outside world. But so many things could go wrong, and it would only take one spark for my world made of paper to burst into flames.

entangled teen

an imprint of Entangled Publishing LLC